PRAISE FOR *COOKING FOR PICASSO*

"A tasty blend of romance, mystery,
and French cooking . . . Read on!"
—MARGARET ATWOOD

"A colorful family saga . . . *Cooking for Picasso*
is a novel about how people take what seems to be
worthless and make it into something priceless.
The characters in Camille Aubray's novel illustrate . . .
that value lies not in what you own, but in who you are."
—WASHINGTON POST

"A quest for the missing Picasso worthy of Cary Grant
and Audrey Hepburn. As with any good quest, the
heroine finds love along the way, too."
—KIRKUS REVIEWS

"This touching and delectable novel invokes the breathtaking
scenery of the South of France and the Côte d'Azur in
1936 . . . Aubray paints a beautiful story of love, art, food,
and the enduring romance of the Mediterranean."
—FODOR'S TRAVEL

"Ondine meets a mysterious figure in her family's café—
with no inkling of how he'll shape her life and that of
her granddaughter Céline, living in present-day
Hollywood. A sweet summer read!"
—COSMOPOLITAN

"This richly crafted tale of love, trust, art, and food is wonderfully evocative of the sun-kissed Côte d'Azur, while weaving in a modern-day mystery."

"With lively characters and a twisting plot, Aubray's novel is a smart and satisfying tale of family, creativity, romance, and intrigue."

"Intrigue, art, food, and deception are woven together in a tale of love and betrayal around the life and legacy of Picasso. Touching and true, this well-written narrative made me long for my mother's coq au vin and for the sun of Juan-les-Pins."

"Camille Aubray takes the reader on a heartfelt journey to the South of France . . . Wise, atmospheric, and plain fun, Aubray expertly blends fact and fiction to create a rich and memorable tale."

PRAISE FOR *THE GODMOTHERS*

"A group of deeply complex and beautifully
written women . . . Aubray marries history, suspense, and
womanhood in a story perfect for devouring."
—NEWSWEEK

"Aubray portrays her strong characters as intelligent,
brave, and even ruthless women. This is
historical fiction at its best."
—BOOKLIST

"Aubray delivers an addictive and tense multigenerational
feminist romp through WWII-era New York City."
—PUBLISHERS WEEKLY

"Setting her tale mostly in the 1930s and '40s, Aubray
uses the dramatic changes in America to highlight the
family drama—a saga reminiscent of Mario Puzo and
Francis Ford Coppola. Unlike them, though, Aubray
focuses on the challenges particular to women . . .
A fast-paced, drama-filled portrait of a family dynasty."
—KIRKUS REVIEWS

"Thrilling! Readers will enjoy immersing themselves in
family drama and watching women's friendships grow."
—LIBRARY JOURNAL

"A fascinating, fast-paced trip into the mob underworld."
—PEOPLE MAGAZINE'S
"People Picks the Best Books"

"We love Camille Aubray's *The Godmothers*!"
—PARADE

"Aubray shines in her ability to bring each woman alive
with distinct personalities, and to weave individual
stories and different plots into one collective story . . .
Enjoy immersing yourself into this family's story."
—HISTORICAL NOVELS REVIEW

"A 'best book to read on a beach vacation!'"
—BOSTON GLOBE

"One of the best books of the year!"
—RED CARPET CRASH

"I couldn't put this down! I can't remember
reading such a juicy page-turner."
—MELANIE BENJAMIN,
New York Times bestselling author

"*The Godmothers* is my type of book: captivating,
well written, and full of love and drama."
—JACQUES PÉPIN,
chef, TV personality, author

THE GIRL FROM THE GRAND HOTEL

BOOKS BY CAMILLE AUBRAY

The Girl from the Grand Hotel

The Godmothers

Cooking for Picasso

THE GIRL FROM THE GRAND HOTEL

A NOVEL

CAMILLE AUBRAY

BLACK
STONE
PUBLISHING

Printed in the United States of America

First edition: 2024
ISBN 979-8-212-41723-5
Fiction / Historical / World War II

Version 1

Blackstone Publishing
31 Mistletoe Rd.
Ashland, OR 97520

www.BlackstonePublishing.com

For Jean-Jacques, Yvan, Pierre,
François, and all my dear friends
at my "home away from home."

PROLOGUE

The French Riviera
Late August 1939

In the summer of 1939, Hollywood invaded the French Riviera.

Annabel and her escort were attending a big party at the Grand Hotel in honor of the very first Cannes Film Festival. The entire hotel and its splendid grounds were all decked out for this gala event, with sparkling fairy lights in the graceful umbrella pines and along the borders of every path so that guests could find their way in the twilight.

Ladies in chiffon dresses and men in formal tailcoats were flitting across the great lawns like butterflies. Laughing and chattering with excitement, they passed under a white satin banner at the entrance to the terrace that spelled out in gold letters: *La Fête des Étoiles*.

"The Celebration of the Stars!" someone translated in a shout, and everyone was eagerly scanning the crowd in search of the human stars to be honored tonight—those mysterious Hollywood actors who'd be here in the flesh instead of flickering elusively on the silver screen.

Annabel had not even reached the main path when she heard the first strains of music wafting toward her on a Mediterranean breeze. A young woman began singing a plaintive, haunting new song called "Somewhere Over the Rainbow."

But instead of hurrying to catch up with the other party-goers, Annabel, dressed in a blue-violet gossamer gown and matching satin shoes, laid a gloved hand on her escort's arm to detain him, explaining that she'd forgotten something.

"I'll only be a few minutes," she murmured apologetically.

He sensed that she was up to something, and he said jokingly, "You've finally become a woman of mystery." Then he added gently, "And I'm not sure I like it."

But he waited there patiently, taking the moment to smoke a cigarette and gaze upward at the real stars in the sky.

Annabel hurried off, knowing that she had to work fast. She glanced over her shoulder to make certain that no one was watching, even though the hotel guests and the staff would all surely be preoccupied with this party tonight. The rest of the world was about to burst into flames, but here on the Côte d'Azur, the parties went on and on.

She felt a little guilty about sneaking into someone else's room with a "borrowed" key. It just wasn't in her nature to be deceitful. But this was no time for second thoughts. She had been warned not to make a mistake tonight. *People have already been murdered just to stop us from obtaining this item.*

She put the key in the lock, pushed the door open, and hurried inside. There was only a small lamp lighting the room, and Annabel preferred it that way, so that she could move about in the shadows and search around without her figure being illuminated in a window. She thought of an old proverb her father once told her: *When skating over thin ice, safety is in speed.*

So she set to work, rapidly pulling out several dresser drawers, carefully rummaging through each. Then she searched beneath the bed and under the mattress, until . . .

She heard a rustling noise, and she froze. No one was supposed to be here, and yet . . . Yes, now the sound was unmistakable. Someone was definitely in the adjoining room—and coming closer and closer with each footstep.

Her heart was pounding fearfully. She cast about looking for a hiding place, then quickly ducked into a nearby closet only seconds before someone entered the room.

Annabel held her breath. She'd been warned about moments like this: *It takes great training to be a spy. You must unlearn natural behavior.*

But she wasn't really a spy. She wasn't anybody important. She was just a girl from America with a summer job. At the beginning of this month, she'd been carefree, trusting, and open to new experiences.

What a difference only a few weeks could make. Thinking back on it now, there had been warning signs all along. Yet everyone was either too busy or having too much fun to notice that, this summer, they were all on a collision course with history.

PART ONE

I . . . would give my life for three years in France.
                                        —F. Scott Fitzgerald

CHAPTER 1

The Grand Hotel
The French Riviera
Earlier that month

Annabel had been working at the Grand Hôtel du Cap des Rêves for only a month when the Hollywood guests began arriving that first week in August. But she'd been well trained by her uncle to rise to any occasion, so on the big day she awakened early, washed quickly, and dressed neatly, then hurried out of the little boardinghouse where she lived on a quiet tree-lined square.

As she hopped onto her bicycle and pedaled through the small, sleepy coastal town, the morning sun was climbing softly up an enormous canopy of incomparable blue.

"Beautiful," she said aloud. Having been raised in the canyons of Manhattan, she was astonished by how high and wide the expanse of sky was on the French Riviera. If this were a painting, the sky would take up nearly three-quarters of the canvas. It seemed to promise limitless possibilities.

She cycled onto the main coastal road, one of three *corniches*, behind which rose the foothills of the Maritime Alps. Between the big cities, the Riviera's shoreline had several peninsulas that each dipped a toe into the sea, like ladies venturing out for a swim.

They reminded Annabel of the rocky capes on the East

Coast of America, where as a child she'd visited friends in the summertime in places like Cape May, Cape Elizabeth, Cape Cod. But in the South of France they were called Cap d'Antibes, Cap Ferrat, Cap Martin, once-modest fishermen's villages now rapidly becoming more and more fashionable and expensive.

A brisk breeze wafting in from the sparkling Mediterranean Sea seemed to be urging her forward as if it trembled with excitement. The entire Côte d'Azur was abuzz about the first-ever Cannes Film Festival.

Officially it would not begin until the first day of September. But the month of August was already scheduled full of "pre-parties": press luncheons, open-air concerts, cocktails on sumptuous yachts, fireworks displays, exclusive charity auctions, pool parties, and countless dinner dances. Everyone who was anyone was fighting like mad to get their fancy invitations. The local shopkeepers and café owners expected it to be the biggest boon to business that they'd seen in quite a while. And of course the hotels would be hosting many of these events.

"This will be lots more fun than the usual fuddy-duddies," the staff told one another, for the imminent arrival of movie stars had already dimmed the luster of even the richest dukes and most august princesses, who now seemed like mere bit players.

The Hollywood visitors were arriving this week from all directions: some from the stylish railway cars of the Train Bleu, others from private ocean liners chartered by individual film studios. They'd be staying at all the fabulous hotels in the great cities of the French Riviera: the Negresco in Nice, the Carlton in Cannes, the Hôtel de Paris in Monte Carlo—and the one where Annabel worked. She must hurry now.

She turned left onto a long, winding road that snaked its leisurely way around the entire lush, exclusive Cap des Rêves, or Cape of Dreams—past pebbly beaches and shimmering sea on one side and, on the other side, the deep-green curtain of dense pine trees.

Scattered here and there were exclusive private villas, their high walls spilling over with bright pink and purple bougainvillea and ancient yellow climbing roses. These hideaway villas were staged on three levels of land that became smaller at the top, like layers of a wedding cake.

And above the highest villas, at the very center of the Cap des Rêves, was a flat plateau, home to a military installation so protected by high concrete walls and wire fencing that it was virtually inaccessible to ordinary folk, who called it the Mound. As far as anyone could remember, it had always been an observation post, originally meant to watch out for pirates, and now relegated to some generally protective purpose.

Now Annabel veered onto a narrow street called the Chemin du Phare, which ended its short run at the old lighthouse on the very tip of the cape. Halfway down this quiet road was a gated driveway with a gold sign that said *Grand Hôtel du Cap*.

"*Bonjour!*" Annabel called out to the security guard who operated the wrought iron gate from a tall, narrow gatehouse.

"*Salut!*" he replied as she cycled past him toward the hotel.

Built in the late 1800s, the Grand Hotel sat serenely on its own hill overlooking the sea. A white Belle Epoque confection five stories high, it had two main wings and a rotunda. The guest rooms were graced with wrought iron balconies, while the suites and penthouses had private terraces with stone balustrades. Many impeccable gardens bloomed along winding paths that were sheltered by old trees of pine, plane, and palm.

Annabel pedaled more slowly now, past a parking area for delivery trucks. Once beyond that, she hopped off her bicycle and walked it down a gravel path that skirted the neatly clipped lawns. She was heading for the tennis courts, which were enclosed by very tall pine hedges, so she couldn't see the players but could hear the usual *pop-pop* of tennis balls being batted back and forth amid triumphant voices floating above the hedges.

She tucked her bicycle into her favorite spot between an old storage shed and the high shrubs. As she emerged, she heard quick footsteps coming her way.

"*Bonjour, mademoiselle!*" exclaimed the hotel's handsomest guest as he came bounding out from the courts carrying his racket. Hans von Erhardt was a tennis star, not a movie star, but his blond hair was the color of buttercups, and his blue eyes shone with endless vitality. Other people played on this court for leisure, but Hans was a fearsome young up-and-coming team player who'd made a big splash in the February tournament on the French Riviera. Then he'd gone off to play throughout Europe, returning here for his well-deserved holiday—during which he nonetheless rose early to faithfully practice his stroke for the two hours a day prescribed by his demanding coach.

"*Bonjour, monsieur!*" Annabel replied shyly. She'd read in the newspapers that this was Hans's first year in serious competition, playing in the highly esteemed "amateur" circuit, which meant that he competed for the glory of the sport and his country, not for money. The youngest son of an eminent German aristocrat, Hans could afford to spend his time in this way, and he was devoted to the game as if it were a religion. There was even talk that next year he might play for, and win, the Davis Cup. He had perfect manners, having been raised to be a gentleman who rode horses, practiced fencing, and eventually produced heirs.

"*Un jour parfait, n'est-ce pas?*" Hans said exuberantly to Annabel as he sprinted past her, heading back to the hotel to wash up after his morning workout.

"*Oui, c'est vrai,*" she responded with a smile.

Employees weren't supposed to fraternize with guests, yet one must politely respond to such casual remarks about the weather; so Annabel and Hans had formed a tacit friendship, a conspiracy of happy early risers, akin to the other morning people whom she saw every day.

But she was glad that Hans's tennis coach had gone off in another direction, for the older man was the complete opposite of Hans: a wiry, sour-faced creature with beady, hooded eyes that seemed to disapprove of everyone.

She watched Hans jog ahead of her on the main, wide stone path flanked with flower beds. When he reached the terrace at the back of the hotel, where breakfast was served under the umbrella pines, someone called out to him, and he paused to chat pleasantly with some guests at their breakfast table.

Annabel had been trained to observe new guests, so she took a quick look around. At this hour there were the usual elderly visitors, but the younger, more fashionable crowd was still sleeping off a night at the cities' casinos and bars.

She spotted a few new arrivals, including an English couple who each looked to be in their late thirties, slightly rumpled in hiking clothes, companionable and cozy over a breakfast of tea and toast and boiled eggs in cups. Somehow they looked vaguely familiar, but they sat with their heads down, each thoroughly absorbed, the man in his newspaper, and the woman poring over a map and making notes as if planning their day's excursion. She had wildly curly reddish hair peeping out from under her hat.

Her husband had a chubby face dominated by big sunglasses. He borrowed her pen and said quietly, "Twelve-letter word for *miserly*, ends with *s*."

"Parsimonious," the wife said. Then she looked up at the waiter and asked in French, "Can you show me where we might find some hiking trails nearby? We'd like to see the local flora." The waiter obligingly bent over to look at her map.

Another newcomer was seated at a small nearby table in the shade of a pine tree. A slender man in his early forties, he had thinning hair and the face of an aristocratic wolf. He drank his coffee while scribbling away with a pointy pencil on a tablet of yellow, lined paper. When he'd filled the sheet, he seemed newly energized, rose, quickly left a tip for the waiter, tucked his yellow pad under his arm, and headed right back into the hotel with great speed.

He looked so distinguished that Annabel could not resist pausing at the reservations podium to look up the man's name. There it was: *Erich Maria Remarque.* As he went by her, she held her breath, wanting to tell him how much she'd admired his novel *All Quiet on the Western Front*, but not daring to "fraternize."

The author nodded to Hans the tennis player, who was still standing at a much bigger table presided over by a well-dressed American matriarch. Her large family of giggly girls and lanky boys looked enthralled. Annabel knew that this was the family of Joseph P. Kennedy, American ambassador to England. They'd checked in over the weekend, and the kids spent most of the day running in and out of their exclusive white tented cabana down by the sea.

"Hans, would you autograph our tennis ball?" said the seven-year-old named Teddy.

Hans smiled and obliged. "Here you go."

As Annabel quietly passed them, she heard the boy named Bobby—who was thirteen and had a face full of mischief—telling Hans, "You should have been down at the cove with us! My brother Joe brought a harpoon gun he got from President Roosevelt, so we chased an octopus! He hid behind the rocks, but we'll get him next time."

After Hans left them, one of the Kennedy girls, Kathleen, whispered something to her mother, Rose, who replied in a firm voice with a Bostonian accent, "Absolutely *not*. Other *people* might allow their girls to run around in two-piece bathing suits, but it is *not* for *us*."

"Oh, *Mother*," the other girls moaned.

Annabel slipped through a side door near the gravel parking lot, past the valets who were moving more quickly now to park the autos of a flurry of new guests who'd arrived via the circular driveway at the front entrance. She smiled to herself, remembering her own arrival just a month ago, right after her junior year at college.

One never forgot one's first experience of the Grand Hotel. Doormen sprang into action at the gold-trimmed doors opening into the palatial white lobby, with its soaring ceiling, marble floors, glass-topped tables with china vases of exotic fresh flowers, and fine lamps with soft lighting.

And beyond the lobby a brief, wide marble staircase led to the *pièce de résistance*—the dramatic rotunda ballroom, a breathtakingly beautiful affair of white-and-gold furnishings, tall gilt-framed mirrors, glittering crystal chandeliers, and enormous french windows with an expansive view of the sweeping lawns, the shining blue sea, and the endless azure sky. The ballroom doors led outside onto another marble staircase that descended to the grand terrace and the main path where Annabel had just been.

Already a flock of guests in swimsuits was flitting down that long main path that bisected the sweeping verdant lawns and led to the clifftop Victorian gardens. There a winding stone staircase led down, down, down to an Olympic-size saltwater pool, carved into the rocky coast with a nearby open-air restaurant. And below the pool area was a meandering coastal path, and a small swimming cove where the Mediterranean Sea sparkled and the sailboats floated in and out of sight.

———

However, all those pleasures were for the guests. Annabel went quickly down a small corridor that led to the employee cloakroom, the offices, the safe-deposit boxes, and the telephone switchboard center. These rooms were smaller and plainer than the guest areas.

"Your uncle is looking for you," said Raphael, the concierge, emerging from his office. A tall, slender Italian man with blue eyes and light-brown hair, he wore a carefully pressed tan uniform. Annabel, like the other female administrators, wore navy and white.

She hurried into the office of the hotel manager, Monsieur Jean-Pierre Faucon, whom she called Oncle JP when nobody else was around. Today he'd assembled the heads of each department—housekeeping, catering, recreation, restaurant, security—for a quick briefing.

"Hollywood will be here in twenty minutes!" Oncle JP proclaimed, glancing at his pocket watch. He was impeccably dressed in a pale-grey suit and white shirt, and, Annabel noticed, he wore his best necktie, the blue silk one he reserved for special occasions.

He was of average height, but he had the high forehead and alert dark eyes of an especially intelligent man who spent his waking hours anticipating and solving every problem before it became a catastrophe. He'd taught the entire staff his "Code of Standards," which was absolutely sacred to him.

"I am pleased to announce," Oncle JP said, "that, in addition to a few guests from Paramount, RKO, Universal, and MGM studios, we will also have visitors from a new movie entity—it's called Olympia Studios—whose president has honored us by booking ALL of his people into our hotel. So as of today, we have a full house, well into September!"

There was a brief burst of enthusiastic chatter among the staff. Then, after quickly going over some staff issues, Oncle JP clapped his hands and said briskly, "*Alors!* I need not remind you that we *never* speak to the press about our guests. Especially now, I expect your utmost discretion at all times. And remember, we do not discuss politics with anyone."

Annabel saw that the faces around her were now quite sober. It was becoming harder and harder to maintain an atmosphere of elegance and charm when Herr Hitler and his fascist pals, Mussolini of Italy and Franco of Spain, had made the world a more angry, dangerous place after bombing other cities into submission.

Yet this aggression had actually inspired the creation of this Cannes Film Festival, for it was designed to be a "freedom-loving counterweight" to last year's infamous Venice Film Festival.

When Annabel first arrived, her uncle had explained the Venice furor. "You see, Hitler and Mussolini outraged the film world by using their clout, at the last minute, to take the prize for the best foreign film away from an American drama that was picked to win, and instead they gave the prize to Leni Riefenstahl's propaganda 'documentary' glorifying Hitler's athletes at the Berlin Olympics. So Italy and Germany will not be represented here in Cannes."

But today, Oncle JP concluded, "Remember: every guest of the Grand Hotel is to be afforded the greatest courtesy, no matter where he comes from."

It was so unlike America, where the bad news seemed like a distant nightmare. Here, the threat of another world war was lapping at every shoreline in Europe, a rising and then receding tide as the diplomats kept working out last-minute compromises that everyone clung to for hope.

"Even if the fascists try to invade *us*, why, our army will stop them cold!" the waiters and porters assured each other. And then, referring to a row of armed, manned forts and bunkers that dotted the border, they'd say, "The Maginot Line will hold!"

———

Now, Oncle JP wrapped up the staff meeting by saying firmly, "*En marche!*"

And the team indeed marched off to their assigned tasks.

Annabel, as usual, waited for a private moment with her

uncle. As the newest member of the staff, she was "on rotation," which she knew perfectly well was really code for "on probation" while Oncle JP watched closely to see for which tasks she was best suited.

She braced herself, expecting to be assigned to whatever department was shorthanded today. Last month she'd worked with the pastry chef for her first week, and she'd smelled of butter and flour all day and every night even after she'd washed up.

After that she'd moved on to the kitchen garden, where she picked fresh herbs and vegetables and fruits until her back ached and her eyes were dazed by the hot sun. Next she'd been assigned to the "recreational" department, which meant working at the pool to hand out dry towels and to collect wet ones, then going over to the tennis courts to retrieve stray balls. Then she was put on the hectic front desk, helping to check people in and out. This was followed by a stint waiting tables in the bar and restaurant; and so July came to an end.

Now a new and important month was beginning, and Annabel sensed that her uncle had reached a point of decision.

Sure enough, he said, "I have had a conversation with the head of Olympia Studios—he and his family have already arrived, ahead of their employees, who will not be far behind—and we think that we may have found a new role for which you are uniquely suited!"

"What is it?" she asked eagerly.

But Oncle JP, in his maddeningly methodical way, said, "Wait for me here while I have the front desk call upstairs to find out if that man from Hollywood is ready to see you!"

CHAPTER 2

Thoughts of
New York and Boston

Annabel sat on the small sofa in her uncle's office, awaiting his return from the lobby and his decision about her fate at the Grand Hotel. What new "role" could she possibly play here that might lead to a permanent position?

She suddenly felt just as nervous as when she'd first arrived. Back then, she'd thought of this as a holiday combined with a summer job, a temporary change of scenery to help her get her bearings.

But on that July day when Annabel had first entered the Grand Hotel, Oncle JP sat her down in his office and made it very clear that in Europe, if you were lucky enough to be taken in as an apprentice and have someone invest that time in you, then you were expected to make a serious commitment to what you'd learned. Your reward was that you could count on doing that same job for the rest of your life. Security, he called it.

Yet to Annabel, who was only twenty, it sounded like a life sentence for some crime she hadn't committed. Still, she'd tried to look enthusiastic. Her uncle saw right through her.

"Ah, I know that expression well," he'd said drolly. "You made the face of Louis—yes, yes, your father looked just like that at your age."

Papa was Oncle JP's younger brother, and although they possessed the same intelligent dark eyes and pale complexion, here the similarities ended. Clearly Oncle JP, a man in his mid-fifties, was cautious and traditional above all.

"What was Papa like—as a boy?" Annabel had asked eagerly.

Oncle JP had sighed but smiled fondly. "He was impulsive and eager for adventure—that's why he left our Riviera and went to *le Nord*." Like a typical Provençal, her uncle referred to the entire rest of France as the dreaded North.

"Paris, you mean," she'd responded in amusement.

"Yes, he worked as a photographer's assistant until the Great War. *Enfin*, when his military service ended with that leg injury, he took the first boat he could get to America. Tell me, what was his life like in New York? His letters sounded happy. Did he achieve his dream?"

So Annabel had told him about her father's life in New York, and how he'd met her mother, Julia—who'd also run away, from a rich but stodgy family in Boston. Julia became a fashion model for a department store, and that was how she met and fell in love with Louis, the handsome French photographer who took her picture. They'd married and then opened their own portrait studio, developing a reputation for magical lighting that brought out the best in the faces they photographed.

"Opera, theatre, and ballet stars adored them," Annabel told her uncle, describing how society people who hoped to look as beautiful as celebrities flocked to her parents' studio.

Annabel had grown up helping out around there, watching her slim, beautiful mother climb up on a stepladder to adjust the lights, while the charming Louis stood below, peering through his camera to get just the right angle that would make a nose less prominent and give tired eyes a glow. Together her parents could turn mildly interesting faces into compelling images of sophistication and dignity.

"But when the Great Depression struck, people stopped spending money, and some of the theatres went dark," Annabel explained. Her uncle nodded soberly.

At first, things had looked bearable for her parents. Yet throughout the 1930s, the clients kept ebbing away. Annabel, tucked safely away at Vassar, had no idea of how bad things had gotten, because her parents didn't want her to find out and drop out of school.

Then, one Christmas when she'd come home, she found her exhausted mother ill with *la grippe*. Mama died shortly after New Year's Day of 1939.

Annabel was shocked that her mother could die before reaching old age. It wasn't fair; it felt horribly wrong. And death itself was utterly unfathomable—how could someone you'd known your whole life just one day *disappear*, forever? Where did they go?

She was simply not prepared to grapple with life's biggest mystery. She'd gone back to school only because her father insisted. And it did force her to concentrate on her studies ahead of her formidable junior-year exams. Some part of her believed that, somehow, Mama was still back there in New York awaiting Annabel's return home.

She hadn't realized that Papa, left completely on his own, never recovered from the loss; this and the strain of trying to hold together his faltering business seemed to age Louis. He was struck with a heart attack just before Easter.

When she arrived home from Vassar for the holiday break, Annabel was met at the door by a doctor, who'd patted her shoulder and said gravely that apparently every man in Papa's family possessed a delicate heart with a "murmur," as he called it. It sounded like a scientific name for dying from a broken heart.

Annabel was by her father's side at the end, holding his hand. He'd whispered, "If I don't make it, go to my brother,

Jean-Pierre. He is not rich, but he's a good man. His address is in your mama's book."

Yet before she could truly cope with this new loss, Annabel was summoned to Boston, to see her mother's family, whom she hadn't ever met because they'd never forgiven Mama for "disgracing" them by running away to Manhattan to marry a "foreigner" who was "in trade."

Nonetheless, Annabel had been eager to finally meet her New England grandmother. It made her think of the Thanksgiving poem about riding a sleigh: *Over the river and through the woods, to Grandmother's house we go . . .*

When she'd entered that imposing old house in the most proper section of Boston, a butler showed her into a dark parlor filled with darker furniture. A severe old white-haired woman sat in a high-backed chair near the fireplace, and she was dressed in black, with a gold-trimmed onyx brooch and a lace shawl. Without any demonstration of affection or sympathy, her eyes glittered as she sized up her granddaughter, who took a smaller seat opposite her.

"You look like your father," Grandmother had said in place of a greeting. It sounded like an insult, delivered as if addressing a scullery maid.

So Annabel replied quietly, "How do you know that? Mama said you refused to meet my father or even look at a photo of him." For her mother had told her of letters returned, unopened.

Grandmother pursed her lips, then said, "You don't look like your mother, but you certainly *sound* just like her." Another appraising gaze. "Well, young lady. What are your plans?"

"I have only one more year left to go at Vassar. My major is poetry, my minor is French, and I've studied a bit of German, too—" Annabel began.

"And how do you plan to pay for another year of school?" her grandmother demanded, leaning on her cane, her bony fingers clasped around its ivory top.

Annabel had fallen silent then. She hadn't been able to bring herself to sort through her father's possessions, but of necessity she'd looked at his bank records. He had a modest savings account with smaller and smaller deposits recorded, but there were still unpaid studio bills to contend with. Evidently he'd been living hand to mouth for some time, always miraculously managing, but only that. She knew that he'd have somehow come up with the last of her tuition, even if he had to borrow it from someone. But he was gone now.

"Your father should have provided better for you," Grandmother said stiffly, and went on to make it quite clear that any money in *her* family was in trust for her sons, not the child of an ungrateful daughter who'd long ago been disowned for her disobedience.

"I can't be expected to pay for the unnecessary schooling of a girl," the old woman continued in a voice as dry as the kindling that crackled in her fireplace. "And where would it get you in the end? Nobody of any quality wants to marry a bluestocking. But you'll be twenty-one in September. You are old enough to be responsible for yourself now. I must know your plans. I don't want this family disgraced any further."

So that's why you sent for me, Annabel thought. *To avoid scandal.* She'd thought her mother had exaggerated her family's stuffiness. Now it was very real.

"A girl like you should enroll in secretarial school," Grandmother had concluded, after mulling it over. "*That* I will pay for. Perhaps you could find work with a bachelor doctor or lawyer who might marry you. I suppose you're pretty enough," she'd said, for the old lady, who was the daughter of a Scottish noblewoman and a whaling captain from Nantucket, had only the vaguest notion of how the rest of the world married off its girls.

Annabel thought it sounded positively medieval. Perhaps she'd inherited some of her parents' restlessness; she wanted to do something special with her life before she settled down.

Which meant that she did have a plan, of sorts. But it wasn't coherently formed yet, so she left her grandmother's house without mentioning that she already *had* a boyfriend—a Harvard man, in fact.

David was the first boy she'd ever contemplated spending the rest of her life with. Their relationship had grown more passionate, and they'd even spoken about having a "future" together. After graduation, of course. David had one more year of law school left.

So she went straight to David's apartment in Cambridge. He took her out to a dinner dance, and then they went back to his place and made love. It was only the second time they'd done so. But that night, he seemed like the only loving person left in her universe.

As they lay there in his bed, he'd asked her how it went with her grandmother; he had always been deeply impressed with this pedigreed side of Annabel's family, who, he'd admitted, made his lineage "look like stowaways" by comparison. Now she told him all about that ghastly interview, and that she was not going back to Vassar.

She'd hoped that he would say, *Let's just get married, then!* But Annabel could see that he wasn't completely listening, as if he had something else on his mind.

Finally he sat up, lit a cigarette, and said regretfully, "Darling, I think you and I should start seeing other people. You need a man with more—resources—than mine."

She'd felt her heart plummet as if she were in an elevator that had just dropped too fast.

He went on, "You're a great girl, and we've had a lovely time together. But I just don't think we're quite right for each other, and it would be selfish for me to keep you all to myself."

She stammered in disbelief, "But—but—just last month you said you loved me and that if we had children together, our kids would be so beautiful and smart and free."

It was humiliating to have to remind him of this. But then he admitted that, over the Easter holiday, he'd kept company with a girl he'd known since childhood that his parents had wanted him to marry all along. Apparently, this time they'd convinced him.

"Edna and I just have more in common, you see," he told Annabel hurriedly. "And when it comes to marriage, that's what's most important—being compatible. She and I have always sort of had an 'understanding' since we were kids. But when I met you, it was like a thunderbolt. I couldn't think of anyone but you," he admitted, as if she were a temptress who'd lured him from the straight and narrow. "But passion isn't enough to make a marriage. I can see that now. And you're the kind of girl who likes to think for yourself all the time."

She'd stared at him blankly, wondering why he was suddenly making this personality trait sound like a defect. Finally he felt obliged to explain that he thought she was becoming "too assertive, even in bed."

"The man is supposed to be the hunter," he said in a tone that sounded like a disapproving minister.

This from the man who'd convinced her that sex before marriage was natural for two people in love; a man who'd taught her how to smoke a cigarette—although she thought those things tasted like burnt matches—and how to listen to jazz. He thought himself "modern" and "progressive," and he professed to support women's rights. Only in theory, evidently.

"You always said you loved my 'spirited nature,'" she said softly, still confused. "Was that just a line?"

"No," he said, looking earnest for the first time. "I do love you. I really do. It's killing me to let you go. But I guess marriage has to be about more than love. A lawyer needs a certain kind of wife who knows how to be a follower. And besides," he added solemnly, "I haven't been fair to Edna, stringing her along. It's high time I did the honorable thing."

Finally, Annabel caught on. "How rich is she?" she asked.

The guilty look on his face was her answer. So, apparently Annabel's Boston heritage had been a large share of her attraction for David . . . until it now looked as if it wouldn't quite pay off.

"See, that's just what I mean," David was saying defensively. "You speak your mind and I admire that; I truly do. But you don't suffer fools, and in certain circles, that would cause offense. I don't want a constant tug-of-war about who's in charge. I want my life to be on an even keel."

He'd held out the flat of his hand and ran it in a straight, level line, to demonstrate.

Annabel said, "If that were a heart monitor, you'd be dead."

She was already getting dressed now. "But you're right about one thing," she added on the way out. "I don't have time for fools."

———

Feeling utterly stranded, Annabel had gone back to her parents' apartment in Manhattan, where the landlord then raised the rent. Despite what her father had said, Annabel couldn't imagine asking a French uncle she'd never met for financial support. Two people had just told her that she couldn't depend on their support. Wouldn't the uncle feel the same? So she took up her grandmother's offer and went to the secretarial school instead of taking her exams at Vassar. She learned so quickly that the head of the school placed her in a job typing for a theatrical agency.

Her plan was to save up enough money to return to Vassar, but on her secretarial pay it would take forever to earn enough. Most of the secretaries she knew were simply marking time until locating a rich boss to marry. Annabel knew that she could no longer bear the mundane existence of a hopeful office girl.

She had never felt so alone in her life. Finally, one Sunday afternoon, she'd worked up the courage to clear out her parents' belongings. There was a stack of magazines about movie stars that her mother used to scrutinize for lighting and posing ideas. As a child Annabel had found them fascinating, for they seemed to tell tales of a more enchanted life, where everyone was beautiful and happy and never bored.

In her parents' closet she found the few possessions that were dearest to them. Her mother had been sentimental about only a few items, like Annabel's baby things.

Her father had a small box of keepsakes. Here Annabel discovered his correspondence with the mysterious Oncle JP. She sat on the floor to sort through the packets of letters and found, to her surprise, that they often discussed the progress of *chère* Annabel.

As she'd sifted through this warm and affectionate correspondence, she saw that Oncle JP had had his sorrows, too; his wife had died when their son was born. Then, when the son was only a young man, he was hit by a car and killed. The son's pregnant girlfriend was too immature to raise a child and was relieved to place it in the care of Oncle JP, who officially adopted his little granddaughter.

The child's name was Delphine, and now eight years old, she was slightly lame from an earlier bout with polio. *I wish that Annabel and Delphine could meet*, Oncle JP had written to Papa. *I think Delphine would like to know an older female cousin, a woman to look up to.*

Annabel had put down the letters with a lump in her throat. Perhaps she could do some good for Oncle JP, instead of merely asking for a handout. These people were the only family she had left. She felt as if she were walking on a tightrope across Niagara Falls, surrounded by thick mist shrouding the past behind her and obscuring the future that lay just ahead.

And so, when her money was running out and all she had left in the world was a suitcase of clothes and just enough for a passage to France, she had written to her uncle, who told her to come at once.

CHAPTER 3

A Hollywood Assignment

Annabel left her uncle's office and peered into the lobby, wondering what had detained him. The reception manager, a neat middle-aged Bavarian woman called Marta, was tending to a newly arrived guest—a bespectacled, spinsterish-looking young woman dressed in a mouse-colored suit, her hair pulled back severely into a bun. She presented a Polish passport but spoke in French.

As Marta checked her in, the elevator doors opened and a man rushed out in a gust of self-importance, barking in tortured French, "My room key has disappeared!"

Herr Wilbert, who'd checked in last week, was a wine importer from Berlin who brought his wife and children to the Grand Hotel every August. He was a rotund man with apple-red cheeks, and he looked as if he should be a jolly fellow by temperament; but he was one of those guests who never entirely settled down.

Glaring at Marta as if daring anyone to accuse *him* of forgetfulness, he said defensively, "I always keep my key on the desk. That stupid room service waiter must have taken it!"

"I'll order you another one right away," Marta said, and she picked up the phone and gave the instructions to her assistant. Marta smiled politely at Herr Wilbert and asked, "Will you be having breakfast on the terrace? We can bring your key to you when it's ready."

Annabel had discreetly slipped behind the counter to collect Herr Wilbert's mail and hand it to him, which he accepted with a grunt. Meanwhile Marta gave the waiting Polish girl her key and said, "Your room is ready. It is rather small and does not have a view, I'm afraid. This is our busiest time of year, and you were the last reservation we took."

Annabel knew just which room this girl would get—small, dark, and facing the parking lot, it was used only when the hotel was truly filled up, and even so, it usually went to a guest's maid or butler.

The Polish girl nodded resignedly; she wore the expression of someone who expected to be treated dismissively. She had only one small suitcase and a battered typewriter valise.

The red-cheeked wine importer, unreasonably annoyed at having to wait for a newly minted key while a mere girl got hers, exploded with, "*Ich habe keine Zeit zu verlieren!*"

The Polish girl stiffened at the mere sound of German being spoken. Annabel understood enough of the language to glean that he'd declared he had no time to waste.

But now Oncle JP returned to the lobby with an air of efficiency, having resolved a delivery problem. Herr Wilbert grabbed his arm and said, "I want my key *now*!"

"Of course!" Oncle JP said instantly. "I'm so glad to find you here. I've been keeping some special information for you about a new winery opening next week. I'm not supposed to give out this brochure until they open, but for you, I think you'll want to know about it."

They stepped aside and became engrossed in the brochure.

Marta hurriedly finished up with the Polish girl, saying, "Your employer paid for his room but hasn't checked in."

"Yes, he has been delayed," the girl responded. "He is a film director. He will surely telephone to let us know when to expect him. Please send for me the moment he calls."

So, Annabel thought, *the poor thing isn't even on vacation*. And yet, at least her boss had put her up here, at the Grand Hotel. Most such clerical types were booked by their employers into cheaper, backstreet inns in the rougher parts of the towns or cities nearby.

It wasn't long before Marta retrieved the new key and handed it to Oncle JP.

"*Alors*, Monsieur Wilbert!" Oncle JP announced, beaming. Herr Wilbert clapped him on the back. But Annabel didn't like seeing her uncle bow his head deferentially to a guest who called Oncle JP *my good man* in a particularly patronizing way, as if speaking to his personal valet, before finally marching off to join his family for breakfast.

Guessing her thoughts, Oncle JP said quietly, "When guests get angry, they are usually just afraid that they aren't being respected. They arrive here with more than suitcases—they bring their troubles, too." He said to Marta, "Send a little box of fresh chocolates to Herr Wilbert's room—he likes that." Then he checked his pocket watch and said to Annabel with a bright smile, "Let's go meet that man from Hollywood!"

They bypassed the elegant guest elevator made of polished mahogany and glass and wrought iron. Instead, he and Annabel went into the plain but more spacious service elevator and rode to the suite level, just beneath the penthouse.

"The president of Olympia Studios is called Sonny Stanten," Oncle JP explained as the elevator ascended. "He is here with his wife, Adelaide, and their two daughters. The older one is Linda, who is married to a man called Alan, who is also a vice president of the studio."

Annabel dutifully absorbed this information. Everyone at

the front desk, pool, and restaurants was taught to know the proper pronunciations of the names of their guests.

"The younger daughter is called Cissy," Oncle JP said, frowning at a small notepad. "We have been given strict instructions that she is to be fed nothing but chicken soup. It is some sort of diet, I'm told. Have you ever in your life heard of such a thing? Morning, noon, and night, nothing but chicken soup, sent up to her room!" He looked disgusted at this attitude toward food. "For 'her health,' they say. No doctor I know would recommend it!"

"It must be some Hollywood diet," Annabel offered. She'd heard plenty of gossip about movie and theatre people, first at her parents' portrait studio, and later at the theatre office where she worked.

"MGM put Judy Garland on such a diet—she's the girl who sings in that big new musical that will be shown at the festival, *The Wizard of Oz*," she explained. "And poor Greta Garbo ate nothing but raw carrots and cabbage until her director, Ernst Lubitsch, insisted that she go out and eat a big juicy steak to put 'roses in her cheeks' before they shot their new movie that's coming out this year—it's called *Ninotchka*."

Oncle JP listened with a puzzled look, as if earnestly trying to understand the habits of an exotic species called actors. "I heard from our room service supervisor that a woman guest named Miss Marlene Dietrich asked for something called Epsom salts. Ever heard of *that*?"

"She must have sprained an ankle or something," Annabel suggested.

"No," Oncle JP said in a droll voice. "She drinks them."

"Oh! To make her feel less hungry, perhaps," Annabel said, but she shuddered.

As the elevator slowed to a stop, Oncle JP continued, "These men from Olympia Studios were very pleased to hear that I have you on our staff—an American girl who speaks both English and French." He smiled at her with affectionate pride.

"You will be a real asset this summer. Most of these Hollywood people don't speak French at all," he added incredulously, as if he could not imagine living on earth without the music of his mother tongue.

When they stepped out of the elevator, the penthouse doors were already flung wide open, revealing the mogul's family and their servants rushing to and fro. Annabel could see trunks and suitcases everywhere as the butler and maid scurried to unpack them.

In the center of the main sitting room stood the matriarch called Adelaide, a stout woman laden with heavy gold jewelry, perfume, and a fur-trimmed wrap, even in this summer heat. She seemed to be directing everything, while two yippy white dogs were snapping at the ankles of every passing bellhop and servant, then jumping up and down on every gold-satin-covered Louis XVI chair in sight. Annabel held her breath, wondering how this lovely furniture, not to mention the bellhops, would survive the season.

"Linda!" Adelaide shouted at her eldest daughter. "Stop tying up the phone line."

Linda, taller and slimmer than her mother, was dressed in a more fashionable outfit of silk and linen that looked straight out of an ad for Coco Chanel's new "resort wear."

"Of course I *had* to get all new clothes, once we stopped in Paris," Linda was saying, gesturing with a cigarette-in-its-holder, as if she could be seen by the person on the other end of the phone. "Everything that seemed so chic back home suddenly looked positively *horrid*. I tell you, the minute you look in a mirror in this country, suddenly you just *see* everything that's wrong. Well, darling, you can kid yourself anywhere else—but *not* in France."

Adelaide turned to a harried maid and said sharply, "Put the hatbox there, not *there*!"

Annabel whispered in panic, "Oncle, I don't have to work

for these women, do I?" She imagined herself as some sort of ladies' maid to such an exhausting family.

"No, no. Come this way. Sonny Stanten said he wants to explain your duties to you himself," Oncle JP said, as the matriarch, who'd given him a flicker of a glance, now tilted her head to indicate that her husband was in another room.

Annabel followed her uncle down a brief, plushly carpeted interior corridor, passing a bedroom where other maids were busily unpacking trunks; and then a bathroom whose door was wide open. A plump young guest was visible, sitting in her underslip on the wide edge of the tub, her face streaked with tears. She looked to be sixteen.

"That's the younger daughter, the one they called Cissy," Oncle JP said quietly. "The one who's on that strict diet."

Cissy was making a strange, low moaning noise that sounded like "Ahh-whoa-whoa-whoa!" over and over again. A severe-looking woman dressed in a nurse's white uniform, poised at the counter before an open black bag, turned briskly, brandishing a hypodermic needle. But before administering it, something caused her to look up and, seeing Annabel and Oncle JP, she kicked the door closed.

At the end of the hall was the master bedroom suite, which had its own sitting room, fitted out with generous white leather chairs and yellow brocade curtains. Two men were ensconced around a low, glass-topped coffee table spread with sheaves of paperwork. Both men wore three-piece dark suits instead of the usual pale flannel sported by men of leisure.

"We're scheduled for cocktails with the distributors from Berlin today," the younger man was saying, completely indifferent to the pandemonium in the other rooms.

The portly elder man glanced up and nodded to Oncle JP. "Ah, it's you. And this is—?"

"My American niece. Annabel, this is Mr. Sonny Stanten."

Annabel thought it a bit incongruous that it was the older

man who was called Sonny. He had thinning grey hair and wore reading spectacles halfway down his long thin nose, which gave him the look of a dormouse in a fairy tale. Except for his cigar. Without removing it, he said brusquely, "Good. We need somebody American around here. Can she type?"

"Of course," Oncle JP said smoothly. "As I mentioned to you on the telephone, she was a secretary in an important theatrical agency in New York City."

The younger man, who Annabel later confirmed was the son-in-law named Alan, now studied her with renewed interest. "Then *you* must be an important girl," he said in a teasing tone as silky as cream. His bristly mustache twitched into a smile; he wore a red carnation in his buttonhole, and he looked as if he spent a good part of his day appraising women.

"Fine," Sonny said, turning his sharp gaze to Annabel, with a keen look that was all business. "I need a girl to take care of two of my people. One is an actor—Jack Cabot—who thinks of himself as a director and a producer, to boot. I only put up with him because he convinced my best actress, Téa Marlo, to delay renewing her contract with *me* unless I let her star in Jack's little independent movie and distribute the damned film! So we're premiering it here."

"Oh!" Annabel perked up at the names Jack Cabot and Téa Marlo; they'd been paired in two other movies for Sonny's studio and were the hottest thing since John Gilbert and Greta Garbo. Sonny allowed a smile, proud that these stars were his.

"You like Cabot and Marlo, eh? Well, maybe we'll pick up some European distributors; they like this arty stuff," he grumbled. "So, girlie, if you see any Frenchie reporters, tell them this new movie is the best thing since sliced bread. It's called *Love Isn't Easy*—you got that?"

The son-in-law said perfunctorily, to no one in particular, "A much better title than what the screenwriter wanted to call it—*Love Is a Pain*."

"Screenwriters are a number-one pain, and actors come in a close second. I'd rather raise racehorses," Sonny muttered. "But we made it into a good movie anyway."

Annabel had met men like Sonny in New York. They were brash, confident, and aggressive, unafraid to gamble on a hunch, but they had surprisingly delicate egos. If somebody crossed or insulted them, such men worked themselves into a lather, and they were prone to proclaiming their grudges to anyone who'd listen—a bartender, barber, or secretary—like a dog worrying an old bone.

Sonny said briskly, "Okay, Mam'zelle Annabel, here's your schedule. In the mornings I want you working with my dipso-maniac screenwriter, who wrote that script for *Love Isn't Easy* because it was based on his unpublished short story. He's still under contract, so I've got him doing rewrites on some other scripts now. He swears he's on the wagon, but nobody believes him. I picked him up cheap after he got dropped from MGM and was loaned out to work on that infernal *Gone with the Wind*. He got kicked off that movie, too."

"Well," said Alan, "every screenwriter in town has worked on *Gone with the Wind*."

"But this one can't type for beans," Sonny said to Annabel. "And he's got handwriting nobody can read. I hope *you* can. Go to him in the mornings and type whatever he gives you. He says he'll lay it out for you on his desk. Look over his correspondence and his calendar, too. He's hopeless with that stuff. And—most of all—make sure he doesn't take a drink. I don't know how much work he'll have for you today, but try to get started and learn the ropes."

Annabel couldn't help liking Sonny. His blunt manner was somehow like a breath of fresh air, filled with verve and energy. It might be fun to be a part of all this, after all, working on exciting films with big stars. Perhaps a door was opening somewhere.

"You'll assist the actor in the afternoons," he continued.

"Make sure Jack Cabot shows up for all the promotional events we've lined up for him, especially the interviews. He's always trying to duck out of interviews. Look over his correspondence and his calendar, too."

But then Sonny eyed her keenly and said, "Report to me about every single angle he's working. I want to know who Jack's talking to and what nonsense he's filling Téa Marlo's head with. I can never tell *what* she's thinking. The woman is an enigma."

"Don't forget, Jack Cabot is meeting with us at lunch today," Alan reminded him.

Sonny said, "Right," then turned to Annabel to amend his orders. "So just go to meet Cabot around three o'clock today; say hello. Then, starting tomorrow, your mornings are with my screenwriter, and your afternoons are with the actor at two o'clock. And at the end of each week, I want a full report on both men. Got that?"

It now dawned on Annabel that Sonny had been using this confidential, engaging tone to ensure her loyalty; in fact, it sounded as if he expected her to be some sort of a studio snoop. She felt suddenly apprehensive.

"*Absolument*," Oncle JP said with a brief bow. "Please let us know if there is anything else you need." He guided Annabel to make a professional exit, politely ignoring the family hubbub that was continuing unabated in the front room as the mother and daughter ordered the servants around, barely noticing Oncle JP and Annabel as they departed.

When they were safely back in the service elevator, Oncle JP rubbed his hands together and said with satisfaction, "This should be 'right up your street,' as you Americans say, because of your experience in that New York theatrical agency. Sonny will pay extra for your secretarial services, of course. Do your best, and then you will develop the reputation of being a competent and reliable secretary whom others wish to hire."

Oh, swell, Annabel thought dispiritedly, her brief hopes for a glamorous future dashed.

"A typewriter is a typewriter is a typewriter," she muttered. If Gertrude Stein had been a secretary, that surely would have been the extent of her poetic response to the world.

"*Pardon?*" Oncle JP said mildly.

"Oncle, why did he ask me to 'report' on the actor and the screenwriter? I'm not a nanny and I'm not a spy!" she objected. She knew from her theatre work that gleeful gossip was the plague of the entertainment industries, and low-level flunkies were only too happy to be given an official reason to snitch on their betters.

"Of course you're not a spy," Oncle JP agreed. "Trust your old uncle, who has been working at the Grand Hotel almost as long as that old frog sitting on the fountain." He was referring to a stone frog carved onto the rim of an ornate fountain in a side garden.

She felt slightly ashamed of her own ingratitude. Oncle JP was the most hardworking person she'd ever met. At sunrise every day, at his doctor's suggestion to maintain the health of his heart, Oncle JP jogged up to the top of the plateau called the Mound in the center of the *Cap*. The military brass up there all knew him well, for he'd served with one of them.

Then he would return to his apartment in the nearby fishermen's village of Saint-Pierre. Patiently he'd feed his little granddaughter, Delphine, her breakfast, then bring her to the next-door neighbor in their apartment building, a kindly older woman who looked after the child in the summer. Having done all this, Oncle JP would report to work earlier than most of the staff at his prized Grand Hotel. He was indisputably the heart and soul of the place.

Moreover, her uncle had gone out of his way to let her know that she was wanted on a personal level. When Annabel had first arrived, he'd already booked her into the nice place at the

rooming house so she'd have her privacy, but she had a standing invitation to join him and his granddaughter every week for
Sunday dinner.

"You are family," he'd said. "Always come to us whenever you
wish. Your joys are our joys; your troubles are our troubles. You
are not alone. We will always be here for you."

———

So how on earth could Annabel complain today, when her uncle
was so pleased to have found her a spot of work that he thought
would reinforce a path toward her future security?

Now Oncle JP said reassuringly, "Just type what they want
you to type, and see that they get their work done. Then we can
tell Sonny that your clients are doing exactly what they are supposed to be doing. If they are not, you come to me, and I will
handle it. These guests are the kind that may never come back
here again; but they will talk about this experience they've had
at our Grand Hotel, for years to come. That is how reputations
are formed."

Annabel nodded. "Yes, Oncle JP. What rooms are my clients staying in?"

"Ah! The actor, this Jack Cabot, he is staying in the Villa
Sanctuaire," Oncle JP replied. "The screenwriter is in the Jasmine Cottage. I've already had a typewriter sent down there.
But as this Sonny fellow said, today is more of a get-acquainted
session. So go and see what you can do for the writer, and if
you have free time afterward, then report to the poolside for
the rest of the morning, because we have a shortage of bar staff
there, today of all days. I will send someone down to relieve you
there as soon as possible. Take a late lunch up here; and if you
have time to bring Delphine into the garden for some air, that
would be good. Then go to help the actor. Let me know how it
all went when you're done."

Annabel found it interesting that Sonny had placed her clients in the two cottages that belonged to the Grand Hotel—perhaps to keep them away from the rest of the guests, for whatever unknown reasons. These cottages were the most private and yet the most simple accommodations, for they stood at some distance from the main building. Sometimes they went unoccupied for weeks, because most guests preferred the convenience and immediacy of the hotel rooms and their proximity to the convivial bars and terraces and services.

Even before the elevator doors opened onto the main floor, they heard raucous shouting coming from the lobby.

"Now what?" Annabel wondered aloud as she stepped out.

The lobby was completely jammed with newly arrived Hollywood guests dressed in bright colors and awash in cologne. Everyone was chattering nonstop in loud, excited voices that seemed to ricochet off the walls and ceilings, making the lobby clang like a great bell as people clamored to get to the front desk and be sure that they were getting the best rooms. The women's voices were high and shrill as they greeted each other with exaggerated affection. The men boomed jovially, their voices flying like billiard balls crashing into one another.

"Hey, get a load of this pretty little elevator!" a dapper young man called out.

Everyone seemed beautiful and bursting with vitality. Dazzled, Annabel would have liked to stay and see if she could recognize any movie stars beneath their stylish hats and behind those fashionable sunglasses.

Oncle JP looked slightly alarmed by his loud new American guests. "Are they all drunk?" he asked, baffled by the voices that were so different from the low-key murmurs of his usual European clientele.

"No, just—giddy," Annabel explained. At his blank look she added, "*Excités.*"

A look of comprehension crossed his face, and Oncle JP

shook his head. "Ah, yes. This season, it's the Cannes Film Festival that has our guests all excited. But last summer, for some crazy reason, they'd all been told that the Earth was going to collide with the planet Mars. I will admit that it *was* hanging very near and red and bright in the sky at the time."

"But people didn't actually believe that Mars would hit the Earth, did they?" she asked.

He nodded vigorously. "*Oui*, they *wanted* to believe. That season our gentlemen guests ordered telescopes and set them up on the lawn, to calculate exactly when the end would come. Some of them bought binoculars and watched from the rocks. The women, meanwhile, all demanded at the same time to see the hairdresser, so we had to hire extra *coiffeurs*. And bring in seamstresses to alter all the ladies' new gowns. In fact many jewelers came to the hotel with great big boxes to display their most expensive pieces, and *they* made a tidy profit, too."

At Annabel's puzzled expression, Oncle JP explained, "The guests were all competing to be the most beautiful corpses in history when the end came. Like the pharaohs."

"But—the world *didn't* come to an end," she said, amused. "What did they do then?"

"*Enfin*, when the designated tragic night arrived, the guests all ordered the most expensive caviar and pheasant and champagne we had. They dined, danced, and drank until dawn. Passed out on the lawn, binoculars around their necks! Not until the next day, when the sun burned bright in the sky, did they realize that Mars, the god of war, had decided to let them all live—at least for another year."

Annabel glanced up sharply, wondering if her uncle was, in his subtle way, trying to warn her of something more than just this humorous aspect of human nature.

But all he said was, "*Ah bon*. Go help your poor scriptwriter. He sounds like a man who could really use some kindly assistance."

CHAPTER 4

The Jasmine Cottage

If you didn't know that there were two cottages on the grounds of the Grand Hotel, you would never find them on your own. Beyond the fragrant gardens, hidden in the tall pine hedges, was a high, locked wooden gate that opened onto a winding, secretive pebbled path flanked by even taller hedges of flowering shrubs and pine.

Annabel reached for the key in her pocket and opened the gate before locking it again behind her. She heard the cries of bossy birds nesting in the hedges, who flitted overhead in alarm at her presence and called out warnings to one another. A small frog hopped worriedly across the path ahead of her feet. Deep in the shade of the pines, a scops owl emitted its wistful call.

She followed the pebbled path, which branched into two forks, both walled by hedges. The right fork led to the larger cottage, whose gardens descended down to the sea.

It was called la Villa Sanctuaire. This, she knew, was where the actor, Jack Cabot, was staying and where she would report for duty in the afternoon. The villa was ringed by a white fence and climbing fuchsia-colored roses. There was a private pool and garden, two bedrooms, two bathrooms, a tiny servant's room off the kitchen, and a parking area behind the building.

The blue-tiled pool sparkled invitingly in the morning sun, but it lay still. The shutters were closed upon the villa windows, and nothing stirred.

"Maybe he's sleeping. Well, Mr. Cabot has had a long journey," Annabel told herself.

She turned down the left fork of the pebbled path, which was narrower and led to the Jasmine Cottage. It had a white gate with two stone urns on each side spilling over with flowering jasmine, their pale-yellow-and-white flowers trumpeting a mysterious scent. A tiny patio on the side was flanked by trellises covered with more jasmine and small pale-pink roses. The cottage had only one bedroom, a small kitchen, a study, a little parlor, and one full bath. No pool, and you had to walk farther down the path to get a look at the sea. So it was easy to see that successful actors were considered far more important than screenwriters.

But Annabel actually preferred this Jasmine Cottage, so endearingly tucked into its private clearing, sheltered cozily by pine hedges at the rear. It seemed like an enchanted hermit's or lovers' cottage that, in movies, inspired a sigh from the enthralled audience.

She reached the front door, and when she knocked, it swung open, since it had been left slightly ajar.

"Hello?" she called out tentatively. Maybe he'd gone to get some breakfast or take a swim. She felt uneasy about this idea of working for a "dipsomaniac," as Sonny had so inelegantly put it. It was no joke to deal with an alcoholic.

She stood hesitantly in a quiet little parlor, which was really more of an anteroom, with an open archway to the adjoining study. Immediately she noticed that the typewriter, sent down here by Oncle JP, was sitting on a small typing table in a windowed alcove of the study, with a chair pulled up to it and a fresh sheaf of paper alongside it.

There was also a larger, more formal desk, heaped with a scattering of books and papers. Annabel remembered Sonny's instructions about what the screenwriter wanted from her: *He says he'll lay it out for you on his desk. Look over his correspondence and his calendar, too.*

A bit uncertainly, she advanced to the big desk to see if he'd left instructions for her.

The screenwriter had evidently been at work already, for there were piles of opened letters, stacked beside an opened ledger. Some letters were marked *File: final*; others were labeled *Reply required.*

The nearby ledger had scrupulous notations with amounts and dates of installment payments made for bills and loans, showing any balance still due. There was a loan from "Agent," with interest, recently paid off. There were overdue hospital bills, from New York, California, and North Carolina. Someone had had to have an appendectomy. Someone else had a bad lung. Another bill was for a stay in a "rest" asylum.

"I hope he doesn't expect me to do bookkeeping," she said under her breath, for she'd had no experience of keeping ledgers.

Her gaze returned to the letters. Many bore the logos of well-known American magazines—*Saturday Evening Post, Cosmopolitan, Esquire*—and one glance made it clear that these were what writers called "rejection slips," citing reasons such as *The ending could be difficult for us, our readers prefer happy endings*, and *This story, while good, lacks the warmth of the author's best work*, or simply *I wish the character was more likable*, and finally, *It doesn't have the incandescent quality we'd hoped for.*

"Whew!" Annabel murmured. She knew the joke that every waiter in Hollywood was writing a screenplay and every screenwriter was writing a novel. This guy was clearly "moonlighting" from his script work by writing short stories—and he was getting

kicked around, but judging from his meticulous records, he refused to give up.

Finally she spotted a stack of typed pages with handwritten changes on them, topped by a longhand note on a sheet of
Grand Hotel stationery: *Type today. Good for Collier's.*

"These must be my instructions," she sighed, relieved. She
estimated that this manuscript was just over thirty pages long.
It wasn't in script format, so it must be a treatment.

She carried it to the little typing area, sat down, put a sheet
of clean paper into the typewriter, and glanced at the title of the
manuscript, handwritten all in capital letters: *THE WOMEN
IN THE HOUSE.* But then he'd crossed that out and put in a
new one: *TEMPERATURE.* The author line said *by John Darcy.*

The handwriting wasn't as bad as Sonny had made it sound;
she'd seen worse. The writer was clearly an educated man,
but there were occasional misspellings, as if he had been in a
great hurry and couldn't be bothered. She began to retype it
with the changes.

She could not help becoming engrossed in the story, chuck-
ling at certain satiric lines. It was about a scriptwriter with a
fever, living in a bungalow on a movie star's estate and wanting
to rekindle his love affair with an actress. But he was also at-
tracted to a new secretary. However, a medical lab had mixed
up the scriptwriter's electrocardiograph with that of another
patient who had a fatal heart condition . . .

Annabel's typing speed usually depended on whether the
material bored her or not. Invoices, sales reports, and memos
could be deadly slow going. But she was very fast when the material was good. And this one was fun. She typed away.

"Hey, what are you doing there?" came a sharp male voice.

A man stood in the doorway between the study and the
bedroom. He was dressed in a rumpled bathrobe he'd thrown
over a shirt and pants. He was slender, with golden-brown hair
touched by some strands of grey. His hair was askew and his

face looked bewildered, as if he'd perhaps dozed off and then just woke up.

He was holding a cigarette in one hand and a stub of a pencil in the other. He stared at her with alert, bright eyes that seemed not entirely blue, not entirely grey, and not entirely green. He looked to be in his early forties, but he was so pale that he seemed almost ghostlike. There was a slight sheen of perspiration across his face.

Annabel stammered, "I'm your typist. Mr. Sonny Stanten said to come here in the mornings."

"Yeah, he told me," the man said ruefully. "You're here to make sure I produce pages for him. He doesn't believe that writers are working unless he hears the clickety-clack of the typewriter keys. No use telling him I get all my best ideas in the bathtub."

Then he saw that she'd started on the manuscript, and his eyes narrowed. "Oh!" he said with some alarm. "Did Sonny also ask you to spy on me, or are you playing house detective on your own?" he asked warily, drawing nearer to see which papers she was working on.

Annabel blushed, since Sonny *had* asked her to be a snoop, though she truly hadn't meant to do so. She said defiantly, "I am *not* one of Sonny's—employees. I work for the Grand Hotel. I'm supposed to type your correspondence and your rewrites. He said *you* said it would all be waiting for me on your desk."

"Ah!" The man relaxed a little. "I said I would leave it all on *your* desk. Not mine," he corrected. "My fault. I forgot to put the damned script there for you. C'mon."

He returned to the bedroom. Annabel rose uncertainly and advanced only far enough to watch from the threshold. The man stooped to pick up pages of lined paper littered on the floor around the bed. He'd evidently had a pot of coffee sent in, for the pot, cup and saucer, spoon, sugar, and milk lay crowded on the nightstand.

But the wooden tray, with which the waiter would have

carried it in, had been put on the bed and pressed into service as a lap desk, judging from what was on it: a pad of lined paper, an ashtray and cigarettes and matches, a scattering of stubby pencils, and a pencil sharpener. He'd moved a lamp closer to the bedside table, too. Clearly he'd been at work from the moment he got here—possibly even on the train ride over, too, judging from the many pages he'd produced. Strange that he was working in bed, like an invalid, instead of at a desk.

She observed that there was no sign of the drinker about him: no bottles, no smell of alcohol. He was sober and clear eyed, so perhaps he truly was "on the wagon." He continued to search the bedroom until he finally found what he was looking for and waved it aloft; yes, a script, for its pages were fixed together with familiar-looking fasteners.

While she waited, Annabel could not help noticing that the man's luggage was laid out on chairs in the bedroom, wide open, as if he hadn't even fully unpacked yet, except for one battered suit and a rumpled raincoat hanging in the dressing room alcove, with a pair of polished shoes lined up neatly below. And there was a single hat perched on the shelf above.

"Do you need some help unpacking? I can call a valet," she asked, politely and automatically. All guests were offered this service.

He shook his head ruefully. "Fortunately," he said in a wry tone, "I travel light."

He handed her the script. He'd made penciled revisions on these typed pages, too. Sometimes he'd crossed out a whole page and stuck a handwritten one over it.

"I hope you can read my scribbling. If you can't, just make up a good line. This movie will never get made, no matter what I or anyone else do to it. I always feel sorry for the guy whose script I'm rewriting, but this one's impossible. It's got a role for a female swimmer who sings. Never met one who could do both. But Sonny's got her under contract."

He was frank and friendly, with a smile that made his whole face glow with life. Yet he had a delicate quality; there were shadows under his eyes, and that sheen on his pale skin, and an occasional cough that followed a spell of talking. His clothes looked slightly too big for him, especially around the neck and shoulders—perhaps indicating a man who'd been ill. That could explain why he was working in bed. She remembered those medical bills she'd just seen.

"I recently finished up an assignment for MGM—*Madame Curie* for Greta Garbo," he said, as if to assure her that he'd had better projects. "But in the end they shelved the whole thing. 'Too much science, not enough romance.' Then Alfred Hitchcock wanted me to adapt Daphne du Maurier's novel *Rebecca*. But I was in the hospital with a lung cavity at the time."

She glanced up quickly. So he *had* been seriously ill, and quite recently.

He looked at her more keenly, his face alight with curiosity. "I suppose I should interview you before we officially commit to working together, right?" he said with a teasing grin, stubbing out his cigarette in an ashtray and following her back into the study. "Say, what's your name?"

She told him, and he repeated rather indifferently, "Annabel. That's my sister's name. I tried to make her into a successful *femme fatale*, but some women just aren't meant to be vamps. You sound American."

"I am," she answered.

"You go to school?"

She hesitated. "I did," she hedged.

"Where?"

"Vassar."

"Ah!" he exclaimed, more interested now. "My daughter goes there. I worry that she'll just get swept up in the parties and neglect her studies. When did you graduate?"

"I—my father died, so—I had to leave early," she said, awaiting the dismissive response most people gave her for this failure.

"Oh, too bad. Well, I quit college early, too," he said conspiratorially. "Princeton. Just as well. Some of those Ivy League
professors were born just to bore students to death and kill all
your desire to learn. What did you study?"

"Poetry," Annabel confessed.

"Really? Do you write poetry? I did, too!" He stared at her
with a strange fascination, as if he'd just found out that they had
the same astrological sign. She suddenly suspected that this
screenwriter was deliberately trying to "draw her out."

"Who are your favorite poets and authors?" he asked in a
teacherly tone, sitting down on the arm of a sofa.

"Emily Dickinson," she said; then, wanting to get this
inquiry over with as quickly as possible, she added, "Elizabeth Barrett Browning. Robert Browning. Keats. Longfellow.
T. S. Eliot." She hoped that would satisfy him. You weren't
really supposed to chat with the guests beyond certain polite
formalities.

He told her a few scholarly anecdotes about each poet's
life, then gestured at the papers on his desk and said ruefully,
"I wanted to be a poet, but here I am writing for Hollywood and
the slick magazines! All they want from me are cute stories
about spirited young girls. I think it's creepy for men my age to
do that. Read any good novels about girls lately?"

"Well, I used to read Louisa May Alcott when I was younger."

He surprised her by saying, "Me too. Read that over and over
as a kid. Who else? And please don't say Jane Austen. College
girls always say Jane Austen."

"Actually, I liked Charlotte Brontë better," she admitted. "*Vil-
lette* made me cry."

"Good! How about a more contemporary author?"

"Well—I loved *The Great Gatsby*," she ventured shyly.

He looked surprised. "Really? Most girls never read it. That wasn't exactly women's fiction. And women, I'm told, are the ones who 'make' a book a bestseller. Or not."

Annabel was hovering over the little typing table, waiting a bit uncertainly.

"Let's make a schedule," he said enthusiastically. "I'm good at lists and schedules. I compose in longhand. Every night, I'll leave the day's assignment on *your* desk. Then you come in just as you did today, and when you leave, drop it on my desk. I'll go over it once more and make any final changes to be retyped the next day. How's that sound?"

Annabel smiled. There was something touching about him; he seemed a bit lonely and yet rather formal in an old-fashioned, gallant sort of way.

"Fine," she said. "But I must be done by noon each day. I am working for someone else in the afternoons."

"Who?" he asked, alert. "Another screenwriter?"

"No, an actor."

"Which one?"

"Jack Cabot."

"Ah!" he said. "Jack is destined to be a *big* star—if he can just get Sonny out of his way."

There it was again: that odd bit of tension around the name of Jack Cabot. Annabel could not help saying, "Sonny seems bothered by Mr. Cabot; why is that?"

The screenwriter nodded. "You figured that out already? Well, some men are just born to annoy each other. Sonny never really knew what to do with Jack Cabot. They put him in westerns, but he was too debonair for that. They put him in romantic comedies, but he's not wacky enough. Then they tried him out in gangster pictures. Those weren't bad, but now Jack knows he can do real drama."

"Yes," Annabel ventured. "Mr. Cabot's performances are so—intelligent, so passionate."

"Yeah, well, Sonny likes the sex appeal but hates the

intelligence. He just wants another contract player to move around on his checkerboard with whatever leading lady *du jour.*"

"But he's as good as Cary Grant and Clark Gable," Annabel said stoutly.

"Great! We want lots of women to think as you do. Because Jack and Téa Marlo just made a new movie based on one of my scripts. It's called *Love Isn't Easy.*"

Annabel nodded, recalling the studio men's discussion.

The screenwriter's eyes narrowed. "You've heard of it?"

"Sonny mentioned it. Sounds like fun," she said diplomatically.

"Well," he sighed, "we rewrote the hell out of it, and they changed the whole ending. But maybe this time I'll get a screen credit—and better pay! They're going to show our movie at a party at this hotel. I've seen some of the rushes. Jack looks terrific; so does the girl."

"I can't wait to see him—I mean, in the movie," Annabel said, feeling embarrassed that she had just revealed a desire she herself hadn't been fully aware of until now.

"I suppose you'll fall in love with him, and that will be the end of my secretary," he said, as if he were already imagining the plot of a movie. "Well, don't elope with that guy till the Cannes Film Festival's over! That's how long my contract is. Depending on how fast you type, I bet we can get a lot done." His face was radiant with visions of great success.

But this burst of enthusiasm must have used up some of his strength, because he swayed slightly now. He sighed. "What do people do around this hotel for exercise?" he asked. "I'm supposed to 'build up my strength' while I'm here. Is there a tennis court?"

"Yes. Also, there is croquet. And a big, lovely swimming pool," she said, reverting to a more formal, hotel-hospitality mode. "And of course you can swim in the sea, although this time of year you must look out for the *méduse.* Jellyfish," she translated at his blank look.

It occurred to her that he looked too feverish for any of these vigorous activities.

He was watching her face alertly and now asked, "What's wrong?"

"Just—just that it gets very hot at midday, and it's better to swim or play in the early morning or late afternoon," she offered lamely.

"You're a terrible liar. Best not to attempt it," he advised. "Lying doesn't come naturally to you, so it shows. You've got an open, honest face; that's why it's easy to talk to you."

Other people had told her this at the secretarial agency; it caused them to confide in her in a way they wouldn't with others. Even strangers on the train, and on the boat ride to Europe, had told her their life stories. It made her feel naive sometimes; as if she were a girl who could pose no danger or threat to anybody.

She took her seat at the typewriter, then hesitated.

"What's the matter?" he asked.

She was holding the screenplay but gazing at the page in the typewriter. "Should I finish the changes on this story first? I started them because I thought that note was for me."

He regarded her appraisingly again. "Sure—if you don't tell Sonny, and you don't mind doing a little moonlighting? I can't pay much for it, just a bit extra. But I'd sure like to get this short story out in the mail pouch today. The screenplay rewrites can wait until tomorrow."

"Certainly," she said. "I can do this quickly."

"Okay, Annabel. When you're done, just let yourself out," he said over his shoulder as he retreated to his bedroom to work. "À bientôt."

Annabel smiled. "You speak French?" she asked.

He shook his head. "Nope. But I've been to the French Riviera before. In happier times."

CHAPTER 5

La Piscine des Sirènes

The air had become hotter and heavier in the blazing sun by the time that Annabel hurried down the zigzagging stone staircase that led to the pool and the sea cove.

The magnificent Olympic-size pool was the pride of the Grand Hotel. It was built into a rocky ledge overlooking the brilliant Mediterranean, and on another ledge below, there were white tents that served as private cabanas. There a narrow flight of stone stairs led to the coastal path and a small swimming cove, where the sea lapped invitingly and one could swim in the company of tiny bright orange-and-blue fish that darted in and out as the waves carried them back and forth. Beyond the cove, the wider sea was dotted with the white sails of yachts gliding slowly and majestically, adding to the billowy, meditative atmosphere.

Most guests lounged by the big pool, called la Piscine des Sirènes, which was made with exquisite violet-blue tiles and sparkled in the sunlight. It was constantly replenished with seawater that came via underground tanks that filtered it. There was a high diving board and a lower one. In the center of the pool, at the very bottom, was a lovely mosaic image of a mermaid or *sirène*, the logo for this beach "club" area.

Annabel loved this spot; a person could just spend the whole day here quietly watching the sun—it would rise softly to your left and then traipse giddily across the blue sea until finally it set on your right in a blaze of tangerine-colored glory.

But today, the scene here was wildly, frantically busy. As she donned an apron to help serve the new guests, Annabel immediately saw that while a few people were in the pool cavorting like children, showing off on diving boards, or gleefully dunking one another, many of the Hollywood people, camped out in the luxurious poolside sunbeds, appeared to be conducting meetings and behaving as if they were still in Los Angeles, impervious to the new scenery and the natural serenity of this place. And all of these newcomers wore enormous dark sunglasses. The regular guests who summered every year on the Riviera found the Hollywood crowd amusing. But the polite French staff had their hands full.

Yves, the pool director, muscular and suntanned from working outdoors, and wearing a white uniform, trotted about supervising the young lifeguards and poolside staff.

He nodded gratefully to Annabel, saying, "You are a lifesaver! A lot of these movie people don't speak French; they make hand gestures at the waiters or point at the coffee or champagne they want. They will be happy to hear you speak English!"

Carefully balancing her tray, Annabel approached a tall, lean, handsome man who appeared to be in his late thirties, ensconced in a corner chair next to a shorter, bald man. They ordered coffee, and when she set each cup down on the small table between the two men, she couldn't help overhearing their conversation.

The tall, handsome one said in an aggrieved but laconic way, "Look, *you're* my agent and *you're* the one who said I should be more careful about the projects I take."

The bald man was perspiring, even in the shade of the parasol. "But for Chrissake, if Selznick ever again tells you he's bought the rights to a bestseller and wants you for the lead, you should tell *me* about it before you say no."

"Aw, I never read the tomfool book! He said it was about a Civil War rogue in Atlanta who makes ladies swoon—all I could think was, can you imagine me playing a lover boy from the South? Mister, my fans would laugh themselves silly and choke on their popcorn."

"Okay, then! You dodged a bullet," the bald man said unconvincingly.

"Oh, sure! Now all the gossips are saying Gary Cooper thought he was too good to play Rhett Butler in *Gone with the Wind*."

Annabel gasped at the star's name, realizing why she'd been mesmerized by the unusual cadence of the actor's voice. He heard her and looked up sharply; then he grinned and said conspiratorially, "Keep it on the QT, huh, baby?"

She nodded shyly, feeling as if she'd just had some magic stardust sprinkled into her life. As she turned away, she heard the agent say, "Was I supposed to tip that girl for the drinks? This could really add up around here."

Annabel selected an iced tea from her tray to serve to a tiny, heavily perfumed blond woman who had a sunbed on the other side of Gary Cooper.

The lady had risen momentarily to rummage through her big beach bag for a sheaf of papers, and then she sat down again. She looked to be in her mid-forties and was barely five feet tall. She had a highly sexualized aura, with pert lips, round pillowy cheeks and bosom, and a bit of a belly, making her look like a child's favorite soft doll.

She'd been shamelessly eavesdropping from under her floppy wide-brimmed cloth flowered hat. Now she pushed her sunglasses down her pert nose and leaned over to eye Mr. Cooper as she said, "Honey, join the club! I lost the role of the whorehouse madam in that blasted Big Wind of a picture, just because I wanted to rewrite the script a little. I *always* work on my own scripts. I would have been a *divine* Belle Watling!"

Gary Cooper grinned and said, "Is that so, Mae? Then welcome to the Anti–*Gone with the Wind* Society." He held up his cup as if to toast her.

With her free hand, the sassy Mae West raised her glass to salute him, gave him a wink with the longest false eyelashes that Annabel had ever seen, and then declared peevishly, "So now they're calling me 'box office poison.' But I've got another little rabbit I can pull out of my hat!" She waved the script she'd been making notes on, flopping its pages airily. "Naturally I had to write most of it. It's called *My Little Chickadee.*"

"Farm story?" Gary Cooper asked.

She shook her head. "Western. With W. C. Fields! He keeps trying to rewrite our scenes. I can't *abide* that fat little drunk! Oh well, here's to the Box Office Poison Club."

Mr. Cooper laughed, then turned his attention back to his agent.

Miss West glanced up at a glamorously suntanned female who was settling into the sunbed on the other side of her. As the stunning newcomer took her seat, she said in a German-accented voice, "Did I hear you say 'box office poison'? They called *me* that, too!"

This woman was in her mid-thirties, slender, golden haired, and so deeply suntanned that she seemed like a bronzed statue— behind sunglasses with round, shocking pink frames. Annabel waited politely to see if she wanted to order something.

Miss West leaned forward and said, "Well, if it isn't my old pal from Paramount! My, what a gorgeous suntan! What's your secret, honey?"

The slender lady slipped a hand into her straw tote bag and pulled out a small dark vial with a handwritten label on it. "It's my own special recipe for suntan oil. Want to try it?"

"What's in it?" Mae West asked, accepting the vial and sniffing it.

"Olive oil, iodine, and red-wine vinegar," the German actress said, in the tone of a *hausfrau* proud of her recipe.

"If it's good enough for Marlene Dietrich, it's good enough for me," Miss West said stoutly, but she didn't use any before she handed it back.

"Gary, darling!" Marlene said rapturously, and she blew a kiss at Gary Cooper.

Although deeply immersed in a quieter chat with his agent, Mr. Cooper looked up briefly to smile and say appreciatively, "Lookin' good, Marlene!" and Annabel recalled steamy, sexy screen chemistry between these two stars in movies called *Morocco* and *Desire*.

"Iced coffee, darling," Miss Dietrich said to Annabel.

Mae West said mischievously, "What's your beau drinking, Marlene?" as she gazed at a gentleman heading toward them; he'd apparently arrived at the pool with Miss Dietrich but paused numerous times to shake hands with people along the way. He seemed at least ten years older than she was; he had a high forehead, a receding hairline, and wire-rimmed spectacles.

As he drew closer, Annabel recognized him as the American ambassador to England, Joseph P. Kennedy, the patriarch of the family whom she'd seen just this morning on the breakfast terrace chatting with the tennis player.

While he was still out of earshot, Mae West murmured, "Hmm, don't know how you do it, honey, juggling your days with *him*"—she nodded toward Mr. Kennedy—"and your nights with the divine Erich Maria Remarque. Yet you don't look the least bit exhausted!"

Marlene looked momentarily startled, then said casually, "Oh, I take my vitamins."

Mr. Kennedy had reached them now and settled into the

other chair next to Marlene. He gave Annabel a quick glance and said, "Coffee."

Annabel went to get their order, but she couldn't help feeling a pang of sympathy for Kennedy's wife, Rose, who apparently chose to focus her attention on her children, ignoring her husband's notorious flirtations with glamorous Hollywood actresses.

When Annabel returned with their drinks, Miss Dietrich was saying to Mr. Kennedy in her low, sexy voice, "Papa Joe, I'm worried about this ridiculous movie that they want me to do. What a strange title, *Destry Rides Again*. Does anyone *really* think I should play a dancing girl in an American western?"

"Absolutely," Mr. Kennedy said firmly. "I just got off that transatlantic call I made to check it out for you. They've got a good script, and a great song for you to sing. And the hero will be played by a very up-and-coming young man called Jimmy Stewart."

"That tall beanpole with a baby face?" Miss Dietrich said skeptically.

"Sure, sure. They say he's really got 'it' and he'll go far." He lowered his voice to add, "The studio expects him to be the next Gary Cooper!"

"Aw, go on, do it, honey!" Mae West, with the ears of a cat, broke in enthusiastically. "At the very least, if you play an all-American saloon gal in an all-American western, it'll really upset the Nazis, and I'll bet Herr Hitler himself will get his knickers in a twist."

"Good!" Miss Dietrich said with feeling. "Then I'll do it!"

But suddenly everyone stopped chattering, as a strapping young man climbed up to the high diving board. Annabel recognized the tennis player she'd just seen this morning, Hans von Erhardt, looking like the epitome of robust youth, health, and vigor, with his sleek tanned skin, his well-toned body, and his butter-colored hair gleaming in the sunlight.

"A definite Apollo," Mae West cooed, watching for his dive.

He raised his arms, bounced lightly, rose up, and for a moment seemed to float halfway between the sea and sky as he neatly folded and unfolded in a perfect dive, slicing cleanly through the dappled pool waters, surfacing to a burst of tremendous applause.

There was a collective sigh from the other side of the pool, where several German, Austrian, and American families had assembled in a shady section near the shallower end. One plump lady was hanging her family's wet beach towels on the beautiful stone railings in her section, unaware of the horrified looks of the French guests who would never be so *gauche* as to create a laundry line to obscure the beauty and symmetry of their surroundings.

But the plump lady, still holding a towel, suddenly stopped, utterly transfixed with admiration for the blond diver; then she said something quite loudly to her friend in German.

"What'd that fat lady just say?" Kennedy asked his companion.

Marlene Dietrich snorted. "She called that lovely young man 'Nietzsche's blond beast,' you know—the great Teutonic aristocratic hero, filled with the ruthless vitality of the victorious life force." Her tone was sarcastic and ominous.

There was a chilly silence, even in the heat of the August sun. Then Mae West broke the tension by tossing her head and saying jokingly, "Well, if I have to choose between two evils, I always pick the one I've never tried before."

———

Precisely at twelve thirty every day, lunch was served both on the hotel terrace and at the poolside restaurant, where guests moved to grab the best dining tables beneath big white awnings that flapped gently in the breeze like the sails of a yacht.

Annabel was glad to see the waitresses who arrived to replace her, and she went up to the hotel kitchen to have a quick
lunch. There she learned that the neighborhood lady who usually tended to Oncle JP's granddaughter had broken a tooth
and gone to see a dentist today, so she'd dropped off Delphine
at the hotel. This was why Oncle JP had asked Annabel to look
in on the girl.

"*Bonjour*, Annabel, *ça va*?" Delphine exclaimed. She was
eight years old, capable of waiting patiently for her grandfather
in his office after her lunch, playing with a coloring book. Her
previous bout of polio made it hard for her to walk; she had to
laboriously drag her right leg. So on busy days like this she was
usually just parked in a wheelchair in a corner.

"It's a wild day, lots of new guests," Annabel answered. Her
heart ached for the girl, who was very pretty: Her pale skin was
as fine and creamy as a china doll, her eyes wide and dark, and
she had a little button nose. Her hair was a soft brown that
naturally fell in such pretty curls that it fascinated people who
passed by.

But Delphine had the sorrowful aura of a child who had
been forced to spend most of her time in solitude, away from
the more raucous play of the other children. When Annabel
had first arrived in France and bent down to kiss her cousin,
little Delphine gave her such a big, childlike hug that Annabel
instantly loved her and soon became a kind of tutor to the girl,
wheeling her around and teaching her the English words for
the things she pointed to.

"Can we go see the fountain?" Delphine asked eagerly.

Annabel hesitated. The fountain was in a section meant for
the guests to enjoy, not the staff. But most people, distracted by
the pool, tennis, and croquet, seldom noticed that quiet corner.
At this hour it was probably empty. Delphine liked to see the
exotic fish there.

"Sure." Annabel pushed the chair in that direction, and at

Delphine's urging, Annabel softly sang a little French children's song that her own father had taught her. Inside the garden they felt a change in the air because of cool water droplets carried on a breeze from the fountain's meditative splashing arcs.

Annabel stopped the chair, and Delphine did what she always did here, out of view of the rest of the world: she used the rim of the fountain to help hoist herself to a standing position, and then, leaning carefully on it, she took the difficult, halting steps that she was capable of, moving around the circular fountain while still holding the rim.

"See? I'm doing it!" Delphine said excitedly as she struggled to the spot on the fountain where the stone frog was poised, spouting water out of his mouth. Delphine giggled with delight as she held out her hand to catch the cool stream from the frog's mouth.

"I should take you swimming someday!" Annabel said softly. "We'll go down to the cove early in the morning, when nobody else is around to get in our way."

"Then I can swim with pretty little fish like these?" Delphine said enthusiastically, and leaned forward to murmur her greetings to the pretty decorative fish that darted in the fountain's waters and came close to her hand, as if they were listening to her friendly tone.

But Annabel heard other voices approaching, and she said, "Delphine, we must go."

The little girl sighed, then obediently used the fountain's edge to turn herself in Annabel's direction so that she could go back to her wheelchair. But as she determinedly hobbled around the fountain, a group of guests emerged at the far end of the path.

Annabel recognized Hans the tennis player and his unpleasant-looking coach. They were walking with a film executive called Herr Volney who'd come here only a few days ago and whom she remembered because of his bushy blond eyebrows and his rather elaborate nautical outfit, replete with gold-trimmed navy blazer, white flannels, and a captain's cap; for he owned a large three-masted schooner with an imposing dark-green hull. Herr Volney had caused quite a stir with the regular poolside crowd when his yacht first sailed into view and anchored out in the sea, in full showy position, while a member of his crew rowed him ashore so that he could lunch with one of the hotel's guests. Apparently he'd been invited back today.

Now these three men were deeply engrossed in a conversation in German that had clearly turned into an argument, and the coach appeared worried and glum. Hans, looking particularly angry, turned abruptly away from the others, stalking defiantly ahead.

He was still scowling, but his expression changed quickly when he saw Annabel and Delphine, and he smiled gently. But as the other men caught up with Hans, they abruptly stopped talking and they stared, first to give Annabel a curt nod, then to observe Delphine.

A surly frown crossed Herr Volney's face; he was finishing a cigar, and he tossed the butt of it into the fountain, in the very spot where the little girl was, at the fountain's edge.

Delphine, still concentrating on laboriously dragging her leg, was startled by the nearby splash, and she looked up, frightened by the man's malicious intent. Her lower lip trembled. She was now close enough to Annabel that she could reach for her outstretched hand.

As the men walked on, Herr Volney said scornfully, "*Schwache Kreatur!*"

The force of this harsh, hostile utterance made Delphine jump involuntarily and then stumble self-consciously into her wheelchair's seat. Herr Volney guffawed as if vindicated.

But Hans gallantly paused to take Delphine's hand and briefly bow over it, saying in all sincerity, "*Bonjour, petite princesse.*" Then he reached into the fountain to fish out Herr

Volney's cigar butt and toss it away under the shrubs before walking off in the opposite direction of the other men.

As Annabel wheeled her cousin back to the hotel, Delphine whispered fearfully, "What did that nasty man say about me?"

"I don't know, sweetheart," Annabel lied. Unfortunately she'd heard this expression before and knew that it meant *feeble creature*. Some people in Europe and even in America espoused a so-called medical theory known as eugenics, which essentially advocated the extinction of any human being who was less than perfect.

Annabel suddenly thought of the Hollywood diets that she'd discussed with Oncle JP. Where did the modern quest for perfection end? How could you condemn a person for the things about themselves that they couldn't possibly change: their handicaps, their race?

She felt a fierce, protective instinct sweep over her. "Some hotel guests are just cranky, Delphine, even here in a paradise like this!"

"It's these bad times that makes people cross, isn't it?" Delphine quavered. "That's what the lady next door who looks after me told Grandpapa."

"Never mind. Maybe tomorrow we'll go for our swim," Annabel promised, hoping to distract her.

Delphine smiled brightly, making an effort to be brave, as Annabel steered her back to the hotel, where the girl would wait in Oncle JP's office, quietly returning to her coloring book until it was time to go home.

Annabel wished she could stay a bit longer, but she was due to go and meet the actor, Jack Cabot. So she kissed the little girl and then hurried off to her next assignment.

CHAPTER 6

The Villa Sanctuaire

When she arrived at the Villa Sanctuaire, Annabel found Jack Cabot sitting in a chair at a table by his private pool, under a sun umbrella. He was wearing blue swimming trunks and an open robe and dark sunglasses. He was frowning over papers, which were held down with ashtrays on the table beside him because an occasional breeze would rifle the pages. He had a red pencil and was making notes here and there.

"Mr. Cabot?" Annabel said. "I'm here to assist you."

The actor glanced up sharply, then nodded. "Oh, hello. You must be the girl from the Grand Hotel." He took off his sunglasses and smiled.

Annabel was not prepared for the effect of his gaze upon her. His soulful dark eyes revealed the lightning-quick vitality within him. On screen he could play a passionate lover or a ruthless killer, because of the fire in those eyes. His sensuous mouth indicated a ferocious hunger and that special thing that the movie magazines called "animal magnetism."

Annabel, who thought of herself as worldly enough not to be silly over celebrities, now experienced an undeniable plunging sensation of pleasure deep in the core of her body, as if she had just dived off a cliff like the local pearl divers who performed for tourists, leaping from unfathomable heights into the rocky, foaming sea below. She actually had to recover herself before answering him.

"Yes, I was told to work with you in the afternoons," she managed. She noticed that Jack had lustrous, curly dark hair and, unlike most men, did not use pomade to slick it back. It gave him a romantic, Byronic air, and Annabel couldn't help wondering what it would feel like to run her fingers through that beautiful hair.

"Have a seat," he said rather absently. As she sat beside him on a white wrought iron chair covered with a blue cushion, she saw that he was reviewing a document on long legal paper, perhaps a contract. He put it aside with a sigh, yawned, and stretched, saying in a melodious voice, "They said you have a theatrical background. Tell me, have you ever worked on a movie set? Know anything about 'lights, camera, action'?"

Annabel admitted, "I haven't worked in motion pictures. But my parents ran a portrait studio—my father was a photographer. My mother did the lighting, and she taught me a lot about it. They are—were—very good at it; they truly loved their work."

She had not spoken about her parents to anyone in France, except Oncle JP, and only once, when she'd just arrived. Having inherited some French reserve about personal matters, she'd developed a tacit agreement with her uncle not to speak any further of their shared loss.

But now the mention of her parents in the past tense was like finally admitting that they would never come back to her. She'd literally left them behind in a graveyard back in New York, without a proper mourning period; everything had happened so suddenly and required immediate action from her about the funeral, burial, and her own survival—overwhelming responsibilities, especially once she was booted out of Vassar and then dumped by her Harvard boyfriend.

Something in her voice must have reflected all her grief, because Jack suddenly lost his distracted air and his dark eyes were fixed on her. But unlike the screenwriter—who seemed to study her as a potential character for a story—Jack looked deeply sympathetic, as if some unhealed wound in his own heart made him especially sensitive to the suffering of others. His gaze seemed to say: *Yes, I have known the kind of grief that never really leaves you.*

But what he actually said was, "How lucky you were, to have had parents like them. Joy of living is something you have to see, in order to learn it for yourself." His voice was deeply resonant, like a well-tuned instrument. Annabel nodded mutely.

Now Jack said more lightly, "And how lucky *I* am, to have you helping me this summer. An expert on lighting! An actor's best friend. Without good lighting, we'd all look like waxworks. Maybe you can help me scout some locations while I'm here. I have an idea for a new film that will be set on the French Riviera. I'd like to see some of the authentic local sights. I have a car, so we can drive around and take photographs. Not today, of course. But soon."

The thought of driving along the blue coast at this man's side was unexpectedly thrilling. But all she said was, "Certainly. Any afternoon."

"Great! Meanwhile, would you keep a diary for me, so I'll know where I have to be? I can't deal with all these messages. Some are in French, from local press and bigwigs. There may be some schedule conflicts we need to finesse. See if you can make heads or tails of it."

He gestured toward his mail tucked beneath a dark-blue diary engraved with the studio logo in gold. "Please write the appointments in pencil so I can change my mind if I want to. And let's schedule a meeting with Scott. I want his input on the script I'm writing; he said he'd help punch it up. You work for him, too, right?"

"Scott?" Annabel asked, puzzled, as she picked up the diary.

Jack looked surprised. "Weren't you down there this morning at his cottage? He went for a walk after you left. He said you were great."

"Do you mean—Mr. John Darcy?" she asked, bewildered.

Jack laughed appreciatively. "Yeah, right, he told me he's submitting his next story without an agent, using a pseudonym so the magazine editors won't know it was written by F. Scott Fitzgerald—they think he's all washed up, and they say his new work is 'too strong' for their readers. Well, *everybody's* looking for fluff these days. Mustn't scare people and say anything bad about all the gangsters running Europe. Can you believe the world we live in?"

Annabel, her mind reeling, didn't know what to say. Was he really telling her that John Darcy, the screenwriter in the Jasmine Cottage, was the famous author of the hugely successful *This Side of Paradise* and all those popular stories in the *Saturday Evening Post*?

Jack rose from the table decisively. "Do excuse me, I have to make a phone call to Paris."

She said automatically, "Shall I place the call for you? It can be tricky here."

He was already on his way back inside the villa, and he waved her off. "Don't worry! I figured out how to do it."

Annabel could still scarcely absorb what she'd learned. Rapidly she went over every bit of the conversation she'd had with the screenwriter, realizing now what it had all meant. She felt like an idiot, blithely discussing *The Great Gatsby* with the very man who'd written it.

Trying to recover her equilibrium, she forced herself to concentrate on the task at hand. Jack's correspondence was far more glamorous than Mr. Fitzgerald's. The international social set who summered on the Côte d'Azur were clamoring for Jack to attend their parties. The world press was equally curious. Requests for interviews, screenings, lunches, cocktail parties, dinner invitations. They were all excited about the nascent Cannes Film Festival; every hostess and events manager was vying to get as many stars as they could snag for their events.

"Sounds like fun," Annabel sighed wistfully as she opened each envelope and noted every appointment and time in the appropriate dates of the new calendar book. It all seemed like a delightful movie itself. Several parties and screenings, she knew, were scheduled to take place right here at the Grand Hotel, including a masquerade ball to benefit a children's charity and the screening party for *Love Isn't Easy*, the movie Jack had made out of Scott's story; the last, biggest event of all here would be the Celebration of the Stars. She could not help feeling a rising hope that perhaps, by proxy, her own life, too, would become more exciting.

She checked to make sure that she had the correct times and the correct spelling of the hosts' and hostesses' names, as well as the addresses. She knew from experience that one little error could cause a catastrophe later. So absorbed was she that she barely heard the soft rustling sound of another guest who came out of the house from a side door, until suddenly Annabel inhaled the scent of attar of roses wafting toward her.

A tall woman went drifting by like a blown leaf, wearing a diaphanous silk caftan the color of her own flesh—a soft peachy pink. Her pale-blond hair was delicate and windblown. Her face was sphinxlike, with a luminous, otherworldly glow; her exquisite nose and mouth and brow and high cheekbones made her appear as if she'd been lovingly carved by a master sculptor. Her eyes were violet colored and had a veiled look from the natural droop of the eyelids and long lashes, in a sensuous, almost sleepy way.

The woman had moved directly past Annabel without even seeming to notice her. Now, poised at the edge of the pool, she dropped her hands to her sides, and the entire caftan, which was already see-through, just slid off her body in a soft sigh.

Standing there naked, poised, Téa Marlo raised one hand to her brow to shade her eyes as she scanned the sky, as if drinking in the brilliant blue view. This gesture made her look like a warrior goddess poised in the blazing sunshine. Her breasts were well set apart, like two perfect fruits. Even her pubic hair glinted in the sunlight, white gold, like corn silk.

And then she simply slipped into the pool with a soft splash.

Annabel glanced away, ashamed of what she was thinking— something catty that her girlfriends at Vassar had told her about pubic hair: *When you see a girl naked in the shower, that's how you know if she bleaches her hair or if she's a natural blond.*

Téa swam in long, languorous strokes, her slender arms and legs slicing through the water, making hardly a sound, her head turning rhythmically on each fourth stroke to come up for air. It was like watching a ballet performed in the water instead of the air. When Téa reached the end of the pool, she flipped over for the return. Her breasts were proudly firm as she back-stroked to where she'd begun. Then she rolled over and swam face down again.

Annabel could not help being mesmerized; she truly understood all the fuss over Téa Marlo. You simply could not take your eyes off her. People had said, *Something incredible happens when the camera sees her.* But in person she was even more stunning.

"There is absolutely no reason why Téa should be in a hurry to sign their new contract." Jack's annoyed voice floated out from the open door of the villa. "Sonny just wants to lock her in his stable for seven years! Who knows what stupid pictures they'll make her do? Yeah, yeah, that's what they said to me, too, but in the end, they just shove you into one asinine role after an-other—and then when the picture tanks at the box office, they blame *you*, the actor. Look, she's free and I'm free. We'll never get another chance like this again to do what we want. The French are willing to put up some money for my next picture, if we shoot it in France instead of in Hollywood, which is fine by me. And I've got a potential American backer interested as well. I don't *care* if Sonny won't like it. He doesn't own Téa."

He paused to listen briefly. Then he said impatiently, "*Of course* I've discussed this with Téa. And I want to make her a partner in my company. Yes, I'm sure. Well, *you're* the lawyer; *you* figure out the details. No, I don't want Sonny to come any-where near *this* picture!"

Annabel worried that Mr. Cabot had no idea how his voice carried outdoors. The less she heard about his business, the better; if Sonny quizzed her at the end of the week, she didn't want to have to spill the beans that Jack Cabot was apparently planning to make another independent film, this time without Sonny's involvement.

She was glad when Jack finally got off his call, rummaged around in the kitchen, and came back outside, carrying a cham-pagne bucket full of ice with a bottle peeping out. He smiled at Annabel, and she again felt that delicious plunging sensation inside her.

"Your calendar is all ready," Annabel said shyly, gesturing toward the open book. "Your first interview is tomorrow morn-ing. I've noted the details in here."

"Good," he answered. But now his gaze followed the figure in the pool as he parked the champagne bucket beside the pool's edge. "Well, thank you, Annabel. That's all for today."

He shrugged out of his bathrobe, looking strapping and suntanned in his blue trunks as he stood at the pool. Over his shoulder he said, "Before you go, could you grab some champagne glasses from the kitchen? Just leave 'em near the champagne, will you?"

She went inside and returned with a tray of two flutes. By then, Jack had already entered the pool and swum over to the far side, where Téa was resting. Annabel saw that he'd left his blue trunks on the ground by this side of the pool. So she quickly set down the tray with the two glasses beside the champagne bucket, and she backed off.

On the other side of the rippling pool, Jack and Téa were pressed close to each other's body, nuzzling their faces and laughing softly. Annabel slipped quietly away.

———

When she returned to the hotel, the concierge was bustling about, trying to accommodate all his new guests' urgent demands. He glanced up, saw Annabel, and waved an envelope at her.

"Do you think you could possibly help me out?" he pleaded. "All the bellhops are off on other errands, and I've got this telegram they say is urgent for Hans von Erhardt. Would you mind taking it up to him? I saw him go to his room about an hour ago. I'll owe you a favor, I assure you!"

Raphael seldom asked for such help, so she said quickly, "Of course."

She didn't feel like going up in the service elevator today. Nobody was waiting for the guest elevator, so she took it, admiring its Belle Epoque charm; it was made of mahogany paneling and glass windows, with a wrought iron door that had a gilt-edged mirror on its exterior and a golden handle. Inside, the gleaming numbered buttons for the floors were embedded in a shining brass plate.

You could view your progress through the windows as the elevator ascended or descended in a glass shaft that was surrounded by a wide, sweeping marble staircase—for those who preferred to walk.

Annabel knew that the tennis player's room was an especially good one, the kind with a small balcony and a fine view of the sea. She walked down the carpeted hallway, passing framed mirrors over tables with beautiful vases of freshly cut and carefully arranged flowers. Discreet lighting came from tulip-shaped fixtures with frosted glass in gold sconces.

When she reached the room at the end of the hall, she knocked on the door. After a pause, she recognized the male voice that said through the closed door, "*Ja?*"

"Telegram," Annabel said. There was another pause. She heard a low murmur of voices but could not make out what was being said.

Down the hall, the English couple she'd seen doing the crosswords at breakfast was now coming up the broad marble staircase, laughing and talking, their arms full of wildflowers and blooming branches. They must have gone hiking, judging from their even-more-rumpled clothes. They arrived huffing and puffing at the landing just as the elevator doors opened and an elderly countess stepped out carrying a small black poodle.

The nervous pet reacted to the sight of the moving branches, and suddenly the poodle wriggled out of the old woman's arms and made a mad dash down the hall, right toward Annabel, just as Hans von Erhardt opened his door.

He was standing there in his bathrobe, his blond hair slightly mussed. Annabel handed him the telegram and he opened it quickly, scanned it, and seemed to turn pale beneath his tan, just as the poodle streaked past his legs and dashed into the room.

"Ho!" Hans stepped back in confusion, and Annabel ran after the poodle.

She caught up with it in the small anteroom just beyond the door and made a quick grab. But when she straightened up, she could see, in the mirrored wall of the bedroom just ahead of her, a reflection of the bed.

A naked woman was propped up against the pillows, looking startled, her large breasts exposed, before she thought to grab the sheets to cover herself. As the woman reached to the night table for her eyeglasses so that she could see what was going on, Annabel got a better glimpse of her face.

It was the mousy little Polish secretary. She was actually quite pretty, with her russet hair tumbled all about her shoulders and her big blue, nearsighted eyes. But she looked so alarmed that Annabel instinctively pretended not to recognize her and retreated quickly with the excited poodle squirming in her arms.

"*Excusez-moi,*" Annabel said to the tennis player.

Hans was still clutching his telegram, and he appeared mightily preoccupied, then looked glad that she was leaving with the dog in tow. He shut the door hastily behind her.

The dog's elderly mistress was slow moving, so she'd just caught up with her errant pet. The poodle licked Annabel's face enthusiastically before it got handed back to its mistress.

"Bad dog!" the countess chided in a frail voice as she accepted the poodle. To Annabel she said with brief hauteur, "*Merci, mademoiselle!*"

Annabel sighed as she headed for the stairs this time, trying to make sense of this entire day. It had been a long one, and she was exhausted. For once, she'd be glad to go back to her little rooming house on the square, where she'd have dinner with the other tenants in a quiet dining room, and then she could tumble into bed.

She hadn't been this exhausted since her first day on the job. After being so eager for excitement, she now hoped the guests would settle down and the rest of the summer would be, perhaps, just a little less stimulating.

For there was something about being in the midst of this circus-like atmosphere that, despite all its dazzling gaiety, gave her an apprehensive feeling of impending catastrophe—like a passenger in a speeding car whose driver was heedlessly hurtling toward one of the Riviera's very dangerous curves.

CHAPTER 7

The Deep End

The next day, Annabel remembered her promise to little Delphine and sent the hotel car to collect her to go to the swimming cove when there weren't any guests about. At this hour, the air was cool and pure and promising.

It was so early that Annabel didn't even hear the *pop-pop* of the tennis player's morning practice on the court near the shed where she parked her bicycle.

Annabel pushed Delphine in her wheelchair down to the coastal path. Yves, the lifeguard director, assured her that there were no jellyfish today because of the tide.

As they reached the swimming cove, Annabel was surprised to find a man sunning himself on the wide flat-topped rock just above the sea. He was dressed in a red swimsuit with a hotel towel slung over his shoulder, and his sandals lay beside him. But unlike the tennis player, he wasn't very suntanned yet.

"Who is that?" Delphine whispered.

"Rick Bladey. He's got the penthouse for the entire month of August," Annabel whispered back. Everybody knew about this rich young American who was waiting to collect his inheritance from a father who owned one of the biggest hotel chains in the world. They were "thinking of buying" the Grand Hotel, which Rick's father said would be "a ruby in our tiara."

But others had tried to make this deal before, and it had all come to naught. The Grand Hotel had previously been owned by an eccentric Frenchwoman who'd died and left it to her five pedigreed dogs in care of a lawyer she'd chosen to represent them. Her distant relatives disputed the will and finally won, and wished to sell. But they quarreled incessantly among themselves and could not agree on anything, ending up leaving the running of the hotel to their business managers, lawyers, and of course Oncle JP and his well-trained staff, who serenely believed that life at the Grand Hotel was ultimately impervious to the whims of the rest of the world.

"He looks like the prince in *Snow White*," Delphine whispered.

"I suppose so," Annabel muttered. But there was something about this guy's supremely confident face that set her teeth on edge. Everybody else found "Ricky" fascinating. Blue eyed, with fine chiseled features and straight, neatly clipped raven-black hair that the hotel barber trimmed every day, he was ten years older than Annabel but acted half as mature. He'd been thrown out of the best schools in the world and was finally banished to France after disgracing his family by peeing into the library fireplace of his fiancée's illustrious father.

The international press always gleefully noted Ricky's latest exploits, whether it was gambling away more money at a throw in Monte Carlo than most people earned in a lifetime, or racing around in his red Italian sports car, which the hotel valets loved to drive back and forth in the front driveway for him. He'd once made a bet that he could race his car against the famed Train Bleu to Paris—and he'd won.

Oncle JP said little about the man, yet from his few comments Annabel suspected that, behind Rick's devil-may-care act of being a rich man on vacation, he actually might be here as a spy for his father, assessing how much the Grand Hotel was worth and who should be fired and what should be changed. But she did not tell all this to Delphine.

The man sensed their presence now, opened his eyes, and then sat up with a bright look on his face. "I know you!" he said to Annabel. "You're the girl who sings those French nursery songs in the garden!"

Annabel was taken aback. His friendly blue eyes sparkled in the soft early sunlight. He gave Delphine a wink and said, "I had a French governess when I was a little boy in Paris living in my papa's hotel. And she sang that same song to me! She was the only person who liked me." He sounded wistful as he said to Delphine, "Do you love your governess, too?"

The little girl looked puzzled at first, then burst out laughing. "Annabel is my cousin!"

"Oh!" Rick said, not the least embarrassed by his *faux pas*. "Annabel, eh? And what's *your* name?" Delphine told him. He said, "Well, listen, Delphine. Anytime you see any big bad wolves in the garden, you just tell them that all you have to do is snap your fingers, and the man in the penthouse will come down and chase them right into the sea."

So, Annabel thought warily, *he really was in the garden that day, eavesdropping.* Just where had he been hiding out when Herr Volney insulted poor Delphine at the fountain?

As if reading her thoughts, Rick addressed his next remark to Annabel. "I was sleeping off a hangover on one of those pretty chairs you've got tucked in secret places around the hotel gardens. When I heard you singing so beautifully, at first I thought I'd dreamed you up."

He actually looked a bit smitten, as if he'd been so in love with his French governess that he was now somehow transferring those feelings onto Annabel, just because he'd heard her sing a familiar lullaby. "I swim early every morning in this cove," he said encouragingly.

He smiled at Delphine. "Do you swim?"

"No, but I want to learn," she said, although she looked a little anxious.

"Nothing to it. Come on, I'll show you," he said enthusiastically, rising to his feet and extending his well-muscled arms to lift her out of her chair and into the water. "I was on my swim team at college before they chucked me out. See? Water's not too cold, and it feels much warmer the longer you're in it."

Delphine looked so eager when she glanced at her cousin for permission that Annabel nodded, still feeling somewhat reluctant.

The little girl squealed with excited fear and delight at the water. She clung to Rick and laughed as he talked her into floating on her back while he supported her with his hand.

Annabel had planned to teach Delphine how to stroke and blow out bubbles to breathe in the water, but Rick had already begun to demonstrate this with Delphine before Annabel had time to take off her cover-up clothes and plunge into the water herself.

It *was* a bit cold at this hour, but not too bad. The tide was gentle this morning, and the little fish darting in and out of the rocks seemed unperturbed by Delphine's splashing around. She was a good student, intelligent and attentive. And in the water, her disability seemed to dissolve into the waves.

When they heard a train whistle, it inspired Rick to sing a song to Delphine that he said he'd learned at Princeton. He sang softly, "so as not to disturb the fish," he said, in a cadence meant to help her keep time with her swim strokes:

I've been working on the railroad, all the livelong day.
I've been working on the railroad, just to pass the time
    away . . .

As he continued singing, Annabel tried not to let him see her smile.

When their lesson was done, Rick deposited Delphine on the warm, flat rock to dry off. Annabel had been swimming within sight, so she returned now, to wrap a towel around the girl and to let Rick go off and get a little more exercise. He swam in clean, strong strokes, then returned and climbed up beside them.

"I once swam as far as the lighthouse," he boasted. The lighthouse was quite a way off, around a narrow curve at the rocky tip of the *Cap*. But Rick said he wouldn't go out there today, and after he toweled off, he smiled at Delphine.

"We don't need that chariot of yours," he declared. "Come on, little one. I'll carry you there; it'll be faster." And before Annabel could demur, Rick scooped up the girl and carried her all the way back to the hotel, while Annabel pushed the empty chair after them.

Delphine, pressed against his broad chest and bouncing along with his jogging gait, giggled with delight at being attended by such a handsome man who carried her as if she were as light as a bouquet of flowers.

"Where to?" Rick asked when they reached the hotel. Annabel pointed to the parking area, because Oncle JP had made an arrangement with the man who delivered the fish to ferry Delphine back to town and to the apartment of the lady who took care of her during the day.

The fisherman waved to Delphine. He sometimes made his delivery with his wife at his side. She was the one who counted his money and kept his books. She was here today, and her severe face broke into a smile at the sight of Delphine. They'd known her since she was a baby.

"Who wants to buy a great big fish?" Rick exclaimed as he deposited the laughing Delphine in her seat in the fisherman's van.

There were tall crates stacked on the ground for the kitchen crew to pick up, of shrimp-like creatures called *langoustines*, each kept in their own cubbyholes within the latticed crate, their orange antennae sticking out inquisitively. There were also crates of oysters and lobsters. And the sole, delivered whole and glistening in the morning light, was destined for a *meunière* sauce; and the big flat turbot would be roasted on long stalks of fresh-picked herbs.

Annabel turned to the hotel heir and said, "Thank you for all your help, Mr.—"

"Call me Rick. All my friends do," he said, then sauntered off through the terrace to return to his penthouse and get dressed.

On the way he passed Ambassador Kennedy, who was reading the newspaper over his breakfast. He rose early each day, ahead of his family. Rick said, "Any good news? Has somebody finally knocked off Hitler?"

Annabel gasped. It was a good thing there weren't any other guests around to hear that.

The ambassador looked up and said mildly, "Now, now, Mr. Bladey. We Americans mustn't abandon our neutrality. The Europeans ought to work something out with these totalitarian states. It's economic maladjustment causing the world's unrest. Good businessmen can always come to terms when they know how to negotiate."

"Businessmen, yes. But bullies can't be negotiated with," Rick said firmly.

A waitress approached tentatively. "Phone call for you, sir," she said to Rick, and he went off.

Annabel headed for the offices, where Oncle JP was pacing the hallways. His brow was furrowed, as if he were mentally juggling seven problems at once.

"Annabel, I must ask you a favor," he said. "The housekeeping supervisor had a family situation to deal with this morning, so she is delayed. Will you please make the preliminary rounds just to see if the maids have all their supplies? It won't take long, about an hour at most. Then you can resume your day's duties. I've written it all down for you."

"Of course," she said, accepting the clipboard he handed her. The fine housekeeping at the Grand Hotel was legendary. Upon returning to a room after a swim, no guest ever had to confront dirty towels, unmade beds, undone laundry, uncollected breakfast trays, wilting flowers in the vases, or a bug of any kind, anywhere. (It was not as if no cockroach, bedbug, mouse, rat, or scorpion existed—but no guest would ever see one.)

Annabel had once said to her uncle, "But most guests don't even notice if a flower has been replaced before its first petals fall; or if a chocolate on their pillow was made today; or if the folds of their towels aren't perfectly matched on the shelf; or if their slippers aren't exactly aligned beneath their bathrobes in the closet."

"They may not notice with their eyes, but they *feel* it," Oncle JP had replied. "Not each small thing, but the cumulative effect. Even if they didn't, *you* know. Our entire staff knows. Their confidence and pride in this hotel affects their every gesture, their voices, their work."

So now Annabel took the keys for the housekeeping closets and began her rounds on the lower floor, which had the smallest rooms and the kinds of guests who got out of bed early. As opposed to the suites and penthouse, where a guest might loll all morning.

The maids in their tidy uniforms and caps were already at work, nodding *bonjour* to Annabel as she passed them with her clipboard and checked their carts to make sure that they had adequate stacks of linen and scented guest soaps. Fortunately the laundry had been delivered early, and the mops and brooms and other cleaning supplies were all in good shape.

The second-floor maids were functioning well, but they

needed more pens and stationery to replenish the guests' desks. Annabel telephoned downstairs to report this.

On the third floor all seemed well as Annabel unlocked the maids' closet and stood before each shelf, dutifully checking the items off on her clipboard. But then, quite suddenly, she heard a shriek from out in the hallway that was just as quickly stifled.

Annabel rushed out and glanced up and down. At the far end of the corridor, she saw a diminutive maid slowly backing out of a guest room, leaving the door open. The girl had both hands clapped to her mouth. Annabel knew whose room this was and hurried over.

"*Qu'est-ce qui se passe?*" she demanded.

The girl pointed inside mutely. She had left her maid's cart in the room, so she'd clearly knocked at the door, gotten no answer, and gone in trundling her mops and dusters ahead of her—then unceremoniously abandoned them.

Annabel, fearing something like a snake, tiptoed into the room and around the cart. The maid trailed behind her, so that when Annabel stopped short, the girl collided with her as they both gazed, horrified, at the naked male figure sprawled on the bed, face down.

"*Le joueur de tennis! Il est mort, n'est-ce pas?*" the maid whispered fearfully.

"The tennis player is *what*?" Annabel echoed, moving closer.

Hans von Erhardt's strong, suntanned right arm, sprinkled with delicate blond hair bleached nearly white from the sun, was stretched outward across the bed, while the other arm was tucked under his head. His broad, well-toned back, his healthy young flanks, and his strong, suntanned legs lay there lightly, with his head turned to the side and the usual debonair lock of yellow-blond hair still hanging over his forehead.

Annabel felt overwhelming pity at the sight of Hans's out-stretched hand, as if he were reaching for help. She forced herself to pick it up gently and seek a pulse in the wrist; but at the touch, she set it down again, for he was already cold as clay.

She backed away, aghast. Taking a deep breath, she picked up the telephone and called her uncle. She had to fight off a wave of nausea before saying, "Monsieur von Erhardt is—I think—dead. We must get a doctor."

The maid, observing the worst being confirmed, began to moan in a string of chants that the French reserved for real trouble: "Oh, *la-la, la-la, la-la, la-la, la-la!*"

"I'll handle it," Oncle JP said instantly into the phone. "Don't touch anything, lock the door, don't tell anyone, and tell the maid to be silent and go to her supervisor's office. And you, Annabel, wait for me there," he added in an appropriately grave tone; yet, she noted, he seemed only surprised, not stunned, as if perhaps this sort of thing had happened once or twice before.

Later, he would tell her about the elderly duchess who'd died sitting up in a small chair in the library with a book in her lap, all alone; and a *sous*-chef who, one night when the others were gone, had sneaked a piece of leftover *filet de bœuf* into his mouth so hastily that he'd choked to death and lay there on the floor of the empty kitchen overnight until the morning crew discovered him the next day.

Now here was a young guest, a kindly soul who'd been such a healthy, rising tennis star with a pure zest for each day of sun and tennis. This was terrible. This absolutely must not be. Annabel felt lightheaded and could not bear to look at the poor man again, so she turned toward the window.

She unlocked the door when her uncle arrived. He went inside and surveyed the situation thoroughly; then, as they stepped into the hallway, he locked the door again, saying firmly, "Come, Annabel."

He led her down an old, seldom-used staircase, hidden behind a nondescript door. The staircase had a brass railing and metal steps and wound itself in a secret spiral along the spine of the hotel. The lighting here was dimmer and the stairs narrower than the grand marble affair that the guests used. It was a relic of the past.

Returning to his office, Oncle JP moved swiftly and efficiently. Annabel, sitting in the chair by his desk, felt stunned and remained there as he conferred with the particular doctor and police detective whom he knew well and thus could be assured of their discretion.

They saw to it that what had once been a man but had now become just a body was taken speedily on a stretcher into the service elevator and whisked into a waiting ambulance at the delivery area, so that the guests wouldn't notice. If any of the staff saw the ambulance, they'd assume that an elderly person had had a heart attack, or some show-off down at the pool hit his head at the diving board and needed stitches. These were the kinds of guesses the staff was allowed to say to a guest if questioned.

It all seemed to happen in such a businesslike blur that Annabel could scarcely comprehend it. Oncle JP had notified Han's tennis manager, who in turn contacted the aristocratic family, and everybody agreed that the entire thing must be kept quiet until they'd figured out exactly what had happened. To her shock, Annabel realized that if the details of this story got out, practically everyone on the Riviera stood to lose: the hotels, the restaurants, the government, the tennis team, perhaps even the Cannes Film Festival itself.

With so much vested interest at stake, everybody naturally knew what to do without being asked, and they all did it thoroughly and dispassionately. The police detective, a weary-looking older man with a lined face and black mustache, made his notes, searched for clues (no suicide note, no pill bottles), and had the room checked and photographed; and he interviewed the maid, and Annabel, in a stern but rapid way.

Annabel answered mechanically, for she felt as if the sun

had seared into her eyeballs the image of that cheerful blond man lying naked on the bed; yet, even now, she somehow still expected Hans to waken and go bounding along the hallway and down to the courts for his usual practice session, racket in hand, giving everyone he passed a bright, elegantly friendly smile.

"Annabel, are you all right?" Oncle JP said, handing her a cup of coffee when the police had finally gone. She nodded and he said softly, "I hardly need tell you not to discuss this with the staff or the guests, no matter what they ask you."

She was slowly emerging from the fog of shock and asked, "What did the police say?"

Oncle JP told her the official line, which the doctors, the police, the boy's manager, and his relatives had all agreed upon: The report would be that the tennis player had died at the hospital of heart failure. Too much sport, too much heat.

Annabel said incredulously, "Is that what they all really think? Even Dr. Gaspard?"

Dr. Gaspard was a semi-retired, esteemed doctor who lived in town nearby and ate lunch at the hotel twice a week, whom Oncle JP could summon quickly for emergencies.

Her uncle said carefully, "We believe it was a suicide." Annabel gasped. He went on, "There were—indications—that he'd taken a great deal of drugs, then smothered in his bed. Asphyxiation and cardiac arrest. But his family back in Berlin has asked us to please keep this quiet. His coach will collect all his belongings to return to the family."

He sat down at his desk, trying not to look troubled.

"But why should the tennis player commit suicide?" Annabel objected. "*You* saw him, Oncle. He was happy and healthy, talking about his future and the Davis Cup next year."

Oncle JP looked at her thoughtfully, then made a decision. "I will tell you this because you may hear about it somehow anyway. Hans was being summoned back to Berlin. They'd decided to drop him from the tennis team because he broke some laws. So when the team abandoned him, he could no longer stay in France, and some men from Berlin were on their way here to 'escort' him. He would have had to stand trial back home, and that would have caused great disgrace to his aristocratic family. So he apparently did the honorable thing."

Annabel absorbed this, then pressed on. "What law could that nice man have broken? Marta told me that he refused to join the Nazi Party; is that it?"

"No, but I'm sure that didn't help matters," Oncle JP said regretfully.

Annabel knew that she still wasn't getting the whole story. "What was the actual charge against him, then?"

"Well, first of all, he smuggled money out of Germany. People must report every item of value they take with them when they travel out of there, even their wedding rings! However, I think, considering his family's connections, they might have settled that matter without incident. But I am told that he also violated some old German law called Paragraph 175."

"What's that?" she asked. From the way he said it, it sounded ominous.

Oncle JP hesitated, then said, "It is a law that outlaws homosexuality. Apparently a young male prostitute in Berlin confessed to being propositioned and 'seduced' by Hans. 'Moral turpitude,' 'sexual delinquency'—they have all kinds of names for it." He sighed. "The Nazis are exploiting a dusty old law as a convenient tool that Hitler's henchmen can deploy at will, to hold over the heads of anyone like Hans who falls out of favor with them."

Annabel shuddered, having heard dark rumors of imprisonment, even torture. From here it had all seemed so unreal. Some accused journalists of exaggerating to sell newspapers.

Oncle JP went on, "It's no joke to get caught. Such men are put in concentration camps, where they are abused by guards and forced to do hard labor. They are humiliated, made to wear pink triangles on their shirts. I only tell you this so that you can understand why Hans must have wanted to spare his family the disgrace, and the agony of trying to rescue him—"

She had already heard of the Nazis forcing Jews to wear yellow stars and go into those awful prison camps. Now this. Were Hitler's men going to put badges of shame on everyone who didn't meet their idiotic ideals, and arrest people just for being who they were?

Then suddenly she remembered something that could be quite significant. "Oncle—I sincerely doubt that Hans is a homosexual. For heaven's sake, I just saw a woman in his bed, only yesterday!"

Oncle JP looked astounded. "What are you talking about? What exactly did you see?"

"I saw that Polish secretary in Hans's bed!" she insisted. "I went up there with a telegram for him; Raphael was busy and asked me to take it there. And I tell you, I *saw* that woman sitting there naked!"

Her uncle shrugged. "That proves nothing. Some men like both sexes . . ."

"Yes, sure, but even if Hans simply didn't want to face charges, I don't believe he killed himself," Annabel objected. "Something isn't right here; I just don't know what."

"The doctor seems certain it was suicide," Oncle JP reminded her. "An overdose."

The more she thought about it, the more it outraged her. "Hans was a health fanatic—he wouldn't take drugs. Maybe something else happened!" She still could not bring herself to say the word that lay beneath all this. *Murder.*

Oncle JP paused thoughtfully, then rose from his chair and went out to the reception desk, asking Marta which room the Polish secretary was in. Annabel, who had followed him there, said quickly, "I remember which room she got. She's in that little one—"

But Marta had already consulted her records. "She's not there anymore. She checked out. The night staff left the information for me, here. The Polish girl said that her employer had canceled his trip and that she'd been summoned home. Her bill was paid in full, and also the remaining fee that they owed on her employer's room."

Oncle JP gave a brief nod, then returned to his office. Annabel followed him.

"This is very suspicious!" she hissed. "Suppose that secretary—or the man she works for—killed Hans? And even if she didn't, she may be a witness; maybe she saw someone. Now we *must* call back the police! They only asked me how I found Hans, so I didn't get a chance to even think of saying that I saw the Polish girl in his bed. But I can tell them all about it now!"

Oncle JP looked up sharply. "You will do nothing of the sort!" he said in a quick, warning tone. "I will speak to the police. But I don't want you involved any further, not at all. Do you hear me? Do not say to anyone else what you have just said to me today—is that clear?"

Annabel was taken aback by his tone. "But Oncle—" she objected.

"Leave it to me," Oncle JP said firmly. Then he added more gently, "The boy is dead. There's nothing more we can do. His family is surely in pain over this; they have asked us to please leave it alone. It's easy to forget that our German guests aren't free, even when they are out of Germany. If they displease the Nazis, there are often family or friends or colleagues back home in Berlin who might pay the price."

He looked at her with the sympathetic expression of an uncle, not an employer. "All we can do now is attend to our guests. I told the maid she could go home for the day, but she said she'd rather work. There's no shame in saying you can't work today—is that how you feel?"

"No," Annabel said. She could not imagine cowering in her

bedroom at the rooming house. It would drive her crazy, trying to figure this all out.

"Good. Then go about your business, and let me tend to everything else."

Annabel went out into the lobby, still feeling dazed.

From the front desk, Marta waved her over. "Well?" she asked in a low voice. "Are they going to investigate that man's death any further?"

Annabel shook her head. "I don't think so. The family has asked them to drop it."

Marta nodded as if she comprehended a great deal. "This is how it happens," she said.

"What do you mean?" Annabel asked.

Marta said quietly, "I grew up in Germany. I was there when the fascists came to power. So I know. It's why I left, and stayed here. But it can happen anywhere. I'll tell you how it works. First, they go after the gypsies and migrants that nobody wants around—with the military on the borders to keep out the 'bad people' and to guard 'the good' ones. Then they attack the Jews—first the poor ones, then even the wealthy ones. And people still look the other way. Then the fascists create strange laws, or unearth old ones, about 'morality' or 'disloyalty.' Anyone who doesn't toe the line is therefore a 'traitor.' By now there are secret police who don't wear uniforms and just show up and take people away in the dead of night.

"All the while they make lists, of teachers and judges and lawyers and doctors and artists whom they call 'degenerates.' At last, some good citizens protest all this—but that gives the fascists an excuse to let their storm troopers 'put down disloyalists and restore order.' Their neighbors and colleagues are only too happy to denounce them to the authorities.

"And ordinary people say, *It's not my problem. I am not an immigrant. I am not an anarchist or a homosexual or a degenerate artist or a bad scholar. I am not a gypsy or a Jew.* Till one day, the 'good people' wake up to find that *they* are all prisoners now—but by then it's too late."

Marta's voice dropped even lower. "Some people back home are even postponing heart and tooth surgery, for fear of what they might say when they are under anesthesia!"

Annabel had been listening with mounting horror. Marta was a calm, placid woman who'd worked here for five years. She never spoke of politics, never criticized guests or got upset about anything; she only set about solving problems. To hear her talk like this was somehow more terrifying than the mutterings of everyone else.

Annabel wondered if Marta, too, had family back home, for whose safety she must toe an invisible line, even while she was here in France, the land of liberty. Annabel suddenly felt very lucky to have no loved ones in Germany.

"And I know what you're thinking," Marta said. "Everybody thinks the same thing. You'd say: *Well, that can't happen here.* And I say to you, *Oh, yes, it can.* It can happen in Spain. It can happen in Germany. It can happen in Italy, Austria. And it most *definitely* can happen in France. It can happen anywhere."

PART TWO

A sunny place for shady people.
                    —William Somerset Maugham

CHAPTER 8

A Frog in the Garden

The disturbing death of the tennis player made hardly a ripple among the guests at the Grand Hotel, which astonished Annabel. In an ordinary summer, Marta assured her, a young man's "heart attack" would be worth at least a week of gossip.

But this year, one Hollywood visitor after another made bigger splashes every day, erasing the previous gossip and prompting excited new chatter about movie stars and socialites mingling in local restaurants, strolling on the Promenade des Anglais in Nice or the Croisette in Cannes, lazing on the beaches by day, and getting roaring drunk in bars at night. Inevitably, there were more than the usual fights: jealous couples breaking up, artistic rivals coming to fisticuffs, lovers throwing wineglasses at those who ignored them.

It seemed that only Annabel could not forget the tennis player so easily. She shuddered every time she parked her bicycle at the shed near the courts. She didn't even like to hear other guests playing and laughing there. Yet her work kept her so busy, and the burning summer heat was so exhausting, that by the middle of the month she'd managed to put her thoughts and feelings about the sad affair on hold.

Her uncle summoned her to his office for weekly reports that he in turn passed on to Sonny. Annabel was glad that she wasn't the one who had to deal with the studio head.

"How goes it with the screenwriter?" Oncle JP asked today.

"He works hard on all his assignments," Annabel said truthfully.

That was putting it mildly. "Scott," as he insisted she call him, was in dire straits.

His life depended on earning any "dime" he could get. But at first he was still so ill that he even allowed Annabel to discreetly call the doctor that the hotel relied on.

It was the same doctor who'd been called for the tennis player. Dr. Gaspard was a man in his mid-sixties, with silver-and-black hair, a fastidiously neat little beard that came to a careful point at his chin, and a kindly attitude. After examining Scott, the doctor advised him to rest for a week. But the patient—with Annabel interpreting—talked Dr. Gaspard into letting Scott dictate from his bed so that she could jot down his correspondence and corrections.

This schedule did seem to help, for the fever came down. The doctor told Scott that if his temperature was normal for forty-eight hours, he could start taking some light exercise.

"Don't tell Sonny I've been sick," Scott warned her. "He'll think it's booze. You must be like a priest and reveal nothing of the confessional."

It was true that while typing up his letters, Annabel had a window into Scott's personal world as well as his professional. It had been his daughter who was hospitalized for the appendectomy and was recovering in the care of her mother, Zelda. Even though Scott's wife was in a mental asylum, she was lucid enough to lovingly oversee her daughter's convalescence and to write beautiful, poetic letters to her husband assuring him that she was certain of his talent and she believed that, despite any setbacks, he would soon be paid better for his hard work and recognized once again for his great talent.

Annabel was astonished to learn that *The Great Gatsby* had failed to sell, or even to support his future efforts in a modest way. Yet Scott and Zelda knew that that book was his masterpiece. And they both believed that he would write another great novel just like it.

"I used to get four thousand dollars for a short story," he'd told Annabel ruefully. "Now I'm lucky to get two hundred." But every cent counted. "Hollywood pays better, but it's unpredictable bursts of work, and then I'm either rewriting someone else's work, or they're rewriting mine," he said. On top of that, his previous novels were already in peril of going out of print entirely.

Since Annabel was now updating his ledger and recording his mail, receipts, and bank statements, she saw all those urgent family expenses—his daughter's tuition, his wife's residency at the asylum. She observed that as soon as any money was earned, it was used up as Scott scrupulously paid off his debts, with interest.

He's like a man laying the tracks for a train that's already roaring toward him, she thought. Any other man might give up and jump off a bridge, but Scott believed unfailingly in his own shining destiny and felt he had an ace up his sleeve.

"I've got a new novel in mind," he'd said yesterday as he dictated "pitch" letters about it to his book publisher and to the editor of *Collier's*, who might serialize it in his magazine.

"But don't tell anyone that I'm writing a book about Hollywood," he'd warned her. "Your Grand Hotel is crawling with spies from the press and the studio front offices and every government on earth. Nobody trusts anybody this year."

Annabel had said cautiously, "Why don't you want people to know about the new novel? Maybe you could make a movie deal—"

"No!" Scott said in alarm. "If people start buzzing that I'm writing tales about Tinseltown, the big shots will try to find out who is who in my characters, for fear that I will make them look ridiculous; then Sonny will do everything in his power to stop it. So you have to *swear* on the souls of your ancestors that you won't tell a single person. Understand?"

He'd stared at her, his eyes darkening in a way that was almost frightening.

"Okay," Annabel had said meekly. "I swear."

"Good!" he'd exclaimed.

———

So now, when Oncle JP said, "Anything else you can tell me about the screenwriter?" Annabel shook her head. She wasn't a snitch. And this wasn't Nazi Germany.

Oncle JP raised his hawkish eyebrows, rather astutely sensing that there was much she was not telling him, but he said only, "Does he drink?"

Annabel said carefully, "He says he allows himself one glass of wine at the end of the day, just so that he knows he can have it and won't have to anguish over it all day. Dr. Gaspard said it would be all right. But I've never seen him drink even that! If he has, I see no sign of any ill effects. He seems healthy. He plays tennis with Jack Cabot sometimes."

"The actor in the Villa Sanctuaire?" Oncle JP asked. "How goes it with him?"

Annabel said, "Fine. He does all his interviews and goes to all the luncheons."

She did not think it necessary to tell her uncle that Jack was secretly advising Téa not to renew her contract with Sonny. After all, this was just something Annabel had overheard on the telephone. She might even have misunderstood the meaning of what she'd heard. So she certainly wouldn't want to indulge in false gossip.

"Is that all, then?" Oncle JP asked, rubbing his forehead. He had much on his mind, as always at this time of year.

Annabel did not say, *And I think I am falling in love with Jack.* She could barely admit it to herself. At first she'd believed that it was just a silly crush on a movie star.

But crushes wore off, and this didn't. Every time Jack looked at her intently with those dark, expressive eyes, she felt her entire body yearn for him. She was shocked by the way her flesh instantly responded to the mere sight and scent of him.

When Jack accidentally touched her—brushed against her hair, tapped her arm to praise her work—she had to put her head down to hide her delight. Just approaching his villa and knowing that he was there waiting for Annabel made her heart beat faster. The more she tried to dismiss these feelings, the more her hunger intensified.

She hadn't even felt like this when she was a schoolgirl. Even her erstwhile boyfriend, David, had not evoked this simple, surprisingly aggressive animal lust that she felt for Jack Cabot. Of course, there was much more to it—a wistful yearning for something that seemed as if it would be forever beyond her grasp.

"Oncle, I must go," she said hastily. "The writer and the actor have both asked me to be there this morning because they are having a big meeting, and they want me to take notes. It's about their film, which we are screening here at the Grand Hotel ahead of the film festival."

She explained that this was the first film Jack had directed, *Love Isn't Easy*, based on *Love Is a Pain*, a charming unpublished story by Scott. Annabel had been given the script to read so that she'd understand the references they might make in the upcoming meeting.

"It's about an American girl returning from Europe, unaware that a handsome foreign spy has hidden something in her suitcase and is now following her to retrieve it," she said as Oncle JP listened intently, for he believed in the power of *le cinéma*, especially this year. "The girl lives with a wealthy grandfather who despises publicity, and she has two American suitors who are highly suspicious of the handsome spy, so the heroine doesn't know whom to trust." Jack had added more complications and dangerous rival spies pursuing them in the chase scenes, which were both funny and suspenseful, worthy of Alfred Hitchcock.

Scott had seen some of the footage and praised Jack's acting talent, especially his ability to convey subtle changing reactions to a movie's situations and people. Scott had said, *It's a rare gift, being able to visualize those shifts of thought and feeling in a human face. Hollywood is full of actors who can't do it, forcing the director to cut away and then cut back, to give those lesser performers time to rearrange their faces. And it never looks right. Jack's one in a million.*

Annabel relayed all this to her uncle. "I think we will have a very successful screening party for that film, here at the Grand Hotel," she concluded with some pride.

"*Eh bien,*" Oncle JP said brightly. "Then I will tell Sonny all is well with your work."

He smiled at her encouragingly, allowing himself a fond expression for his niece. She always felt warmed by this, and today she deeply appreciated that he was shielding her from being called on the carpet to report to Sonny. It was Oncle JP's way of letting Hollywood know that Annabel belonged to the Grand Hotel, not to them.

So she nodded gratefully to her uncle and then hurried off. This big meeting was taking place at Jack's villa.

———

When she got there, she immediately felt tension in the air. Five men were seated around the table beside the pool: Jack, his handsome face frowning at some pages before him; Scott, his hair neatly brushed, and dressed in clothes that looked to be of high quality but a bit worn; Sonny, puffing on his cigar; his son-in-law, Alan, wearing a gardenia in his buttonhole; and a German visitor whom she did not know, a man with light-brownish hair streaked with grey, a squarish jaw, and chilly, pale-blue eyes. He was wearing a sober brown business suit, and he sat very straight and rigid.

"Herr Hardtman, this is my secretary—" Jack began.

The man waved his hand dismissively. "Yes, yes, all right. She can stay." As if it were up to him to decide this. He spoke in accented English, biting off the words as if to be precise.

"Have a seat, Annabel," Jack said, gallantly pulling out a chair for her. She sat down and waited, with her pad and pen poised to take notes.

"Where is Téa Marlo?" the visitor asked stiffly, glancing around.

"Hmm? Oh, Téa. She went for a fitting for her gowns," Jack said absently.

Herr Hardtman looked particularly displeased, yet Sonny appeared smug at having this desirable, prized racehorse of an actress in *his* stable.

Alan cleared his throat. "Well, I'll get right to the point. Jack, we allowed our foreign consultant to review the film of *Love Isn't Easy*, and the long and the short of it is, Herr Hardtman has advised us not to show it without making certain changes."

"What!" Jack exclaimed. "For God's sake, that's not possible. The film is finished. You people saw the script months and months ago, before we shot a single frame!"

"Well, actually, Herr Hardtman didn't really get a look at the script until last month," Alan said, appearing a trifle guilty. "Apparently it got lost in the shuffle. An awful lot of movies are being released in 1939. It should be a banner year for all the studios!"

There was a brief, awkward silence. Annabel understood

perfectly what was being left unsaid. Scott had told her that the major studios were rushing out as many of their films as they could, "in case" there was a war with the fascist countries.

The German consultant leaned forward now. "Perhaps there is no need to reshoot. Perhaps you could dub in new words," he said firmly. "Simply make the fascist spies into communists. That would do."

Jack, quietly seething, now said sarcastically, "Oh, that's all, eh? Piece of cake!"

Alan said to the consultant, "The spies aren't specifically referred to as Nazis, just fascists. The accents are indeterminate. They could just as easily be French or Russian accents."

"No!" Herr Hardtman said vehemently. "You'll have to do better than this."

"Key-hrist," said Scott, "it's *Three Comrades* all over again. I don't think Erich Maria Remarque will ever forgive us for the hatchet job that MGM made us do to his novel."

"And if they didn't respect the author of *All Quiet on the Western Front*, what chance have *we* got?" Jack replied. He glared at Herr Hardtman. "Your Mr. Goebbels banned *that* masterpiece, too, and revoked Remarque's citizenship for good measure. Are you going to drive all your best talent into exile?"

Annabel suppressed a gasp, for she had not heard of all these troubles of the aristocratic-looking man she'd seen scribbling away with his pointy pencils on yellow lined pads at his breakfast table on the terrace.

Herr Hardtman's face reddened with silent fury.

Sonny shot an alarmed look at Jack. "Let's not dredge up unpleasant things," he advised. "People do what they have to do, these days."

Jack smiled at Herr Hardtman for the first time. "Not to worry. Mr. Remarque is perfectly happy here on the French Riviera in the clear blue light of Western freedom. When you Nazis denounced Marlene Dietrich, you inspired her to become an American citizen! So just keep that talent coming."

"Knock it off, Jack," Alan said testily now. "Herr Hardtman is only trying to help. You should see the fellow he has to answer to, and be glad *that* guy isn't sitting here now."

"I advise you to take this seriously. I should regret being forced to invoke Article Fifteen," the man said coldly.

"What the hell is that?" Jack demanded.

"You want to be a producer, you ought to learn the business side of things," Alan snapped impatiently. "Article Fifteen is the law in Nazi Germany. It means that if a studio makes one film which these men decide is antifascist or 'anti-German,' then *every* single other film produced by that studio would also be banned from their market."

"Which is why MGM canceled the production of Sinclair Lewis's novel *It Can't Happen Here*," Scott said meaningfully to Jack.

"Oh, no, no, I heard that Louis B. canceled it only because it cost too much to make," Sonny said hastily.

Hearing the title of the Sinclair Lewis novel, Annabel recalled what Marta, the head of reception at the front desk, had said to her on the day of the tennis player's death. *You'd say: Well, that can't happen here. And I say to you, Oh, yes, it can.*

Sonny tried to steer this ominous discussion in a lighter direction. "Now, now, gentlemen. Jack's little movie is really just a pleasant comedy. Moviegoers will be looking for laughs, not politics. Nobody will pay any attention to the accents, nor take any of the spy stuff seriously! It's just window dressing."

He glanced at the other Americans for support, but they were sulking. Out of default, Sonny's gaze rested on Annabel now. She was surprised to see that this normally confident boss looked a bit like a drowning man seeking a helping hand wherever he could find it.

"It's really a romantic love story," she piped up.

Sonny seized on this in relief. "There you go! It's a love

story!" he exclaimed. "A perfect showcase for Téa Marlo, proving she can do comedy as well as tragedy. She will make us—and Germany—proud."

"Ah, yes, Téa Marlo. Which reminds me," Herr Hardtman said smoothly, reaching into his pocket, "I wish to directly deliver an invitation to Miss Marlo, from Herr Volney, one of our most esteemed film executives, who is hosting a little party in her honor on his yacht. He is a personal friend of Joseph Goebbels himself."

It was the second time that the name of the propaganda minister of Germany had been invoked in this chilly conversation, which was becoming downright frosty now. Annabel could not imagine attending a party thrown by Herr Volney, that disagreeable film executive with the bushy blond eyebrows who'd been so nasty to little Delphine at the fountain in the garden.

"Annabel handles Téa's calendar and will see that Téa is made aware of your invitation," Jack said, quickly improvising. "So you can give the invitation to Annabel."

Herr Hardtman leaned toward her and pressed into her hand an envelope of heavy linen stationery embossed with gold. She forced herself not to recoil from his stern gaze.

"You *will* personally give this to Miss Marlo," he said. There was no question in his voice. It was a command. "Tell her that there will be people at this party whom she is very eager to see. You will remember that?" He stared harder, clearly insisting upon an answer.

Annabel, trying not to show any fear, said stiffly, "Of course."

Herr Hardtman rose to go, unilaterally ending the meeting. He said to the other men, "As for your film, I think I have made our position clear. The choice, of course, is yours. But I do hope you realize that the wrong decision could create certain—serious difficulties—for you with my colleagues, not just now but in the not-too-distant future."

He gave a short, stiff bow and strode off. A momentary silence hung in the air.

"What the hell does that mean?" Jack said finally. "Is this that Article Fifteen jazz again?" He turned to Sonny. "How can you and Louis B. stand for it? Aren't *you* Jewish?"

Sonny smiled wryly. "As Charlie Chaplin said, 'I do not have that honor.' But everyone thinks I'm Jewish, so I might as well be."

Jack persisted, "But you *know* what the Nazis are doing to innocent people! Why play ball with them? Who gives a damn what the Germans think?"

"We do," Alan said shortly. "Germany is a big market for films! We also have employees living and working in Berlin. Know what it's like to live there, these days? People who piss off the Nazis disappear off the streets, and nobody tells you why. We've got money invested in German productions, German banks. We can't take that money out of the country—that's a law, too. We get on their bad side, we stand to lose a great deal. An actor is not supposed to *lose* money for his studio, Jack. He's supposed to *earn* money for us. So you'd *better* start to care."

The remark about the law against taking money out of Germany struck a chord with Annabel, reminding her of the cheerful tennis player who'd been accused of doing that very thing and had ended up dead. She shivered, even in the warmth of the Mediterranean sun.

"I believe," Scott said, "that our guest was not talking about Article Fifteen or any other law in that parting shot of his. No, sir, this sounds like more than just *we won't sell your films in Nazi Germany this season.* They're looking at a much bigger 'picture,' no pun intended."

Annabel glanced at him questioningly. Jack seemed to understand.

"It means," he said, "that if we fight another world war—this time *they* could win it."

Sonny and Alan left the villa without really deciding what, if anything, was to be done about *Love Isn't Easy*. Sonny had at least agreed that he would not cancel the screening party at the Grand Hotel.

"Leave it to me," he said with a wave of his hand. "I will resolve this matter."

Annabel thought that sounded hopeful, but after Sonny and Alan left, Jack and Scott remained at the table, gloomily prognosticating about the fate of their film.

"Sonny might go ahead with the screening here in France but then pull the plug on the distribution by 'postponing the actual release,'" Jack predicted. "I'll ask my lawyer to check my contract, because if Sonny reneges on the American distribution, then maybe I can take the film to Warner Brothers. They don't bend to the Nazi pressure. Neither does Charlie Chaplin's company! He just thumbs his nose at Hitler and keeps making movies to annoy him."

"As long as his new picture doesn't upset the fascists in the U.S. of A.," Scott observed.

Jack looked sober but said, "One thing's for sure—I don't see that we can do anything to our film now to help Sonny."

"Dubbing is out," Scott agreed. "This isn't a simple matter of plugging in new dialogue. Why do people like Herr Hardass think you can change fascism to communism with the flick of an audio switch?"

"Sonny just has to stand up to them," Jack said vehemently. "Not only for our sake. For his. If he kowtows on this picture, he'll have to kowtow to everything else they demand. They want Téa to go back to Germany and make pictures for Hitler. They think everybody on earth will end up answering to them. World domination."

"Those fascists keep more lists than I do," Scott said wryly. "Of everybody who ever crossed them. Or offends them. They've even got Picasso on some list, for God's sake."

They fell silent, once again contemplating the unthinkable. Jack said more quietly, "Hell with it. We're all at the point of no return. People like us have got to stop looking the other way, pretending we don't know that the Nazis want to annihilate a whole race!"

He looked passionate about it now, and Annabel admired the way he'd said flat out what most guests were avoiding saying directly this summer.

Scott nodded, and they shook on it. Then he rose and yawned wearily. "If you need me, you'll find me back at the salt mines."

"Tennis tomorrow morning?" Jack asked. "I keep seeing Hitler's head every time I hit that ball."

Scott grinned. "Sure."

"Do you need me to type something for you today?" Annabel asked Scott, for this morning meeting had taken up her usual time at the Jasmine Cottage.

Scott replied, "Just for about a half hour, to go over the mail. See you tomorrow, Jack."

Annabel followed him down the path to the Jasmine Cottage.

It was not a good day for the mail. One glance at the envelopes told Annabel that there were new rejections of Scott's short stories to be recorded in his book.

Scott saw them and commented, "A prizefighter once told me that a publisher asked him to write his memoirs. The fighter said after twenty years in the ring, he'd never received a blow as devastating as the sight of a manila envelope with a rejection letter inside." He went through each quickly, tossing them, one by one, onto her desk with instructions about which ones to file away and which ones he'd try to revise.

"Well, there's always tomorrow's mail," he concluded philosophically. "No choice but to keep on going. I'm too old to be a gigolo." He grinned. "If only I'd played my cards better when

I was a younger man, hanging out here with the Murphys and Cole Porter and all those crazy rich dowagers and tycoons."

His eyes had a far-off look now. "The Riviera was a swell place to be back then. Everybody I knew was writing a novel or a ballet, or making a painting, or composing an opera. And there was always some heiress or her husband around to pick up the tab."

Jack had told Annabel, *Ernest Hemingway had no qualms about abandoning one wife for a richer one. But Scott wouldn't think of abandoning his first wife to be supported by another woman!*

This was Scott's quixotic quality of a knight-errant. He'd confessed that as a boy he'd devoured stories of Greek heroes and English princes and French knights, giving Scott the idea that all men should strive to be heroes seeking a prize for their lady fair—and Zelda would always be his lady.

Sorting the last of his mail, Annabel said indignantly, "How can anybody turn down a story by you? I read those magazines, and most stories that they *do* publish aren't *nearly* as good as yours. Even a grocery list written by the author of *The Great Gatsby* would be more interesting than most of the stuff they print! I don't know how you put up with these letters!"

"Bless you for that!" he said. "When you really care about your work, you can't stop wanting to make something even better and better, whether the rest of the world gives a damn or not. And that, in its own way, is some sort of epic grandeur."

He stopped and stared at an unfamiliar envelope. "Say, what's this?"

Annabel recognized it because she had seen ones for Jack and Téa just like it. Scott opened it and said in surprise, "It's for a party coming up at the Grand Hotel that I've actually been invited to. *Un Bal Masqué pour les Petites Colombes Blanches.* What's that about?"

"It's a masked ball to raise money for a children's charity," she explained. Rick, the hotel heir staying in the penthouse, was hosting it.

"Are people going to dress up in costume, like pirates and harem girls?" Scott asked, intrigued. Annabel smiled at his penchant for imagining situations taken to their dramatic limit.

"No. It's a black-tie affair. But everyone must wear a mask, until midnight."

"Hmm." Scott inspected it more closely. "They don't usually put writers on lists like this. It's for me and 'a guest.' I don't know anybody here this year who's available. Would you like to come with me to this little shindig?"

Annabel replied regretfully, "We're not supposed to mingle with the guests—"

"Nonsense," he said brightly. "You're not a hotel clerk. You're a Vassar girl traveling in disguise. Besides, this summer you're helping me and Jack. That makes *you* Hollywood. You're coming and that's that. Gussy up," he advised. "Everybody's going to look sharp."

CHAPTER 9

A Cathedral on the Croisette

After Annabel finished working with Scott, she set off to help Jack. He was just coming out of his private swimming pool, his body glistening wet in the sunlight.

"You have an interview in Cannes this afternoon," Annabel reminded him.

Jack groaned. "I wanted to scout locations today! Come with me to Cannes. Then you can point out a few choice spots along the way; I only speak *un petit peu* of French."

At that moment they heard a car door slam, and then Téa came drifting toward them from the villa's small parking area, which led to a very narrow access road that few people knew about. The studio's French driver followed, for he'd taken Téa into Nice for her fittings, and now he slipped into the villa, carefully carrying some of the gowns that she was going to wear for the balls and galas and screenings. Then he departed, quickly and quietly as he always did.

Jack kissed Téa as she sat down beside him and tossed her pale straw hat on the table.

"You missed all the fun and games with Herr Hardtman today," he said dryly.

Téa shrugged lightly. It crossed Annabel's mind that Téa had carefully timed her jaunt to Nice to avoid being seen this morning by Sonny, Alan, and their Nazi consultant.

"Alan cornered me at the hotel gate just now," Téa said. "Stood in front of the car to stop me, just to say Sonny doesn't like the publicity photos we took before we got here. Says I don't look blond enough—he wants me to *bleach* my hair! Like all those platinum blonds."

"Don't do it," Jack said instantly. "In my next film, you'll be playing an innocent French girl from a little Provençal village. I don't want you looking like some peroxide floozy."

"I heard that the bleach the studio uses, it can burn the scalp and make you lose a lot of hair that never grows back," Téa said mournfully. "But what can I do?"

This was the first time that Annabel had heard Téa speak at length about anything. Off camera, Téa had a more pronounced German accent. She also had a tremulous quality, and this fragility made people want to help her.

Annabel, thinking of her parents' studio with her mother up on the ladder chattering about the lights, said shyly, "Miss Marlo, your hair is already golden. You don't have to bleach it to make it look blonder. You can get a wonderful effect just from the right lighting."

Téa said despairingly, "The studio photographers apparently failed to do so."

But Jack said, "No, listen to Annabel. Her parents had a portrait studio."

Annabel nodded. "I can show you how to do it, if we get some professional lights to work with. It will make a beautiful glowing halo of your hair. Sonny's got to love it!"

Téa's eyes widened, and she grasped Annabel's hand as if

she were a lifesaver. Her fingers were cold, even on an August day. "Can you really do that?" she asked, enthralled.

"Yes, I helped my parents. We did it for special clients and publicity stills."

"Wonderful! If I have the photographer come to the hotel to take the pictures, would you assist him by doing the lights?" Téa asked intently. When Annabel agreed, Téa squeezed her hand once more, her expression one of boundless gratitude.

Jack said, "Listen, I've got an interview in Cannes today. Wanna come meet the press?"

Téa made a face. "Those people! They latch on and won't let go. Grab, grab, grab."

Jack laughed. "Annabel's coming. We're going to scout some locations. Maybe we'll find some nice little café and discover a great cup of coffee. Sure you won't come?"

Téa smiled faintly but shook her head. Her glance flickered at Annabel, and a slight frown came over her beautiful face. She said, "You can't go into Cannes like that. You need to look special. Come with me," she ordered, suddenly maternal and bossy.

While Jack went off to clean up and get dressed, Annabel followed Téa into her room and over to a dressing table, where Téa rummaged through a few drawers and pulled out some silk scarves, which she held up to Annabel's face.

Annabel watched in the mirror as Téa discarded them one by one, murmuring, "Yellow, no good. Green is worse. Purple, too much. Blue, not bad. Ah—this one, the red and white, perfect for your pale skin and dark hair."

Deftly Téa draped the scarf around Annabel's shoulders and said, "Wear it *comme ça*; don't just tie it at your throat." Annabel loved how the scarf settled on her in a rustle of silk wings. Then Téa pulled out a long strand of lustrous pearls, which she draped around Annabel. "Doormen and journalists—they always notice good jewelry."

The pearls undeniably gave a lovely glow to Annabel's complexion, and she felt that the face that stared back in the mirror looked more sophisticated, giving her a glimpse of the person she'd always wanted to be and might yet become.

Téa reached for a glass perfume atomizer that had a rubber ball you squeezed to spray it. But she sprayed it just on herself. "When staying at home, you need only to wear perfume to be beautiful," she advised as she wafted outside, trailing the scent of attar of roses.

"Well, that looks fine!" Jack said when he saw Annabel, but his smile was for Téa.

"Go take your interview," Téa replied, giving him a playful shove.

"Oh!" Annabel exclaimed. "I almost forgot. Miss Marlo—"

"Call me Téa. It's short for Tibelda. But Marlo is a name the studio made up, because nobody could spell Meinrad."

"Well, Herr Hardtman—the man at the meeting this morning—he said to give you this," Annabel said, reaching into her notebook, where she'd tucked the formal invitation.

Téa looked at Jack, puzzled, and he explained, "Courtesy of the German 'adviser' to our film. He was here, it turns out, for a pleasant morning of arm-twisting."

Annabel said, "He insisted that I say to you, 'Tell her that there will be people at this party whom she is very eager to see.'" She disliked the taste of that man's words on her tongue.

Téa's face froze. Dispassionately she tore open the invitation, scanned the contents quickly, and tossed it aside on the table. "Grab, grab, grab," she said again. But she suddenly looked like a frightened German schoolgirl, afraid of disobeying a teacher.

"I may have to go to this party," Téa murmured. "It's on Herr Volney's yacht—and he *is* the German distributor for Sonny's films. Alan told me to be nice to him and get him to use his influence so Hardtman will stop fussing about our little *Love Isn't Easy* film." She sighed.

"Maybe there's another event scheduled that day, and you can beg off," Jack suggested. "Why don't you let Annabel take a look at your diary and see what she can do?"

"No!" Téa said emphatically. "I don't use that diary. It makes things too—permanent."

"Okay, okay," Jack said. He turned to Annabel. "A secret admirer gave Téa a diary—and those pearls. I think it was Sonny, but she won't say. Come, Annabel, the press awaits."

———

Annabel loved going off with Jack at the wheel of his baby-blue convertible. But she had an embarrassing moment when he stopped the car at the front of the Grand Hotel just as Oncle JP stepped out to have a word with the porters. He moved toward her as Jack hopped out to exchange some American money for French with the concierge.

Oncle JP registered Annabel's presence in the car with one of his raised eyebrows, then leaned over to hear her explanation. She told him that Jack had an important interview and some location scouting to do and needed her to show him around and translate if necessary.

"Ah," said Oncle JP, nodding sagely. But she could see that he was sizing her up and surely noticed the silk scarf and pearls, which she hadn't been wearing this morning. She blushed. Jack came strolling back, and the two men exchanged pleasantries.

Then Oncle JP's eagle eye spotted a small fallen twig lodged between the windshield and the wipers. With one deft gesture, he reached out and removed the twig.

In a low voice that only Annabel could hear, he murmured, "Even little distractions can cause big accidents."

Jack didn't notice, for Sonny's plump daughter, Cissy, was returning from a forced jogging workout with her nurse. They were in exercise clothes, and the poor girl was covered with sweat. Cissy paused at the driver's side to say hello to Jack, who obliged her with a smile and a mild comment about how nice the weather was. Cissy watched wistfully as he drove off.

"Poor kid," Jack commented. His departing car caused a small sensation as hotel guests waved at him, the men shouting hello and the women coquettishly blowing kisses as if they half expected Jack to stop the car and scoop them up into his arms. It all had such a strange urgency that it was almost violent, and seated beside Jack, Annabel flinched involuntarily.

"God! I thought those women were going to jump right through the windshield!" she exclaimed. "So weird—they looked almost angry while they cheered you."

Jack nodded. "Téa says adulation is just a disguise for 'the rage of envy.'"

As they passed the black wrought iron gate and the guard's booth at the stone pillars, Annabel breathed a sigh of relief. The wind that blew in from the sea ruffled her hair, as if to dispel the feverish frenzy they'd just experienced. They breezed along a road that followed the curve of the coastline, until traffic slowed them down as they approached the city of Cannes.

"There's the Carlton Hotel," said Annabel, pointing out their destination. The color of whipped cream, this hotel had a fairy-tale quality, with white columns, a multitude of tall french windows and little balconies, and two large, dusky domes rumored to have been inspired by the breasts of a fiery Spanish courtesan and performer.

The hotel overlooked a famous promenade called la Croisette, where strollers could "see and be seen." Beyond it was the beach, dotted with the hotel's signature umbrellas and sunbeds; and the breathtaking Mediterranean Sea, sparkling in the sun like a sea of sapphires.

Once again, Jack's pale-blue convertible caused everyone to stop and stare. Even Annabel was being admired and scrutinized now, for no one knew who she was. She was grateful for

Téa's silk scarf and pearls, which helped Annabel to hold her head high as flashbulbs popped when they alighted from the car at the entrance to the Carlton Hotel.

The valet bowed to them. A smiling doorman ushered them inside. Everyone in the lobby stepped deferentially out of the way, and Annabel went gliding through with not a single obstacle to impede her progress. *So this is the good part of being famous*, she thought.

They went down a long corridor to the hotel lounge, where Jack was hailed by a bartender, who seemed to know and like him. So did a dapper Englishman drinking at the bar—a man with a longish face, a well-tailored suit, a silk kerchief in his breast pocket, and a white carnation in his buttonhole—who shook hands with Jack and nodded politely at Annabel.

"Wasn't that Noël Coward—the man who writes those clever songs and plays?" she whispered to Jack when they were out of earshot. "I saw him in New York at one of his opening nights taking a bow onstage." She half expected the playwright to stand up and sing "Mad Dogs and Englishmen," because this lounge looked like the sophisticated stage sets where his lightning-quick comedies took place.

Now a woman in an apricot-colored suit with an outrageous hat decked with false flowers stood up and waved vigorously to them.

"That must be the British movie columnist," Annabel said. The lady had commandeered a low table and plush chairs. She was accompanied by a photographer who had his camera and flashbulb slung over his shoulder. A waiter arrived with a pot of tea.

"We'll take the pictures later, outside," the woman said to the photographer, who drifted over to the bar and waited politely as the interview commenced.

"Espresso," Jack said to the waiter. Annabel diplomatically had the tea. The interview began with a polite discussion about the upcoming film festival; Jack was as tolerant of inane questions as he was of the better ones, without giving away too much of himself. Annabel could see that this was as vital a skill as the acting itself.

But then the woman said archly, "Do I hear wedding bells for you and Téa Marlo?"

"No," Jack said shortly. Evidently this was a sore subject for him, and the interviewer seemed to have expected that, for she patted his hand with false solace.

"Is it true that the Führer has summoned Téa to return to Germany and the UFA studio?" she asked, her small gold pen poised above her notepad.

"Téa loves America, and she belongs in Hollywood," Jack said firmly. "No one is going to be summoning her anywhere."

The woman made notes and then leaned in, purring confidentially. "What's Téa Marlo really like? Is she beautiful when she wakes up in the morning? Does she snore?"

Annabel gasped indignantly, but Jack only laughed. "I sleep late," he said. "The whole world is awake and on the move before my feet go into my slippers. But once I'm on my feet, I *do* like to work hard. Now, this new picture of ours, I think you're really going to love it . . ."

Annabel was glad when they finally stepped outside into the blazing sunlight and crossed the street so that the photographer could snap a bunch of photos of Jack on the beach, his smile as dazzling as the sun. After the reporter and photographer left, Jack obligingly signed a few autographs for the cluster of fans who'd gathered to watch.

Annabel had strolled off a few paces and waited for Jack in front of the official poster for the first Cannes Film Festival. She studied it idly. The artwork showed a very elegant man and woman in profile, seated against a cream-colored background, as if they had good seats at a theatre and were leaning forward attentively. The man was formally dressed in black and seemed to be wearing a monocle. The woman's hair was swept up into a dramatic pompadour, and she wore a strapless gown with a plunging back. She had long, slender arms, and extremely long fingers raised as if she were applauding. There seemed to be great deal of peach-colored billowing clouds beside her.

"Is that her gown all around her? It's a little odd," Annabel observed as Jack joined her.

He peered at it and said, "Looks more like flames, as if the whole theatre is on fire and that couple doesn't realize it, because they are so riveted by the movie they're watching."

"Here's some posters for other films showing at the festival in September," she pointed out. "*The Wizard of Oz, Only Angels Have Wings, Union Pacific, The Four Feathers.* Some lineup!"

There was a sudden shout a few yards away from a team of workmen who were raising an enormous cardboard display on the beach. It took ropes, pulleys, and more shouting to get it up, but when they succeeded, the watching crowd said in unison, "Ahhhhh!" and applauded.

For it was a huge replica of the Parisian cathedral of Notre Dame.

"Looks like RKO Radio Pictures has spared no expense to promote *The Hunchback of Notre Dame*," Jack observed. "It's a new movie being presented on the opening day of the film festival. I bet the French will love it, because the story's from Victor Hugo's novel."

"Can't wait to see *that* one!" an Englishman in the crowd exclaimed.

"Hooray for Hollywood." Jack grinned. "Come on, let's sit down somewhere. I want to tell you the plot of my next movie so we can make a list of locations for you to show me."

They took a discreet table at a seaside café where Jack, in his panama hat and dark glasses, might not be noticed. He ordered rosé wine, so cool and refreshing on this hot day.

"My film takes place in France, during the Great War . . ." Jack began.

Annabel obligingly took out her pad and pencil to make notes. "Does it have a title?"

"I'm calling it *Farewell at Dawn*," Jack said enthusiastically. "Our story begins at the onset of the Great War, about a village girl who came to Paris with stars in her eyes and went to work for a fashion designer—a tough bird like Coco Chanel or Elsa Schiaparelli—but our girl becomes disenchanted." He paused as Annabel's pencil flew across the page.

Then he continued, "When war breaks out, she rushes home to the little Riviera village where she was born, where her parents—and childhood sweetheart—still live. But the war takes her man to the trenches. A mobster from Nice, who's running a black market in wartime, wants our girl to marry him. Her family's starving, and she's told that her boyfriend is missing in action, presumed dead. Of course, he returns. We'll shoot it right here on the Côte d'Azur."

She had been jotting it all down rapidly, imagining the whole film as it unfolded scene by scene. Jack had been staring at her as if contemplating Annabel for the first time.

"You can help me 'see' my heroine's motivations. For once, I'd like to do a story about how a woman really feels, if she were truly free from the tyranny of ancient, silly fears of men. Her hero will be something special, too. You ever been in love?" he asked rather unexpectedly.

She recalled David's disapproving remarks and wholesale rejection of her prospects as a good wife, and she blushed. "I—yes, but—it didn't work out."

"Oh. Sorry," Jack said softly. Then he added rather astutely, "Some men can't deal with a woman who's smart *and* beautiful. His loss, the fool." He looked as if he meant it, as if he'd discovered in Annabel something others had overlooked, something precious, like a perfect seashell on the beach, and he leaned forward, saying intently, "Don't ever let *anybody* make you scrunch yourself into something smaller and more manageable than what you are."

The waiter quietly deposited the check on their table. Jack said brightly, "Say, we've got to find the perfect village for the hometown of the girl in this story. I want to see it, smell it, taste it! I want to see all the best sights of the French Riviera through your eyes."

Annabel nodded, glad to focus on business once again instead of her past. They made a list of preliminary locations, then returned to the Carlton. A valet brought their car round.

There wasn't enough time for them to actually stop at potential locations, so Annabel pointed to various turnoffs where they might come back another time. But all the while, she felt acutely happy just to be here with Jack beside her, with his strong arms guiding their car on this sunny day, gliding alongside the sea, feeling so utterly peaceful.

When they reached the road that would eventually take them back to the Grand Hotel, with the fiery sun dancing behind them, Annabel simply rested her head back and closed her eyes, feeling the wind caress her cheeks; and she found herself wishing that the sun would never set, so that her day out with Jack could go on forever.

CHAPTER 10

An Invitation

In the next few days Annabel sensed a strange, excited tension in the air. It began with a new influx of visitors, indicating that the pre-festival parties had begun.

"Tyrone Power is here, with his pretty French bride!" The word spread like wildfire as the newlyweds entered the lobby of the Grand Hotel and were mobbed by guests clamoring for autographs, and reporters who'd sneaked in with flashbulbs popping. The American actor, with his jet-black hair and fiery gaze, smiled shyly and obligingly.

Annabel, passing through the lobby, paused to watch in fascination. Journalists were shouting questions about Tyrone's new film, *Jesse James*, in which he portrayed the legendary outlaw as a hero.

The society photographers kept snapping many pictures of his bride, a French actress, smiling at his side. Tyrone had married her recently in Rome against the strenuous objections of his studio boss, Darryl Zanuck, who wanted the "heartthrob" actor to remain a bachelor so as not to upset the fantasies of female fans that translated to box office success.

Annabel saw the same English lady who'd interviewed Jack,

now smirking as she said in a stage whisper to her photographer, "My dear, don't you know? Zanuck tried to bribe the bride
with a multi-movie deal if only she'd stay away from Tyrone—but
she turned it down and got married anyway! French women are
so romantic; no American actress would do that! So the bride
is now being blackballed in Hollywood. They say she'll never
work there again."

It made Annabel wonder just how far Sonny was willing to
go to hold on to Téa.

Annabel hurried off to the grand ballroom, where flunkies
from Olympia Studios stood guard, allowing no one to enter
who wasn't on their "list." She entered.

Téa was sitting in a chair with a makeup bib tucked under
her chin. A slim, middle-aged Frenchwoman in a pink smock
was putting the finishing touches on the star's lovely face.

At the same time, a fastidious-looking local hairdresser, a
tall man with blond hair and carefully manicured fingernails,
was hovering around her possessively.

"I *really* wish you'd let me give you a color rinse," he whee-
dled in a French accent.

"You ought to listen to him," Alan said testily to Téa. "He
does all the best people on the Riviera, and even the richest
women wait months to get booked into his salon in Cannes."

Téa spotted Annabel and cried out triumphantly, "There is
my expert! You must all listen to her. Come, Annabel, I *need* you!"

An American photographer was waiting beside his camera
to take the publicity stills. He eyed Annabel skeptically. "This
is your lighting person?" he said to Alan.

"Téa's secretary," Alan said significantly. The makeup woman
and the hairdresser all stopped what they were doing to stare
at her in disbelief.

"She needs her hair lightened," the hairdresser insisted
with a venomous look.

Annabel, mortified to be at the center of a power struggle,

was rescued by a fellow in workman's clothes who said, "Are you the lighting lady? Here's the equipment you asked for. Please check it out and see if it's all here."

It gave her some real business to focus on, and this restored her confidence. "Yes, please put them there," she said firmly. "Téa, your hair looks fine. Sit here." She pulled out a chair.

She heard the hairdresser say in French to the makeup girl, "That little bitch is going to ruin this shoot."

Annabel turned on him and said sharply, "*Tais-toi!*"

The man jumped as if he'd been bitten. Alan, amused, said, "What did you just say?"

"I told him to shut up," Annabel retorted. "I want him out of here."

Téa fixed her violet gaze on the hairdresser and said, "Do as she says."

The man glared at Alan, who just threw up his hands. So the hairdresser turned on his heel and stalked off. The makeup woman, seeing where the power was today, murmured in French to Annabel, "Just as well! He goes up and down the coast eavesdropping on all the clientele, because he's spying for the fascists, you know!" She looked utterly serious.

"How is my makeup?" Téa whispered gratefully to Annabel.

She assessed it and said, "Fine, but the matte red lipstick is too strong, even for black-and-white photos. A sheer pinky rose would be less harsh and reflect the light better."

The makeup lady scurried to her table and returned with a cloth to wipe off the old lipstick and a new pot of color to replace it.

Annabel arranged some lights and then climbed a ladder and put a few above. Téa sat looking out the window, as immobile as a marble statue, while Alan paced around the room. Jack stopped by to lend moral support. The photographer grunted over his camera. All these men were as impatient as caged lions, but Annabel ignored them until at last she turned the lights just so and got the effect she wanted.

"Ready!" she announced.

Téa immediately snapped into her best poses, assuming that luminous yet tragic quality that she seemed to summon as if she'd gone off into a trance. She was a professional; she knew her "good" side, knew how to tilt her chin at a certain angle, raise her eyes so that they became like pools suggesting hidden depths, while she let her mouth drop slightly open in an expression of both purity and desire.

And as for her hair—it looked like a soft golden cloud with an otherworldly glow. The photographer had been peering into his camera with a frown of concentration, but then he said excitedly, "Hey, that'll work!" and, inspired, he snapped away, saying, "Beautiful, beautiful. Look this way, please. Excellent!"

Alan had stopped circling the room and now stood at the ladder below Annabel, even holding out his hand to help her down when the shoot ended. But she didn't like the way he said, "Well! Our little American secretary has hidden talents."

When she returned to the villa with Jack and Téa, they opened a bottle of champagne to celebrate. Téa kissed Annabel on each cheek, then collapsed into a chair and murmured, "Thank God—no bleach for me!"

———

Shortly after that session, Téa quietly vanished. Jack explained that she had accepted the yacht party invitation and gone sailing off on Herr Volney's yacht to meet his friends in Monte Carlo. "Sonny and Alan told her to go," he said. "But I don't think they realized how long she'd have to stay there."

Annabel nodded, saying sympathetically, "I guess she has to be nice to them. Does she have family stuck back there in Germany?"

Jack said briefly, "Sure. Her father and a brother. They depend on her financially. But personally, I think she's just glad to get away from Sonny and his seven-year contract." His gloomy tone indicated that he felt abandoned, too.

It was obvious that Jack and Sonny were engaged in a tug-of-war over Téa, both wanting her absolute allegiance and expecting her to denounce the other man. No wonder she'd gone off to Monaco, even if she had to use the devil's own yacht to get there.

Jack sighed. "Well, Sonny says Téa's been very helpful with Herr Hardass; so we're going ahead with the pre-festival screening of *Love Isn't Easy*. If we succeed in Cannes, then even the Nazis might allow the German distribution."

Annabel was secretly glad to have these afternoons completely alone with Jack. He was now concentrating on the script he wanted to write and direct for his next project.

Unlike Scott, who was only interested in Annabel's life in the United States, Jack had become intensely curious about her French lineage. So she dutifully answered his questions about her father, Oncle JP, even Delphine. Then they plotted their location scouting.

"We'll start with a tour of the old town of Nice, because it's got cobbled streets and ancient churches," she told him, ticking off her list. "Then the old seaport in Cannes with the colorful fishing boats; and we should swing by the high *corniche* road where Napoleon marched back to Paris from his first exile. The view is breathtaking."

"Sounds good," he said, leaning his head closer to hers to peer at the map. Annabel once again felt something magnetic pass between them.

Her feelings for him just seemed to intensify. Each day when she arrived and found him seated in a poolside chair waiting for her with an inviting smile, she had to fight off the urge to sit in his lap just to feel his fine, hard leg muscles beneath her. Simply thinking about it made her body ache with longing. At such times she would duck her head and wait for the feeling to subside so he wouldn't see the exquisite agony of her desire.

———

One afternoon, exhausted from their sightseeing, they returned to the villa and sat in the chairs by the pool, drinking iced tea with sweet lemons from the coastal town of Menton.

Jack said thoughtfully, "We've got good locations, but we still haven't found the right hometown village for my heroine! These coastal towns and fishing ports have all become too touristy." He took a gulp of tea and then said, "Tell me about the Maginot Line."

She glanced up in surprise. "How do you know about that?"

"Well, it's not exactly a secret, is it?" he said. "The French are proud of it, *n'est-ce pas?*"

"It's a series of forts scattered at key places along the border," she said soberly. "But it wasn't built until after the Great War, so you can't use it in your film. It was built *because* of the Great War."

"I could use it at the end of the film. To show why it was built—to stop men like Hitler, right? Is there one of those forts around here?"

She hesitated. "Yes. Up in the mountains above Menton and Roquebrune. It's on one of the highest spots in the Riviera. It's so high up they say you feel like an angel in the clouds. But Jack, the fort isn't a tourist area, especially these days!"

"I know," he said enthusiastically. "That's what makes it so intriguing. Are there any unique, old-fashioned little villages near that fort, in those mountains, like, on the border? A place that time forgot?"

She told him she'd heard of a charming town called Sainte-Agnès, poised on the highest peak. Jack leaned forward. "What'd you say this place is called? What's a Sahnt Ann-yez?"

"No, no, it's *Sainte A-ǵ-n-è-s*," Annabel explained, writing it down.

"Oh, Saint Agg-ness. Why didn't you say so?"

"I did. The French do not pronounce the *ǵ* in *Agnès* as the English do." Then she warned, "Some roads there are so narrow you can barely get a car through; they were probably donkey trails! And there are no safety rails. Raphael, our concierge, says if you fall off a cliff, you tumble into a gorge that seems to have no bottom."

"Sounds perfect! I want to see the town and the fort," Jack said, suddenly fired up with so much enthusiasm that Annabel felt slightly alarmed. Hollywood people were so mercurial, their moods so sudden and extreme.

"Well, you can't go up to Sainte-Agnès too early in the day, because it takes longer for the sun to come up over the mountain. And you can't go this late in the afternoon; we'll never make it down the mountain before dark—and in the dark, you will fall into a gorge for sure."

As if to prove her point about the time, the antique clock in the villa began chiming the hour. Annabel rose to go. "We must plan ahead for this one," she advised. "Midday is best."

"Fine, you pick the date, and put it on the schedule!" He clapped his hands and said, "Great!" Then he rose beside her. "You're great, too," he murmured, leaning closer.

Annabel felt that same delicate tension between them, and she waited for him to withdraw from the intimate moment, as usual—but this time he did not. He paused, as if to make sure that she wanted him, too. She tilted her head upward, feeling her heart beating faster. Her lips parted softly with that unbearable hunger for him; suddenly all she wanted was to press her body against his and devour him.

He pulled her closer, put his arms around her, and sought her mouth with his. The first kiss was gentle and friendly; then harder, again and again, each time making her catch her breath, each kiss longer and hungrier, taking their time, until ending in a long, languid, lingering one before they finally broke free and sighed for air.

"You are lovely," he said softly. "So very lovely."

Her lips were still wet from his kisses, and she felt that she was also wet where her *culottes* were. In this dazzling August heat she even felt as if she might actually swoon, which she had never believed possible outside of romantic movies.

Jack was still holding her hand, but now he let it go as they heard a car pulling up on the gravel driveway. A moment later the studio's French driver came up the walk, carrying a suit of evening clothes from the tailor, which he deposited for Jack in the villa, then departed discreetly. He was a middle-aged man with a quiet step and his uniform hat pulled low over his eyes.

But the spell had been broken just by his fleeting presence. Jack said thoughtfully, "There's going to be a party tonight. A masked ball. They say it's the Grand Hotel's first big pre-festival event. But Téa warned me she won't be back from Monaco in time for this party. Anyway, I've got to show up at this damned thing, but I can't ask another actress without setting the gossip columnists into a frenzy and upsetting Téa." He gave her his most winning smile. "So, Annabel dear, I would be honored if you'd be my guest."

She felt a wild surge of joy at the realization that her only real rival for Jack's attentions wouldn't be here tonight. She didn't even mind that she herself wasn't important enough for either the gossips or Téa to take seriously.

"Oh, but how could I?" she said softly. "I've nothing to wear."

"Téa's got plenty of stuff inside, and you're the same height and size," he said appraisingly. "Come by tonight and we'll outfit you like a princess, mask and all."

"All right," she murmured, for it was simply inconceivable to say no to Jack.

But then she remembered. "Oh, Jack! I think Scott asked me to go with him."

"Tell him I asked you first, and you didn't realize it was the same gig," he suggested with a wink.

———

The next day Annabel had a guilty morning, working with Scott. She didn't want to hurt his feelings, but she simply could not give up this opportunity to be with Jack all night long in such a glamorous setting.

"Scott," she said finally, "I'm so sorry, but when I agreed to go to the charity ball with you, I didn't realize that it was the same event as Rick Bladey's party."

The playboy heir was hosting this gala because he was the biggest donor to the children's charity, so he'd paid for the party itself as well, in order to show off his stature at the Grand Hotel to all the other rich people who'd flocked to the Riviera in the hopes of meeting so many glittering movie stars in one place.

So Annabel thought her excuse was entirely plausible. "I'd already accepted another man's invitation, um, first, you see," she said bravely to Scott, for this was the truly dishonest part of her speech. "I'm afraid I can't—"

Scott said directly, "Who are you going with, instead of me?"

"Jack Cabot," she said, hoping that she wasn't blushing.

"Ahhh."

She waited to see if he was upset, insulted, angry. But Scott's fine, sensitive face revealed nothing, except for a passing glint in his eye that flashed like lightning and was gone. Then he broke out in a grin.

"I told you before," he said in a paternal tone, "and it bears repeating, *you are a terrible liar.* You have a tell, and I am not going to say what it is, because I intend to rely on it. So truly, I advise you never to lie to me again, and don't lie to others unless absolutely necessary."

Annabel felt insulted to be tagged as naive.

"And don't pout," Scott said. "You ought to be glad I'm taking it so well. At my age, all I have left is my dignity. I'll be forty-three next month."

Well, you are a married man, after all, she thought.

"Just save me a tango," he said jokingly. "And if you see me surrounded by a bevy of thirsty starlets who expect all men to buy them drinks, come rescue me."

She realized that part of her job was exactly that: to keep this man from "falling off the wagon." So she said playfully, "I will *definitely* be keeping an eye on you."

"No, you won't," he said ruefully. "Not when you're dancing with Jack Cabot! You know why he got his first big break? The secretaries in the studio. They were called in to view his screen test, and they all said, 'Oh, he's so divine—he's like Cary Grant and Clark Gable and John Barrymore and John Gilbert all rolled up in one!'"

Now she felt slighted at being referred to as a girl from the secretarial pool. She wasn't sure what she wanted from life, but she certainly didn't want to be a secretary forever.

"How come Jack's not going with Téa?" Scott asked suddenly.

"She's in Monte Carlo with that Nazi who owns the big yacht," she said. "You know. The 'personal friend' of Goebbels. Sonny and Alan made her go. Jack's worried about it."

"Hmm. Well, don't *you* worry about Téa and Jack. They're killers, too. Be careful, Annabel. These movie stars seem like nice people who desperately need our love, but they're not like you and me. They're highly strung, so when they get nervous, they rear up and break things—and when they cause accidents, it's usually the other guy who gets killed."

It was just the kind of thing that Oncle JP would say, Annabel thought impatiently. She didn't want advice, nor to even think about her uncle right now. She was counting on the fact that this party was a masked ball and nobody would recognize her to report back to Oncle JP. He himself would make sure that everything was in its proper place before the party began, but then he'd go home tonight to have dinner with little Delphine, as he did every night.

Annabel loved them both, but their modest, quiet routines sometimes made her feel quite old. She was only twenty, and the larger world with its fun and frolic beckoned, even with all its dangers supposedly lurking behind every bush, in this terrifyingly modern century.

———

When Annabel arrived at the villa, Jack was in the pool but hanging on to the side of it so that he could speak to a man standing above him outside the pool, bending down to talk. The visitor was dressed in light white flannels, and as he straightened up and headed toward Annabel, she recognized him as the young hotel heir.

"*Bonjour, mademoiselle.*" Rick glanced at her curiously. "What are you doing here?"

Annabel felt this was unduly nosey. "I do secretarial work for Olympia Studios."

"Oh, is that so?" Rick asked, gazing at her with those smiling blue eyes. "Well, I just may invest in Jack's new project. Maybe you and I will end up working together."

She gave a polite smile but felt her usual irritation with him. Yes, he was handsome, but in a way that he himself clearly knew about; and that finely sculpted face never seemed to reflect any serious care in the world. In fact, his features were more perfect than those of most movie stars, who all had some quirky aspect, even a flaw, that made them uniquely fascinating.

Rick was evidently accustomed to women being enchanted by both his looks and his father's money, which Rick would one day surely inherit. Perversely, Annabel enjoyed not being impressed by him as she gathered her steno pad and pencil to put away in her bag.

This seemed to make him try even harder to charm her. "And how is little Delphine?" he asked finally, this with a genuine smile. "Has she kept up with her swimming lessons?"

Annabel relented slightly, for Rick was the only guest who'd ever really noticed Delphine, much less cared about her, except for the tennis player. Annabel gave him a warmer smile and admitted, "Delphine and I haven't been swimming much lately. Maybe we'll go back to our lessons in the autumn, when it's not so hot outside and things are quieter here."

"Good idea. The water will still be warm enough. Wait till the tourists are out of the way. That guy who runs Olympia Studios is making his chubby daughter take swim lessons in the pool with the head lifeguard early each morning, before it officially opens up," Rick said. "Poor Cissy. I made the mistake of going there early one day, and she insisted I watch her practice her dives, over and over again. Man, what a splash. She looked like a baby hippo in a watering hole." He shook his head. "What a family," he said as he sauntered off.

Jack had climbed out of the pool and was toweling off. He came up to Annabel and said easily, "Why don't you have a look around Téa's closet for that gown they sent over, the one with the mask? Don't worry, she won't mind. She lets friends borrow clothes all the time. Unlike most women, Téa doesn't get attached to baubles and things. That's why big men so often fail to impress her with showy gifts."

Despite his assurances, Annabel found herself tiptoeing into Téa's bedroom like a thief. She opened the closet door to a feast of silk and chiffon. There was a low-cut, slinky silver lamé number; a bouffant gold gown that looked like something from the Sun King's court at Versailles; a midnight-blue taffeta; and a chic ruby-red silk number.

Upon closer inspection it was obvious that the beautiful bouffant gold was destined for this party, for it had a matching mask pinned to the hanger, as well as a matching wrap, slippers, and tiny purse—and even a golden wig that Marie Antoinette would have coveted.

Annabel had brought her own makeup, and now she went to Téa's vanity table and carefully did her face. But she discovered that she'd forgotten to bring her powder compact.

She studied the array of Téa's cosmetic paraphernalia on the table. A black-and-gold lacquer box contained several jars of makeup. A matching cup held brushes. There were cut-crystal bottles and jars whose tops were all a matching black-and-tan enamel trimmed in gold, with gold scripting indicating that they contained custom-made creams of varying hues.

Some bottles were apparently missing from their slots, and there didn't seem to be any pressed powder. Perhaps Téa had taken those things with her to Monaco.

Cautiously, Annabel opened a small drawer, next to the one with the silk scarves. There was no makeup there, just more scarves, and a book covered in pink satin that had *Diary 1939* scripted in red embroidery in three languages. She recalled how Téa had scornfully said she didn't use that diary. And right next to it was a tangle of that beautiful string of pearls, just thrown in the drawer without so much as a box or velvet pouch to protect it.

Jack had said that both of these were gifts from Sonny. Well, Téa was a woman who simply refused to be bought, and Annabel admired her for it.

In the last drawer, she found a large box of loose powder and a fluffy puff. She powdered herself lightly, then dressed quickly and carefully, feeling as if she were discarding her old life and stepping into a more glamorous future. She put on the wig and the gold mask, which was trimmed with sequins and gold feathers.

Gazing at her image in the mirror, she found it almost frightening. She looked like a firebird from a Stravinsky ballet. Well, maybe she *could* scare a few people tonight. She'd never done so before. It gave her the sense that, at least on this occasion, she could be anybody she wanted to be, even a dangerous woman! That would be fun.

Suddenly she heard a loud, angry male voice, which at first she did not recognize, coming from the next room. "I absolutely will *not* do it!" Jack Cabot was shouting in a tone she'd never heard from him before. "You tell Sonny he can find somebody else to babysit that brat of his! I tell you, I've already asked someone else. Never mind who."

Annabel had come to the doorway, aghast. Jack was standing at the entrance to the villa, already dressed beautifully in a pale-grey summer tailcoat. His shined shoes gleamed. His black mask lay on a small hall table.

A short, bald man stood beside him, imploring, "Gimme a break, willya, Jack?"

Then both men glanced up at Annabel; the other man did not recognize her because of the mask, but he looked startled. "I thought Téa was in Monte," he said.

"She is," Jack said shortly, not looking up as he furiously lit a cigarette.

The man's face registered the fact that an unknown female had just emerged from one of the bedrooms in the villa. Then he resumed his pleading. "Jack, I been Sonny's PR man for thirty years. And I tell you, if you don't do this favor for Sonny, he'll never let you forget it. He's already livid about Téa skipping out on this party. He thought she'd be back in time. So you just *gotta* escort Cissy to the ball."

"Aw, dry up. Don't tell me they waited till the last minute to find her an escort! Somebody *else* bowed out, right?" Jack demanded.

"Nope, it was Cissy who turned *him* down. Some cowboy extra who sings while he throws a lariat. Sonny's trying to turn him into something bigger, a movie star. Anyway, she was s'posed to go with him, but she said *he* said something rude to her today when he saw her in her swimsuit."

"Then get a lifeguard to escort her! Why should I be rude to *my* date?" Jack demanded.

"Sorry about this, Miss," the man said briefly in the direction of Annabel. But he was not to be dissuaded. "Jack, believe me, you don't want to piss off Sonny right now, when he's moving heaven and earth to rescue that film of yours."

"Sonny could have gotten *any* actor to play Prince Charming tonight. He's doing this just to humiliate me," Jack said furiously, exhaling smoke from his cigarette.

"No, no. You don't understand. The poor kid's been on a starvation diet just to be presentable for parties like this one. It's a big deal, for her, for Sonny. And this party is a charity event. So *be* charitable. Look at it this way: if you're kind to Cissy, she and her mom will be singing your praises to Sonny forever."

Jack looked at Annabel. She didn't dare speak and reveal her identity, but she nodded slowly. He raised his eyebrows in disbelief, so she nodded again, this time more firmly.

Jack muttered, "It would almost be worth it, to drive Sonny crazy by making him hear his daughter and his wife rave about me for the rest of his life."

"Attaboy!"

"I didn't say I'd do it."

"Man, if you *don't* take Cissy, then Sonny will want to know who *this* girl is that you're taking instead, and he'll go out of his way to make trouble for *her*, too," the PR man said meaningfully, jerking his head toward Annabel.

She froze, thinking of what Oncle JP would say if this whole thing blew up.

It was that last bit that seemed to convince Jack. "I never thought of that," he admitted.

"Sure, you don't wanna make trouble for this nice lady, do you?" the PR man agreed.

Jack gave a deep sigh. "Get Cissy presentable. Will you at least do that for me?"

"Sure, sure. That family's had everybody working on her all week. Masseuse, manicurist, seamstress, hairdresser, makeup lady, the works."

The PR man pumped Jack's hand in a grateful handshake and then hurried off.

Jack turned to Annabel, still scowling. "I'm so sorry," he said. "You look beautiful."

"Thanks," she said in a small voice. Jack took her hand and kissed it as if he meant it.

He picked up his mask, an ornate black affair with gold trim and black feathers. He took her hand again, and she followed him outside. They stood by the pool for a moment.

"You'd better not keep Cissy waiting," she said, resuming her old role of a hotel employee.

He sighed. "I'm going straight to the bar to get a stiff drink. Looks like I'll need it tonight." And he went off with the attitude of a man heading for a firing squad.

Annabel watched him go down the path to the hotel. The moon had already risen in the blue sky, which would soon darken and be dotted with stars. It was a beautiful night for a ball. She could even hear, very faintly, the stirrings of the first big party at the hotel, the sounds of a band tuning up, the distant murmur of voices. There would be other big parties this month. But she surely wouldn't be invited to them.

She walked out to the front gate of the Villa Sanctuaire, still unwilling to give up her borrowed wings from Téa's closet, feeling like a Cinderella who hadn't even gotten a single dance with her prince before her carriage turned back into a pumpkin.

"*Bonsoir, princesse!*" came a voice from the path. She knew who it was; Scott was probably on his way to the party, too.

"Stood you up, did he?" Scott could not resist saying. "The bum."

"It wasn't his fault," she began, but he waved her off.

"I know, I know. I heard the whole thing. How could I help but hear him howling? Personally I think Jack should have stuck to his guns. Suppose Cissy falls in love with him tonight? And her mama and papa demand he marries her? Then he's really in the soup."

"You imagine the most extreme things—just to turn them into your short stories!" Annabel chided jokingly. Scott was always so fatherly with her that she could not help teasing him sometimes, the way a daughter would scold.

"That is *precisely* why people like me become authors," he replied. "The human race is so damned unmanageable that we have to invent a new world we can at least influence, if not control. You like my mask?" he asked, producing a small, foldable one from his pocket. It was a simple style, just an eye mask. "They're giving these out at the hotel for people like me who don't have those elaborate custom-made ones. See? Blue for the men, red for the women."

Annabel said suddenly, "Where did you get that tailcoat?"

"I borrowed it out of Jack Cabot's closet while he was swimming," he said easily. "The studio sent him three of them to choose from. So he never even missed it."

"This is Téa's gown," she confessed. "But *I* at least got permission."

"For the gown, or for the man?" Scott could not resist saying slyly. Annabel pretended she hadn't heard him. He said, "Well, at least I don't have to go stag to this party, after all."

She hesitated only a moment, then followed him down the path. "I don't know how I'm going to get away with this," she confessed, suddenly nervous. "If any of the staff or guests recognize me, someone is bound to report me to my uncle!"

"I'll tell everybody that you're a princess who speaks only Arabic," Scott suggested. "Don't worry. Everybody's in disguise tonight."

CHAPTER 11

A Masquerade Ball for
the Little White Doves

The Grand Hotel's first formal party ostensibly had nothing to do with the film festival. The invitations had announced its purpose in gold lettering: *Un Bal Masqué pour les Petites Colombes Blanches*, and the ballroom was decorated with white papier-mâché doves to represent the inmates of the children's hospital that would benefit from the proceeds.

Yet the images of the "little white doves" had now become a symbol not only for the welfare of the children but for universal peace, flying in the face of relentless tyranny: Mussolini's Italy, which had invaded Ethiopia; Nazi Germany, which had annexed Austria and Czechoslovakia; and Franco's Spain, where the dictator's gang had overthrown the freely elected government with a shockingly brutal bombardment aided and abetted by Hitler.

Annabel felt a rush of patriotism in the air from "the free world." It seemed to her that the rotunda ballroom of the Grand Hotel shone like a beacon of goodwill, with its gold and marble illuminated by crystal-and-gold chandeliers that reflected dazzlingly in the large gold-framed mirrors. The midnight-blue ceiling was dotted with gold flecks that twinkled like stars.

Scott was surprisingly at home in this highly charged

atmosphere, elegant in the way he expertly led her into the ballroom. As he showed his invitation to a doorman, Annabel kept her head down for fear of somehow being recognized by the staff despite her disguise.

Masked guests, champagne flutes in hand, were already milling around, perfuming the air with their cologne like hot-house flowers. The blue smoke of their cigarettes rose in brief clouds until it was carried away on a breeze through the tall windows, which were flung open to an expansive view of the star-filled sky and the moonlight that made the sea shimmer.

Scott immediately danced her right out onto the ballroom floor, navigating the room with ease. Annabel said teasingly, "Something tells me you've waltzed with queens."

"Coupla duchesses," he replied. "Ladies-in-waiting, sopranos, an aviatrix, several ballet dancers. Ah yes, I remember them all—but I never felt happier than I did in one moment of solitude, when I stood at the top of the Riviera on a cliff, and I felt like the whole world was supporting me, because it, and I, felt young and full of possibilities. Like you are, now."

As they whirled past other dancers, he murmured sly observations about the guests for Annabel's entertainment. "See that actress in the corner? That's Norma Shearer. She's the only one in Hollywood who knows how to throw a decent party."

Annabel glanced over his shoulder and saw a petite woman in a daringly tight flame-red gown and matching mask who'd positioned herself in a corner under the especially flattering light of a pink lamp. She was surrounded by a throng of men who leaned in to capture her attention and evoke her high, airy laugh, which was, astonishingly, somewhere between a loud giggle and a yodeler's shout.

As Scott and Annabel drew closer, he said to the actress, "Salutations, lady fair!"

Norma peered at him with an exaggerated effort. "Is that

Scott?" she cried, putting the back of her wrist to her forehead, as if about to swoon. "I don't *believe* it! Could it really be he?"

"Shhh!" Scott said to her playfully, and he put a finger to his lips.

Norma put her red-nail-polished fingertips to her matching red lips and theatrically blew Scott a kiss. He danced Annabel away and explained, "I once had such a crush on her."

"Oh! She was wonderful as Elizabeth Barrett Browning in *The Barretts of Wimpole Street*," Annabel murmured.

Scott said, "She's got a new film called *The Women* that George Cukor directed. I bet you'll like that one. I worked on the script before the studio chucked me out and hired Anita Loos. It opens on September first. Irv—her husband—would have loved it."

"Irving Thalberg?" Annabel asked after pausing to figure out who he meant.

Scott nodded. "Now *he* was one of the greatest Hollywood producers that town has ever known. He died young, from over-work. His heart gave way." Scott's voice dropped even lower when he admitted, "Thalberg was the inspiration for the hero of our Project Top Secret."

He was referring to his new Hollywood novel, which he had now named *The Love of the Last Tycoon*. Annabel liked that he called it "our" project.

The band gave a drumroll, and suddenly an athletic-looking man leaped from the outside terrace through the open french windows and landed nimbly on his feet in the center of the dance floor. The crowd gasped, then laughed and applauded as the band struck up a new tune. The man, sporting a dash-ing mustache, was wearing a bandit's black mask and a black Spanish hat like in the movie *The Mark of Zorro*. Even with his disguise, Annabel could see that he was extraordinarily sun-tanned, which made his smiling teeth look even whiter.

"That's Douglas Fairbanks," Scott murmured. "He was *the*

king of Hollywood silent pictures—you'll never see a better action hero. But I guess he was before your time."

Now Annabel spotted Jack Cabot, looking handsome as ever but wearing an aggrieved expression, visible even behind his mask, because Sonny's daughter Cissy was clinging to his arm as if she would never let go. "That girl is a nervous wreck," Scott observed.

"But she *has* lost a little weight!" Annabel said. "She looks very nice, actually."

Cissy was wearing a black-and-white gown, but she was teetering uncertainly on heels that were perhaps higher than she was accustomed to. She took a few dainty steps, cast a longing glance at a tray of canapés that a waiter was whisking by on a silver tray, and finally accepted a glass of champagne.

Her family was following closely, and Cissy's mother, Adelaide, immediately snatched the champagne out of her daughter's hands and handed it to Alan, who obligingly drank it.

Alan's wife, Linda, wore a green gown with Grecian draping, making her look like a slightly angry goddess, carrying her cigarette in a long silver holder as if it were a weapon. Sonny was dressed up, too, but to Annabel he still looked like a grey mouse in a fairy tale, his spectacles catching the light and making his eyes seem to glint intently.

The band members conferred, then suddenly launched into a Charleston. Scott was mopping his brow with his handkerchief. "I think I'd better sit this one out," he said.

Waiters were flashing by with more trays of canapés and champagne. One of them stopped in front of Annabel. "Champagne, *mademoiselle*?" he asked. Annabel recognized him but kept silent, hoping he'd never guess that she was Oncle JP's niece.

"Yes, the lady would like a champagne," Scott said, handing a flute to Annabel. "And I would like a glass of Coca-Cola."

The waiter stiffened. "I am so sorry, sir. There has been an unusual amount of requests for cola, and we ran out of it an hour ago. I believe that more is on the way."

Scott sighed. "Ginger ale, then," he said resignedly. "At least it's gold, with bubbles."

The waiter said in relief, "Right away, sir," bowed, and went off.

"I thought you allow yourself one glass of wine a day," Annabel whispered.

"Sure. I'd love some champagne. But I don't want to give this crowd the satisfaction of saying that old Scottie fell off the wagon again," he said wearily. "Of course, they'll see the ginger ale and assume it's champers, anyway. By tomorrow they'll say I fell under a table. Oh well. Whatever they accuse me of, I've surely done it at some point in my life."

He was calm and deliberate as he slowly drank the ginger ale that the waiter brought him. Annabel sipped her champagne. Her father had taught her to be discerning about wine, so she knew that this was a nice, dry *brut* with lively bubbles that danced in the chandeliers' lights. In fact, the whole room seemed like one big glass of shimmering champagne.

Mom would have loved this, Annabel thought, vividly recalling how her mother pored over the movie and theatrical magazines and the newspaper stories about the departures and arrivals of famous people who obligingly posed on the decks of fashionable ocean liners. It had all seemed like a fairy tale, full of magical creatures with strange powers.

Now here was Annabel, right in the thick of it.

As the band launched into a tango, a slim, wiry man in a white eye mask grabbed Norma Shearer and skillfully spun her onto the dance floor. Soon the other dancers stepped back to give this couple room at the center of the floor, but all eyes were on the man this time.

"He's very good!" Annabel whispered to Scott.

Someone had grabbed a rose from a vase and handed it to

Norma, who stuck it between her teeth. Scott had been study-
ing the man to try to figure out who it was behind the mask.

"That's George Raft," he announced triumphantly. "Just did
a prison picture with Jimmy Cagney called *Each Dawn I Die*."

"I know about Mr. Raft!" Annabel said eagerly. "My mother
told me that he grew up in Hell's Kitchen, and it was his mama
who taught him how to dance, so they could win prizes at dance
competitions at carnivals and amusement parks."

At the finale, George Raft gave Norma Shearer a dramatic
kiss that looked as if he meant it. Annabel had heard that these
two stars were having a "secret" affair, in total violation of the
"morals" clauses in their Hollywood contracts. Evidently here
in France, they didn't seem to care who knew about it.

Scott was watching Mr. Raft with a look of admiration as he
said in a low voice, "The FBI 'interviewed' Raft last year because
they think he's a member of the Jewish mob. He's a self-made
man. I think Raft and Gatsby would have gotten along very well."

"I never read *that* in a magazine! How do you know all these
things?" Annabel asked, still speaking in a low voice so that no
one would notice her.

"Oh, I know an English gal back in Los Angeles who's a
gossip columnist." Something in Scott's tone indicated that
he had some sort of relationship with the English columnist.
Not wanting to embarrass him, Annabel pretended she hadn't
picked up on it.

There was a sudden stir in the crowd, like a loud rustle of
leaves, as a couple entered, unmasked, flanked by deferential
members of their party. A hush fell over the entire room as
the crowd parted for the new couple to pass through. Annabel
watched in fascination as the male guests bowed low and the
female guests curtsied. The bandleader led the musicians to
play a stately tune.

Under cover of the music, a murmur spread through the
crowd like wildfire: *That's the Duke and Duchess of Windsor!*

Today's Hollywood royalty had just deferred to a real king, who'd given up the throne of England to marry a divorced American.

Everyone seemed starstruck, except Scott, who watched the Windsors impassively.

"Those two," he said dryly, "are just a little too palsy-walsy with Adolf Hitler himself."

He eyed a stiff, arrogant-looking group of men whose entrance had passed largely unnoticed because of the hubbub surrounding the Windsors. "Hmm," Scott said broodingly.

"What's the matter?" Annabel asked, following his gaze.

She saw the rotund, apple-cheeked wine merchant, a man Annabel vividly remembered from that little episode at the front desk when he'd impatiently demanded a new room key. It took her a moment to recognize him because Herr Wilbert was the only one in his group wearing a disguise—a furry eye mask that made him look like a plump fox.

He and his friends moved to the outdoor bar on the terrace. The tallest man among them had such a severe military haircut that there was hardly any hair on the sides of his head, and he sported a pencil-thin mustache. He reminded Annabel of a painted toy soldier from another era. The others also wore slightly contemptuous expressions, as if daring anyone to challenge their supremacy.

"Who are those men without the masks?" Annabel whispered.

"New guests; they just checked in. Jack and I saw them on the tennis courts. The tall one is Herr Ubel—he's Nazi military brass," Scott added dryly. "The others are the German millionaires who shoehorned Hitler into power. They're all on vacation with their wives. You should see them play tennis. No etiquette whatsoever, and they cheat." He snorted. "Don't let anybody tell you that the working class brought the fascists into power. It's the businessmen who smile and sell us all the things we want— cars, cosmetics, kitchen machines, pills. Then the press gets on board and legitimizes the Führer's gangsters with loads of free publicity."

Annabel heard a small cry coming from the terrace, so she peered out the open doors just in time to see Sonny, with a look of displeasure, ordering two hotel porters to escort Cissy down a side path that would take her back into the hotel without re-entering the ballroom.

"Her face is streaming with blood!" Annabel gasped as Cissy, who'd been so prettily made up, was hustled by. The rest of her family was pretending that nothing had happened, and they determinedly joined the crowd inside.

Jack, returning from the outdoor bar on the terrace, looked startled by the commotion and exchanged a brief word with Alan before hurrying over to join Annabel and Scott.

"What happened?" Scott asked.

"Cissy fainted and fell right on the main path. The flagstone sliced her face, poor kid," Jack said, shaking his head. "She told me she's been lightheaded all week. That damned diet that her father put her on. Sonny's kept her on such a short leash ever since she got here, so she's a bundle of nerves. I think that foul nurse gave Cissy a shot so she'd calm down for the party. Well, she calmed down, all right. Keeled right over on her face."

"Poor Cissy," Annabel murmured.

"So you made it to the ball, after all," Jack said to her in amusement. He looked at Scott, who was still carefully nursing his ginger ale. "Mind if I dance with your date?" Jack inquired.

"Ask the lady," Scott replied.

Jack held out his hand, and Annabel quickly took it. He led her across the dance floor with long, smooth strokes. He danced differently than Scott, for Jack was obviously professionally trained, perhaps at his studio, so his moves were more theatrical. Annabel knew that actors were expected to learn fencing, too, among other debonair movie skills.

"You look lovely this evening," Jack said in her ear. "So glad fate has put us together again." They glided past other dancers, as if skimming on the surface of a reflecting lake. Annabel was enjoying the very warmth and scent of him as he held her closely. She was mightily sorry when their dance was done.

A stout blond dowager now beat a small mallet against an antique bronze Chinese gong, startling the crowd into silence. "*Mesdames et messieurs*," she trilled in badly accented French with an American twang, "*faites attention, s'il vous plait!*"

"This looks serious. I think we'd better get out of her way," Jack said, leading Annabel back to the sidelines where Scott stood.

The lady was evidently chairing the ceremony, and she declaimed, "It is *mon grand plaisir* to introduce to you the man who has made this entire evening possible—a magnificent benefactor to the children's charity—I give you Mr. Rick Bladey!"

The crowd broke into applause and cheers, but Scott could not resist saying, "I never understood why people clap for boys who inherited every penny they've got."

Annabel was feeling indulgent tonight and could not help smiling at Rick's boyish enthusiasm. "Well, he really likes kids; he's good with them. I think he's sincere."

"But that's not why they're clapping for him," Scott observed.

Rick, his dark hair slicked back like patent leather, was wearing a black silk mask with a red crest of his father's hotel logo in the center of the forehead. He nodded and grinned, which gave him a devil-may-care, schoolboy appearance.

Yet he seemed a bit bashful as he spoke. "Thank you. And what a stellar night it is!" he exclaimed. "I have never seen a livelier or lovelier party. We are here for the children, but first, I confess that my father pressed me into service tonight to make an announcement for him."

The crowd, which had murmured appreciatively at his first words, now hushed itself again in anticipation. "I am happy to report," Rick continued, "that this beautiful, beloved Grand

Hotel is now the Riviera jewel in my father's crown. On September first I will officially christen it as the Grand Palais of
the Bladey Hotel Group!"

The crowd broke into even wilder cheers as an enormous
bottle of champagne—the biggest Annabel had ever seen in her
life—was wheeled out on a trolley by four waiters who carefully
negotiated the turns, because they were heading toward a table
that was piled high with cocktail glasses stacked in rows atop
each other in a pyramid shape.

With great care, the champagne bottle was mounted on a
stand above the pyramid of glasses, then opened with a pop
that sounded more like a cannon firing. The bottle was then
mechanically tipped, so that the champagne flowed out into the
top glasses first, then went tumbling into the ones below, then
the ones below that, like a sparkling waterfall.

"Ahhh!" The crowd's cheers were even louder now. Rick
ducked his head, looking relieved that he'd done his duty to his
father. He moved on to his next announcement.

"But as I said, tonight, we are here for a higher cause," he
continued, then launched into his speech about the worthy children's charity, urging all to give generously. "And that's why, at
midnight, we will all be unmasked, and we shall auction off,
to the highest bidders, some kisses from the brightest stars of
Hollywood!"

Everyone applauded and then surged forward to get their
champagne. The band struck up a new tune. A giddy masked
woman came over to claim Jack for the next dance.

Scott said to Annabel, "I'll get you some of the champagne
from that big bottle. I want to know if it tastes any better than
what you had earlier, so you'll have to sip it for me."

"Okay," she said, happy to oblige.

But as she stood there, she wondered if Oncle JP knew
about this seismic change of ownership of the Grand Hotel.
Of course, the staff had all been dreading something like this

for years. The previous owner—the eccentric childless French widow who'd fought off buyers and speculators by leaving the hotel to her fleet of dogs when she died—had said, *I'd rather have it go to the dogs than to strangers.*

Even when those distant relatives had won their suit against the dogs and tried to sell the hotel, they'd been so unable to agree, and negotiations dragged on for so long, that prospective buyers had walked away. Annabel had found all this vaguely comforting, thinking that no other sale would ever go through and disturb this oasis of good taste and tranquility.

Yet apparently Rick and his kin had managed, at long last, to do the impossible, which was to get the heirs to agree on their price.

Scott returned with the champagne, and Annabel dutifully assessed it. "Very dry and bright, like stardust," she reported. "And yet it's very silky, almost creamy, not as rough as ordinary champagne bubbles going down your throat. A hint of lemon blossom, too."

"Excellent," Scott said, and he actually pulled out a small notebook with an even smaller pencil attached and jotted it down. Then he warned in a low voice, "There's cocaine being passed around tonight. Nasty stuff. Keep away from it—and any man who offers it to you." Nothing seemed to miss his sharp gaze, as if he were memorizing the entire event.

Annabel felt another presence near her now.

"May I have this dance?" a masked man at her elbow asked in French. And even before she could reply, the strange man whisked her off across the dance floor.

CHAPTER 12

A Dance with a Stranger

As a dancer, this masked man was the antithesis of Scott and Jack. He was powering Annabel around as if he were pushing a lawn mower with speed and determination. His mask covered his entire head; it gave him the face of a goat with horns, trimmed with silver around the eyes. Perhaps it was meant to be a satyr, but it looked demonic.

Annabel felt herself struggling to catch her breath. He was pushing her backward, so she could not see where they were going until they reached a curtained area well beyond the dance floor, just outside the ballroom, in a dark hallway that led to the restrooms.

Now he backed her into a corner and shoved her roughly past the crimson damask curtains. She literally had her back to the wall, and he was gripping her arm.

"Stop it! Let me go," she exclaimed.

"*Du weißt, was ich will!*" he said, switching to German now that they were alone. His tone was low but harsh, completely different from his polite request to dance with her.

"*Pardon?*" Annabel said uncomprehendingly. She searched her brain for her schoolgirl German. What had he said? She thought it meant, *You know what I want!*

He shook her by the shoulders, impatient for an answer, and sneered, "*Spiel keine Spielchen mit mir!*"

She thought he was accusing her of playing games with him, as if she'd been flirting but was now being coy. Disgusted, she used both hands to push his chest away.

"Leave me alone!" she cried, raising her voice now. But he only grabbed her arm harder as she tried to twist free.

A gnomish-looking man in an apple-green tuxedo emerged from the shadows at the other end of the hallway, where he'd been standing as if waiting for someone. "Come, come, now, sir!" he said in an affronted English accent. "That is no way to treat a lady!"

Annabel took advantage of the distraction and managed to wrench free, then felt herself actually stumble into the arms of her stout savior. He was shorter than she, but his wide girth and proud demeanor gave him the reassuring quality of an immovable boulder.

"There, there," he said. She realized that this was the Englishman she'd seen at the terrace, doing the crossword puzzle with his wife over breakfast.

"Shall I call a *gendarme* for you, milady?" he inquired, half in jest.

She straightened up and looked fearfully over her shoulder, then realized that her assailant had managed to vanish into thin air. She knew that the last thing Oncle JP would want was the police summoned here. So she shook her head and said, "It's not necessary."

"Very well, not to worry, that villain has vamoosed. But my dear, you're shaking," the kind man said. His green mask contributed mightily to his elfin appearance. "The ladies' room is yonder. Why don't you go inside and talk to my wife; she can fix anything. Just ask for Elsa, and will you do me the favor of telling her that her long-suffering husband patiently awaits her? I dare not intrude upon *la chambre des dames*."

Annabel hardly knew what he was saying, but she hurried down the hall and into the ladies' room for the simple reason that she feared that her assailant might return, and the safest place seemed to be where only females were allowed.

There was the usual cluster of women leaning into the mirror. They'd removed their masks to fix their hair and to powder their noses and bosoms and shoulders.

When a vivacious woman with enormous blue eyes emerged briefly to raise a gilt comb to her hair, another lady exclaimed, "Bette Davis! I had no *idea* you were so tiny!"

Miss Davis sighed. "Yes, darling," she said crisply, "I have to be shorter, to make the men look bigger." And with that, the star of *Dark Victory* and *Jezebel* swept out.

Annabel sank onto a tufted round ottoman that resembled a white-and-gold mushroom. She waited until the cluster of women had all donned their masks and left in a gust of chatter, leaving only one other person behind—a woman with fluffy, reddish-brown curly hair. The lady wore a purple gown and was just putting her matching purple mask back on. She was the Englishwoman whose husband stood patiently outside, and as she glanced into the mirror, she saw Annabel in the reflection.

Annabel took off her mask, but her fingers were trembling. Her wig, she saw, was askew, and she had to take it off and smooth it out before putting it back on.

"Good gracious!" the Englishwoman trilled. "You're the girl from the Grand Hotel, aren't you? My, that has such a mysterious ring to it, doesn't it? But I never forget a face. I've seen you whizzing about here with such a charming smile. What *is* your name, my dear?"

Annabel told her, then said hastily, "But please don't tell anyone I was here tonight. I was helping out a friend who had no date. I never should have come. A man—a man—"

"Yes, dearie, I know," the woman said soothingly. "They *can* be such beasts at times. Don't worry, ducks. A little powder is a marvelous thing. Just dab away those tears on your cheeks," she said knowingly, in the steadfast tone of a school headmistress, waving around her own pink powder puff, which looked like a rabbit's foot.

Annabel hadn't realized that there were tear streaks on her cheeks. Still feeling shaky, she opened up Téa's gold purse but then remembered that she had no pressed powder.

The English lady had been watching her and now moved closer with her own powder puff. "Now tilt your head up and don't look down, as they say to the acrobats on the tightrope. Not too much, mind you. One does not wish to look like a dusted doughnut."

Annabel allowed the lady to pat the powder under her eyes, grateful for this woman's cheerful, chirrupy tone, as if everything bad could be banished by simple common sense. She was as soothing as the plump man outside the door had been. This was the same couple whom Annabel had seen returning to their hotel room after a hiking expedition, carrying those flowering branches that had caused a countess's dog to dart into the tennis player's room as Annabel delivered a telegram.

"Is your name Elsa? Your husband asked me to remind you that he's outside waiting for you," Annabel remembered to say now.

The woman nodded. "How he detests these parties. At first, it was all I could do to talk him into wearing that mask tonight. But by now I rather think he's enjoying being incognito and flirting with young things like you. Well, at least you're not that pretty little co-star of his. She's a good girl, I suppose, but I don't trust a girl who does such fastidious sewing. Nice, neat, tiny little stitches. Only nuns and murderesses can make such perfect stitches.

"Believe me," Elsa continued as they went out of the ladies' room together and entered the hallway, "it's not easy being the wife of the Hunchback of Notre Dame."

"Ha! It's no picnic being married to the Bride of Franken-stein, either!" exclaimed the man, still patiently waiting for his wife. He'd temporarily removed his mask to wipe his brow with a handkerchief, and he had the face of a charming, intelligent bulldog. A familiar bulldog.

"Oh! Why—are you—Charles Laughton?" Annabel gasped, then glanced at the wife, who nodded in amusement. "Then *you* must be Elsa Lanchester!" Annabel babbled, not caring if she sounded like any starstruck fan, because she was.

"Yes, I suppose I must be," Elsa agreed. Seen in person, the actress was much more glamorous than those eccentric char-acters she played on screen.

Annabel said, "Oh my goodness, you were both so wonder-ful in *Rembrandt*, and I loved that funny card-playing scene with the two of you in *The Private Life of Henry VIII*."

Elsa gave her a wink. But Charles, laying a finger beside his nose, said, "Shh! Must keep our identities a secret until midnight, for the great unmasking. It says so, right on the in-vitation. Until then we must all skulk around the Grand Hotel like spies and assassins."

As they reached the ballroom, Charles noticed Jack and Scott waving vigorously at Annabel as if they were relieved to see her again. Now they were heading her way.

"I see you have two handsome swains searching for you," Charles commented, adding mournfully, "They say the princess kissed the toad and he became a prince. My wife, Elsa, kissed a toad, but I became Quasimodo. Not much of an improvement on the outside, but inside, I assure you, I try my best to be a prince among men."

A young woman with large breasts peeping out from her strapless gown apparently had overheard him and cooed at Charles, "Oh, Mr. Laughton, I just can't *wait* to see you in your hunchback costume!" She snuggled up to him suggestively.

Elsa pushed herself firmly between the two. "Buy a ticket,

sister," she said cheerily over her shoulder. Charles smiled sheepishly but allowed himself to be led away.

The buxom fan said aloud, "Well, I never!" as Charles and Elsa glided into the ballroom.

Everyone was adjourning to the terrace, where the dowager lady who was chairing this party with Rick was once again commanding attention, ready to make another announcement.

"*Mesdames et messieurs*," she intoned, "prepare to remove your masks, and then we shall auction off our kisses from the stars! All in a good cause, to raise money for the children's hospital. Come one, come all!"

Jack had somehow disappeared, but Scott caught up with Annabel and demanded, "Say, who was that masked man who danced you out of the room? You got a boyfriend we don't know about? No? The way he swept you away, Jack and I thought some sheikh had kidnapped you for his bride." He peered closer at her. "You okay?" he inquired.

She nodded but still felt anxious. "Where is Jack?" she asked.

"He just ducked out for the night," Scott explained. "He's supposed to be part of this kissing auction, but he claims that all those rich ladies will save their money to kiss a bigger star than he. Jack says he doesn't want to sell himself cheap. Who was that couple you were just talking to when you came into the ballroom?"

"Charles Laughton and Elsa Lanchester," she whispered. "He's the star of *The Hunchback of Notre Dame*, the big film that's going to officially open the film festival!"

Scott paused. "Wonder if any of these biddies will bid to kiss the Hunchback?"

"Gather round for the countdown to unmask!" Rick boomed into the microphone.

That meant it was nearly midnight, Annabel realized. "Scott, I can't take off this mask," she said in panic. "Any one of the staff might recognize me and tell my uncle."

"Ladies and gentlemen, quiet, please." Rick was now at the front of the room, waiting for silence before he intoned, "We are counting down . . . ten, nine, eight—"

"Okay, come on, Cinderella, let's escape through the pine trees," Scott advised.

But they were unable to get past the outdoor bar because suddenly there was a raucous eruption of angry shouts coming from the men who had gathered there and were blocking the exit to the path beyond the pines. Scott instinctively pulled Annabel aside.

"How dare you say that, *here* of all places!" an American guest bellowed at a smirking Nazi visitor who belonged to that group that Scott said cheated on the tennis courts.

The American had yelled so loudly in outrage that everyone heard him and froze; Rick had even stopped his countdown. Amid a chorus of whispered *What did the German guy say?* Annabel heard someone else, after a pause, whisper back, *He said there are too many Jews here!*

"Take it back, sir!" the American insisted.

The other man, defiant and scornfully undaunted, simply laughed.

People were pressing forward across the terrace now, some out of curiosity, others spoiling for a fight. A tall Frenchman stepped up and said to the Nazi, "If you hate democracy, go back to the Venice Film Festival! Because here in France, we are gathered to strike a blow for freedom, against all hatred, bigotry, and fascism!"

And suddenly the group of men at the bar were pushing and shoving each other.

"By God, I'll strike a blow for freedom, too!" an elderly guest quavered.

"You absolutely will *not!*" his white-haired wife exclaimed.

There was more shouting and shoving from both sides now, and as if a flag had dropped, the terrace suddenly turned into a free-for-all fracas, with men punching one another, breaking glass, and throwing chairs. The poor French waiters, so polite and impeccable, froze momentarily before making a few attempts to break it up.

Annabel heard someone say, "Hotel security is on its way. They were guarding the front gate and the grounds by the sea."

Stunned, Annabel now saw that Douglas Fairbanks, George Raft, Tyrone Power, and a host of other men had rushed into the fray, at first to pull the pugilists apart, but then finding it necessary to throw punches to defend themselves. It looked as if this could only get worse—until, finally, the plump blond chairwoman startled everyone by raising a racing pistol straight up above her head and firing it into the air.

The astounded crowd fell silent. "There will *absolutely* be no more fighting here!" the lady boomed. "This is a night of peace! We are going to raise money for that children's hospital, and we're going to do it NOW."

The security guards had arrived, firmly quieting the pugilists. The chairwoman said sternly, "Everybody calm down—and let the kissing auction begin!"

———

The white pebbles on the private walkway shone like pearls in the moonlight, so it was easy enough for Annabel and Scott to find their way back to the cottages. When they reached the Villa Sanctuaire, she saw that there was a light on inside.

"Looks like Jack made it back here," Scott observed.

"I have to go in," Annabel said. "I must return this gown; I left my clothes in a suitcase in Téa's room." She was feeling more and more like Cinderella. She'd only had two glasses of champagne, but after this wild evening, she'd had enough of a world that seemed to be suddenly spinning in the wrong direction.

Scott, looking tired now, said, "Okay. Tell Jack I'll bring his tailcoat back tomorrow morning. Take care of yourself, Annabel," and he went down the path to his Jasmine Cottage.

The villa seemed like a serene safe haven. Jack was nowhere to be seen, so she entered Téa's room and turned on a tiny lamp on the dressing table. She removed her wrap and wig, then slipped out of the golden ball gown and carefully hung it up. She sighed as she crossed the room to open up her suitcase and resume her old role in life.

"Who's there?" Jack said a moment later, coming to the threshold of Téa's room and peering into the dimly lit area with some alarm. "Téa, is that you?" he asked cautiously.

"No, it's just me," Annabel said from the dark corner where she stood. "I came for my clothes."

"Annabel," he said gently. "You are never 'just' you." He turned to politely retreat.

"Don't go," she said softly. She had put on her blouse, but it was unbuttoned as she stood there in her slip. She had not yet put on her skirt.

Jack came toward her, close enough for them to look into each other's eyes. They exchanged a smile, as they had so many times when working together, in which they delighted in something they agreed on. Only this time, she saw that he was truly acknowledging the deeper feeling that lay between them. She thought triumphantly, *I didn't imagine it. It's not just me who feels like this. He does, too.*

Jack came closer and put a hand to her cheek. "You are so lovely," he said. "I've never met anyone like you before."

He stroked her face until his fingers reached her lips and traced their shape, too. Then his hands traveled down the sides of her neck, to her shoulders, where he slowly removed the unbuttoned blouse. He lifted her hair so that he could kiss her neck, and then he put his arms around her and gently pushed the straps of her underslip off her shoulders, cupping her naked breasts in each hand.

She raised her face to him, and his mouth found hers. Then they moved together toward the bed. Téa's bed. As they slid beneath the soft sheets and into each other's arms, Annabel felt the moonlight all around her, shining in soft ripples that undulated like the sea itself across the bed, making her feel that she was floating on a tide of love.

CHAPTER 13

A Favor for a Friend

The morning after the masked ball, Annabel left Jack's villa at sunrise, terrified that someone from the staff might spot her coming from the Villa Sanctuaire at this early hour.

Jack had stirred sleepily when she sat up in bed, and he said, "You're so beautiful—heart, soul, and body." He'd pulled her back down into his arms and started kissing her passionately, protesting when she told him that she had to leave. Then he understood why.

"All right," he'd whispered, "I don't want to cause any trouble for you—dear, sweet Annabel." He stroked her hair and then watched her as she slipped out of the villa.

The lawns were still wet with the morning dew. She took a circuitous route to avoid seeing anyone as she stole away from the Grand Hotel. She did not have to work this morning. Most of the staff had "rotating weekends," which meant that they took two days off, like a Sunday and a Monday on one week, and then a Friday and a Saturday the next. But since Annabel was doing office work, she had the usual weekend of Saturday and Sunday.

When she returned to her room at the boardinghouse, she

had an odd moment when she felt as if she were entering the room of a stranger—the girl she used to be, who didn't really know what she wanted from life. Now she knew she wanted a life with Jack, and she even felt as if she could become the kind of woman who could get what she wanted.

She floated through her Saturday routine of washing out some clothes and then going for a walk until she found a bench under a tree to read a book. On Sundays, Annabel often visited her uncle and little Delphine to share their cozy supper. But on two Sundays a month, Oncle JP went to see a friend of his—a widow who lived in Èze. At first, Annabel had found this *liaison* a bit shocking. Yet apparently in France it was not uncommon for a widower Oncle JP's age to seek such discreet companionship.

So on this particular Sunday, Annabel had promised to visit Delphine, who loved to read a recipe aloud from the cookbook as Annabel prepared their dinner. Delphine was an excellent reader and took the job very seriously.

"*Attention!*" she chided. "You're using more pepper than the book says!"

Cooking in that tidy kitchen, then eating with Delphine and tucking her into bed afterward, Annabel felt two ambitions warring within her. Part of her wanted to be a sophisticated, independent woman, free to go off to Hollywood for a far more lucrative career than she would have here in the hospitality business in France. But another part of her wanted her own version of this sweet domesticity, married to Jack with a lovely daughter of their own. Was it possible to have all of what life had to offer with the man she loved?

At the end of the day, when she returned to her own bed, she lay there remembering their night together. For the first time in her life she had made love to someone who wanted her to be exactly who she was—as passionate, hungry, and greedy as he.

"He *liked* me that way," she whispered wonderingly to

herself as she lay there recalling his caresses before drowsing off to a blissful, contented sleep.

———

So it wasn't until the Monday after the masked ball that Annabel returned to the Grand Hotel. Entering this palace of beauty, she now felt taller, like a goddess returning to her castle, as if, for once, this paradise belonged to her, and she now had the stature to own it.

Oncle JP awaited her in his office, looking up expectantly. He gave her the brief smile of approval that a Frenchman often gives a female who has enough pride and self-respect to know how to enter a room. Annabel felt as if she'd just learned how.

Then he said, "Your screenwriter left a message that he only needs you for an hour today. This is good, because that man Sonny wants to speak to you personally, to get a report directly from you this time. He's down by the pool today, playing cards with some men, but said you could come anytime before noon. Simply tell him what you've been telling me."

She groaned. She could feel herself crashing back down to earth and tried valiantly to resist the sensation of being put in her place to resume her duties.

Oncle JP had a wry expression now as he said carefully, "And did you enjoy the dancing at *Un Bal Masqué pour les Petites Colombes Blanches*?"

Annabel felt her face growing hot with a telltale blush, so there was no use denying it. "Who told you?" she asked in a small voice, wondering which staff member had reported her presence that night—or, worse yet, seen her sneaking out of the villa the next morning.

"It was *I* who 'told' me. I stayed late awhile on Friday night to make sure that all was well at the ballroom. And I know the graceful way my niece moves, even when wearing a borrowed disguise. When I left, I saw that you dance well," Oncle JP said with Gallic irony.

"Oh," she said lamely. "I didn't see you."

"No," he said, "you did not." He waited patiently.

"I'm sorry, Oncle," she said, but even now, it was hard to feel truly contrite.

"Annabel, we are not guests of the Grand Hotel. We are in service," he reminded her.

She'd heard him say this to other staff members when they forgot their place, but she wished she didn't have to hear it now. Usually, such an admonition was followed by Oncle JP pointing his right finger at his right eye and saying, *I've got my eye on you*, which meant that you were on his bad list. He did not say that now, but his tone of disapproval was enough.

"But you are American," he said regretfully. "I have never yet met an American who understands the concept of service; that is why I avoid hiring them whenever possible. And," he sighed philosophically, "you are young. I think you miss being young, and being in New York. You are like your father, in that way. I expect that one day you, too, will leave me, to seek your fortune by returning to 'the land of the free and the home of the brave,' as the song goes."

He sounded so mournful that Annabel said hastily, "I won't leave you in the lurch."

"Well, at least not today," he agreed. "At least not until summer's end. So please, be careful, Annabel. Movie people and rich people can be dazzling, but like diamonds they often have sharp edges."

She nodded, unable to look him in the eye. Then she remembered Rick's big announcement at the ball. "Oncle JP, did you hear that Rick's father bought the Grand Hotel?"

"Of course," he said in a noncommittal tone.

"But what will happen to us—to you—to everybody?" she asked.

"So far, Rick has assured me that his family will continue to leave the management up to us, with business as usual," he said in a tone that was not a hundred percent convincing.

Now she did look him in the eye to say, "And do you trust that man and his father?"

Oncle JP shrugged. "As much as one can trust anyone these days," he replied. "If you see Rick, just be friendly in a professional way. He likes you, I think, because you don't like him. But we are not here to 'like' or 'dislike.' We are here to serve."

Annabel felt irritated by her uncle's compliant attitude. She wished that, just once, he would lose his temper with a guest. Maybe tell Rick and his father where to get off. That would be impossible, of course. Yet some of the older staff had told her that her uncle could yell with the best of them when it was warranted. She'd like to see it for herself.

So she was glad to escape his office today. At the front desk the concierge, Raphael, looking as if he were juggling six things at once, stopped her; he had another telegram, this one to be delivered to Mr. Charles Laughton. "Have you seen him?" Raphael asked. "He doesn't answer his telephone, but the maid says she thinks they're still up in their room. Well, if he's not up there, please bring the telegram back to me in case he comes through the lobby."

Annabel couldn't help being a little fascinated by Charles and Elsa. Their chipper, eccentric attitude was both liberating and reassuring. It was thrilling to be able to say that she'd met the brilliant actor who'd played everything from the Scottish king in *Macbeth* to Captain Bligh in *Mutiny on the Bounty* to a comic British valet in *Ruggles of Red Gap*.

She had just stepped off the elevator on the Laughtons' floor when she saw a strange figure at the other end of the hall, outside a guest room near the staircase, making furtive movements that instantly put Annabel on the alert as she drew nearer.

It was a young woman dressed in a stylish swim coverall

outfit, crouched over a room service cart that had someone's discarded breakfast tray on it; and she was actually foraging among the plates, wolfing down half-eaten croissants and other breakfast pastries.

As Annabel drew nearer, she saw that it was Cissy, Sonny's daughter. It was such a heartrending sight, like the homeless men Annabel had sometimes seen in New York City rummaging through garbage bins. This wealthy girl was acting like a starving animal, stuffing food into her mouth and fearfully glancing over her shoulder.

When Cissy saw Annabel, she froze, looking ashamed. Her face still had scratches on her forehead and chin from when she'd fallen at the party.

"Oh, please!" Cissy whimpered. "Don't tell."

"Of course not," Annabel said. She assumed a voice that she hoped was somewhat like Oncle JP's, kind but authoritative. "But this won't do. Come with me—I'll take you to the kitchen and we'll give you some real food, and nobody will ever have to know."

She had made this decision and didn't care if it got her into trouble. Perhaps it was because Oncle JP had hinted that she might not work at the Grand Hotel forever, and the mere thought of release was what made her feel emboldened. Or perhaps she just didn't like being told that she couldn't go to the ball and be happy. She was feeling defiant.

"I have to deliver this telegram first," she said. "Won't you come with me?"

Something in her tone must have inspired Cissy to dare to commit full-out mutiny, for she looked intrigued and awed as she followed Annabel down the hall. "You're American," Cissy noted. "I thought you were French. What part of the States are you from?"

"New York," Annabel replied.

"Oh! I went to finishing school there," Cissy said, sounding wistful. "I liked New York. I liked the other girls. They all went on to college. Did you go to college? Where?"

"Vassar," Annabel said.

"I wasn't so good at school. I got mostly Bs and Cs," Cissy said in a chatty way, as if she were starved not only for food but for female friendship. "I was good at music, though. Classical music. The teacher wanted me to take voice lessons and study opera, but Father wouldn't hear of it. He says I don't belong in the limelight."

"Well," Annabel suggested slyly, "lots of girls don't listen to their fathers *all* the time. If you became a professional opera singer, nobody would insist that you go on a diet!"

Cissy looked astounded, then snorted with laughter. They were approaching the Laughtons' room, but before they got there, the door opened and a small, dark young man came backing out of it, stealthily, his arms around something he'd hidden under his jacket.

"Oh! I've seen him before," Cissy whispered. "He paid a 'visit' to a cowboy star I know, who told me that this boy steals things—he took a silver-and-turquoise belt buckle from the cowboy—who didn't report it; he didn't want that kind of publicity," she added hastily.

Annabel did not know of this particular boy, but she'd been warned of his ilk skulking around the backstreets of Villefranche and Nice. There were all kinds of names for these young male prostitutes, and they absolutely were not permitted in the best hotels. But sometimes they found their way in, especially if a guest was paying to keep them; such boys were known to charge all kinds of expenses to their "sponsor," ringing up a tab of prized champagne, cigars, even clothes and jewels sometimes.

"*Arrête!*" Annabel said to him. She noticed with some pity that he had his bare feet thrust into a battered pair of shoes that were too big for him.

The boy jerked his head in surprise, then lifted his chin resolutely.

She eyed his bulging jacket. "Hand it over," she said in French, holding out her hand.

"The lady, she say I can take it," the boy objected unconvincingly in uneducated French.

Annabel concluded that he might have been casing out the hotel for a door left open by a maid or a guest. She continued in French, saying severely, "Give me what you're hiding there *now*; if security finds this in your jacket, you'll be arrested and it will go harshly for you."

With a pout, he handed Annabel the item. It was a brown, wooden sculpted African figure of a woman holding an urn on her head. It looked like an antique artifact that could be of some value. Annabel kept it.

"What else?" she asked sternly. The boy handed over a silver corkscrew from the hotel, then held his jacket open to show that there wasn't anything else.

Annabel knocked on the Laughtons' door. The silence that followed made it seem that they weren't inside. She got a key from a passing maid, then went in, saying, "Housekeeping!"

Cissy remained in the hallway looking fascinated, but the boy followed Annabel into the room, too, looking around as if he was still sizing up what else might be worth taking.

The Laughtons were nowhere to be seen. The room was a good one, with the hotel's artwork on the walls—prints of drawings by Matisse, Braque, and Picasso. Annabel saw that Charles and Elsa had rather artfully arranged those flowering branches they'd collected on their recent hike, putting them in vases they'd moved to various corners. The effect was Oriental, lovely.

Annabel put the corkscrew in the desk drawer where it belonged. She picked up a clean laundry bag provided by the hotel and put the artifact inside it, intending to lock it in a safe place until she could ask Elsa about it. It didn't seem right to just leave it in the room.

Then she telephoned Raphael downstairs, to alert him that a certain unwanted visitor was up here. Raphael immediately sent a security man up to escort the boy to the security office via the service elevator, to search him and make sure he had nothing else. Annabel and Cissy took the fancy guest elevator, straight down to the lowest floor. Annabel led the way through the swinging kitchen door, where Albert, the chef, was busy with his team.

She said, "Albert, this is an important guest. Will you please give her breakfast at the chef's table any day she wants it? How about fresh fruit, two boiled eggs, some toast, and tea?" She turned to Cissy. "The chef's table is a special place in this kitchen. Only certain guests get to eat at it. But people don't usually ask for breakfast here, so it should be available to you any morning. Breakfast is included in your room fee. But still, this must be our little secret. All right? Good. *Bon appétit.*" Cissy squeezed her hand gratefully and sat down.

Annabel hurried off to the lobby. She still had the artifact and thought it wise to put it somewhere safe. There was a regular lost-and-found cupboard, for abandoned umbrellas and forgotten hats; but items of greater value usually went into her uncle's special private safe within his office closet, to which only he had the key. She would leave a note for the Laughtons along with the telegram and give it to Raphael so that someone could page them.

But in the lobby she spotted the Laughtons just returning from a morning swim. Elsa's hair was ever more wild, and Charles was flushed red with sunburn, despite the straw hat he wore on the back of his head. Elsa was darting her head about in little birdlike motions, which reminded Annabel of the way the actress had performed in the movie *Bride of Frankenstein.*

"Oh, *hallo* there, Annabel! Dear me," Elsa cried, "there's been a terrific muddle here. They say they gave you a telegram for my husband?"

"Yes, here it is," Annabel said, and she handed it over.

Charles tore it open and perused it, then said drolly to Elsa, "Hmm, it's from Alfred Hitchcock, about the New York party in October for *Jamaica Inn*. I daresay we may never work together again. He sulked all through the filming, and I'm not sure Daphne du Maurier will recognize her novel on screen, as Hitch made my character quite perverse."

Annabel turned to Elsa and said delicately, "I believe this belongs to you?" Discreetly she handed Elsa the sack with the little African artifact. "We have a hotel safe, if you'd like to keep it there."

Elsa peered at it quickly and said sharply, "Yes, that's mine. Where did you get it?"

Annabel said uncomfortably, "Well—a—boy removed it from your room. A stranger—not hotel staff," she amended hastily. "I don't know how he got into the hotel, but security will deal with him. You might want to inspect your room to make sure that nothing else is missing. I imagine security will want to talk to you—"

Elsa comprehended this swiftly. So did Charles. His smiling, expressive bulldog face changed suddenly, in a vulnerable way, and his eyes filled with quick tears that he winked away. "A search will not be necessary. Let the boy go," he said. Shamefaced, and without another word, he turned and made his way speedily to the guest elevator.

Annabel suddenly realized her own *faux pas*. Clearly Charles knew the boy.

Elsa sighed and watched Charles go, then murmured to herself, "Poor lamb." She recovered and gave Annabel the smile of a Girl Scout leader determined to forge ahead no matter what the obstacles. "You'll handle security, yes? Thanks. And we'll say no more about it to anyone else, then," she said brightly, then added in a low voice, "Thanks a lot, ducks."

———

When Annabel was heading for Scott's cottage, she ran into Rick on the main path. As usual, he gave her a most charming smile.

"Have you heard the news?" he asked breezily.

"That your father has bought the Grand Hotel?" she said carefully.

"Yeah, it's gonna be great," he said, pleased that she'd taken an interest.

Annabel said rather tartly, "I hope you understand that there are people working here who have given their whole lives just to make the Grand Hotel what it is today."

Rick had the surprised look of a man unaccustomed to being held to account. "And what exactly is it that the Grand Hotel 'is today,' would you say?" he asked.

"An oasis of beauty, elegance, and good taste," she shot back, undeterred. "It takes years to train the staff to make it so."

"Did your uncle tell you to tell me this?" Rick asked, amused.

Annabel said hastily, "Of course not. My uncle would never dream of saying such a thing. But *I* would."

Rick said, "Well, Annabel, I can sure see the value of keeping *you* on."

"Never mind me," she said, annoyed. There was something about this man, with his smooth, untroubled brow, charming blue eyes, and insouciant attitude, that made her want to puncture that sublime confidence of his. "Just take care of this incredibly well-trained staff. You don't want to drive them into the arms of the competition," she added slyly.

Rick smiled gently. "You are so right," he agreed. "Please don't be angry, but you do have the most beautiful voice I've ever heard."

She remembered what he'd said about her singing in the garden and how it reminded him of his childhood governess. Despite his influential family, there was still something of the wistful orphan about him. In spite of herself, she felt sorry for him.

But as she left, Annabel reminded herself of what her uncle had just told her: *Movie people and rich people can be dazzling, but like diamonds they often have sharp edges.*

———

Annabel hurried over to the Jasmine Cottage and discovered why Scott only needed her for an hour today. He was back in bed, sitting up with a long writing pad against his knees. His hair was tousled and his face flushed.

"Are you ill?" she asked alertly. He nodded. "What's your temperature?" she asked. She knew that he was careful to monitor it when he felt this way. She was reminded of the main character in that short story of his that he'd renamed "Temperature."

"A hundred and two," he admitted, but when she gasped and offered to call Dr. Gaspard, he said in alarm, "No, no! Last thing I need is a doctor buzzing around here like a fussy bee. If Sonny hears about it, he might replace me on these projects, and I'll end up on some Hollywood sick list again. That's how I lost out on Hitchcock's script for *Rebecca*. No, I just had a little too much tennis today with Jack. I'll be fine; I know what to do. There's just some letters for you to type. Then come early tomorrow, and I'll have plenty for you to do."

She knew that he would, too. He was working on his new novel, on short stories, on rewrites for whatever scripts Sonny and Alan threw his way; and he was now advising Jack on his new film about the French village girl and the Great War, which Jack was writing himself.

"At least let me call room service for you," Annabel insisted.

"You should have some beef *consommé* to give you strength." She was already dialing the phone to call in the order to Olga, the room service supervisor.

"Okay," Scott said without looking up. "Ask for some cola and a bucket of ice, too, and some aspirin."

As Annabel left the Jasmine Cottage, she could not help thinking that perhaps the fates were working in her favor today, to give her this extra time with Jack. They'd planned to go to see the little town high up in the mountains this afternoon. Jack wanted to take some home movies so he could determine the best locations for his next film.

All she had to do now was get through this little meeting with Sonny. She hurried over to the steep stone staircase that led to the pool area. An attendant told her that Sonny was in the white canvas cabana that he'd rented for the entirety of his stay. His tent was at the very end of a row of these exclusive spots on a lower terrace, closer to the sea. The canvas doors flapped in the breeze, looking like those of a rich sheikh's tent.

She found the one that belonged to Sonny. You could not exactly knock on a tent door, so she called out, "Hello?"

"Come in," said a male voice. She pushed aside the flap and entered. Alan, Sonny's son-in-law, was sitting on a canvas chair that resembled the kind that film directors used. He was wearing a white towel around his hips, and his hair was wet.

"I was looking for Mr. Stanten," Annabel said. "I mean, I heard he was looking for me."

"Yeah, that's right. He'll be back in a little while; he's expecting you."

Annabel suppressed a groan. How long was she supposed to wait? This might mess up her outing with Jack today.

"Come here—you've got something funny in your hair," Alan said.

She moved closer, despite a strange feeling that had come over her that she could not identify, until Alan, at first pretending to reach out to pluck something from her hair, stood up, made a sudden move, and released his towel, proudly showing her his alert penis as if he imagined she'd be delighted.

Annabel backed away, idiotically unable to say anything but "Well, goodbye."

"Oh, come on!" Alan said in annoyance as he advanced purposefully toward her. "You did it for Jack, didn't you?" he added in a sly, silky voice. "You can do it for me."

Annabel grabbed the first weapon that she could find—a white wooden stool, which she brandished in the air between them, like a lion tamer.

"Keep away from me, you creep!" she said with more bravado than she actually felt, for she was trembling with outrage and fear, because Alan was now lunging toward her.

But at that moment Sonny opened the tent flap. "That phone call didn't take long after all," he began. But when he saw Annabel brandishing the stool at his naked son-in-law, Sonny said in exasperation, "What! Alan, not *again*. Will you never learn?"

He looked at Annabel with some amusement and said, "Attagirl. Crack the whip when a man acts like a mad lion." Alan scowled and reached for his towel.

"If you don't put a leash on him, I'll tell my uncle to throw him out of the hotel," Annabel said, her voice trembling now. Sonny saw how upset she was.

"Okay, okay, calm down, girlie," he said hastily. "It won't happen again, I promise you. Here, want a nice cold bottle of Coca-Cola? No? All right, all right. Look, just take this contract to Téa Marlo when you go to see Jack, and tell Téa I need her signature on it *tonight*."

He handed her a manila envelope with a thick document inside it. "Thank you, Miss."

At this point, Alan's pride had evidently kicked in, for he looked at Annabel and, as if throwing down a trump card, said,

"You're not even my type. You're not pretty enough—you're too tall and skinny. I like 'em shaped like an hourglass."

Annabel gave him a withering look and said, "Buster, I'm *way* out of your league."

Sonny laughed heartily as she turned on her heel and went out.

———

When Annabel walked past the pool, she must have still had a distressed look because Yves, the lifeguard director who was busy assembling clean towels, glanced up, and his dark eyes seemed to register what he saw on her face. He raised his eyebrows and said astutely, "Something you want to report to me?" But when she shook her head, he sighed, glancing at the crowd. "Don't worry, Annabel. Soon enough they will *all* go home."

There was a sudden shout at the shallow end of the pool. "Now what?" Yves muttered.

A male guest stood at the edge of the pool gesticulating at Hugo, the young swim instructor, who was teaching some of the guests' children how to swim.

Hugo was becoming legendary; he was an Austrian medical student who'd arrived in France just a few years ago with only a backpack of possessions but an ambition to excel. In his homeland he'd financed his studies by working as a lifeguard, and he'd developed an excellent swim technique. He could calm even the most rambunctious of children.

Today he'd been patiently instructing the little ones, who gazed up at Hugo with the utmost trust and adoration. But now more parents came to the edge of the pool and began pulling their children out of it.

"Maybe one of them had a little bathroom 'accident,'" Yves said worriedly, as one set of parents came marching over to Yves with a furious expression.

The wife said loudly in a Germanic accent, "Our children will *not* be instructed by a Jew!"

"You ought to drain the entire pool!" her husband spat out.

There was a shocked silence. Annabel glanced back at the pool, where the trusting looks on the faces of the children had now been replaced with an expression of wary disgust; and it was the children's reaction that seemed to affect Hugo more deeply than the ugly words that the parents had hurled at him. He looked as if he had been punched in the gut, and the expression on his face made Annabel want to cry for him.

"Well?" demanded the outraged father, glaring at Yves.

Yves looked straight back at him calmly, as if dealing with just another *gauche* guest. "*Monsieur*, you are not in Nazi Germany now. You are in France," he said firmly. "*Liberté, égalité, fraternité.*"

There was a strange glint in the woman's eyes as she hissed, "Not for long!" before she and her husband stalked off with their children, wrapped in hotel towels, trailing behind him.

———

Annabel left the pool area feeling shaken by everything she'd seen today. First Alan, then those nasty people yelling at Hugo. Who did these arrogant guests think they were, throwing their weight around with such a foul sense of entitlement?

She was halfway to the Villa Sanctuaire when a thought occurred to her. *Who told Alan that I made love to Jack?* She wondered uneasily if Jack had bragged about it over the weekend. She didn't think he was that type—but what did she really know about Jack? She'd have to look him in the eye, perhaps even ask him, point blank, if he'd told anyone.

By the time she reached the villa, she had worked up a head of steam and was determined to confront Jack. But her indignation evaporated when she saw him sitting at the poolside table with Téa, leisurely finishing their morning coffee and croissants and laughing together. So Téa had returned from her jaunt on the yacht with the Nazi film distributor.

Annabel felt her resolve plummet. She just wanted Jack all to herself today. But how could any girl compete with a sensuous film star destined to be "the next Greta Garbo"?

Jack looked up at Annabel, and his expression softened, as if he perfectly well remembered their night of love. But when Téa glanced at him with a flick of those long eyelashes, he quickly assumed a more neutral expression. And in that moment, Annabel knew that no matter how much Jack cared for her, it was Téa who was his master.

"Sonny asked me to give you this," Annabel said to Téa, placing the manila envelope with the contract on the table. "He says he needs your signature on it by tonight."

Jack snorted. "Oh, he does, does he?" he said. "Well, you can just tell Sonny—"

"Tell him yourself," she snapped, unable to suppress her tension any longer. "I don't ever want to go near that man or that Alan ever again!"

Now both Jack and Téa looked up in surprise. Jack said quickly, "Annabel, come inside and have a look at a map I got for our trip today."

She followed him into the kitchen area, where he poured a fresh cup of coffee and handed it to her. "Rough morning?" he asked in a soothing tone.

She was trying steadfastly not to be susceptible, but she found that she needed to tell somebody what had happened, and she simply could not tell Oncle JP. But all she said was, "Did you tell Alan that you and I—that we—the other night, the night of the ball?"

A look of comprehension crossed Jack's handsome face. "Good God, no. Did that fucker try something with you?" Annabel nodded, trying to recover some iota of poise.

"Want me to sock him for you?" Jack inquired. "Alan is a man who 'wants punching,' as the Brits say."

"No, I think I took care of it myself," she said without elaborating.

Jack looked amused now. "Good for you, kid," he said. "Use it as leverage against Sonny. He can't afford to have his staff get arrested in France. You watch—from now on Sonny will be sweet as pie to you."

Annabel had not considered that she'd gained some leverage from this situation. "The whole thing makes me sick," she said, and that included participating in any power games.

"Look, if you don't feel like going up in the mountains today, I'd completely understand," Jack said consolingly.

She said quickly, "Oh, I *want* to get away from this hotel and all the people in it." The idea of an entire afternoon alone with Jack, beyond any prying eyes, gave her the hope that such intimacy and privacy would allow them to really talk, heart to heart.

"Good!" Jack replied briskly. "*Allons-y*—isn't that what you say here? I'll load up the car. Téa had room service pack us a picnic hamper. There's plenty of food."

"That's because I'm going with you," Téa's voice said unexpectedly. She was standing in the doorway. Jack grinned with some surprise.

Téa said softly, "You are right, Jack. I don't want anything more to do with Sonny and his contract—it's for seven years! And I'm sick of UFA and their Nazi producers. I want to be a real partner in your new company, Jack. We will make beautiful films together!"

CHAPTER 14

A Village in the Clouds

Jack took the wheel of his pale-blue convertible, and Téa slipped into the passenger seat beside him—where Annabel usually sat when she'd had Jack all to herself.

So Annabel had to take the little back seat instead. She watched as Téa tied a silk scarf around her head and popped on an enormous pair of dark sunglasses. Jack had sunglasses, too, and his panama hat. Annabel had neither sunglasses nor a scarf.

But she didn't mind the wind and sun. It was an unexpectedly fine afternoon, and they made good time. On their right, the bright blue sea sparkled beneath a brilliant azure sky and a lemon-yellow sun; to their left, the grey-violet mountains rose protectively.

They passed Monaco and headed toward Roquebrune-Cap-Martin and then Menton, the last little coastal town of the French Riviera just before the Italian border. Here was where the "old guard" of distinguished elderly ladies and gentlemen took seaside walks on the promenade and then dozed on park benches in the sun with their contented poodles asleep at their feet. Then these elders returned to the dark, old-fashioned coolness of hotel parlors, to take tea and play cards, their well-bred voices seldom rising higher than a murmur.

When Annabel told Jack and Téa about this illustrious retirement crowd who flocked to Menton year after year, Jack nodded and then theatrically declaimed, *"Whispering of old kings come here to dine or die."*

"Yes, that's a perfect description of it! Who said that?" Annabel asked.

"Scott," Jack replied. "It's from his novel *Tender Is the Night.*"

"Such an uncommon man, that Scott," Téa observed. "Face like a choirboy, but eyes like cut glass that can see right through you."

Téa was unusually animated today, and as they glided along with the wind at their backs, she peppered Annabel with questions about their destination.

"How high up is this village?" Téa demanded.

Annabel had already been doing research for Jack, so she checked her notepad and announced, "Sainte-Agnès is measured at over two thousand five hundred feet. It is the highest village on the entire Côte d'Azur. It was built in the tenth century—people say by a Saracen pirate who met a local girl, and they fell in love. She got him to become a Christian, which is why the town has a saint's name. So they say."

"See?" Jack said triumphantly. "I knew this was a 'local girl' kind of place. That's just what I want for my movie, only our story will begin at the onset of the Great War."

Téa smiled at him indulgently, reaching out to stroke Jack's curly dark head. Annabel experienced a twist of longing in her heart. She knew what it felt like to touch his soft, beautiful hair.

"And what about this military fort Jack told me about?" Téa said over her shoulder.

"It's part of the Maginot Line," Annabel said obligingly. "They say that out of all the forts on the Line, this one has the strongest concentration of weapons."

"Do the soldiers stay there all the time? Really?" Téa said as Annabel nodded. "How many soldiers live there?" she asked curiously. Annabel shrugged. But apparently, Téa had learned all she cared to know about the town, because now she picked up one of Jack's cameras and snapped pictures of him as he drove and grinned and made faces at her.

But soon the driving took all of Jack's concentration as he turned off the main road and they began their ascent. Up, up, up, round hairpin turns as the road zigged and zagged, which was the only way to make such a steep climb. They followed each curve carved into the rocky mountainsides, skirting past one precipitous ledge after another, and there were no guardrails.

"Whew!" Annabel said, for sometimes the way was so narrow that she held her breath as they squeezed through rocky cliffs on one side and what looked like a bottomless gorge on the other. The higher the car went, the more they seemed to be floating on a flimsy ribbon of clouds circling the mountains, spectacularly dizzying as the road rose higher, even higher.

Téa had grown suddenly quiet, gripping her seat as if afraid of falling out of the car and tumbling into one of the endless ravines below. Her face was pale and her lips were dry.

"How—how much farther is it?" she whispered.

Jack was focusing mightily on steering the car through a narrow underpass beneath an ancient rocky archway, so he didn't immediately notice Téa's change of attitude, even as she shrank closer to him, shying away from her car door and window as if unable to bear looking at the sheer drop below every turn of the road. She sucked in her breath and closed her eyes.

Annabel herself hadn't realized how terrifying this ascent would be. She'd never been here; she'd only heard about it from the concierge, Raphael, who'd been born just across the border in Italy. Raphael knew all the hills along the frontier between the Italian and the French Riviera; he'd left home when Mussolini came to power. Raphael had told Annabel, *I was sorry to leave my grandmother. We used to hunt for mushrooms in the* *hills. She always told me the Italian mushrooms were better* *than the French ones, even when they were only a yard apart!*

"Oh God, is it much longer?" Téa cried out finally, her eyes wide now. "I don't think I can bear it. No, I must go home at once."

Jack glanced at her quickly. "Almost there," he said soothingly.

Téa moaned and shut her eyes again.

At long last, they reached a high, flat plateau with a viewing and parking area. There was still something dizzying about it; wisps of clouds were drifting around like a heavenly vapor. A few other tourists had parked, and some were unpacking their picnic baskets. But most visitors set off for the tiny little town, tucked safely away from the cliffs.

"What a view, Téa!" Jack exclaimed. "They say that on a clear day you can see as far as Corsica!"

"All I can see are angels with their white wings, sitting on the clouds just waiting to escort us to our death!" Téa exclaimed, almost tearfully.

"Come on, let's go shoot some film to see how it plays!" Jack said, briskly slinging the straps of his camera over his shoulders. He had brought an assortment of equipment—home movie cameras and snapshot cameras—and he handed one to Annabel and one to Téa.

"You two go take your pictures," Téa whispered. "I can't bear to move. Let me just sit here awhile and catch my breath."

"But it's worse *here*!" Jack said with a trace of exasperation now. "The village is more protected. It's a nice place. What you need is a good strong cup of coffee."

"I said NO!" Téa exclaimed vehemently. "Leave me alone! I'll take my pictures from right here, in the car, thank you very much!"

Annabel had never heard the dreamy-tempered Téa speak in such a forceful tone before. But Jack seemed to recognize this attitude and said, "Okay, baby. Don't upset yourself. Annabel and I will go down the main drag of the town and keep a look-out for you, in case you change your mind and want to join us. Just don't wander too far."

"Hardly a chance of that happening!" Téa cried.

As Annabel and Jack set off, he said, "I really hated to leave her like that. But when Téa gets that mulish tone, it's best to leave her be. I had no idea that she had a fear of heights. How the hell am I ever going to get her to come back up here again to shoot this film?"

"She did look pretty upset," Annabel agreed. But she was secretly thrilled to have Jack all to herself again.

"Well, let's get a look at this village, now that we're finally here!" he said exuberantly.

Sainte-Agnès turned out to be as enchanting as Raphael had described it. The place was like something from a fairy tale, and Jack and Annabel wandered its cobbled streets and mysterious vaulted passageways near picturesque little shops and medieval houses, where the locals, moving calmly about their business, used simple homemade, old-fashioned brooms to brush off their doorsteps, occasionally pausing to chat with one another.

Jack was enraptured by the faces of the villagers. "Look at these great elderly men, with their hats and canes and deeply wrinkled faces! And those wonderful, vigorous older women, with their kerchiefs tied around their snowy hair," he enthused.

He got some of them to pose obligingly as he snapped pictures; then he and Annabel filmed shots of each other walking down quiet stone alleyways where their footsteps echoed, with Jack asking her about lighting techniques and discussing camera angles.

They crossed a tiny town square, pausing as Annabel jotted down possible locations in her notebook. Her favorite place was a charming old church with stone steps. Jack filmed her as she ascended them and went inside, dipping her finger in the fountain of holy water and crossing herself at the altar. They paused awhile in the hushed, cool, dark interior.

"You're perfect here," Jack said as they left and emerged into the bright sunlight. "It's as if you really did come from this enchanted place, just like in my story."

He hadn't written much of his movie treatment, but he had a lot of it in his head and he developed the story more and more as they walked and talked.

Annabel loved his company, enjoying his warmth and scent, which was a combination of clean linen, vetiver aftershave, and his own mysterious maleness. He had the sleeves of his blue shirt rolled up to his elbows, revealing his strong, suntanned arms.

"You know, I should star *you* in the new movie," he said, stopping short suddenly, looking deeply inspired. He gazed at Annabel as if seeing her in a new light.

"I'm not an actress," she reminded him, as they paused to sit on a stone bench.

"Oh, sure you are," he said. "There's nothing to it, if you know how to concentrate, and if you have an expressive face. Which you do. It's all in the eyes. Fire in the eyes, fire in the belly. You have all that fire within you."

It was the first time he'd spoken to her in that intimate tone since the night they'd made love. She looked up at him quickly, and he leaned in and kissed her deeply. Then he sighed.

"Dear, sweet Annabel," Jack murmured. "You truly are the rose of the Riviera."

She wanted to say it. *I love you.* But she didn't dare speak and break the spell. She just sat there with his arm around her, feeling wanted, feeling beloved.

Finally the church bell tolled the hour, slowly and sonorously. A little gust of wind played with their hair, indicating that the sun was sinking lower.

Jack said, "I'd like to stay up here in the clouds with you forever."

"Can't we?" Annabel said softly.

He smiled but said regretfully, "Alas, we mortal creatures must go back down to earth. Well, let's have a look at that Maginot fort, while there's still good light, shall we?"

She rose with him but hesitated. "I don't think they'll let us get near it," she warned. "It could be dangerous. That fort is manned with soldiers and guns!"

Undaunted, he said, "I still want to see it. But let's first stop back at the car and see how Téa is doing. She might be feeling better and want to come with us."

But when they returned to the car, they found it empty. There was no sign of Téa anywhere. Jack didn't think this unusual. "I knew she'd calm down once we left her alone. She's always been a loner at heart. Probably went for a walk to get some air. Most people don't recognize her when she's out and about with those dark glasses. She looks completely different from the way she does on film—where she has that ethereal quality—but in real life, she's really just one of those well-scrubbed, healthy outdoorsy types. Let's wait here for her. Here, have a sandwich." He reached into the hamper, and they nibbled on the delicate little sandwiches.

They sat in the car, with Annabel up front this time. She was thinking, *If you love Téa so much, why do you kiss me? Who am I to you?*

"I—I wish I understood you better," she said. She was surprised at how angry she sounded.

Jack, attuned to her, said gently, "I wish I were ten years younger. Then I could be your true lover and suitor." She eyed him skeptically; after all, he was only in his early thirties. That wasn't so old. She told him so.

He smiled and said, "Oh, but I was born old. So was Téa. Her father was a policeman with a foul temper. Her mother, she said, was 'a doormat.' Her brother is brilliant but deeply disturbed. Not a great home environment! When Téa was only thirteen, a theatre director spotted her, but he was a tyrant, too. Finally she just ran away to Hollywood."

Annabel, feeling a tumult of confusing, mixed emotions, tried to steer the conversation away from Téa, asking curiously, "What were *you* like, as a kid?"

"I never was a kid. My mother worked in a brothel in New Orleans. First washing dishes, then doing—other things. They say I was born there; I don't remember," he said, his dark eyes taking on a distant look. "I only remember when we moved to New York City and lived in a one-room flat, in the theatre district. I had to go out on the street and play every time my mother had a 'visitor,' day or night, rain or shine, snow or sleet, like the postmen say. That's why I hung out backstage in the theatres, watching the shows until someone chased me out. At least it was warm inside there, and sometimes they felt sorry for me and fed me. It felt more like home than anywhere I lived."

He shrugged, looking embarrassed, then grinned as if to shake off the past.

Annabel had pictured Jack as a dark-eyed little waif and felt a surge of sympathy; yet she suspected that by describing a fairly sordid upbringing, he was trying to discourage her.

And sure enough, he said, "So you see, my dear, Téa and I are damaged goods. I guess the scars eroticize each other. Whatever we do, wrong or right, Téa and I, we can't let go."

She heard the word *scars* and wondered if this was why Jack felt guilty about his attraction to Annabel. Did he think Téa needed his protection? Was that her real hold on him? Annabel's mother had once told her, *Some people rule with weakness, some with strength.*

Annabel found herself repeating the same question that the lady reporter in Cannes had asked him, "So—why aren't you and Téa married, then?"

"We almost did tie the knot," he said after a moment. "Set the date and everything. She panicked at the last minute—told me the bond between us was unbreakable, but she couldn't bring herself to slip into a harness. She has a horror of repeating her parents' marriage."

"Don't *you* want a family of your own?" she asked, wanting to add, *with me*. For she was convinced that Téa truly did not love Jack as wholeheartedly as Annabel herself did.

Jack looked earnest, as if he really wanted to be honest with her. "You're so young and fine. You deserve a young man who's just as young and fine as you are. But people like me don't become actors because we're heroic, or even normal. Some of us become actors because we *aren't* heroes and we know we'd make a lousy husband or father or soldier or prince. But we keep hoping if we act like one, we'll learn how to become a hero." He seemed genuinely pained, as if he'd revealed more of himself than he was truly comfortable doing.

But Annabel suddenly discovered her own surprising streak of ruthlessness, and she leaned in and deliberately kissed him, hard. "You *are* my hero. Don't you love me?" she said softly, kissing him again. "You know you do," she murmured. "Don't you?" she kept saying, pressing her advantage by kissing him again and again, as if to say firmly, *No more talk about Téa!* She was fed up with everyone telling her that she could never have what she wanted, starting with her grandmother, then Oncle JP, and now Jack. No, she just didn't want to hear it.

Jack at first was taken by surprise; then he seemed helpless to resist her kisses and his own desire, ending up groaning helplessly, "Ah, God! You're killing me, you little angel."

Two small girls eating ice cream cones had stealthily approached their car and now cried out in unison, "*Oooh, la-la!*" then burst into laughter as Jack and Annabel stopped kissing and looked up, startled. The girls' parents shooed them away, but the spell was broken.

"Come on," Jack sighed, giving Annabel a playful shove. "I've got to get a cup of coffee before I face that drive back down the mountain. Let's lock the cameras in the trunk."

Annabel relished her triumph over him. She now felt hopeful about her future—with a tantalizing vision of herself starring in Jack's new film, working even more closely with him. It would be a new role for her. She wouldn't just be the girl from the Grand Hotel. She would be his muse, his star, his lover.

As they approached the little town again, Jack glanced at another path leading away from the town. "Where does that go?" he asked. "To the Maginot fort?"

"Maybe. I don't know," she said, still feeling blissful.

"Why don't you check it out while I get the coffee for us?" Jack suggested. "We came all this way. I just want to see what the damned thing looks like. I'll meet you right back here."

"Okay," she said, feeling happy about everything now.

The path Annabel took was of narrow beaten earth flanked on both sides by trees, scrubby growth, and not much else, and it was all uphill. Stones stuck out of the earth and made for unsteady walking, and there was no one else about.

Soon she could see the Maginot fort looming up against the sky, like something medieval even though it had been built in this century—a formidable fortress that was smooth and rounded like a tall, fat tower, with no windows, only some slits for soldiers to peer out of or to poke their artillery at their enemies, she imagined. She hesitated, wondering if someone would pour hot oil or tar on anyone who got too close. She decided that she had gone far enough and would go back and tell Jack about it.

But before she turned away, she saw a woman ahead of her, snapping pictures like a tourist, who then turned, spotted Annabel, and waved, coming toward her with a bright smile.

It was Téa, looking calm and playful again. "I can't wait to show Jack *my* pictures," she said proudly. "I bet they're better than his! Where is he?"

"He went for coffee. He's coming," Annabel said, amused

that Téa had recovered from her fright and now wanted to one-up Jack. Actors were so competitive.

But suddenly there was a strange rustling sound in the trees.

"*Arrêtez-vous!*" came a commanding shout.

Annabel and Téa were immediately surrounded by young French soldiers. Terrifyingly, two of them had their rifles trained on the women.

An older man with a ferociously bristly mustache appeared out of nowhere and seemed to be in charge. He looked severely at Téa and barked in French, "What are you doing here?"

Téa recovered and smiled sweetly. "We are tourists, of course!"

"Tourists are not allowed here!" he retorted, unconvinced.

"We're just looking for a friend, and we took the wrong path," Annabel said quickly.

The older man could see that she was fibbing and said furiously, "Who are you two spying for?" He motioned to one of the young soldiers to take Téa's camera from her.

"Hey!" Téa objected. Annabel was truly frightened. Surely Téa must see the seriousness of the situation. Who cared about a few travel pictures at this point?

"We will have to arrest you both," the older man declared. "Where are your passports?"

Annabel tried to explain that they were kept at the Grand Hotel, where she herself worked, and that Téa was a guest who'd asked for a tour of the village nearby. The man looked stern and disbelieving, and the two younger men still hadn't put down their rifles.

Now Jack appeared on the path, carrying three cups of coffee in a box. So Annabel had to start explaining all over again. The older man looked more recalcitrant than ever. But then Jack took charge, asking Annabel to translate for him.

"Tell him we're actors; give him our names," Jack said

confidently. Then he mentioned the first film that he and Téa had done, which had been dubbed and distributed in France.

A light dawned on the stern man's face. He was unimpressed with Téa, but he recognized Jack indeed, asking him about the character he'd played in the film—a soldier in the French army fighting the Napoleonic Wars. Yes, a real man's man. Did Jack really do his own stunts, especially the one where he leaped from a burning building into a passing hay cart?

Jack, Annabel, and the officer were talking very fast, the translations flying back and forth. Even in translation, Jack was utterly charming and mesmerizing. The young soldiers put down their rifles without being told to, listening in fascination, mostly just watching Jack's animated face as he gestured and explained that he was here to scout locations for his next big film, and he might even want to hire some soldiers to play extras.

The older man relented somewhat but still sounded severe when he said in French, "It is a nice idea, to make a film about this place, but none of that can be shot *here*, at the fort. No, no, impossible. Perhaps in Sainte-Agnès, yes, but even there, one must go through the proper channels with the cultural minister."

"Of course," Jack said agreeably.

In perfect French, Téa suddenly said, "Can I have my camera back, please?" Annabel wanted to strangle her. Couldn't she see how tenuous this whole situation was?

The man's mustache twitched as he exclaimed, "*Mais, non, c'est impossible!*" and launched into a fresh tirade. "Perhaps you Hollywood people do not truly understand the gravity of the situation!"

Annabel and Jack had to step in again, and the man did not relent until all three visitors nodded solemnly and contritely. Finally, after the official was convinced that they had comprehended his stern warnings, he allowed them to go.

Annabel held her breath all the way to the car. They drove

off, with Téa in the front seat beside Jack again, and she defiantly reached into her pockets and pulled out a few rolls of film,
slipping them into her purse with a triumphant smile. Apparently she'd taken more pictures earlier today than the single
roll that was in the confiscated camera.

"At least *I* managed to get some photos of that silly old fort
for you," she teased him.

Jack was too busy driving to react much, and at this point,
Annabel just wanted to reach the safety of the hotel before anything worse happened. As they went down, down, down the
zigzagging road, she kept her eyes on the setting sun, as if it
were her lodestar.

———

"I think that old general sent a car to follow us. They just turned
away now," Jack observed, glancing in the rearview mirror as he
finally drove through the open gate and into the curved driveway
of the Grand Hotel. Oncle JP was already standing outside at
the front door, looking furious. As he spotted Annabel, he motioned severely for her to come to him.

"Uh-oh," Jack said. "Looks like you're going to catch hell.
But how could he possibly know what happened to us?"

"Oncle JP knows, sees, and hears everything," Annabel said
fearfully.

"Want us to go with you?" Jack offered. "We can explain it all."

"No, I'd better see him alone," she said, resignedly getting
out of the car and watching the two of them drive off to the
Villa Sanctuaire.

Oncle JP waited until he and Annabel were alone in his
office. He shut the door.

"Really, Annabel, this is insupportable!" he began.

He told her that the official at the fort had telephoned, asking
Oncle JP to verify that Annabel indeed worked at the Grand

Hotel and that the two people with her truly were the Holly-wood guests that they'd claimed to be. Her uncle had had to smooth things over.

"And believe me," Oncle JP exclaimed incredulously, "one does not go about ruffling the feathers of the French military intelligence! It is fortunate that I have my own military service connections. But even so, this is a blot on the hotel's reputa-tion—and mine!"

His face looked so ashamed, so wounded. Annabel was truly contrite. She had not only violated his sacred Code of Stan-dards, but she'd gotten him into trouble with his military friends. Weakly, she tried to explain why Jack had wanted to go up there.

But Oncle JP was not interested in excuses. "This must never happen again! *Jamais!*"

"It won't," Annabel promised meekly. If only he'd really shouted at her, she might have felt defensive, defiant. But he hadn't even raised his voice.

He stared down at his desk and shuffled his papers, as if he could not bear to look up at her again, perhaps because he did not want her to see how hurt he was.

"I'm sorry," she whispered again. "*Désolée.*"

She really *did* feel desolate. Even after she left his office and scurried to her little rooming house on the square, she could not shake off a fearful feeling that had begun up at the Maginot fort with the threat of imminent arrest.

Until now, the war talk had seemed like a dark fairy tale happening to other people. Now she could feel that beyond the secure gates of the Grand Hotel, there really was a big, bad world out there, coming ever closer like an advancing tide of terrifying life-and-death struggles. She would need her family more than ever now.

Yet she sensed that this latest breach of hers would not be so easily repaired. Fretfully, she tossed about in bed for hours that night before she could finally escape into a heavy sleep.

CHAPTER 15

Love Isn't Easy

The next day, Oncle JP informed Annabel that Jack Cabot had said he would be too busy to work with her, as he was now getting ready for tonight's screening party for his first independent film, which Sonny's company was distributing. Annabel knew that Jack was also secretly working to nudge forward a deal with Rick to finance his next film about the village girl in the Great War, so that Jack wouldn't have to rely on Sonny for future pictures.

"So for the time being, Monsieur Cabot does not require your services," Oncle JP said crisply, sitting at his desk and fiddling with a pen. "However, I am told that the screenwriter is very busy now, so you can continue with him into the afternoon if necessary."

Oncle JP's expression betrayed nothing else, but Annabel had her suspicions. "Did you talk to Jack about—" she began indignantly.

"That little escapade of yours yesterday? Yes, of course I had a word with him. Even an esteemed guest must learn that there are limits, here in France. And I must tell you, Annabel, that there are also limits for the staff of the Grand Hotel. People have been fired for less."

This was worse than when she was a scared child who'd been sent to the principal's office for whispering in class. She felt her face scalded with shame as she sat there under her uncle's stern gaze, and she said, "Did you tell Sonny about it? Is he the one who's fired me?"

"No, of course I didn't tell him, but the directive came from him, and you are not fired; you are merely reassigned." Oncle JP saw her distress, and in spite of himself, his face softened and he sighed. "Well, you are a woman in love—that's the trouble," he concluded, making it sound like a character flaw.

Startled, Annabel said nothing; there was no use in denying it. She reflected bitterly that this was the first time her uncle had called her a woman instead of a girl. Yet it didn't feel so great, for in her first outing as a woman she'd essentially been told she was a disgrace.

What was she supposed to do, be discreet like her uncle and his visits to the widow in Èze? That simply wasn't possible when you were young and in love with a movie star.

Oncle JP said, "One more thing. Do not interfere with Sonny's family again. He is displeased that you violated his daughter's diet. The girl's nurse got suspicious and followed her to the kitchen one morning. The chef said it was *your* orders. So Sonny is sending Cissy and her nurse back to Los Angeles on the first available passage that they can book for her."

Annabel was stunned. "But she'll miss the whole Cannes Film Festival!"

"He says it is necessary 'to teach her some discipline.' I suspect the truth is she has become an embarrassment to him. In any case, the girl and her nurse are already on the train to Paris. From there they'll switch trains and eventually board an ocean liner home."

"That Sonny is a . . . a . . . fascist!" Annabel sputtered. "And so is the damned nurse."

Oncle JP said gently, "There are some people you cannot

help; if you try, it only does them harm. This is why we must not interfere with our guests. That will be all, Annabel. Do your work, and keep your head down."

Annabel slinked away, still feeling guilty about Cissy. She had wanted to simply nourish the starving girl; it wasn't a crime, and yet they acted as if she'd murdered someone.

And what about Jack? Had he really said he didn't want her services? She doubted that he would phrase it that way. But perhaps someone else had talked to Sonny. Perhaps Téa had put her foot down and said she didn't want Annabel hanging around the villa anymore. Maybe Téa wasn't so happy about An-nabel borrowing a gown and literally filling her shoes.

What if someone like Alan had told Téa that Annabel and Jack had enjoyed each other, dancing away the night at the masked ball? One thing Annabel was learning was that news traveled fast these days, gossip even faster. And Scott was right. This hotel was crawling with Hollywood spies. Cissy's nurse was only the least of them, no doubt.

———

When she arrived at the Jasmine Cottage, she could see that Scott was indeed swamped with work. There were pages on every surface of every piece of furniture, it seemed. He was editing Jack's treatment, finishing his rewrites for Sonny, and polishing his short stories.

"Let's get all these other assignments out of the way," Scott said. "Maybe I can sell a short story or two that will put more money in the piggy bank and buy me time to write nothing but *The Love of the Last Tycoon.* I just need three solid, uninter-rupted months to do it."

Annabel quickly set to work typing the letters that Scott was sending to his book editor and also to the editor of *Col-lier's* magazine, where he hoped to serialize this new novel. He was seeking an advance of money from both men, but they'd all insisted on seeing a treatment before they would invest in Scott's new novel.

"Personally, I don't think treatments really capture the heart and soul of a novel," he said. "But if that's what it takes to get the advance, well, then let's tell them I'll do it. I wrote some new pages for the treatment. We still have to watch out for Sonny's spies," Scott warned. "He came by the tennis courts to ask me how my work is going. He was just fishing around."

"But why should anybody care what you—or I—are up to?" she asked, taking the sheaf of new handwritten pages to type up and add to the treatment in his Top Secret file.

Scott said, "It's never about us; it's always about *them*. Guys like that forever have their dicks on the line. Oh, excuse me, Annabel. I mean, they live in constant terror of ridicule."

"But your novel—it's about greatness," she said. "A genius of a movie producer. What's wrong with that?"

Scott sighed. "Well, men like Sonny know *they're* not the hero. They think idealistic heroes exist just to show them up. I still have people mad at me because they saw their own reflections in the less likable characters of *Tender Is the Night* and *The Great Gatsby*. Remember, the rich and the mighty—they have absolutely no sense of humor about themselves. Beware of people with no sense of humor, Annabel. They are more dangerous than you might imagine."

Scott went back to his desk and continued scribbling on a long, lined pad of paper. Annabel sat down at her little typing table in the alcove and plugged away devotedly to get his letters and then his script rewrites done so she could then type up his stories.

They worked in companionable silence. At lunchtime, Scott suggested sending for sandwiches and cola from room service. After that brief lull for lunch, they continued.

She felt suddenly content. There was something—holy—about

Scott's devotion to his craft, like a priest at his altar. For, like Oncle JP, Scott had his own code of ethics. If he took an idea or a passage out of one of his old short stories and used the material in a new novel, he'd mark the story *Not to Be Reissued in a Collection* because he felt it was "used up." For a man who needed money so badly, he was still unwilling to compromise the integrity of his work.

She turned to the two short stories he wanted to sell to the magazines, racing to input his edits in time to go out with the last mail pouch of the day. She found them absorbing.

One was called "Salute to Lucy and Elsie," the sensitive tale of a rich boy who feels that he can't just abandon his pregnant girlfriend; it dealt with serious issues of birth control, religion, and honor, as the wealthy father tries to discourage his son from marrying such an unimportant girl. The editors at *Esquire* magazine had asked for significant revisions to handle this "controversial" material.

Scott was also polishing an earlier story, "Thank You for the Light," about a woman who works as a traveling salesperson and is so exhausted that, in between two sales calls, she stops into a church and feels desperate for a cigarette; the ending was mysterious and touching. Annabel was thoroughly engaged as she typed each page.

But suddenly, her typewriter stopped dead. It simply conked out without any warning. She tried again. Nothing. The keys just would not respond anymore. She opened it up, checked the keys, the carriage, and the ribbon, which would not advance. She tried everything she knew how to do, but nothing helped.

"Oh no!" she cried, frustrated to come to a halt so close to the mail deadline.

Scott said, without looking up, "Hmmm?"

"It's the typewriter," she wailed. "It's broken. I mean, maybe it can be fixed, but not by me. I'd have to call in a repairman. That could take forever!"

Now Scott had the look of a champion swimmer briefly coming up for air. He said, "Why don't you use the typewriter that's out in the tennis shed?"

"What typewriter?" she asked blankly.

Scott put down his pencil. "I saw a typewriter case in that storage shed near the tennis courts. The door was tied shut with twine. I don't think anybody's been in that shed for years—it's piled high with old furniture and parasols, all decorated with spiderwebs. I was looking for a tennis racket. I guess most people bring their own. Jack went out and bought me one. Anyway, why don't you take a look? The typewriter was near a bunch of tennis rackets that need to be restrung, and they're all covered with tarp."

"I guess it's worth a try," Annabel said glumly, imagining that if it had been stored in there for so long, then it, too, would require major repairs before being usable.

But she dutifully walked over to the tennis courts. It was so hot today that there was nobody playing there, for the burning sun was straight overhead, baking the courts. In the sleepy haze even the birds sounded drowsy in the trees.

The shed's door latch was indeed tied shut with twine in a complicated way. It took some doing to unknot it. She opened the door cautiously; this was just the sort of place that a snake would like. She reached into her pocket for the tiny flashlight that her uncle insisted she carry everywhere. Now she knew why.

The shed smelled of a dry mustiness, and every item was thick with dust. She worked her way through the old lounge chairs and parasols. Sure enough, as Scott had said, there was a tarp thrown over some forlorn old tennis rackets. And there, too, was the typewriter case.

"Oh!" she said softly. For she recognized it as the Polish girl's typewriter valise. She must have left it behind, so perhaps it got swept up by housekeeping; but it should have been taken to the hotel's lost-and-found cupboard.

With a small jolt, Annabel was reminded of that moment when she saw the girl sitting in the bed of Hans von Erhardt—the last time Annabel had seen him alive.

"Could he have rescued it and put it here?" she wondered. She supposed she really ought to take it to the lost and found. But she wanted to help Scott make his deadline.

She picked it up. It must be an old model, for it was heavy. She hauled it back to the private path that led to the Villa Sanctuaire and the Jasmine Cottage. As she passed the villa, she saw Téa, who was standing outside on the front path and now came right up to Annabel, looking surprised and delighted to see her.

"*Bonjour!* We felt so bad about getting you into trouble after Sainte-Agnès," Téa exclaimed. "Jack said we must do something for you. Come, let's have lunch," she suggested warmly. "It will be just us girls, because Jack is with Sonny right now. They're both nervous wrecks about the screening of our movie tonight. So I am all alone today."

In all the fuss, Annabel had managed to forget that tonight's party was for the screening of *Love Isn't Easy*, being shown as a pre-festival event. Well, it was no longer her business, since Jack or Sonny had essentially fired her and nobody had invited her to the party.

"I'm sorry, Scott is waiting for me," she said.

"Cocktails then," Téa insisted. "Come to the villa when you're done with your work."

She wouldn't take no for an answer, so Annabel agreed, secretly hoping that Jack would be back from his meeting by then, and she'd be able to read from his face whether he really didn't want her around anymore.

When she returned to her typing table by the alcove, she moved her broken typewriter out to the hallway and set the Polish one down on the table with a loud "*Uf!*"

Scott was sitting at his desk with his writing pad, gazing

upward as if searching his mind for *le mot juste*. Quietly, Annabel opened the metal flaps on the wooden case.

"Whoa." Strangely, her first reaction was fear. She shook it off and stared at the Polish typewriter, baffled.

It was made of wood and steel, with black and silver fittings. But there were odd metal knobs and gadgets. She could see the usual three rows of keys for the letters of the alphabet. They looked fine. Yet above them, inexplicably, there was another set of three rows of letters like a duplicate keyboard, but these weren't keys; they were just circular windows that you couldn't press.

Above *that* were some toothed metal wheels. Maybe it was a way of switching to a foreign alphabet? Was the alphabet different in Polish? Yet the second set of letters seemed identical to the first.

"Wonder if it still works," she muttered. Tentatively she pressed a key on what looked like the main keyboard. She pressed an *A*, but immediately, one of the little circular windows in the second set of letters lit up, flashing a *T* at her.

She tried again, this time pressing the *Y* key, which only made an *S* light up in the set of round windows.

"This is really weird," she said aloud. "And where is the paper supposed to go?"

Scott was scribbling, but he looked up. "What's the matter?" he asked distractedly.

"I've never seen a typewriter like this," Annabel said in exasperation. "It seems to have two keyboards, but when you press a key *here*, it doesn't type it onto paper. It just makes a round window light up *there*—but it lights up the wrong letter of the alphabet!"

"Lights up?" Scott echoed. He rose from his desk and came over to inspect it.

"And I don't even know where the paper feeds," she continued. With Scott at her side, she was emboldened to press a latch beneath the keyboards, thinking a paper roller might be there. The latch made a click, and then a door at the front of the machine dropped open.

"Wow, look!" she gasped. The opened door revealed a compartment that had mystifying rows of plugholes, each with letters above them; and there were also a lot of strange wires, all with forked strands ending in metal tips.

"I've never seen anything like this!" she exclaimed. "Except maybe a telephone switchboard that the operator uses."

Scott stared at the machine in fascination. "Annabel," he said solemnly, "to paraphrase the artist Magritte, *ceci n'est pas une* typewriter."

"Not a typewriter? Then what is it?" she asked dubiously.

"A radio? A telegraph machine?" Scott said enthusiastically. At first Annabel thought he was just making up a short story about it. He lowered his voice. "Looks like the kind of thing the military use. Like a field-office piece of equipment. Wonder who this belongs to?"

That fearful feeling was returning to Annabel as she said slowly, "I believe that a Polish girl brought it here. But why would she leave it behind when she checked out? Even if she forgot about it when she left so late at night, why wouldn't she have telephoned the hotel later, to have it sent back to her?"

"What Polish girl?" Scott muttered, admiringly pressing a letter and watching another one light up. "It looks to me like some sort of cipher machine," he said finally, in a low tone.

"What's it for?"

"For spying!" Scott was examining the wires now. "For making coded messages. I've been telling you that our French Riviera is lousy with spies this summer. *Real* spies, Annabel, not just our Hollywood spies—who are amateurs compared to these guys."

Annabel shuddered with an involuntary chill down her spine. "Oh God! I'd better give this to my uncle," she said nervously.

"He'll know what to do. Meanwhile, I'll tell the hotel office to send us one of their typewriters, or else rent us another one."

Scott helped her close it back up. "I don't think you should walk around the hotel with this thing," he advised. "Leave it in my closet, and tell your uncle to hotfoot it over here. Don't worry about doing any more typing today. You've got bigger fish to fry now."

She could see the wisdom of this. But when she telephoned Oncle JP's office, he wasn't there. Marta said that he'd gone to inspect something but was expected to return.

So Annabel let Scott haul the thing into his closet. Then she hurried off down the path to look for her uncle.

CHAPTER 16

Nightmare

But Annabel got no farther than the Villa Sanctuaire when Téa flagged her down.

"Darling!" she called out, as if she were truly glad to see Annabel. Téa seemed lonely here without Jack. She'd changed into a pink-and-white dress that buttoned down the front.

"I knew you wouldn't forget me," she said with a soft, touchingly eager smile. "I've already been mixing up Jack's favorite cocktails. He's on his way down here, and he wants to talk to you. Come, dear Annabel, come sit with me."

It was hard to resist being wanted so much—like having a queen bestow her shining light of approval—and the ethereal Téa could be very forceful when her mind was set on you. She took Annabel by the arm and hauled her determinedly into the villa. It was dark and cool inside, a welcome relief from the burning August sun.

"Would you like a martini or a champagne cocktail?" Téa inquired, busily going behind the counter of the kitchen area and tying an apron around her waist. She looked as if she were enjoying playing house.

"Champagne cocktail," Annabel relented. This might be

her only chance to find out who exactly had stopped her from being Jack's assistant. Maybe he would show up while they were sipping drinks, and she'd see what he really felt about all this.

Téa busied herself pouring drinks into two stylish cocktail glasses. Then she took off her apron, and carrying one glass in each hand, she floated over to the sofa and set them down on the low table. She went back to fetch the champagne bottle to bring to the table, then plunked herself down chummily beside Annabel on the sofa.

Seen this close, Téa was incredibly beautiful. Her skin was like peaches and cream, her lips plump and moist as berries, and her eyes sparkled with fun.

"What lovely, delicate hands you have, Annabel. Such long, slender fingers!" Téa observed admiringly, seizing one and holding it this way and that. Then she ruefully raised her own hand. "Mine are as big and wide as a man's. Good for chopping wood. The wardrobe ladies always give me gowns with long, dramatic sleeves to hide them." She paused, looking so intently at Annabel that her violet eyes seemed to darken with pure energy.

"Tell me," Téa purred. "How long have you been in love with Jack?"

Annabel quickly took a fortifying gulp of her drink and attempted to be lighthearted about it. "Goodness, I've just met him," she said lamely. "I mean, he's very nice and handsome and all, but, well, he's a movie star."

"Yes, yes. But you *are* in love with him," Téa said, her sensual lips caressing the word *love*. "You are sensitive enough to see how good and sweet a man he is. Perhaps too good for this world." She added softly, "And he is a bit fond of *you*, I think."

Annabel allowed herself one brief moment of delight before alarm set in. She didn't like this game of cat and mouse, and she wasn't about to confess to anything, so she said with a modest expression, "Jack talks about *you* all the time and says you are made for each other."

Téa sighed. "Well, yes, of course. We are soul mates. But *you* are young. You have it all ahead of you. You can give a man all the adoration and children that he wants."

Annabel was surprised to hear the genuine wisp of pain behind Téa's matter-of-fact tone. Feeling rather guilty now, Annabel said delicately, "You're not—too old—"

Téa squeezed her hand with a grateful expression. "No, I'm not old. But when I was a girl, I had to have a—surgery," she said simply. "So there will be no children for me."

It took Annabel a moment to recall such code words that she'd learned at Vassar for the one word that women still hesitated to say aloud, even among themselves. *Abortion.*

Téa recovered and said lightly, "Oh, but men are so bossy when they're in love. They want you to *do* this, sign *that*. And they insist, *Don't do what* he *wants; do what* I *want*. They always like to put a harness on you, like a horse. But I think it's more important for a woman to be free, don't you agree, *chérie*?" She reached for the champagne and topped off their drinks.

Annabel decided to be direct. "Did you ask Sonny to stop me from working with Jack?"

Téa looked truly shocked. "Of course not! Did Sonny do that? Well, don't worry about it. Jack loves working with you. When he returns, we'll get him to deal with Sonny."

Annabel suspected that Téa's interrogation was at an end; had she taken her rival's measure and concluded that Annabel didn't pose any real threat regarding Jack?

Sure enough, Téa changed the subject, speaking of clothes and fabrics and fashion. Or perhaps Téa truly didn't care if there was something between Jack and Annabel. It was almost as if Téa was giving them permission to be happy. Jack had basically said that Téa didn't form attachments to people, jewelry, clothes. It must be true.

"You should wear pink, blue, and red," Téa was saying affectionately. "Those are the colors for you." Listening to Téa's reassuring tone as they sat together companionably sipping their drinks, Annabel was beginning to feel calm, peaceful, as she hadn't been for some time in the company of men. She'd missed having smart and sophisticated girlfriends to talk to.

And something about Téa's soothing voice was reminding Annabel of a poignant memory, long ago buried, of her own lost mother. Annabel had pushed aside all those feelings of adoration, loss, and grief. The memory of her mother as alive and busy at work in the photography studio was already fading.

But now an earlier, physical memory was insistently pushing its way to the surface, refusing to be suppressed any longer, from when Annabel was a little girl—the wonderful, comforting feeling of her mother's arms around her, her mother's hands undressing her for bed, brushing her hair away from her face before she went to sleep on hot summer nights. Her mother's lovely scent and soft body holding her close, rocking her to sleep. Her mother's lips kissing little Annabel good night, caressing her face.

Annabel sighed deeply and closed her eyes as this sweet, intimate memory seemed to envelop her like a soft, protective blanket. She felt herself getting drowsier, slipping off into the most serene, sublime sleep of a contented baby. She even thought she heard her mother's voice saying, *That's a good girl. You're such a dear, good little girl.*

Like an infant, she felt hands bigger than hers stroking her face, her throat, her shoulders. Dimly she felt her blouse being unbuttoned and peeled away, her skirt being gently hitched up, and then she was being kissed all over, by soft, loving lips that caressed her breasts, her thighs, her belly, even the tips of her fingers and toes.

That's it. Good girl. Yes, my sweet.

Something soft and smooth and heavy and warm brushed against Annabel's mouth, and she felt a surge of emotion, kissing it as if she were sucking at her mother's breast.

Aren't you a hungry little baby! Tell me all your secrets, little one; don't hide anything from me. Do you have something for me? Tell Mama.

And now Annabel felt as if multiple pairs of hands were stroking and caressing her entire body everywhere at once, eternal and all-encompassing. But in some places these hands were soft and soothing, and in others they felt rough and scratchy.

Annabel's eyelids fluttered open, but all she could see were dark shadows at the foot of the sofa. Everything felt so blurry, cocooned in cotton wool. She closed her eyes again.

Then suddenly the rough hands grabbed Annabel hard by the shoulders, shaking her. Téa's voice sounded strangely shrill, and she was saying something that was both furious and wheedling at the same time, yet Annabel had a hard time making out the words. It sounded like, *Would you like coffee?*

"No," Annabel whispered. Confused and fearful of Téa's inexplicably angry tone, Annabel made a monumental effort to force her heavy eyelids wide open.

In the darkness of the room, with only small shafts of sunlight peering around the edges of the drawn curtains, she could just make out Téa's face looming at the foot of the sofa, her expression distorted into something harsh, her mouth twisted with fury; yet the voice that emerged from it now sounded oddly desperate, even pleading, as if her life depended on it: *Would you like coffee?* It was all the more terrifying because it made no sense.

Annabel gasped, "I said no!" as in her foggy haze she glimpsed Téa coming closer now, stark naked, revealing her slim figure—with a man's genitals. She smiled in a strange way as she pushed Annabel back down on the sofa.

Annabel screamed out, "Leave me alone!" Immediately a rough hand clapped over her mouth to silence her. She could hardly breathe, but she bit at the hand, which quickly withdrew with a cry of pain before it returned to slap her across the face.

"Stop it!" Annabel cried. Still reeling from the blow, she summoned every fiber of her strength to shove the figure away from her, just long enough to get off that sofa. Stumbling to her feet, and clutching her open blouse and unbuttoned skirt to her body, she made a furious dash for the door and plunged out of the dark villa, into the liberating evening air.

———

She could tell by the night sky that she must have been with Téa a lot longer than it had seemed. Scott was just now strolling down the path from the direction of the hotel and moving toward his cottage, smoking and looking deep in thought. He was all dressed up, as if he'd been to a reception. But when he heard Annabel's cry, he looked up sharply, just in time to see her burst onto the path, her expression terrified.

He threw down his cigarette and came rushing toward her, quickly guiding her to the Jasmine Cottage and banging the door shut behind them.

"Sit down," Scott said, alarmed. "I'll get you a glass of water."

Annabel was gasping for breath, as if she'd run a marathon instead of taken the few steps to get here. She sank onto the sofa, trying to get her bearings. Then she looked down at herself and hastily buttoned up her clothes.

"Did Jack do this to you?" Scott demanded incredulously as he returned with the glass of water.

She shook her head firmly, but her hand trembled as she raised the glass to her lips and sipped the cool water. Every time she tried to tell Scott about it, her voice got stuck in her throat. Finally she cried out, "I don't know what happened! Téa gave me champagne cocktails, and the next thing I knew—I felt I was floating out of my body. I saw—Téa—doing strange things I can't even talk about." Lamely she concluded, "Téa kept wanting to give me things to drink. Champagne . . . coffee . . . and—I saw her—changing—shapes—" she quavered. "It—it was like *un cauchemar.*"

"Ah. That's one French word I learned, from my wife's doctors in Switzerland," Scott said dryly. "Nightmare. A demon that comes into your bedroom and sits on your chest."

At the mention of Swiss doctors, Annabel recalled that, according to that ledger she'd seen with the hospital bills, Scott's wife had been consigned to an asylum.

"Am I crazy?" she whispered fearfully.

"No, no, no," Scott said. "You're the healthiest, sanest person I've ever met. A nightmare? Sounds more like a hallucination. I think Téa slipped you a Mickey Finn."

At her blank look, he sized her up and said, "I think you're under the influence of some drug she sneaked into your cocktail, probably. I've heard of people doing that to their housemaids, just for kicks." He added quietly, "And I've heard the stories about Téa, but I chalked them up to vicious Hollywood gossip. She's a morphine addict, they say. She pals around with others who like the stuff. They claim that Coco Chanel introduced her to it."

Annabel could scarcely comprehend any of this. Scott said, "I think she was trying to get revenge on you. Jack gets a certain light in his eyes when he sees you."

Annabel groaned. The love between her and Jack—did everyone on earth suspect it?

Scott said cautiously, "Shall I call that Dr. Gaspard, just to make sure you're okay?"

"God, no! I don't want to tell *anybody* else about this!" she cried out.

Scott said, "Okay, okay, take it easy. Look, you can't go walking around the hotel in this condition anyway. Do you want to just lie here on the sofa and sleep it off?" he advised, going to the closet for a blanket. "When you wake up, you'll feel better, and you'll figure everything out. Nobody can bother you here.

I won't let them in; I'll guard you like a faithful old dog. I've got some more writing to do. But holler if you need anything."

———

Hours later, Annabel awoke, feeling strangely calm. The room was in darkness, except at the far corner, where a faint light spill from the bedroom indicated that Scott was working there. It was so quiet that she could hear his pencil scratching against the pages of his pad of paper, as if he were a devoted monk transcribing in his cell.

She did not want to disturb him, so she lay there silently on the sofa, trying to sort out what had happened to her. She still couldn't make any sense of it. What she thought she'd seen was simply unimaginable. What could it mean? Was Téa really a man?

She sat up, slowly and cautiously, testing her equilibrium. She felt that what she really needed was some fresh air. Tentatively she rose to her feet, went to the front door, and opened it, breathing in the cooler night breeze, redolent with the spicy scent of the pine trees.

She walked a little way down the path, in the opposite direction of Jack's villa. Beyond the Jasmine Cottage was a small outcropping with a glimpse of the sea and a path leading down to a tiny pebbled beach below. People who stayed in the cottages sometimes launched small boats from here, to take them to the big yachts anchored out farther.

As the salty sea air filled her lungs, Annabel felt her mind clear. She was remembering the very first day she'd seen Téa, wearing a diaphanous caftan and drifting out of the house to the pool, dropping her clothes to swim naked, with that golden skin and her blond hair glistening wet in the sunlight, with even her pubic hair as gold as corn silk.

At the time, Annabel had been reminded of something catty

that her girlfriends at Vassar had told her: *When you see a girl naked in the shower, that's how you know if she bleaches her hair or if she's a natural blond.*

"I saw everything that day! Therefore, I could not have seen otherwise tonight; I must have imagined the whole thing," Annabel murmured to herself. "Maybe that's what those drugs do—they make you hallucinate all kinds of strange images."

Perhaps, too, that little episode when Alan had exposed himself to her in Sonny's tent had upset her more than she'd realized. She must have conflated the way he'd menaced her with the way that Téa had just punished her for loving Jack.

From the other side of the cove, the lighthouse was casting its beam around the rocky coast. As its light swept the little beach below, she could now see a man standing there. Then all went dark again, as the lighthouse beam swept to the other side of the cove. But now the man on the beach was waving a lantern at a yacht that was anchored some distance away. The yacht, as if in response, flashed a blinking light.

"What is *that* all about?" Annabel muttered as she ducked into the shadows.

Moments later she could hear the man with the lantern coming up from the cove, breathing hard with the effort. He went right past her as if in a great hurry. She did not raise her head until she was sure he'd moved on. Then she went out on the pebbled path and cut through the trees to follow the man, who had veered away in the direction of the wide main path that led straight up to the hotel.

That path was well lit, and now Annabel, peering through the trees, could see clearly that the signaling man was Rick, the hotel heir.

He was moving with a quick, long stride and a pensive expression, but as he drew closer to the hotel, he smiled as if in preparation to greet the other guests who were out on the terrace drinking and laughing after a party.

"Hey there, Ricky!" A few guests straggled somewhat tipsily down the path to meet Rick halfway as he waved and then joined them.

Annabel retreated, back to the Jasmine Cottage. Scott was standing in the doorway, looking worried. His face cleared when he saw her.

"Lord, I was getting ready to call security," he said. "I thought you'd been abducted by an opium ring. Feeling better?"

She nodded, but she still felt so confused. He peered at her. "You look upset," he observed.

"I just saw Rick signaling a boat," she said, a little breathless. "Scott, I think you were right when you said that this hotel is crawling with all kinds of spies this summer."

Scott chuckled. "Oh, I saw Rick do that once, too. He says he's signaling his valet to get the cocktails ready. He's probably planning to head out there soon with a girl."

Annabel snorted. "You believe that?"

"Yes! That guy is not the sharpest pencil in the box, and he's definitely too lazy to be a spy."

All this talk of spies reminded Annabel that she had a task awaiting her. "I have to put that weird typewriter in a safer place. I can lock it up in my uncle's office so he can take a look," she said, heading for the closet to retrieve the Polish girl's valise. "But I don't want to go past Jack's villa again," she added with a shudder.

"I don't blame you," Scott said. "Not a good time to see Jack. Tonight was the big screening for *Love Isn't Easy*, Jack's first—and last—independent film. I stopped in earlier, before I ran into you—long enough to see that the whole thing is a disaster."

Annabel had forgotten all about it. "What do you mean, a disaster?" she demanded.

"The entire international press was there. And by all accounts it was a big, fat flop."

"But—but—no, that was a good script—" she objected.

"Yeah, it was, thanks. And a good film, too. But apparently Sonny and Alan got their fat little fingers into the editing room, and they cut the picture to shreds—they say they did it to please the German distributors, 'to save the film.'"

"Baloney!" Annabel said indignantly.

"Yes. So Jack accused Sonny of deliberately sabotaging his film. Jack was already in a lousy mood, because Téa didn't show up for the screening. So when he saw how the studio butchered his movie, he actually punched Alan in the face. Which I must say was quite satisfying to see, even if it means my screenplay is now an *equus mortuus*."

"But why would Sonny and Alan sabotage a film that they are distributing?" Annabel asked, confused. "They care so much about profits—"

"They did it to kill two birds with one stone. First, to satisfy Herr Hardass and his band of Nazi censors. Second, to break Jack, who's been the thorn in Sonny's side all along. Sonny and Alan don't want Jack around anymore. He's too much trouble. Sonny thinks Jack is the reason that Téa hasn't renewed her contract, and that's probably true. And Jack is a stallion who can't be tamed; he wants independence—which means there's always a chance that Jack can lure Téa away, if he makes a deal with another studio like Warner Brothers or MGM. So Sonny's out to ruin Jack Cabot's reputation, so that he'll never make *any* other picture with anybody else."

It all sounded horribly feasible to Annabel. Hollywood people were ruthless.

Scott concluded, "See, Sonny's gambling that Téa may love Jack but she won't throw her whole career away for love. Like, maybe that's why she didn't come to the party to support Jack. She may be betting against him."

Annabel felt as if everything she'd thought of as solid fact was actually only a dream. It was like being in her father's photography studio and staring at a negative of a picture—where black was white and white was black.

She turned her attention back to the closet. When she opened the door, she saw only the empty floorboards where the Polish girl's valise had been.

"It's gone!" she exclaimed in panic.

Scott took a moment to realize what she was talking about. Then he said, "Oh, that. Not to worry. I locked it in my trunk of books and manuscripts when I went out."

He went over to his bedroom, took a key from his pocket, and opened his trunk. He reached in calmly and picked up the Polish girl's valise. Annabel breathed a sigh of relief.

"You want me to go with you to the hotel?" he inquired. "Just to make sure you don't get ambushed by some international spies?"

"Yes," Annabel agreed, taking a deep breath. Oncle JP would know what to do.

CHAPTER 17

Hidden Assets

Annabel felt jittery as they went up the path to the hotel. Scott, who was carrying the Polish typewriter for her, said soothingly, "Just look at those stars above us tonight. I could reach out and pluck them right off that velvet sky and make a necklace for you."

The screening party had been breaking up for some time, but there were still a few diehards lingering on the terrace, gazing out from the railing, chatting, and sipping drinks. The exhausted band was playing for the few couples who insisted on just one more dance.

Annabel saw Norma Shearer, seated there like royalty, laughing uproariously at someone's joke. "Yoo-hoo, Scott!" Norma cried out, beckoning him. "Come over here, this minute! I want a word with you." Scott actually blushed.

"Go ahead," Annabel said, taking the valise from him, for she'd spied Oncle JP standing at the wide hotel door that was opened upon the terrace. Her uncle had stayed on very late tonight, to oversee Jack's doomed screening party. Oncle JP gave the remaining guests on the terrace an appraising look; then he retreated inside, not having seen Annabel in the shadows.

"Okay, go ahead, but if you need my help, put a lantern in the window," Scott teased. *"One if by land, and two if by sea; and I on the opposite shore will be . . ."*

Annabel bypassed the terrace and went to the side door that led directly to the staff rooms. She passed the general lost-and-found cupboard, where unclaimed hats and umbrellas or other such mundane items were kept. She knew she couldn't leave the valise here.

But Oncle JP was not in his office. Where was she going to put the Polish girl's strange contraption? Her uncle would probably say that it belonged in his special locked closet safe for valuables, but she didn't have the key to his closet. She would have to wait for Oncle JP to return. She saw that he hadn't gone home yet, for he'd left his hat hanging on the rack.

Annabel peered into the hallway, hoping to see him returning, and she realized that the outside door had not closed properly behind her when she'd just come through.

As she went back to shut it, she heard a faint, peculiar beeping sound, like a bird or a cicada chirping. Sometimes such creatures did find their way into corridors and chimneys and got trapped and had to be helped back out.

Sighing, and still carrying the valise, she followed the sound and opened a narrow door that led to a place she called her uncle's "secret staircase"—the dimly lit, spiraling wrought iron stairs that had small landings and doors at each floor all the way up to the penthouse.

Oncle JP once told her, *At the turn of the century, these stairs were used by kings and duchesses when they—or their lovers—wanted to come and go unnoticed.*

Nowadays, no guests were allowed to use it, so the doors on each landing were kept locked from the staircase side. But her uncle used this secret place from time to time, when he wanted to slip upstairs and check up on the staff.

This was the very staircase Oncle JP had used the day that

Annabel discovered the body of the tennis player. Remembering that now, she felt a faint shiver.

Annabel paused at the foot of the stairs to listen closely to
the beeping sound, which was more distinct here.

Cautiously she followed the sound up the winding staircase.
The lighting was very dim, and the metal steps got narrower
and narrower, making for a dizzying, rather perilous ascent.
Carrying a heavy valise only made it worse, but she was not
going to leave this thing out of her sight.

Now she saw that on a small landing just below the penthouse level, there was a nondescript door, probably for a broom
closet. And yet, the beeping noise seemed to emanate from
there. She ascended and put her ear closer. Now she could hear
a quiet male voice, urgent, staccato, and brief. She waited until
she was sure that it was Oncle JP's voice.

She knocked twice. There was a silence. "Oncle, it's me,
Annabel," she whispered.

There was another pause; then the doorknob turned. Oncle
JP peered out.

"What are you doing here?" he said in a rough tone.

"Please let me in; *c'est très important*," she pleaded, glancing over her shoulder as if she feared—what? She didn't even
know; she just sensed evil forces lurking in the shadows of this
entire hotel tonight.

"Go to my office and wait there," he said tersely.

A part of her wanted to do just what he was telling her to
do—scurry away like a naughty little girl, free from responsibility, not needing to hear any ugly truths of life. But she was not
a little girl anymore. She would not allow anyone, even him, to
treat her like one.

"No, Oncle, we must talk, here and now. Let me in, before
someone hears us," she said firmly. She'd never stood up to him
like this, but by now she was prepared to leave him, the hotel, and
France if he turned her away tonight. Her voice made this plain.

Oncle JP grabbed her by the arm and pulled her inside, then closed the door behind her.

They were in a tiny, windowless room with weak light coming from a bare bulb dangling overhead. This place was furnished only with a small card table and a single chair.

But on the card table was a machine, which beeped right now and gave off the sound of static, like a radio. Annabel gazed at it.

"Sit down and be quiet," he said sharply as he went to the table. He put on a pair of headphones, listened as he leaned over a notepad, and wrote something down rather quickly. Then he responded with one word, which Annabel didn't catch. Finally he shut it off, took off his headphones, and looked up.

His face looked so different tonight, the features sharper. Clearly her uncle had been keeping some very important secrets from her. She could see now that his mild, deferential attitude toward haughty or rude guests was a mask, disguising a much fiercer man. All along, this tiger had teeth and claws that he had simply not deigned to reveal to anyone.

"So you have discovered my little hobby," he said with an attempt at lightheartedness.

Annabel gave him a hard stare. "Oncle—are you a fascist spy?" After all, she'd heard that all across Europe people were willing to betray their own countries.

"*Non!*" he said, looking momentarily amused at her guess.

She saw instantly that he was telling the truth, but still she eyed him intently. Now his tone became more scolding. "You should not have come up here. But now that you have, it's better for you if you put it out of your mind and just go about your duties."

"Did you speak to my father like that?" Annabel asked softly. "Perhaps that's why he left. Don't push me away, Oncle. You cannot ask blind loyalty from me. We are family. If you can't trust me, who can you trust? I asked a reasonable question. What are you doing here?"

It was the first time she'd ever invoked their blood ties, but it indeed registered with him, as did her calm, rational tone.

He said in a low voice, "It is simply that my old colleagues in French military intelligence have asked me to take messages for them here."

Annabel had always known that her uncle had such connections from his earlier years of service. But now she thought about Oncle JP's daily jogs up to the Mound, that plateau at the top of the *Cap*, where there was a military observation post of some kind that everyone seemed to know about and yet spoke of in only the vaguest of terms.

She said, "Is that what you do when you go up to the Mound every day? Do you meet with your military contacts?"

Her uncle looked surprised at her perspicacity, then nodded and said, "Now I have given you your answer. You are not to discuss this with anyone. Go to my office and wait for me there— and put all this completely out of your mind. This truly does not concern you."

"Oh, yes it does! I must show *you* something," Annabel said quickly, then added, "I believe that you—and your contacts—will surely want to know about what I've found."

She moved out of the shadows and said, "This is some kind of a typewriter that belonged to that Polish secretary who left so suddenly, right after the tennis player's death. But it's not like any typewriter I've ever seen." She stood it on the floor.

He watched alertly but said nothing. She felt a little unnerved; her uncle was like a stranger to her tonight.

"Where did you find this object?" he asked sharply.

"In the old shed behind the tennis courts. It was hidden under some tarp."

Oncle JP moved his radio over and gestured for Annabel to put the valise on the table. She unsnapped the metal latches and flipped open the cover.

"See," she said, "it's most peculiar. If you press one of the typing keys *here*, like so, it makes a completely different letter light up in one of those little round window buttons over *there*—the ones that can't be pressed for typing."

Oncle JP examined this closely, testing different keys to see what corresponding letters lit up.

"And look at this!" she said, opening the front panel beneath the keyboard, where all the plugs and wires were. "It's like a telephone switchboard, isn't it?" she said curiously.

Her uncle did not reply, only kept examining it from all angles. Finally he said, "Who did you say this belonged to?"

"The Polish secretary," Annabel said. "You know, that mousy girl with the spectacles. Only, she didn't look too mousy when I saw her in bed with the German tennis player!"

Oncle JP allowed himself a wry look. Annabel continued, "There was more to that man's death than anyone was letting on, wasn't there? Why was it hushed up?"

He fell silent. She persisted, "What are *you* doing up here? You must tell me the truth, now. People know we are family. They may already assume that I know more than I do. In that case, ignorance is dangerous to me. I've heard that there are Nazi spies up and down the Côte d'Azur. What's really going on here at the Grand Hotel?"

He paused, then made a decision to tell her. "We know that some of our fascist guests have been receiving encrypted radio messages from Berlin, right here in their rooms! We are able to hear these radio messages, but we can't decode them."

Annabel nodded toward the Polish machine. "Is this a radio, too?"

He shook his head. "*Non.*"

"But this is very important, isn't it? What is it?"

Oncle JP said with great seriousness, "Annabel, I am going to make you my deputy. This means that you cannot speak of these things you've seen and heard to anyone, not anyone at all, do you hear me?" His tone was more warning than inviting.

"Yes, Oncle," she said solemnly.

"You swear that you will not reveal anything about this machine to a single soul?"

"The screenwriter has seen it," Annabel confessed. "But he can be trusted."

Oncle JP looked startled at first. Then, rather abruptly, he closed up the Polish case. "I will see if I can send a radio message to Paris tonight and find out what this is."

Annabel, still watchful, asked, "But you have some idea about it, don't you?"

He said only, "You say you found this near the tennis courts?"

"Yes, in that old shed that nobody uses anymore."

"*D'accord*," Oncle JP said slowly. "*Oui*, that fits."

"Why? Did Hans put the machine there?" she asked softly.

"Perhaps. We have learned that the tennis player was working to stop Hitler. He is from an old, aristocratic family who does not support the Nazi Party and feels it will be the ruin of their country. But you were correct—the Nazis *were* pressuring him to join their party, because they didn't want such a popular German sports figure to continue defying them."

"Ah." Annabel recalled that time when she took Delphine into the garden and they witnessed the argument Hans seemed to be having with his tennis coach and Herr Volney.

"And perhaps the Nazis even expected Hans to spy for *them*—because athletes have a legitimate reason to travel to foreign countries, where they can meet—and spy on—all kinds of people without being suspected," Oncle JP said. "In any case, their pressure campaign seemed only to push Hans into total defiance and resistance, because he smuggled money out of Berlin. If we are correct, he was planning to give money and some documents to his courier. But perhaps someone got to him first."

"Then . . . you *do* think his death *was*—?" Annabel still couldn't say the word.

He said, "*Oui, c'est un meurtre.*"

It was the first time he'd allowed any speculation that someone else had taken Hans von Erhardt's life. Annabel felt relieved to have this out in the open at last, yet she was frightened, too.

"What courage he had," she whispered.

Oncle JP said, "Yes. And perhaps he managed to accomplish his mission before he died. But we fear it's more likely that someone caught on to him—before the poor man could succeed at his task. At this point, I have more questions than answers."

PART THREE

A woman's guess is much more accurate than a man's certainty.

—Rudyard Kipling

CHAPTER 18

An Enigma

The next morning, Oncle JP summoned Annabel to his office quite early, saying he finally had some information for her. But he was careful not to actually discuss this in the hotel—not even in his office. He told Annabel to "come take a walk," and he led her away from the hotel, down the Chemin du Phare, the narrow road that led to the lighthouse.

This precaution reinforced the seriousness of the situation. She walked silently beside Oncle JP as he strode, straight backed and deliberate, glancing about to make sure that there was no one nearby to overhear them. Finally he spoke in a low tone.

"This item that you discovered is, as you say, *not* a typewriter. It is a model of a German coding machine called Enigma," he explained.

Annabel could not help thinking, *Scott was right about this. Too bad I can't tell him; he'd love that name.*

"There have been various versions of this machine, over the years," her uncle continued. "Businessmen use a simpler edition when they travel, so that nobody will steal their secret formula, say, for a pharmaceutical or their latest design for a car. So at first I thought that this was all our hotel guests were up to—just business."

Annabel gave him a skeptical look. "Is that what Hans died for? Business?" she said pointedly. Then she thought to ask, "Is the Polish girl's machine a business model?"

"I doubt it," he admitted. "You see, there have *also* been much more advanced German *military* models. Over the years, their Enigma has evolved into a fearsome thing. Our Polish comrades have been working for some time on 'breaking' these coding machines. You see, the Poles were wise enough to fear being invaded by Germany—unlike the British and we French, for we have been, perhaps, a little too confident. But we must all now admit that the entire world should be preparing for a serious confrontation with Hitler."

"Ohh!" she said in dismay. "You don't think—the Germans will take it *that* far and actually invade *us* here in France, do you?" she could not help asking.

"In April, the Nazis declared they would no longer be bound by various promises they've made—including their non-aggression treaty with Poland. So Hitler's assurances of peaceful intentions mean nothing anymore," Oncle JP said bluntly. "It's clear that things are going to get worse before they get better. The Poles believe that they are next on Hitler's agenda, and they will put up a valiant fight when the bombers and tanks head their way, but . . ." He left it at that.

Annabel's heart sank. "Can't Hitler be stopped, Oncle?"

"I am told that the Nazis have built up a formidable war machine. But the Poles have done great work with espionage, making amazing progress. They've actually managed to construct various copies—or 'replicas'—of the German Enigma coding machines. I believe this is what you've found—a Polish-built replica of the very latest model of the Enigma!"

"A replica," she repeated, fascinated.

"But as quickly as our Polish comrades work it out, the Nazis keep improving *their* new models. It has been a constant race to keep up. Now the Poles are running out of money—and time. So they are passing the baton to us, and to the English. The Poles are desperate to protect their code breakers and everything they know, by scattering all that research and equipment to various European countries that they believe are safer from Nazi invasion than Poland—for now. Their couriers work at great risk."

"Then the Polish secretary—ah! Was *she* the courier who was supposed to meet with the tennis player, as you thought?" Annabel asked excitedly.

"Yes, but that girl was much more than a courier. I have been told that she's one of their best code breakers. She's a young mathematics student from the Polish university of Poznań, where many of them were recruited to become top-flight cryptanalysts. They studied patterns, numerous combinations, in order to figure out how the Enigma machines work."

Oncle JP now turned back in the direction of the hotel. Annabel followed, watching seagulls circling overhead as she tried to sort it all out.

He drew a deep breath. "I was just informed that the girl's mission was to bring this machine to the South of France and make contact with the tennis player, who would then give her money and documents so that she could eventually continue on to Paris."

At the entrance to the Grand Hotel, Oncle JP nodded calmly to staff members, but he continued walking with her in silence until they were back in his office. He perhaps expected that she would be satisfied with what she'd heard and go about her business now.

Instead, she said, "Can I see the machine again?"

He paused. "Lock the door," he said decisively.

When he opened the machine, she studied it anew. "Why is it that when you type one letter on the first set of keys, another letter lights up in the second alphabet?" she asked.

"That is how you decode a message. If you are a spy and you get a message over your radio, you write it down—but it will be only a jumble of letters that makes no sense, because the sender used *his* Enigma to put his message in the day's code, and then he transmitted those jumbled letters by radio to you."

"Ah! Is that why, Oncle, when some of our German guests were sending radio messages, you intercepted them but were still unable to make out what they meant?"

"*Précisément*," he replied. "You see, the receiver of the message must also have one of these Enigma machines; then he can type in the jumbled letters of the radio message he just got, and his Enigma machine will show him the correct letters—spelling out the fully decoded message. So he writes *that* down. In other words, if he gets a radio message that says *AQ* and he types an *A* into his Enigma and gets an *H* and types a *Q* and sees an *I*, now he knows that the radio message says *Hi*."

"But why doesn't the Enigma print it out on paper, like a typewriter? That would be so much easier than having to write everything down," Annabel said pragmatically.

"Because it would make the machine much heavier than it already is."

"So as long as both the sender and the receiver of the messages have the same kind of Enigma machines, they can translate each other's radio message, right?" she concluded.

"No, no, no. It is not so simple! You must first know which *settings* to use for your machine," he explained. "These Enigma settings must be changed *every day*. And they are all worked out in advance—and put into a monthly codebook! Which contains all the settings for every single date of the entire month. Every day it's different!"

At Annabel's puzzled look, Oncle JP pointed to the metal, saw-toothed wheels just above all those rows of letters.

"First you must change the position of these rotors," he said, demonstrating that each wheel could be turned to change its position.

"On top of that, you must also change the settings of the plugboard," he said, now opening up the area beneath the keyboards—where all those wires with the metal plugs on their tips could be inserted into various holes, like a telephone switchboard operator plugging each one into its correct hole.

"*Alors*," said Oncle JP, "when you have adjusted all of today's settings, now your machine will know what to do to create or receive a message. Let us say we want to send a warning to another spy. First we must encrypt it. Like so."

He typed the letters *BEWARE*. Annabel watched as this caused completely different letters to appear in the lit windows: *XAPQAD*.

Her uncle said, "You write down those letters, and then you transmit them by radio, or in a letter, whatever. If the person who receives your message has a codebook, he can set his own machine to the day's settings. Then he will type in this jumble of letters, and *his* machine will now light up with the message of *BEWARE*. Note that the letter *A* in *XAPQAD* means *E* in the first instance and *R* in the second. In the old days, we could be sure of a consistency, but not with Enigma! That is one reason it is so diabolically hard to decipher."

Annabel, realizing the full significance of all these details, said slowly, "Then, even if you *have* an Enigma machine like we do now, and even if you intercepted the Nazis' coded radio messages, you *still* can't decode them unless you have the German codebook to tell you how to change the settings every day. So all you need is to get your hands on a codebook."

"Not just one codebook! Every month, a new one must be created and sent to spies."

"Wow." Annabel suddenly comprehended the extent of this spying business. "So—where can *we* ever get such a codebook?"

"From an insider in Germany who can get his hands on it

and is willing to share it with us," Oncle JP said quietly. "Some people sell such information for profit; others offer it simply because they love their country and want the current government to be replaced with a democratic one. Hans refused to work for the Führer, whom his family despises. And we have learned that his good college chum worked in Berlin's 'encrypted communications' center, so it's entirely possible that the friend was in league with Hans and passed a codebook to him so that Hans could in turn pass it on to those of us who are working against Hitler."

Annabel, recalling the tennis player's cheerful, friendly attitude, could not help marveling, "I never would have suspected Hans of espionage!"

"Just so!" Oncle JP said with a droll look. "Yet we are told that the tennis player was carrying this month's codebook to give to the Polish girl so that she could take it to Paris or London, along with the replica, to demonstrate all that she knows."

"Do you think Hans succeeded in giving it to her?" she asked hopefully.

He shook his head. "Our contact in Poland tells us that they suspected that the girl was being watched here at the hotel, so she was told to leave without taking *anything* incriminating in her possession—not the machine, not the codebook. She was also told that even Paris was becoming too risky for her. So she was instructed to go to Marseille and wait until they could get her to London."

"Then—where is the Polish girl now? Did she reach London?" she said apprehensively.

Oncle JP paused, then said, "Our agents have been looking for her ever since she left the hotel. I received an answer only this morning. She was found dead in an alleyway in Marseille. We believe she was captured by Nazi agents, because what actually killed her was a poison that some spies carry in a capsule to put in their mouth and commit suicide. She must have done so to avoid giving up any real information to the enemy."

They fell silent for a long moment. Then Annabel said, "How very brave she was, too."

Oncle JP nodded. "So, I'm told that Hans was sent a wire saying to 'hide the birthday gifts' until another 'friend' could come to our Grand Hotel to take it all to London."

Annabel drew in her breath sharply, realizing that the telegram she'd delivered to Hans had perhaps been those very instructions.

"But Hans didn't realize that the Nazis figured out that he was working against Hitler and carrying that codebook," Oncle JP continued.

Her mind whirled to keep up. "Then—either Hans hid the codebook in the shed . . ."

Oncle JP finished her thought. "Or as a precaution, he kept them separate, and the Nazis found it. You see, I have searched the shed. It wasn't there. And before that, when you discovered that Hans was dead, I came up right away and made a thorough search of his room—yet I never found any documents among his effects."

He sighed deeply. "*Enfin*, it is possible that Nazi spies, right here at this hotel, have deprived us not only of that fine young man but also of the codebook that he so desperately wanted to pass on to the free world."

"This is terrible," Annabel said in a small voice.

"Yes—but our enemies did *not* succeed at one very important thing. They were unable to locate the Polish girl's valise, because, as you see—*you* found it."

There was an unmistakable note of pride in her uncle's voice, which Annabel had never heard before. It made her want even more to help him, just to hear him speak of her again in such glowing terms.

Oncle JP unlocked a drawer in his desk and drew out a photograph. "This is a picture of a torn page from an older codebook, from a previous month this year, which our French spies got hold of," he said. "So this is what the codebooks look like. We are told to keep a sharp eye out for anything resembling it."

She studied the picture. It was a single page with a column of boxes marked for every date of the month, parallel with more columns of more boxes, each with its own jumble of letters to indicate corresponding settings for the machines' rotors and plugboards.

"Annabel, you have been working on rotation this summer and therefore have had a unique chance to see a lot of the hotel. Have you ever seen anything like this? In the maids' closets, down by the pool, anywhere?" Oncle JP inquired.

"No," she admitted.

"Well, I have instructed the maids not to throw out any papers that came from certain hotel rooms. They are to bring everything to me before it goes in the trash."

But now they heard a loud voice from the lobby.

Oncle JP quickly locked up the Enigma machine in his closet, then hurried to investigate. Annabel followed, still holding the photo of the code page, which she hastily stuffed into her pocket so no one else would see.

A newly arrived female guest stood at the front desk, glowering at Marta. She wore gold jewelry and a silk outfit. She was scowling as she repeated her loud demand, tapping her long, polished fingernails on the marble counter and saying over and over in a shrill voice: "*Wo ist der Koffer? Wo ist der Koffer?*"

"What's the trouble?" Oncle JP asked.

Marta explained, "Her luggage is delayed. She sent it on ahead, but it did not arrive from Paris, and it should have been here by now."

Very calmly, Oncle JP picked up the telephone to place a call with the proper railway person who could investigate.

Annabel asked Marta, "What does *Koffer* mean?"

Marta murmured patiently, "Suitcase."

Oncle JP turned to the new guest with a promising

expression, and Marta translated for him as he assured the guest that the authorities would move heaven and earth to find the missing item. His voice was so authoritative and yet soothing that the woman seemed suitably impressed with his confident manner. She held out her hand for him to kiss, then allowed a bellhop to take her up to her room.

Annabel was still thinking of the codebook as she followed her uncle back to his office. She took the photo from her pocket, studied it anew, and then handed it back to Oncle JP. For some reason, the angry guest's shrill demand still echoed in her mind: *Wo ist der Koffer?*

It was as if a tide were pulling her right back to that weird night at Jack's villa, when Téa had undressed her, so lovingly at first, but then handled her roughly and had spoken to her in German, saying . . . something about coffee . . . it had sounded like *coffee* . . . but it also sounded exactly like what she'd just heard that woman in the lobby saying so angrily . . . in the same angry tone that Téa had used with her . . .

"It wasn't *coffee* that she was saying to me! It was *Koffer*," Annabel murmured to herself. "Suitcase. She wanted to know, 'Where is the *suitcase.*'"

Oncle JP had accepted the codebook photo from her and then turned to lock it away in his safe.

Now he said, "One more thing, Annabel. I am told that the codebook was disguised, as if it were a gift for a girlfriend, so that the tennis player could give it to the Polish girl. It had a special cover of pink satin with the words *Diary 1939* scripted on it in red embroidery, to make it look like a book for a woman to keep her engagements in. So that the Polish girl would be able to carry it and it would seem quite ordinary. If you should see anything like this, anywhere in the hotel—"

Now Annabel felt as if someone had abruptly splashed her face with icy water and awakened her from that nightmare at last. For a moment she could scarcely breathe. Everything was suddenly falling into place. The suitcase . . . the date book . . .

"We must be careful about everything we do from here on in, Annabel. We are dealing with dangerous, clever men," Oncle JP concluded.

He turned to face her, then said quickly, "What is it?"

"Oncle JP," she said slowly, "It's not a man we're looking for."

"What do you mean?" he asked.

Annabel said firmly now, "I think I know who our Nazi spy is at the Grand Hotel."

CHAPTER 19

The Last Dance

"I *have* seen that date book," Annabel declared. "Téa Marlo has it."

"The Hollywood actress?" Oncle JP sounded doubtful.

"The *German* actress! Yes, I saw it in her dresser drawer."

"I will not ask you why you were looking in there," Oncle JP could not help saying.

Annabel said excitedly, "It all makes sense now. Téa left Berlin for Hollywood. The Nazis have been pressuring her, ever since she arrived in France. Everybody said it was because they want her to make films for Hitler. And I'm sure they do, but there must be more to it than that. If they want people to spy for them, she's a good pick; she travels, meets people. She went off on a yacht with those awful men—it was that night of the masked ball, which is why I attended the dance in her place, wearing her gown and her mask."

She gave a small gasp of comprehension. "*And* a man cornered me and spoke to me in German; he said, 'You know what I want!' I thought he was just trying to pick me up, but—"

Oncle JP looked shocked. Annabel, rapidly reassessing

everything now, said, "And—ohhh! The day I went to Sainte-Agnès with Jack and Téa—she acted afraid of heights and wouldn't leave the car. But as soon as we left her behind, she went traipsing off to take pictures of the Maginot fort! She acted like a tourist, but she took a lot of photos—"

"*What!* Pictures of the Maginot? You should have told me right away," Oncle JP said sternly. "I think perhaps there is much more that you should tell me, right now?"

Annabel blushed, thinking of the champagne cocktails that Téa had pressed upon her and that whole nightmarish scene. Was it just sexual jealousy over Jack—or something more?

"Oh God! Téa Marlo saw me come back from the tennis shed with the Polish girl's valise, and *that's* why she drugged me—to find out where I put it!" she blurted out.

"Drugged *you*?" Oncle JP exclaimed, aghast.

"Yes. Last night she insisted I have a drink with her, and she put something in it. She said, '*Wo ist der Koffer?*' I ran away before she could find out where the replica is." Deeply troubled now, Annabel said, "Oncle—if Téa has the codebook, did *she* take it from Hans?"

"Undoubtedly. Perhaps she convinced him that she, too, was working against Hitler. Everyone admires famous people; even famous people admire each other. Perhaps she flirted with him and got herself invited into his room," he concluded.

Annabel could picture Téa charming her way in. "Did she *have* to kill him to get it?"

"I doubt she meant to. You see, Dr. Gaspard found out something from Hans's family: One of the reasons Hans took up sports is that he is allergic to most medicines, so he wanted to build himself up and keep healthy. Even a small dose of, say, a barbiturate could have killed him." He sighed. Then he gave Annabel a worried look. "Téa failed to find the Enigma machine, but then she saw *you* with it. And she is surely still looking for it."

"Oncle, what if the Nazis think that *I* am the new agent that Hans was waiting for!"

He said worriedly, "I just had the same thought. My colleagues and I must keep a close eye on you. And somehow, we must get that codebook."

"Do you want me to get it for you?" she asked. He shook his head. "Why not?" she demanded. "You *said* I was your deputy now. So, what's the plan?"

Oncle JP said carefully, "I can tell one of the maids to retrieve the codebook, now that you've given us a clue as to its whereabouts. We have a woman here who is working for us."

Annabel absorbed this *we* and *us* with some surprise. "A maid? Which one?"

But Oncle JP said he could not tell her. "If you are being watched, I don't want you to accidentally betray the maid with a flicker of recognition in your eye if you should see her. It takes great training to be a spy. You must unlearn natural behavior. No, I think it's best if you just behave normally today," he said thoughtfully. "What are you scheduled to do?"

"I go to see the screenwriter in the morning," she answered. "Then tonight—he asked to escort me to the dance at *la Fête des Étoiles*." Privately, Annabel suspected that Scott wanted her on his arm just to impress Norma Shearer and perhaps make her jealous.

The "Celebration of the Stars" was to be the last dinner dance at the Grand Hotel before the official opening of the Cannes Film Festival, and from then on the biggest events would take place in that city. Tonight's *fête* was in honor of Charles Laughton—star of *The Hunchback of Notre Dame*. Rick's father thought it would be good publicity for the Grand Hotel.

"I see," Oncle JP said broodingly. Then he made a decision. "Yes, stay away from those actors at the villa. But you *should* go to that party. If what you say is true, then Téa Marlo will be looking for you and following you, so it's better to have you out in public. Therefore you can keep an eye on Miss Marlo—and my people can look out for *you*."

———

Now that a new typewriter had been sent to the Jasmine Cottage, Scott and Annabel were very busy that morning with Scott's correspondence and writing. His story about teen pregnancy, "Salute to Lucy and Elsie," had been turned down by *Esquire* magazine even after the valiant changes that Scott made, because, in the end, the editors still found it too controversial for American readers.

But by now Scott had Hollywood on his mind. Not only his novel but also his short stories were about people struggling in Tinseltown. The one about the feverish scriptwriter, called "Temperature," got rejected by the *Saturday Evening Post*. Another story, called "Last Kiss," was a sad tale about an aspiring English actress and a director who discovers too late that he loves her; but it was rejected by *Collier's* and *Cosmopolitan*. Scott remained undaunted.

"Never mind. I've got a new Hollywood character whom I call Pat Hobby," he enthused. "I think I could write a whole series of amusing short stories about him, poor devil. He's a hack screenwriter, all washed up, but he'll die trying. Here's the first story; would you type it up right away? I'm going to send it to *Esquire*."

And of course, he'd also written new pages of the treatment for his novel, ready for her to type up. It was just what Annabel needed now—something to focus on and keep her mind off what lay ahead tonight. Besides, she could not help but share in Scott's excitement. "It's fun to see Hollywood through your eyes. It sounds like a dream world," she told him.

"But Hollywood is such a slack, soft place compared to here," Scott mused. "It just doesn't have the vitality and excitement of Provence."

Annabel privately thought, *I could do with a little less excitement around here.*

At midday, they went outside for a breath of air. Jack was coming briskly down the path, looking energized. The sun was shining on his beautiful, curly hair, and Annabel felt her heart lurch at the sight of him, despite her uncle's warning to stay away from the villa.

"He's in a good mood this morning, strangely enough," Scott observed. "You'd think after that disastrous screening party for *Love Isn't Easy*, he'd be a depressed dog. But I bet he's relieved to make a clean break from Sonny. Jack's a fighter. Maybe he's still got Rick backing his next picture."

Indeed, Jack had a broad smile on his face when he saw them. "Annabel, where have you been?" he said eagerly. "I got our films from Sainte-Agnès developed. It all looks great—you should see it! The footage you shot is especially good. You've really got an eye." He paused. "And Téa's been looking all over for you. Why don't you stop by tonight when you're done?"

Annabel felt her blood freeze. She gazed at Jack and wondered, *Do you have any idea what Téa really is? Are you her collaborator?*

She'd kept her promise to Oncle JP and said nothing to Scott of what she'd learned about the Enigma replica, even when Scott told her this morning that Téa had been "nosing around here looking for you" earlier. Annabel's face might have betrayed something then, for she'd had a moment's panic when Scott asked her if "everything went all right with your uncle and that funny typewriter"; but when she'd simply nodded, Scott had studied her for a moment, sensed her discomfort, and let the issue drop.

Now, however, he saw that she was still frightened by that night at Jack's villa, and he instinctively stepped in front of her to create a protective barricade with his broad shoulders as he said meaningfully to Jack, "You'd better tell Téa that Annabel's working with me all day. And as for tonight, she's *my* date. So you might say Annabel is spoken for."

Jack glanced from Annabel to Scott, then said lightly, "Oh, well, good, see you both at the party tonight. Téa and I will be there, with bells on."

Scott watched warily as Jack retreated to the villa. "Someday, I ought to write about those two characters," he said darkly. "I suspect it will involve something quite nefarious."

———

Oncle JP did an extraordinary thing that afternoon—he came down to the Jasmine Cottage to check up on Annabel, clearly wanting to make sure that she was still safe.

Scott had stepped out to go for a walk and clear his head. When Annabel opened the front door, Oncle JP looked supremely relieved to see that she hadn't been spirited away by Nazi spies.

She told him that Scott was being very helpful without asking probing questions and that he was escorting her to the ball tonight, as planned. She also told him about Jack's visit. She half expected her uncle to tell her not to go to the dance tonight after all.

But instead he said thoughtfully, "Fine. We can all keep an eye on one another tonight."

"I guess I'd better find something to wear," Annabel said, wondering if any of the things she'd brought with her from America would be appropriate. She doubted it. "I've got lots of work to do for Scott, so I won't have much time to buy a dress."

They had walked together to the front gate of the cottage. Oncle JP said briskly, "Don't worry about that. I can borrow something from one of the good shops and have it sent here; just write down your size." He took a small notepad from his pocket.

Annabel smiled gratefully and obliged. "You'd better have

the dress sent to me here at the cottage," she suggested. "I won't have time to go back to my rooming house to get ready."

"*Ah bon*. Then I will have a chambermaid bring it to you. So stay put. And remember, at the dance, act normal in every way. Never let on that you have any suspicions of anyone."

When Annabel heard the word *chambermaid*, she was intrigued. "Is that . . . *the* maid—the one who's 'working' with you?" she whispered.

"Yes." Oncle JP nodded. "I thought you should know, after all, in case you need her help."

"Did she find the codebook at Jack's villa?" she asked.

Oncle JP shook his head ruefully. "She was told by Jack Cabot that Téa Marlo was sleeping and he did not wish to have her disturbed. So the maid was not allowed to go into the Villa Sanctuaire to clean today at all."

"Oncle," Annabel said quickly, "I could get it for you." He hesitated. She went on, "I can watch from here and wait until Jack and Téa leave for the party. As soon as they are out of the villa, I'll slip in and get it. Scott will wait outside to escort me to the party, so I'll be safe. And I can bring the book to you up at the hotel, and it will just look as if I'm arriving at the party."

Oncle JP gave her another of those rare approving looks. "Yes, all right. But be careful, Annabel. Two people have already been murdered just to stop us from obtaining this item."

They had moved out along the pebbled path, and her uncle glanced back at the Jasmine Cottage as Scott returned from the other direction. He waved at them, looking preoccupied. Annabel knew that expression; it meant that he'd gotten an idea for something while out walking, and he wanted to hurry inside and write it down before he forgot it.

"What's on *his* mind?" Oncle JP asked, bemused. "Another movie?"

Annabel said, "He does all that the studio asks, but he's also been writing something very special all his own, which you mustn't tell Sonny about. Scott's a great author and he writes his heart out. It's as if he's on fire—nothing can distract him, not me, not the time of day, not sun nor rain, not even if he feels ill. He just lives to write."

Oncle JP's expression softened. "Ah," he said. "Then he is an artist."

After her uncle left, Annabel momentarily reflected that the French greatly respected their artists, even naming streets after their authors and painters and musicians. She reentered the cottage quietly so that she would not disturb Scott.

———

The maid who came to deliver the dress was a small, unassuming middle-aged woman named Nadia who wore her dark hair pulled into a no-nonsense bun at the nape of her neck. She carried the gown as if it were made of butterflies' wings. And indeed it had that gossamer quality, in chiffon colors of violet and blue. She had even brought a pair of blue satin pumps to go with it. And then she reached into an apron pocket and pulled out a small wrapped item.

"It's a gift. Your uncle said he bought it for your birthday next month, but he wants you to have it for tonight," Nadia said with a smile. Annabel unwrapped it—a jewel box, containing a small but fine sparkling diamond pendant on a gleaming gold chain nestled against the dark velvet lining of the box.

"Oh, it catches the light so beautifully!" Annabel said in delight. "Will you help me put it on?" They went into the small cloakroom so that Annabel could get dressed.

Scott was down the hall, in the bathroom, shaving and humming to himself.

She slipped into the gown and shoes. The maid said, "Here you go," and draped the pendant around Annabel's slender neck and adjusted the clasp.

Annabel drifted over to the mirror in the hallway to see herself at full length.

"*Comme un beau cygne,*" Nadia murmured as she stepped back to examine the impression that the whole outfit made.

"What'd she say?" Scott asked as he emerged, looking dapper in his evening outfit.

"She said I looked like a—beautiful swan," Annabel said shyly.

"You do!" Scott said approvingly.

"You look pretty spiffy yourself," she said, adding teasingly, "Is that another one of Jack's outfits that you 'borrowed' from the studio?"

"It is *not,*" Scott said. "It's mine. I keep it for emergencies." He disappeared into the kitchen area and reemerged carrying a cellophane box with a white gardenia corsage in it.

"Back home, a man can't take a girl out without bringing her a flower," he said simply. The maid helped Annabel pin it on, as Scott stepped outside to light his cigarette.

Nadia handed her a pair of gloves and then a blue purse. "For the codebook," Nadia murmured. "The key to the villa is inside the purse." Then she hurried off.

"Ready?" Scott asked. Annabel nodded, and they set out. Music was wafting from the hotel; the band was playing a lovely tune called "Somewhere Over the Rainbow," sung by a young woman with a powerful yet yearning voice that floated across the lawns in a ghostly, poignant way.

But as they drew nearer Jack's villa, she said lightly, "Just one thing. I left something in Téa's room the last time I was there. But let's wait until Jack and Téa leave the villa before I go get it. I'll only be a few minutes."

Scott gave her a meaningful look. "I said it before; I'll say it again. You are a terrible liar. Your uncle was here, so I assume he's aware of what you're up to and it's okay with him?" She nodded. Still, he said gently, "But are *you* sure you want to go back into that villa?"

"Yes," Annabel said. "And I need you to be my lookout. If anyone comes, whistle to warn me so I can get out without being seen." She laid a gloved hand on his arm to detain him. "I'll only be a few minutes," she murmured apologetically.

Scott sighed. "You've finally become a woman of mystery." Then he added in a fatherly tone, "And I'm not sure I like it."

They went partway down the path, pausing at the turn before the villa. It was already growing dark outside now. Clouds were scuttling overhead, cloaking and then revealing a half moon that peered down at the partygoers.

Annabel heard Jack's laugh and Téa's sultry tone as the pair sauntered out onto the path and headed toward the hotel, away from where Scott and Annabel were lingering, hidden by the tall shrubbery. As the voices progressively faded away, Scott dramatically put a hand to his ear, exaggerating his caution.

"The coast is clear," he whispered, and they drew nearer to the Villa Sanctuaire.

He waited for her at the path, smoking meditatively, while she slipped noiselessly up to the villa. She opened the purse, took out the key, unlocked the front door, and entered.

It was dark inside, except for the small lamp on Téa's dressing table. It shed weak light, but to Annabel it was like a star beckoning her.

She hurried over to the dressing table and went straight to the drawer where she had seen the satin-covered date book. She pushed aside the handkerchiefs and scarves.

It wasn't there.

Annabel stifled a groan. She glanced wildly around the room. Had Téa given the book to someone else? If not, where might she have hidden it? Annabel checked the other drawers in the dressing table, then the ones in the little night table by the bed.

She peered under the bed. She eyed the mattress doubtfully,

realizing that Téa surely knew that this would not be a good hiding place if a maid came to change the sheets while Téa was out. But Annabel checked under the mattress anyway. No date book.

Finally her eyes, adjusting to the poor light, spotted Téa's matching luggage, lined up neatly in an alcove near the closet. It was leather, every piece handmade by Hermès.

"Suitcase," Annabel murmured. "*Koffer.*" She opened each gently. The interiors were a sensual cream-colored suede. One for hats. One for shoes. The largest was a trunk, where one side had a silver rod for hanging clothes; the other side had a series of satin-lined lingerie drawers. Annabel checked them all, until at last she found, buried beneath a tissue-wrapped peach-colored peignoir set, the pink satin diary with the year embroidered in red thread.

"This is it!" she gasped in amazement as she glanced inside briefly; for the pages did, indeed, resemble the photo of the code sheet that her uncle had shown her. Hastily she closed up the trunk and put the diary into her purse, feeling her heart pounding with triumph.

Suddenly she heard a rustling sound. She froze. She heard it again, more clearly now. Someone was in the next room and moving closer. Hastily she slipped into the closet, leaving the door slightly ajar because, if she shut it completely, it would make a telltale click.

She held her breath and waited. Someone entered Téa's bedroom now and was moving about. If the intruder yanked open the closet door, he'd find Annabel standing there in her evening gown with a German codebook in her purse and no plausible excuse.

The floor creaked as the person moved about. Someone was using the telephone. It was a short conversation. The man in the room said in a low, gruff voice, "*Tout est prêt. Oui, d'accord.*" He replaced the receiver but then stood there, as if waiting.

Annabel waited, too, straining to hear if the man on the other side of the door had sensed her presence. It seemed like an eternity, until, at last, she heard his footsteps retreating, then silence. She waited longer before cautiously slipping out of the closet, then paused again in the bedroom, silently listening.

Now she could distinctly hear footsteps leaving the parlor and then the sound of the back door being shut behind the man. She could even hear a rustling sound in the shrubs out there. Whoever it was must have taken the little side street behind the villa.

Finally, all was still. Annabel hurried out the front door, locked it behind her, and rushed away. Scott was still standing by the path, smoking and gazing up at the sky.

"Mission accomplished?" he asked in a low voice.

"Did you *see* him?" she asked breathlessly. "Why didn't you whistle to warn me?"

"See who?" Scott asked, baffled. "Nobody came here."

"*Somebody* did!" she hissed. "He went in and out the back door."

"Who was it? Did he see *you*?" Scott asked worriedly. She shook her head.

"Look," Scott warned, "whatever it is you're doing, I think you've got to stop. Let's get off this dark path and get over to that party, where there are people and lights, instead of spies and owls and bats. Frankly, I'm beginning to wonder about *you* and your mysterious errands."

"I'll tell you all about it one day, and you can put me in one of your stories," Annabel promised, taking his arm.

When they reached the main path, the sky had darkened, for the moon was now completely shrouded by clouds. They walked carefully, following the tiny footlights at the outer edges of the path. As they approached the terrace, Annabel could not help feeling a burst of pride in the Grand Hotel, sparkling like a jewel for this event, with a dramatic white satin sash draped across the entrance bearing letters in gold, heralding *la Fête des Étoiles*.

"You said it means 'Celebration of the Stars'?" Scott mused, then turned and gazed up at the sky. "I keep trying to see the heavenly ones, but they've been playing hide-and-seek with those sheeplike clouds. Wonder where the Big Dipper is from here."

"Well, there's plenty of Hollywood stars to see," Annabel said, gesturing at the other arriving guests, who at a distance looked more like a flock of exotic birds crossing the lawn.

It was one of those sweet summer nights when, even in this turbulent year, everyone was happy just to be together, relaxing in the warm night air that blew in from the sea. Out in the darkness, small lights winked and gleamed from several yachts anchored in the distance.

"Cary Grant is on the guest list. I wonder if he'll actually show up!" Annabel said, scanning the crowd for a sign of the incredibly handsome, dark-haired thirty-five-year-old actor, who had the grace of an acrobat, brooding dark eyes, and a romantic cleft in his chin. After a string of light roles, Cary Grant had surprised the Hollywood press this year with his intense, dramatic portrayal of a tough, daring pilot in *Only Angels Have Wings*.

She didn't spot him, but the night was full of other glamorous guests. The women came fluttering across the garden paths, their jewels occasionally catching the light and looking like fireflies. The men's silhouettes appeared so sophisticated in their finely tailored evening wear.

The young woman who'd been singing "Somewhere Over the Rainbow" had been asked to sing another song, so she stood at the microphone under a spotlight, her sad, dark eyes as big as saucers, her voice both strong and plaintive as she sang "You Made Me Love You."

"It's Judy Garland," Scott said. "She's seventeen years old, but she's a real pro."

Annabel thought fleetingly of poor Cissy, who loved to sing but had been sent home like a delinquent schoolgirl. She should be here to be inspired by the power of a good voice.

As Scott and Annabel approached the staircase to the terrace, a couple arrived via a side path and stepped deliberately in front of them. It was Téa, but she was not with Jack; she was walking with that man who Scott had said cheated on the tennis courts—the one called Herr Ubel, a man with a severe military haircut and the attitude to match.

Téa cried out, "Annabel!" and grasped her by the wrist, kissing her on both cheeks as if they hadn't seen each other all summer.

Annabel caught the scent of attar of roses. Her heart began to pound as she wondered, *Did someone see me come out of the villa? Does Téa know? Do they suspect that I stole the code-book, and that I have it in my purse, this very minute? Was Herr Ubel the man in the villa?*

Téa pulled her away from the men and whispered, "Darling, I'm so sorry about the other night. I've been under such stress, and I guess the champagne went right to my head. Let's go sit somewhere where we can talk."

Annabel felt Téa's firm grip still on her arm. Yet there was something almost hysterical in Téa's manner; she looked so desperate, waiting for an answer as if her life depended on it.

Even now Annabel started to feel a tug of pity, but then she steeled herself and said meaningfully, "Oh, don't worry, Téa. I understand perfectly."

Téa gasped and stepped back, startled by Annabel's unflinch-ing gaze and this unusually firm tone from a girl who'd been so malleable and admiring.

Herr Ubel moved forward impatiently now. "Come, Téa, there are some people here tonight who are eager to meet you."

Annabel caught her breath, for she recognized *that* voice, oh yes. It was not the same as that of the man who'd just been in the villa speaking French. But it most definitely belonged to the man in the satyr mask who'd backed her into a corner on the night of the masked ball.

Scott took Annabel by the arm and steered her away from them. "And now if you will excuse us," he said firmly to Herr Ubel, "my date and I are going dancing tonight."

CHAPTER 20

La Fête des Étoiles

Annabel glanced about the terrace, looking for her uncle. Waiters moved swiftly through the crowd, perfectly balancing large, terrifyingly loaded silver trays of filled champagne glasses, as well as plates of canapés of assorted puff pastry delights with various tastes to offer: cheese, ham, shaved truffles, mushrooms, smoked salmon.

She knew that this was just a prelude to a splendid dinner of caviar and lobster. She'd seen the seafood truck this morning, laden with all the red and blue lobsters being delivered in large crates. The fisherman believed that keeping lobsters in water tanks was an abomination, so they were nestled in moist seaweed and stacked in their boxes, then placed in a refrigerated room at the entrance to the kitchen.

"There's your uncle," Scott said in a low voice. Oncle JP was standing unobtrusively at one side of the terrace, talking to his staff and surveying everything with that appraising, eagle-eyed gaze of his.

As Scott stepped away to say hello to someone, Annabel hurried over to her uncle.

"Ah!" he said, smiling. "I see you got your birthday gift.

Delphine helped me select it. It suits you, as I knew it would," he said modestly.

"Oncle JP, thank you so much. I love it!" Annabel said, putting a hand on the beautiful pendant, then giving him a kiss. He actually blushed with pride.

"Step over here," Oncle JP murmured, still gazing at the crowd and nodding whenever someone smiled at him. He drew Annabel into the shadows. "The sooner you get rid of that 'package' in your purse, the safer you will be," he said in a low voice.

She opened her purse, and her uncle, without even looking down, skillfully reached inside, took the codebook, and put it into his jacket pocket.

With some satisfaction he said, "I will photograph its pages right away, and then I'll see that it is returned. Where was it? Did anyone see you?"

She told him exactly where she'd found it, then added that she'd had to hide in the closet when a man briefly entered the villa.

"But he didn't see me," Annabel assured him. A thought occurred to her now. "Did you send a man to the villa?" she asked.

"*Non!*" Oncle JP shook his head.

She said, "He spoke French, and he said 'all is ready.' What can that mean?"

Her uncle's eyes narrowed, but all he said was, "Hmmm." So she told him about the little confrontation that she'd just had with Téa and Herr Ubel.

Oncle JP glanced sharply around at the crowd. Téa was now standing close to Jack, and the two of them were smiling and posing obligingly whenever a photographer asked. Herr Ubel had gone over to the bar under the pines.

Oncle JP said calmly, "You did well, Annabel, but from now on, avoid engaging with Téa or Herr Ubel. Your job is done. Just relax, and try to enjoy the party. You do not have to watch anyone; I have people on my staff looking out for us tonight. But if you should see anything unusual, or need any help, tell me at once. I will be in my office. So go; dance with your date."

Annabel found Scott in a corner, talking and laughing with a bright-faced, blue-eyed Irishman who had a very high forehead and a dazzling smile, which made his whole face light up with sharp intelligence.

"Annabel, meet James Cagney," Scott said.

"Oh, it's such a pleasure!" Annabel exclaimed. Here was the actor who'd just starred in the prison movie *Each Dawn I Die*, and now he had a new gangster film coming out with his co-star Humphrey Bogart called *The Roaring Twenties*, which sounded fascinating. Annabel told him so, and she loved listening to Mr. Cagney's soft voice with its strong New York attitude.

"Why, thank you very much, you're very kind," he said, looking at her searchingly as if he feared he ought to recognize her.

"Annabel is my amanuensis," Scott offered grandly.

"You said a mouthful, brother," Cagney teased him.

But his gaze alighted upon a group of rather unpleasant-looking men standing with Herr Ubel at the bar under the pine trees on the terrace. Nazi cohorts were laughing and talking loudly in German.

"There's always a skunk at every garden party," Cagney remarked in his most fighting-Irish tone. "But tonight I'd say we've got a whole passel of them stinking up the joint. Who invited that lot?"

"They seem to be celebrating something tonight," Scott observed. "They've got the giddy look of people who've won big at a casino and are showing off their winnings by buying drinks all 'round."

"They're not all hotel guests," Annabel commented. "Some of them get invited to lunch by the ones who *are* guests, and they hang out for the cocktail hour. The bartenders say the Nazis have made that side of the terrace their hangout, no matter whose private party it intrudes on, and they just refuse to budge."

"The French are too damned genteel for those thugs," Scott muttered. "That's what Cary Grant told me." He turned to Annabel and grinned. "You just missed Cary. He was skulking around, trying to duck Mae West after she pinched his cheek and told everybody that she was the one who discovered him, when he was a 'sweet' English boy just off the boat."

"Is that so?" Cagney chuckled. He winked at Annabel, saying for her benefit, "You know, I remember when Cary used to sell shirts on the studio lot, to make a little extra on the side. I bought one once. Sky blue. It was fine."

A fresh roar of rough laughter from the bar caused Cagney to return his gaze to the interlopers. He said, "Don't those rats know we've got half the Hollywood Anti-Nazi League here tonight? What are we supposed to do, make nice?" But then he just shook his head and said, "It's enough to make me want to go right back to the farm."

"Heard you got a hundred acres in Martha's Vineyard," Scott said curiously.

"You bet. No concrete roads, no traffic, no fascists," Cagney said. "And the land—it's the best soil I ever saw. A man could be completely self-sufficient out there." He and Scott launched into an earnest discussion of soil conservation.

"May I have this dance?" Rick suddenly appeared at Annabel's side. He looked especially spiffy tonight, with his dark hair sleeked back with violet-scented pomade, his clothes impeccable. But he acted almost afraid that she'd turn down his request, so she gave him a gentle smile and took his hand as they moved out to dance.

Rick was not a natural dancer; he seemed to take a more athletic approach. Yet he managed to keep time and not step on her toes. "You're light as a feather," he murmured in her ear. "Like a beautiful bird, all in blue and violet." He put his cheek near hers and held her like a boy cherishing a favorite teddy bear. As the music ended, he gave her a quick, enthusiastic hug, and she could feel his heart beating excitedly.

Yet no sooner had they stopped dancing than a woman with a high, nervous laugh swooped over to him and said, "Ricky, dance with *me* now!" and dragged him away.

Annabel stood with her back to the stone balustrades, watching Jack and Téa moving across the dance floor to the admiration of the crowd.

"Hello, ducks!" Elsa Lanchester said in a cheery tone, gliding nearer with a smile. Her curly hair had been tamed into an elegant, upswept swirl tonight. She wore a green gown and a paisley silk shawl with gold fringe.

"Hello! And where is Mr. Laughton?" Annabel asked.

"Oh, some photographer made him pose over there with Norma Shearer, just because they made *The Barretts of Wimpole Street* together," Elsa said tolerantly, nodding in the direction where flashbulbs were popping. "Poor Charles, he's a nervous wreck. It's quite a responsibility, with the *Hunchback* screening kicking off the film festival in a few days. He says that on that big night, he'll simply hide under his seat in the dark."

"Well, he can't do that tonight," Annabel said in amusement, searching the crowd for a glimpse of him. "He's the guest of honor at the Grand Hotel!"

Elsa spoke sotto voce. "Charles loves acting, and some people think he's a ham, but I tell you for a fact, he's not so fond of the limelight when he has to play himself among his peers."

"He seems to be holding his own!" Annabel observed, now spotting Charles across the terrace, surrounded by reporters, appearing to answer their questions with aplomb and charm.

Elsa murmured, "Some journalist actually asked him to wear that dreadful Quasimodo costume for publicity shots, but Charles will never climb into the horrid thing again. My dear, it was made of rubber and weighed a ton. They put rubber makeup on his face, too. And they made a hump on his back that was four inches of foam, covered with just a thin layer of rubber 'skin' that went all the way across his bare shoulders and arms."

"That sounds torturous!" Annabel exclaimed.

Elsa lowered her voice and said in contempt, "On top of *that*, the nasty director tied Charles to a revolving wheel and *whipped* him, over and over again, take after take, day after day, and he came home with painful welts on his body, poor lamb."

"Who was the director?" Annabel asked.

"That ghastly Dieterle—we shall never forgive him. Such a strange man. Shows up on the set wearing white gloves, because he's terrified of picking up germs. All sadists and bullies are actually cowards at heart, dearie."

Envisioning the whole scene as Elsa described it, Annabel was both enthralled and horrified. "I'll never be able to think of anything else when I finally see the movie," she said.

Elsa waved her hand. "No, no, it's all just human sacrifice on the altar of art."

Annabel noticed that Jack and Téa had stopped dancing, and Téa, with a charming smile, went over to Herr Hardtman, the man who'd demanded changes to *Love Isn't Easy*.

Jack, unwilling to join Téa with the very man who'd caused the ruination of his first independent film, had crossed the dance floor and was heading toward Annabel.

Seeing him coming so purposefully to her, she felt suddenly lightheaded, torn between sensual attraction and the fear that he might be in cahoots with Téa.

Elsa, observing Jack approaching, whispered knowingly to Annabel, "Handsome curly-headed devil. Just remember—we are *all* only make-believe." And she floated away.

"Annabel, let's dance!" Jack said with his beautiful smile, offering her his arm.

Oncle JP was nowhere to be seen, but she was mindful of

what he'd advised her. *Act normal*, she told herself. So she allowed Jack to lead her out and join the other dancers.

Jack moved in perfect time to the waltz, turning and turning slowly at first, then progressing with the speed of the music. Annabel found her thoughts and feelings whirling, too, in an impossible mix—she felt joyful to be in his arms, yet wondered why he was still involved with Téa. Couldn't he see that Téa belonged with Herr Ubel and his friends?

"What's the matter?" Jack asked, drawing his head back to get a good look at Annabel. "Are you all right? You feel so tense."

She could bear it no longer. She had to know the truth. "Where do your loyalties lie?" she said, looking him straight in the eye. "With the free world—or with Nazi Germany?"

He looked astounded. "What's come over you?" he inquired.

"Why do you love Téa? Don't you know what she really is?"

"What do you mean?" he asked, wary now.

Annabel could not go so far as to say *She's a spy for Hitler!* But she surprised herself by blurting out, "Well, for one thing, Téa—she—she assaulted me at the villa!"

"*What?*" Jack asked, bewildered. "You can't possibly be serious!"

Feeling defensive, she told him that Téa had drugged her, undressed her, and sexually attacked her. "She behaved worse than Alan!"

The music stopped, and there was a brief silence before the band started again with a new tune.

Looking deeply concerned, Jack led Annabel to the other end of the terrace, where they could speak in private. "I don't know what happened to you, but it couldn't have been Téa."

"It was too," Annabel said stubbornly. "She was horrible to me. You should have heard her voice that day, so shrill and—and—angry. Of course, she acts sweet as pie when *you're* around. But she was like a completely different person when she had me alone!"

A light seemed to break across Jack's face. He glanced over his shoulder and said in a low tone, "Listen. I'm going to tell you something you mustn't tell another soul. I think the person you saw was Téa's brother, Georg." He pronounced it the German way, *Gay-org.* "He was in prison in Germany. Téa's been sick about it, but she finally got him out—for now, anyway."

Annabel sucked in her breath. "Her brother!" she repeated. Then she realized that Jack *had* told her about Téa's family back in Berlin.

"Yes. He's a rather brilliant scientist, but also unstable, as brilliant people can be sometimes. Especially when being bullied! You can imagine what the fascists want from him."

Jack gazed out toward the sea. "Herr Ubel and his gang brought her brother to Monte Carlo, but at first they only allowed Téa to see him on Herr Volney's yacht. She finally got them to let Georg come ashore here and spend a day with her at the villa. But they've still got him on a short leash. That's why Téa has to make nice with the Nazis. Those bastards have been using the situation to yank *her* chain the whole time we've been here."

Annabel observed him guardedly. Clearly he trusted Téa utterly. Was he deliberately "looking the other way" about the strange goings-on, as so many people did nowadays, or was he simply blinded by Téa's overwhelming vulnerability?

Looking sympathetic now, Jack said, "I'm sorry you were at the villa when Georg was. He shouldn't have fooled around with you. Téa and her brother used to play tricks on people, pretending to be each other, taking turns, as it were. They've been doing that for years, because they look so much alike in that ethereal way, same hair, same eyes. When they were kids, Téa's mother actually dressed them up in identical clothes, as if they were twins: as two boys on one day, and then as two girls the next day. Really screwed them up. Their mother died in an asylum. Georg never really got over that. He makes a lot of emotional demands on Téa, and he's jealous. Because he's never really been able to fend for himself."

Annabel thought of the rough hands that had shaken her during that drugged episode on the sofa. And the voice that was like Téa's—and yet so unlike it, so demanding and angry, but somehow frantic and pleading at the same time. It was not the voice she'd just heard in the villa, though. Something else was going on there that clearly Jack knew nothing about.

"But Téa and Georg *both* attacked me that awful night," she told him.

Jack felt her shudder and said gently, "It's hard to understand, I know, but try to. Berlin was a pretty weird, perverted place after the Great War. The fat cats got fatter and the poor were starving, so people did what they had to do to entertain the wealthy and catch whatever scraps they threw. That's why Téa left. When she came to Hollywood, she had to leave her brother behind, and he didn't handle it well. They'd been so close, and she was his anchor. But she sent him money and thought he was safe in Germany—until the Nazis put him in jail for 'lewd behavior, moral delinquency, gross indecency, and perversion.'"

"Oh," Annabel said quietly. "Yes, I've heard of that awful law."

"The Nazis keep telling Téa that the only way her brother will be truly safe is if she returns to Berlin to make films and propaganda for Hitler; they say she and Georg can live in style and comfort there for the rest of their lives," Jack said darkly.

Annabel felt that things were making sense, in a ghastly way. Having just found out that Herr Ubel had been the man in the satyr mask at the masked ball, she knew only too well what a bully he could be. He'd literally shoved her into a corner to imperiously demand that she do what he wanted. *Herr Ubel saw me in Téa's costume, so I bet he thought he was dancing with Téa and he was threatening her*, she thought.

Jack took her by the shoulders and gazed deeply into her

eyes. "I'm telling you all this because I know you are a good person at heart—so you *must* keep this to yourself, promise? For Téa's sake and mine. Can we count on you?"

Annabel said gently, "Téa's been pretty cozy with those guys tonight—maybe she's already made up her mind to go back to Germany."

"No, no! Téa's only pretending to go along with them, but she's *really* hoping to convince them to let her take her brother to America with us, right after the film festival. We all want to put Europe behind us, for good!"

"But—what about your new film at Sainte-Agnès? Aren't you going to stay here and shoot it?" Annabel asked in a small voice, thinking, *Wouldn't you rather stay in France with me?*

"Europe is finished," he said flatly. "For now, anyway. I can shoot a lot of that film on a Hollywood studio set."

An errant, chill breeze made Annabel shiver. She glanced across the terrace and saw that Téa and Herr Ubel's group were no longer standing over by the bar but were leaving the terrace. "And where is Téa going now?" she asked pointedly.

"There's a party on that film guy's yacht—Herr Volney's—they're celebrating something, probably somebody's birthday, so Téa must make an appearance, to stay in their good graces."

Annabel felt so impatient now that she wanted to blurt out, *But Téa is doing more than that to keep the Nazis happy! She killed the tennis player and stole his codebook and hid it in that fashionable luggage of hers. You really think she and her brother molested me just for fun? They wanted to know what I did with the Enigma machine.* But Oncle JP had sworn her to secrecy.

So all she could do was say angrily, "Open your eyes, Jack! She's one of *them*! Don't you even care that she may be working against France and the entire free world?"

Jack looked truly alarmed. "Please, Annabel! Don't say things like that. If you go around spreading rumors about Téa, I'll *never* get her out of France!"

As they stood staring at each other, Annabel heard a low rumble of thunderclouds. But now Jack seemed to comprehend that she might know a lot more than she was letting on.

"Is there something else that you're not telling me?" he demanded.

"I can't give you the details," she said earnestly. "I can only say that Téa is just *not* the person you think she is. She belongs to those thugs—not to you."

He drew in his breath. "Well, if an innocent girl like you believes such things, then whatever Téa is being forced to do, her cover is blown. She can't stay here at the Grand Hotel."

Lightning suddenly split the sky, and there was an enormous clap of thunder. The guests shrieked like excited children, covering their ears. The storm was creeping closer, like a prowling beast. Annabel noticed that the heavens had blackened with quick-moving clouds that looked ready to explode. And the sea had turned a steely, battleship grey, its waves roiling and crashing in a spray of angry white foam against the rocky coves.

As everyone looked up, another enormous bolt of lightning flashed in a fiery branch, looking as if it had just torn the curtain of the sky in two. Then there was a cracking sound and an earthshaking thud, like the fall of a giant's dead body.

"Watch out!" someone shouted, for a tree had been struck and fallen right near the hotel; and on its way down, part of it had hit the side door that led to the kitchen, damaging the door so that it fell off, exposing the little hallway to the kitchen.

The kitchen crew had just hauled the tower of lobster crates from the chilled pantry to the hall, but the broken door caused the whole tower to topple over and crash open.

"Look!" Annabel exclaimed as, incredibly, the lobsters themselves broke free, so desperate were they to escape from all the terrifying noise and confusion of the storm and the flurry of workers all around them.

Now the lawn seemed to be filled with escaping lobsters

as they streamed across it, instinctively heading for the sea. It was a sight that, for the rest of her life, Annabel would never forget—all those terrified, hard-shelled creatures scurrying for freedom.

At first, everyone just stared in disbelief as the kitchen staff went chasing after them, their white uniforms bobbing across the lawn. Then the guests began to shriek as they, too, dashed out after the madly escaping lobsters, as if everyone were on a scavenger hunt.

The women in chiffon dresses flitted down the main path amid shrieks of laughter. Annabel saw a few men drunkenly staggering up the lawn, brandishing their shellfish captives and yelling, "Got one!"

But then the clouds finally burst, and the rain came down hard in sudden, heavy sheets. Everyone shouted and made a run for cover, back to the hotel.

All except Jack. He had been momentarily distracted by the sight of the lobsters, but now he was evidently thinking hard. Unexpectedly he kissed Annabel, as if he really meant it.

"*Adieu*, darling," he said softly, turning away.

"Wait—where are you going in this pouring rain?" she exclaimed, putting a hand on his arm to detain him. They were both getting soaked, but she refused to budge.

"To find Téa. The Nazis were celebrating tonight. Maybe something's really up this time," he said worriedly. "And it might be a trap for Téa. If she gets on their boat, she may never be able to get out of Europe and come back to the States. We can't wait until the end of the film festival. She's got to get out, *now*."

"Jack, please—just let her go!" Annabel said urgently, still holding his arm.

He shook her off, more roughly and decisively now. "Go inside, sweet girl. Be safe."

And he turned and ran out into the night and the pouring

rain. Annabel stood there, staring, until someone put a hand on her shoulder.

"Your uncle is looking for you," Scott said. "Come on, Annabel. Come in from the rain."

———

In the cool marble lobby, Elsa and Charles Laughton had escaped the downpour and were watching events unfold. Now Elsa spotted Annabel, so she took off her pretty evening shawl to put it round Annabel's shivering shoulders.

"Mustn't catch a cold, ducks," Elsa said gently. "Heartache is one thing—you can get over that—but pneumonia's a real killer."

The other guests poured into the lobby and were milling about, chattering excitedly, waiting out the rain. But the storm, which had come so quickly, was already abating.

Annabel hurried into her uncle's office. He had been giving instructions to the head waiters to usher the crowd to the indoor restaurant.

Now he turned his attention to Annabel.

"Thanks to you," Oncle JP said in a low voice, "we have photographed everything we needed, and the codebook has been returned by the maid to where you said it belonged."

Annabel quickly told him about her conversation with Jack, fearing that her uncle would scold her for having revealed too much about their suspicions. But Oncle JP seemed oddly resigned. "Téa Marlo doesn't matter now. All things will have to take their course."

"Oncle, what do you know?" Annabel asked apprehensively.

"The Germans have stepped up their radio activity. So have the Russians," Oncle JP said. "Something is imminent. I was working on this, but now the storm is affecting my radio. But we will keep trying."

"What does it mean?" she asked worriedly.

"We think the Germans and the Soviets have made a deal not to fight each other. If this is so, then Hitler will not have to worry about sending his armies to the Russian front. He can focus on the rest of us. There is nothing to stop him now. War is only a matter of days away—maybe even hours."

CHAPTER 21

Exodus

The next morning, the air was clear and bright, the sea sparkling as if nothing terrible had happened the night before, as if the storm had merely served to clear the air.

But the day's headlines were stark. The Germans had indeed signed a "non-aggression pact" with the Soviet Union. And that, apparently, was enough to send people all along the Riviera scurrying in panic, all at once, to get out of France.

When she showed up for work at the Grand Hotel, Annabel saw the suitcases piling up in the lobby, the telegrams coming and going in a frantic flurry. The reception desk was completely besieged, with loud voices of frightened guests and overwhelmed staff ringing out across the lobby.

"You don't understand! I *must* go, *now!*" they all said, indignant with impossible demands, tearful when told they could not immediately get what they wanted.

The guests were all trying to do the same thing at the same time—book a ticket on any ocean liner or train or plane or even coal ship or fishing boat that would carry them away—but already these were being declared "sold out."

Those who had succeeded in booking passage departed,

mostly in pairs, Annabel noted, as if they were exotic creatures specially chosen to get a seat on Noah's Ark.

Seeing all this, she was reminded of the lobsters scurrying across the lawn trying to escape the storm.

The gossip was flying among remaining guests breakfasting on the terrace while enviously watching luckier, triumphant departing guests fluttering out the door.

"I hear that Winston Churchill left the casino at Monte Carlo and just flew off to London without paying his gambling losses, which they say were *quite* significant," a local dowager said as she dealt out a game of cards to play with her visiting friend. Their jeweled fingers sparkled in the sunlight.

"And what about the Cannes Film Festival?" her companion wondered.

In fact, the management staff of the Grand Hotel had had a quick meeting about that very subject. At first, most events for the *Festival de Cannes* were declared postponed for ten days. But soon it became clear that this, too, would be untenable. People were mournfully saying that the whole idea of the Cannes Film Festival was an infant strangled in its cradle.

Oncle JP told Annabel that Olympia Studios was one of the first to cancel its festival events. "Sonny is ready to cut his losses and get out of Europe. He had already secured a private liner to take all his stars home after the festival anyway," he said, "so now Alan managed to bribe, cajole, and threaten the captain into agreeing to sail ahead of schedule. They sail tonight. Sonny let me know that your services are 'done,' Annabel, so you are assigned to the pool area for the morning shift."

And there she discovered that one single event had not yet been canceled: the screening of the festival's showpiece, *The Hunchback of Notre Dame*. Apparently that was still to take place, making it the gala opening—and probable closing—of the festival.

Therefore, Charles and Elsa were not leaving. Annabel

found the couple sitting stoically and serenely at a table and chairs poolside, wearing sunglasses and hats, and drinking coffee.

"The show *must* go on, so they tell me," Charles said drolly to Annabel, his jowly bulldog face reflecting wry amusement.

"You know, I'm beginning to wonder—*why* must the show go on?" Elsa commented languidly.

Then she sat up suddenly and leaned forward, as they all heard shouting coming from below. It was Yves, the pool director, calling to his lifeguards to abandon the pool area and help him at the swimming cove.

"What's going on?" an older English guest—a walrus of a man with a great big white handlebar mustache—called down to the lifeguards. Someone shouted back at him.

Perplexed, the guest turned to the few people left around the pool and asked, "I say, can someone translate? I can't make out what the devil that lifeguard fellow is trying to say."

Annabel obligingly went to the stone balustrades and peered over. Yves was looking upward, saying in French, "The body of a drowned man has been found on the coastal path."

Dr. Gaspard, emerging from the men's locker room after a swim in the pool, heard this and immediately hurried down toward the lifeguards. Annabel advanced farther so that she could hear what was going on.

She watched Dr. Gaspard disappear around one curve of the coastal walkway and then reappear at another. He moved carefully out among the shoreline rocks, crouched, then lowered himself, evidently to where the body was. Annabel still could not see it.

Elsa had come to the railing. "What happened?" she asked, as one lifeguard shouted to another about what he was being told by the doctor.

Annabel listened and then translated, "The lifeguards thought the man drowned in the storm last night. But now the doctor says no, his neck is broken, so maybe he fell from the cliffs. They say perhaps he'd been drunk and fell down and got washed into the sea. But the tide brought him back."

"How awful! Do they know who he is?" Elsa asked.

Annabel shook her head, and she felt compelled to descend the stone steps and open the gate to the cove. The lifeguards had put the body on the stretcher and were getting in position to carry it up the path. The doctor was about to cover the man's face, but Annabel got there just in time to see it.

The dead man was Jack Cabot, still in his evening clothes from last night.

Yves glanced over at Annabel, and what he saw in her eyes made him look stricken with sudden sympathy. She felt herself slipping, as if the ground beneath her feet were giving way. She'd never fainted before, but now it was as if she were dissolving and being sucked down a drain; she could even hear the suction sound whooshing in her ears. But perhaps it was just the sea.

Someone else caught her before she hit the ground. It was Rick, who'd been jogging along the coastal path and had caught up with this tragedy. When he'd spotted Annabel, he sped over to her.

As she came back to full consciousness, Annabel felt herself being lifted up by strong arms, and then she was bobbing up and down as Rick hurriedly carried her back up to the hotel, just as he'd carried little Delphine.

Yves had telephoned Oncle JP, so he was waiting at the door, and he told Rick to lay Annabel down on the sofa in his office. Dr. Gaspard had followed her and now took her pulse, listened to her heart, looked into her eyes.

"She'll be all right," he concluded. "I must go now and fill out the dead man's medical report." Annabel moaned at the way she was hearing Jack being described.

"Anything I can do?" Rick asked worriedly, gazing at her.

"Thank you, she will be fine. She must rest," Oncle JP said quietly.

"I'll be on the terrace. If you need anything at all, don't hesitate to ask," Rick said as he left. Oncle JP thanked him and moved to shut the door.

But Elsa and Charles had followed her, too, and were hovering worriedly. Now Elsa bustled deliberately past Oncle JP to hand Annabel a glass of water, which she drank slowly.

"I am so sorry about Jack," Elsa said softly, sitting beside her.

Annabel looked up at her uncle, still dazed. "Jack was trying to warn Téa," she said in a choked voice. "To tell her that I knew she was working for the Nazis."

She was past caring who heard her or what secrets she was revealing. She hated the whole rotten world. Especially herself, for causing Jack to panic and go after Téa in the pouring rain. If she hadn't opened her big mouth, surely Jack would not have thrown caution to the winds and dashed away so impetuously.

"Which one is Téa?" Charles asked his wife, baffled.

Elsa said, "You *know*, darling. The one you were admiring at the party last night. The one they call 'the next Garbo.' Although from the sound of things, it turns out Téa was more Mata Hari than actress."

Charles whistled. "A regular female Iago," he marveled.

"Please excuse us now," Oncle JP said. "I must speak with my niece in private."

Elsa rose and said reassuringly to Annabel, "We'll be right outside at the tables on the terrace, pretending to read the newspaper."

Annabel thanked her and watched them go. Then she turned to her uncle and said in an anguished tone, "I told Jack not to go after Téa. I tried to stop him."

Oncle JP said regretfully, "You cannot prevent a man from running headlong into his fate. Sooner or later, he will arrive at the destination that he is determined to reach."

He looked so sympathetic that she instantly said, "I saw Dr. Gaspard whisper something to you. Was it about Jack?"

Her uncle nodded. "He may have been—strangled—before his body fell into the sea."

Annabel received this as another blow upon a bruise. "But why? Why did someone have to—kill *him*?" she said in a burst of fury.

"I imagine that he knew too much about them already," Oncle JP said thoughtfully. "The Nazis don't want some movie star going back to America, where he could run around telling everybody what Téa—and the Nazi spies disguised as helpful Hollywood consultants—are really up to. They want America to stay neutral if Europe goes to war."

"Where is Téa?" Annabel asked suddenly. "Does she even know that Jack—?"

Oncle JP shrugged. "She has left the Grand Hotel. We believe she sailed off with Herr Volney on his yacht, back to Monte Carlo. I would bet that she's ultimately headed for Germany; I sincerely doubt that *we* will ever see her again."

"How do you know all this?" Annabel said dully.

"The studio's chauffeur," Oncle JP said. "Unbeknown to Sonny, the man was working with the fascists all along. He was the voice you heard in the villa, speaking in French. The police caught up with him and are interrogating him still."

Annabel, shocked, recalled the quiet man she'd seen occasionally at the villa, carrying clothes for the actors. *All is ready*, he'd said. She asked in a horrified voice, "Did *he* kill Jack?"

"He denies everything, of course. Says as far as he knew, Téa and Jack both got on that yacht last night. But we'll get the truth out of him yet." Oncle JP sighed. "I won't need you until the lunch and dinner service, Annabel. If there are still guests left here to feed!"

Annabel suddenly remembered Scott. "I have to see if the screenwriter needs anything," she said, rising.

"Are you sure? Your work with him is done," Oncle JP reminded her.

"Yes, I want to say goodbye," she said. Her uncle understood and nodded.

But she also wanted to ask Scott if he'd heard anything more about what happened to Jack last night. So she hurried off to the Jasmine Cottage.

She had to pass the Villa Sanctuaire. When she arrived, the front door was open, and cautiously she went in. Nadia the maid was there—the same woman who'd given Annabel the key so that she could remove the codebook.

For a moment, they both exchanged a look. Then Annabel glanced around, walking through the front rooms, surprised to find the villa so quickly being emptied of the previous tenants' personal possessions, with drawers and closet doors yawning open.

She paused at Téa's bedroom and saw that all of her scarves, her perfume bottles and cosmetics, her shoes, the suitcases, were gone. Only the faint scent of attar of roses remained.

The maid glanced up and said, "Miss Marlo departed sometime last night or early this morning. She left the gowns the studio sent her, so they've been returned to the designers from whom they were borrowed." She lowered her voice. "But last night, before the storm, when I came to return the codebook, her suitcases were still here. So I was able to put the diary back where you found it. When I left the villa, I saw her coming away from the party with Herr Ubel, but they didn't see me. So they won't know that it was ever missing."

Annabel imagined Téa hastily departing in secret, and she thought, *Perhaps that was her plan, all along, to leave with her brother—and without Jack. Does she even know that Jack is dead? Or did she leave because she heard about it? Is she working with his assassins, or did they do it to scare her?*

And yet, she suddenly recalled something Téa had said to her when she sat her down on that sofa: *You can give a man all the adoration and children that he wants.* It struck Annabel that perhaps Téa, in her own strange way, had been giving Jack away to Annabel.

Nadia gestured toward Jack's bedroom. "But Mr. Cabot's things—they are still here. Your uncle has made inquiries, but the head of the studio told us that Mr. Cabot has no living relatives to claim his possessions. The studio doesn't want them, either. I have instructions to pack them all up for the lost-and-found cupboard, in case someone turns up to claim his things—but we will probably end up disposing of it all, if nobody asks for it."

"Wait a moment." Annabel felt that it was her duty to go into Jack's room and examine what was there. She felt as if she were protecting him somehow.

Immediately upon entering his bedroom, she could feel his presence and was overwhelmed again as she stared at his things. His clothes, his shoes, his panama hat. His sunglasses. Some cuff links, a wristwatch. Soap and aftershave. His comb-and-brush set, neatly arranged in a black, silk-lined lacquer box. All looking so normal, awaiting his return.

Annabel sank down on the bed. A sudden clear thought had entered her mind, and now it seemed to make her heart swell as if it would burst: *Why didn't I ever tell Jack that I love him?*

She'd been too fearful that such a declaration might put him off and cause him to say something she didn't want to hear. How utterly silly that was. Ultimately it would surely not have made a difference if she'd declared her love; she knew that. And yet, at this moment, it would have been the only thing that might console her right now, to know that she had unreservedly given him all that she had to give.

Her sorrow was so overwhelming that she couldn't move, just sat there like these few touchingly modest possessions of his, mutely waiting for his return. The clothes still smelled like him. The jaunty hat and sunglasses seemed still imbued with his bright energy.

And his camera bags. She reached out to touch them.

She remembered the fun they'd had shooting some film at Sainte-Agnès, with all the twisty narrow streets, and the old stone church with the sonorous bell in its ancient tower. She could not bear to lose all that. So she picked up the camera bags and film, and then, at the last minute, she took his handkerchief with his initials monogrammed on them in dark blue. *J.C.*

The maid had been busy in Téa's room, changing the bedding, polishing the furniture surfaces. Now she looked up at Annabel without asking any questions. They merely nodded to each other, as if they'd both been assigned to give some kind of last rites to the dead.

———

At the Jasmine Cottage, Scott was packing up, too. He'd already thrown his clothes into the open suitcases rather quickly and haphazardly. But now he was patiently, methodically sorting through his papers, pens, and notebooks with special care. *Like a priest undressing the altar after Mass*, Annabel thought, admiring Scott for the things he valued, even when the world was going all to hell around him.

He seemed relieved to see her. "Annabel!" he exclaimed. "Are you all right?"

She nodded. Scott said ruefully, "It's like the Great War all over again. But strangely enough, I feel revitalized instead of defeated. Animal instinct, I suppose."

"Can I get you anything?" Annabel asked. "Do you need a ticket, a taxi—?"

"It's all done. I'm sailing with Sonny's crowd," he announced. "That's one good thing about being under contract. Sonny feels he hasn't wrung the last drop of work out of me yet. He'll have me doing rewrites across the Atlantic, even if the Germans torpedo us all the way. Well, I figure I'd be lucky to even get a seat on the poop deck."

He paused, his eyes alight, as if suddenly struck with a great idea. "Why don't you come with me?" he suggested. "I'm sure I could say you're my secretary and get you a seat. Or else you can just be a stowaway. Once we're miles out to sea, you're home free. Come with me to Hollywood, and help me finish my secret novel."

Annabel shook her head sorrowfully. Scott said softly, "I'm sorry about Jack."

With a small gulp, Annabel sank onto the sofa and burst into tears, the first ones she'd shed since finding Jack's body. Scott said in some alarm, "There, there, now!" and sat down beside her, holding her hand and letting her cry until her tears were spent.

"Annabel, you're a very remarkable girl," Scott said finally. "You are bright and talented and beautiful. You may be feeling very old at the moment, but you *are* young, and where there's youth, there's always hope. Even though this world we've shared may come to an end, take it from me—nothing lasts forever, not even war. One day the whole mess will be over. You'll drift around like a sleepwalker for a while, trying to figure it all out. Well, don't bother—it can't be done. I went through all of this in that last war, so I know, believe me. But then, one day, the sun comes out again—you feel it on your face, you breathe in the new, clean air, and you're so damned glad. Because for you, life is just beginning. Trust your old Uncle Scott."

"You're so nice," Annabel said quietly.

"Sure I am. If you ever get lonesome, come look me up. Anytime."

He hesitated, then leaned over and kissed her on the cheek. Then he rose, to finish packing up his pages, his manuscripts, his letters, his ledger, and his dreams.

She watched as the porter came for his bags, and Scott tipped him generously, as if he were glad to do it. She'd seldom seen a rich man be so happy to share his money like that.

On his way out, Scott doffed his hat at Annabel with a wide grin. "You know what they say. 'See you in church,'" he said jauntily.

And he went off down the pebbled path, whistling. She sat there listening, until he was gone.

———

The official opening-night screening for the first Cannes Film Festival took place on August 31 with *The Hunchback of Notre Dame*. Annabel attended it with Oncle JP and Rick, thanks to Elsa, who'd secured balcony seats for them. There were still a lot of people here—mostly those who'd expatriated to France years ago and simply refused to leave their beloved Riviera residences—so the theatre was filled with an eager audience.

Annabel peered down at Charles and Elsa when they made their entrance, looking so glamorous as they walked inside amid flashbulbs popping, until they reached their orchestra-level seats and graciously bowed before sitting down.

The lights dimmed, a curtain rose, and a hush fell over the theatre as Victor Hugo's great novel sprang to life on the screen. Annabel gasped when she first saw Charles, for she could barely recognize him in his Quasimodo costume and makeup. The poor Hunchback's face was all twisted, his nose like a pig's, his eyes and mouth barely able to move at first.

But soon Annabel saw Charles's compassion, intelligence, and wit shining through the sad creature's eyes, lighting up the face of the Hunchback. His voice was low and humble. With his every gesture Charles gave the poor, bent body of the bell ringer the breath of life. In this fine actor's skillful hands, the suffering Hunchback became the real hero of the story, more so than the dashing man whom the gypsy girl fell in love with.

The young and beautiful Maureen O'Hara made a compelling heroine, but Annabel couldn't help giggling when she first saw her, thinking of what Elsa had said: *I don't trust a girl who does such fastidious sewing. Nice, neat, tiny little stitches. Only nuns and murderesses can make such perfect stitches.*

And Annabel winced throughout the terrible scene when the Hunchback was tied to a wheel and publicly whipped. With each lash she remembered what Elsa had said about how painful that scene had been for Charles to endure.

But throughout the film he was astonishingly graceful and acrobatic as he leaped about the towers of Notre Dame cathedral and rang its big bells, illustrating the childlike pathos of his character, leading up to the breathtaking moment when all seemed lost for the gypsy girl, and even her handsome hero could not save her from the gallows—so it was Quasimodo who rescued her, jumping on a rope and, in one long great swing, heroically scooping the gypsy off the scaffolding and away from the hangman, whisking her back to the safety of his bell tower sanctuary.

Finally, when the humble creature had to watch the girl go off happily with the young man she loved, leaving the cathedral and her silent admirer behind, there was one last brilliant moment. The Hunchback sat high on the ramparts beside a stone gargoyle, watching the girl who was far below on the ground walking away from him forever—and now Charles delivered the final line of the film, with painful, perfect feeling, as the heartbroken bell ringer voiced his agony to the impassive gargoyle figure on the cathedral tower beside him:

"Why was I not made of stone like thee?"

Annabel felt his grief as her own. As she sat there quietly in the dark, mourning the loss of Jack, tears spilled out of her eyes, and for a moment she wished that she were made of stone, too—but no, no, not really. For grief was still a form of love, and love was clearly the only way to survive in a world of cruelty.

Afterward, Elsa and Charles were whisked off to a gala dinner, surrounded by a mob of admirers and press. As the audience filed out behind them, Annabel still felt the emotion of the movie and the thrill of being here to see it on this special night.

"Say, Annabel," Rick said, appearing at her side like an eager dog, "I and some of my friends are going off to a party at the casino in Monte Carlo. Want to join us?"

Annabel still associated Monte Carlo with Téa, even though Oncle JP had told her that he believed that Téa was long gone by now.

"No, thank you, Rick," Annabel said gently. "I need to be near my family tonight."

He seemed to understand.

Oncle JP turned to Annabel and said, "Tonight, you and I will take a taxi home. But we must first stop at the Grand Hotel."

Little Delphine was already home after having had an early supper with the neighbor who cared for her, and then Delphine had been tucked into her own bed. Oncle JP was eager to dispense with his duties and return home to her.

"I have to check in with my associates," he explained to Annabel as he unlocked his office door. "I will be in the radio room. You wait here."

For a short while, Annabel remained on the sofa in his office, dozing a little. When her uncle returned from that mysterious room at the top of the spiral staircase, she jerked awake with a start. Oncle JP looked preoccupied and grave.

"What is it?" Annabel said, alert now.

"We know nothing new yet," he said cautiously. "We can only wait. And hope."

"Doesn't the codebook help you intercept messages?" she asked.

"Well, we aren't picking up any messages tonight. Our Nazi guests have all checked out. Anyway, that codebook is only good for the month of August. Tomorrow, you see, is September first, so the codebook will be useless then. But perhaps our fellow code breakers in London might be able to work with our replica machine and the old codebook to uncover more secrets of the Enigma and ultimately to 'break' it. Perhaps one day, we will even invent a machine more clever—and diabolical—that will render the Enigma an open secret."

Their taxi had waited, and they now drove through the quiet streets in silence. The first stop was Annabel's rooming house. Oncle JP had told her she could stay with him tonight, but she knew that they didn't really have space for her, and she said, "I'll be all right in my room."

"I would like to buy a little house hidden up in the hills, where you and I and Delphine could be safe," Oncle JP said suddenly, as Annabel bade him good night. It was the first time she'd ever heard this modest man express a longing for something he didn't have.

Upstairs in her room, Annabel was so tired that she undressed automatically and then tumbled into bed. She fell asleep instantly.

The next day, the news was everywhere, in the boarding-house and out on the streets.

Germany had attacked Poland this morning.

CHAPTER 22

Come September

On that first day of September, Annabel could see the irony of the new film festival—a gathering for peace, freedom, and good-will—being canceled for an imminent world war.

But it could no longer be avoided. Every bit of strength had to be mustered for a tragedy that had already begun, at the ungodly hour of 4:45 a.m., when a Nazi warship opened fire on a depot in Poland's Free City of Danzig.

"Typical of the tight-assed fascists, to wake everybody up before dawn, just to start a war," Raphael the concierge grumbled that day. "You'd think they'd at least let those people have their breakfast before being bombed into rubble."

The last departing German guests were also not the least bit enthusiastic about the prospect of another war and returning home to a country where, as Marta told Annabel, the Berlin housewives were already being forced to line up to get ration cards.

"They'll have to deal with a black market, all over again, just to feed their families," Marta said resignedly, thinking of all the friends she'd left behind.

Suddenly on the Côte d'Azur, there were French soldiers

everywhere—camped out in tents in the woods, driving in jeeps down the boulevards, marching past merchants on the streets. The Mound at the top of the *Cap* had been turned into a complete military fortification now, with trucks filled with serious-looking uniformed soldiers coming and going.

The Grand Hotel was eerily quiet, as if those who remained were collectively holding their breath and praying for the impossible—a last-minute reprieve, the world returning to its senses. Yet already, every male of draft age had been called up to register and prepare for war. So the staff was being severely depleted of its young men—bellboys, porters, waiters, lifeguards, valets, bartenders, kitchen help. Only the elder male workers could remain.

But it didn't seem to matter, because there were hardly any guests left to serve; and those who were still here were floating about in a daze, too stunned to make many demands. The lobby seemed to ring with its own hollow emptiness. The only chatter was in the restaurants and bars, and even here, people spoke in hushed tones as if in a funeral parlor.

The Jasmine Cottage and the Villa Sanctuaire were clean and neatly ready for new guests—but the doors were locked, the windows shuttered.

Down by the sea, the big swimming pool lay still as glass, except for an occasional soft splash of a lone swimmer slicing through the water.

"There are machine gunners posted along the cliffs, and they even put antiaircraft units at the little road leading to the lighthouse," Yves, the pool director, told Annabel, raising his gaze to scan the hills above them. Because of a knee injury he had not been summoned to fight. He gestured at the sea. "The waters along the coast are being planted with mines."

Annabel, gazing at the sparkling sea, imagined that the baffled fish were wondering what had possessed humanity to destroy its own paradise.

She had taken Delphine for an early swim in the pool before

its opening hour. It was against the rules, but Annabel didn't care; she simply could not bring herself to go down to the swimming cove, and she averted her eyes from the coastal path because she knew she could still "see" Jack lying there on the stretcher. He had been buried in a cemetery at a nearby town that overlooked the sea. Annabel, Oncle JP, and the priest were the only ones in attendance.

"Everyone's so quiet!" Delphine said in a scared, hushed voice as Annabel wheeled her back to the hotel. The fisherman, who'd just made a small delivery today, took the little girl back home, where she would play with her friend who lived nearby and whose mother would look after them. Delphine's school had postponed its opening day.

Annabel helped out at the reservations desk that morning, assisting the few remaining guests to secure their train tickets, which were as rare as rubies now. At noon, she went to work at the bar on the terrace, where luncheon was being served. There were more diners than she'd expected; local people who'd remained at their villas now seemed to want one another's company in the safety of a hotel restaurant where information could be exchanged.

She saw Dr. Gaspard calmly taking his *déjeuner* today just as he usually did twice a week. But this time he had the company of two men who were both fastidiously dressed with silk ascots and handkerchiefs: a tall, rather dapper-looking gentleman who looked to be in his mid-sixties and had a wrinkled, watchful face just like the stone frog on the fountain; and his companion, a younger man with a neatly trimmed mustache and a cigarette poised between his long fingers. All three men sat there smoking, drinking, and talking in low voices.

"Who is that distinguished-looking older man with Dr. Gaspard?" Annabel whispered to an elderly waiter.

"He's the playwright William Somerset Maugham. He has a splendid villa overlooking Villefranche." The waiter gave Annabel a sly look. "He's with British intelligence, they say."

Annabel had heard about Maugham from Elsa Lanchester, who'd said that the man had had a "rather Dickensian childhood" after his beloved mother died and he was sent from the Parisian home he'd loved to his dour uncle's vicarage in England. *That's when the poor fellow started stuttering*, Elsa had told her. *Childhood trauma, you know.*

The diners ate quietly, their silence punctuated by occasional comments that carried across the terrace. The younger man seated at Maugham's side was telling Dr. Gaspard, "The lobby of the Carlton Hotel is mobbed. People convene there, waiting to get out. And Willie and I saw invalids being brought down to the piers on stretchers, desperate for the last ships out. Some will stop at Gibraltar to refuel. We're going to sail Willie's yacht as far as it will take us."

Mr. Maugham said to the doctor, "I once v-v-very nearly drowned in a tidal wave off Burma, so I have had a fear of d-d-drowning ever since. If our s-s-ship is attacked by the Germans and starts sinking, what's the b-b-best way to drown, do you suppose?"

Dr. Gaspard put his fork down. "Don't struggle," he advised. "You see, if you just open your mouth and let the sea in, you will go unconscious within a minute."

Then Marta, the reservations manager, came to the hotel doorway leading out to the terrace. "Dr. Gaspard, please come at once!" she said, her usual composure altered just enough so that Annabel instinctively hurried over.

"What is it?" she asked in dread.

Marta said, "It's your uncle, Annabel. He's had some sort of attack."

———

It was Rick who volunteered to drive Annabel to the hospital, in his sporty red car. This was a godsend, since most forms of transportation—trains, autos, even horses—were being commandeered by the military. Rick followed the ambulance through the clogged traffic that had complicated the usual route.

On the way, he astounded Annabel by actually confessing to her—all the while with both hands on the steering wheel and eyes forward—that he loved her.

"You can't be serious," Annabel said. "Stop it."

"No, I mean it," Rick insisted. "I was hooked the first day I saw you—*heard* you, actually, singing French lullabies to little Delphine. I've been smitten ever since. You're beautiful, Annabel, and you're exactly what I want for a wife. I was just waiting for things to blow over with you and—"

"Please!" Annabel said abruptly, unable to hear him speak of Jack.

"Right. Well, I told myself that if you were free by the end of the summer, I'd marry you and take care of you. I thought I'd wine and dine you, but now there's a war, well, there isn't any time to waste, is there? So come away with me to America, where you'll be safe and comfortable, for the rest of your life. Marry me!"

"For God's sake," she exclaimed as Rick careened into the parking lot of the hospital, "I can't think about anything else right now except my uncle."

"We can take him with us!" Rick exclaimed jubilantly. "And Delphine, too. You are the family I've always wanted."

"You'll change your mind after you take some time to seriously think this over."

"No!" he assured her. "I've waited long enough. I only held out this long because your uncle said to wait until September, when you turn twenty-one—and then, he says, you can do what you want. You see, I've already asked his permission. He says it will be up to you."

Annabel distractedly sensed that there was a bargain being offered here. Something to do with the Grand Hotel and her uncle's position there. She realized that she must tread carefully at a time like this, when the whole world was on the brink of self-destruction and no one could afford to refuse a helping hand.

"Can we please discuss this later?" she said more gently.

"Of course. Meanwhile, I'll wait for you in the hospital lounge off the lobby. Holler if you need me to shout at the doctors or to get you any other help with your uncle."

Annabel remained in the waiting room for hours, because the hospital had to run tests. She was not permitted to see her uncle until the doctors got some answers. Rick returned twice, to bring coffee and to get an "update." Then he went out for dinner, promising to bring her back a sandwich.

She had no appetite but was feeling strangely passive, in the way that waiting people can succumb to the combination of anxiety and boredom. Finally she was told that she could go in.

"How is he, Doctor?" she asked, pausing in the hallway.

"Well, you know, he's had that hereditary heart condition. We always knew it could be trouble," Dr. Gaspard began.

Annabel's heart sank. She'd heard something just like this before, when her father died.

"He's going to be all right, for now. What he really needs is the care of a certain sanatorium in Switzerland which I've told him about. But for the time being, he must stay home until I feel it's safe for him to make such a journey."

What hung in the air, unspoken, was that, quite soon, it might be impossible for anyone to travel anywhere at all, if France officially declared war on Germany.

"I'll keep him here in the hospital for a day or two, but we may become overwhelmed soon, and I don't want your uncle to be here when *that* happens. He's already like a horse champing at the bit to go back to work," Dr. Gaspard said with some admiration. "Perhaps it's best to get him back to the Grand Hotel as soon as possible and let him recuperate there. Otherwise, he'll just lie here chewing his heart out. But he mustn't overdo it, Annabel. You must be vigilant. Don't let him work his usual hours; don't let him climb stairs or get distressed."

The doctor left, and Annabel was finally allowed into her uncle's room.

Oncle JP, his hair slightly mussed, was sitting up in his bed looking furious, having been forced to wear a hospital gown. His severe attitude seemed incongruous here as he sat there frowning, with feathers ruffled, like a displaced, disgruntled owl. Annabel sat in a chair alongside his bed, taking his hand. He let her hold it.

"How do you feel?" she asked softly.

"Like a fool," Oncle JP replied. "A useless fool. At a critical time like this! For all I know, the German tanks are already rolling into France, and I can't do a thing about it."

"But we have the Maginot Line," Annabel said hopefully. "People are saying that we can hold off the Germans for at least six months."

Oncle JP looked her in the eye. "That is a fairy tale that certain men in our government recite to the populace like a bedtime story. Meanwhile, there are *other* forces in France that *want* Hitler to take over and 'straighten us out.' You can't fight a war if some of your leaders secretly wish to ally with such a man. No, I give us a month at best to hold the Maginot Line."

"You're scaring me," Annabel said.

"Good. You *should* be frightened," Oncle JP said with some passion. "If more people in this country feared fascism, we'd all be better off. Our soldiers and sailors will fight bravely, when the time comes, but some of their leaders have already failed them."

Annabel found it all so nightmarishly inconceivable. Would France be taken over, like Czechoslovakia, Austria, Poland? How could that possibly be? Marta at the front desk had warned her: *It can happen anywhere.*

Oncle JP looked so agitated and disgusted that she said

soothingly, "You mustn't upset yourself. We will survive this, all of us, together."

He gazed at her compassionately now. "You should go back to America with that screenwriter you work for; or with Rick, or anybody who can get you a ticket out," he urged. "And don't wait to do it. Go *now*. You may not get another chance."

Annabel considered this. Suddenly the life of a secretary in New York no longer seemed drab. It sounded incredibly more hopeful than staying here, waiting for war. But she said in a light, teasing tone, "Oncle, then who would take care of you? That nice widow in Èze?"

He looked embarrassed, then recovered and said calmly, "*Non*. She left France two weeks ago. She's gone to Quebec in Canada, to live with her daughter and son-in-law."

For some reason, it was this bit of news, more than everything else, that suddenly made Annabel understand what was at stake. She thought of the terrible things she'd heard that the Nazis did to anyone and everyone that they didn't like; the thuggish way that "might made right" in Germany. She recalled how those arrogant men in the garden had scorned the crippled Delphine at the fountain; she shuddered at the thought of what might happen to that sweet, gentle little girl and to Oncle JP if they were left to fend for themselves in France. The fascists had killed Jack. They would kill anybody.

Somehow, she had to help get her family to a safe place. There was, as Oncle JP had warned, no time to lose.

"Go to America," he repeated softly now.

Annabel said firmly, "I will never leave you and little Delphine behind."

———

Two days later, the British government sent Hitler an ultimatum. As the world awaited his reply, Oncle JP was released from the hospital and brought back to the Grand Hotel. Rick drove him there and helped to get Oncle JP situated in his office.

"I'll be up in the penthouse," Rick said to Annabel. "Let's talk later, okay?"

"Yes," she replied, reminding herself that this was a time when one needed all the friends one could get.

As soon as Rick left, Oncle JP said quickly to her, "They won't let me climb stairs. But someone must go up to my radio room and see if there is anything they want us to do. I am going to tell you how to operate that radio, Annabel. Just do as I say, nothing more."

She listened intently to his instructions, then went up the spiral staircase to the tiny locked room. At first, just putting on the headphones and switching on that radio was a terrifying task, to communicate with people who were already preparing for war. It seemed as if she could *feel* the rest of the world reaching out to her across the airwaves, asking for help.

Carefully, she gave the coded greeting, waited for a response, and then diligently took their message. Then she removed the headphones, switched off the radio, locked the door behind her, and hurried down the stairs to her uncle's office.

He was sitting at his desk, but already he looked tired.

Annabel told him breathlessly, "Paris and London agree. They want us to get 'the Polish package' out of France. I assume that means the Enigma replica, right?"

"Yes," Oncle JP said, looking troubled. "Our replica is destined to go to London. But we can't use ordinary channels, especially now, because there are German spies everywhere, and they will be looking for anyone who appears to be a courier or an agent."

At that moment, there was a knock at the door, and a woman poked her head in.

Elsa Lanchester's wild reddish hair was topped with a small

round hat at the crown of her head, making her look all the more like a Girl Scout leader.

"Sorry to disturb!" she trilled in that high, theatrical voice. "But we simply couldn't leave without saying goodbye to our dear girl from the Grand Hotel."

She smiled at Annabel, then turned to Oncle JP. "And how is the patient? Are you feeling better?"

"Yes, thank you," he said, looking nonplussed at such a lively, forthright creature. "Do you have everything you need?"

Charles Laughton peered over Elsa's shoulder and said, "Yes. We have somehow managed to secure seats on a private flight to London. We are told that one must bring cotton wads for one's ears on the aeroplane," he added, a trifle apprehensively, his plump face puckered with thought. "To drown out the roar of the engine, you see."

"Yes, and I hear that the pilot has to use a small megaphone just to communicate with his passengers!" Elsa said, wide eyed. "I daresay that if Charles gets hold of that megaphone, he'll be reciting Hamlet's soliloquy over the English Channel."

"Do you suppose you could take one more passenger?" Oncle JP said suddenly. "My niece needs to get to London. She has a friend there awaiting a birthday gift from us."

Annabel just stared at him, astounded. "I can't leave you, Oncle, just for a package," she insisted. She meant it. She was not going to save the world only to lose him and Delphine.

"Besides," she said meaningfully, "if I leave, someone might notice and follow me." She did not have to say aloud what else she was thinking: *The Nazi spies might still think that I was the tennis player's contact here in France.*

"My, that sounds ever so cryptic," Elsa observed, exchanging a meaningful look with Charles, which they held for a brief time, as if they comprehended somehow that Annabel's mysterious errand had to do with the fate of France, of their country, of the free world. Slowly, Charles and Elsa nodded to each other.

"Now what about this birthday person of yours, waiting for a gift from you? Perhaps we might carry this little parcel for you?" Charles suggested. "Would that help resolve your dilemma?"

Oncle JP looked at Annabel inquiringly. She knew what he was asking her. *Can these people be trusted?*

"Yes," Annabel said firmly.

"*Eh bien*, if you would be so kind," Oncle JP said, turning to Charles now, man to man. "As long as you don't mind taking a certain amount of risk. I do not think you will be in any real danger, but one must be careful. Your government, and ours, would be most grateful."

"Ahhh!" Elsa interjected, then said softly and wisely, "Well, I assure you, I am very good at cloak-and-dagger. Apart from being an actress, you know. As a child, I, and my mother, managed to give many a landlord the slip when our rent was a tad overdue."

Charles rolled his eyes. "I always knew it would come to something like this. Elsa is descended from a long line of renegades and radicals. Her father was a labor organizer, and her mother was a suffragist who made the headlines—people still speak of that court case, to this very day. As for me, well, I come from a family of hoteliers. Modest ones, but we did face our share of—occasional *dilemmas*, shall we say; and so, as a young man, I was the family bouncer. Therefore, I assure you, I can toss out the worst of troublemakers and give as good as I get. In short, you can count on our unwavering support."

"Bravo!" Oncle JP said with a smile. "May I ask, where is your luggage at the moment?"

"Upstairs in our room, all set," Elsa said briskly. "We haven't yet called for the porter."

"I will take care of that," Oncle JP said. "But first, if you would be so kind as to wait in your room for Annabel, who will bring the package to you. It must be secured amidst other rather innocent items, so that it will not be noticed."

"Good show!" Charles said. "See you upstairs."

When they were gone, Oncle JP sighed. "I suppose you are right, Annabel. No one would suspect that couple of carrying one of the most important items of military intelligence. I just hope they don't overdo their performance."

"Not them," she assured him. "Those two are pros."

———

Soon afterward, Annabel entered the service elevator carrying the Enigma replica, all closed up in its wooden case. When she reached the Laughtons' room, she saw that the tray of coffee she'd ordered for them had already been delivered. She'd also had the chef pack some sandwiches and cookies into a box for later, with a small bottle of wine.

Charles thanked her profusely for her thoughtfulness. She smiled, feeling a burst of affection for these two, with all their boundless enthusiasm, stoicism, and good cheer.

Elsa stared at the valise in fascination.

"Mercy, that *is* a sizable package," she observed.

Annabel said nervously, "My uncle says it's best to pack it into a larger suitcase with other items piled on top of it, so that it won't be noticed."

"We shall have to chuck some of our own things overboard, and you can send them on after us," Elsa said determinedly. "Let's bury the 'birthday gift' under a pile of our pyjamas and my unmentionables. I've yet to see a customs man who wanted to touch ladies' corsets."

She gazed at the wooden case. "What—exactly—is *it*?" she asked delicately.

"I can't tell you that," Annabel said regretfully.

"Hmm. I'd say it looks rather like a typewriter case," Charles suggested.

"Yes," Annabel answered, "and as far as you know, that's all it is. Oncle says that if anyone asks, you should say it belongs to your French secretary—me—who left it behind when she went on to London ahead of you."

"Righto, got it," Elsa said briskly.

Annabel continued, "When you reach London, a man from British intelligence will meet you at the gate. He will pretend to be your press agent. He will greet you with the code words, *Hello, Hunch!* It's short for *Hunchback of Notre Dame.*" She herself had suggested this code to her uncle and his contacts.

"Ahh! That's fine," Charles agreed, as if relishing the whole subterfuge.

"Thanks again for the picnic food," Elsa said, kissing Annabel. "And darling, 'I'll See You Again,' as the Noël Coward song says—" She hummed the mournfully sweet lines. Then she added softly, "We won't be in London very long, dear Annabel. Hollywood beckons with its siren song. So, ducks, be sure to look us up, if you ever go back to the land of the free."

The porter arrived to pick up their things. The Laughtons sailed through the lobby, out the front door, and into a taxi. Elsa waved and blew kisses, calling out, "*À bientôt!*"

Annabel stood staring long after their car had passed the hotel gate.

That very morning, Hitler did not meet the British demands, so the United Kingdom declared war on Germany.

CHAPTER 23

I'll See You Again

That afternoon it was France's turn to hand Germany an ultimatum and then, when Hitler resisted it, to declare war.

The French military set up command posts on the rooftop
of the Grand Hotel. Rick moved out of the penthouse and into
the Villa Sanctuaire.

"I always liked this spot," he said as Annabel came down to
see if he needed anything.

He'd already told her last night, over cocktails and dinner,
that he wasn't planning to stay here long. It had been a
sober conversation, discussing what to do about the Grand
Hotel. Rick thought he should just board it up and "fill it
with hungry Dobermans who'll tear to pieces any invading
armies."

"Oncle JP says that it will probably be commissioned as a
hospital," she told him now. She was feeling apprehensive about
everything these days; it all seemed up for grabs.

"Sit down, Annabel," Rick said, gesturing at the table near
the villa's pool. It was strange, but already this villa no longer felt
as if it belonged to Jack and Téa. In the way of all hotel rooms,
it had somehow, skillfully, been reverted by the staff into the

anonymity of a place where people came and people left and still others replaced them, until the end of time.

"What are your plans for the staff?" she asked warily.

"Most of them are gone, anyway," Rick pointed out.

"Marta and Raphael said they would stay on, if we want them to," Annabel replied. "They both became French citizens, years ago. I did not know this, until now."

"That's fine," Rick said noncommittally.

"And my uncle," she reminded him. "He cannot be moved, just yet."

"I've already offered to let him stay at this villa or the cottage, whichever he wants, for him and Delphine," he replied. He'd kept his eyes on Annabel the whole time, waiting.

"That is kind of you," she answered carefully. "But first I want to move Oncle JP to Switzerland as soon as he's able. If we can get in. Dr. Gaspard said it would be a good idea for Delphine, too. There is a clinic, he says, that specializes in helping polio survivors."

Rick understood what she was saying. "Done," he said briskly. "Don't worry about getting them in. I'll arrange for whatever paperwork they'll need, and cover the cost. But sooner is better than later. Say the word and I'll get them both safely out, *tout de suite.*"

Annabel nodded slowly. She felt as if she were seeing the future already. Rick's handsome, happy-go-lucky face had a new seriousness now. But he was young, raised to think of the world as his oyster, expecting to get anything he wanted. He and his kind would somehow pass through this war unscathed. He wasn't yet facing the sorts of pressures that his father would surely bring to bear on him, once Rick actually began to take over the Grand Hotel and, eventually, the entire business empire that his family had built. With such responsibilities, there might come a change in attitude. How long would Rick be able to resist the pull of his father's orbit, before he adopted his father's hard, transactional values and became more like him each day, a ruthless businessman and womanizer?

"I love you, Annabel," Rick said gently now.

His face looked so sincere that she finally allowed herself to feel the affection that had been steadily growing between them despite her best efforts to resist it. Still, these warmer feelings toward him did not alter what she knew to be true about Rick and his family.

Annabel took a deep breath. She also knew in her soul that the kind of love she'd been raised on could never be bought and sold. She still ached for Jack, for her parents, even for an unknown suitor who might offer a modest but truer love, instead of a bargain. She'd never been taught how to be ruthless, and she knew that if one truly hardened one's heart, love might never find its way in again. But she must not be naive today. So she was seeking a way to be pragmatic without surrendering her humanity.

"If we got married, you'd never have anything to worry about," Rick promised.

Nothing that Annabel had ever known had lasted forever. And at least she'd learned a sense of duty from Oncle JP. So perhaps she could use her love for him and Delphine to find a way to tread this line with Rick. She must simply seize what life gave her and make the most of it.

One thing was clear: she would never be in a stronger position with Rick than now, when she was, for him, like that golden ring he kept reaching out for every time his pony on the merry-go-round circled past her.

"I hope you'll understand what I am about to ask," she said softly. "I would like you to put in writing all of these lovely promises you're making to me today. I will depend on you to make good your offers of protection—financial and otherwise—for me, for Oncle JP, for Delphine, and—if you and I have any children, for them, as well."

Rick had looked slightly taken aback at first, but now, at the mention of children, he smiled. "Of course," he said in a light, gallant tone.

"Would you also lease the Villa Sanctuaire to Oncle JP, *and* the Jasmine Cottage to me?" she asked.

"You can have a ninety-nine-year lease on both if you want," Rick said with a sweep of his hand. "We're going to build an annex down the street, which will essentially be like a second hotel."

"That's very generous, thank you," she said earnestly. "I have only one other request. I want the staff of the Grand Hotel guaranteed to have their jobs restored as soon as the war is over. Especially Oncle JP, if he is up to it, and if he wants it."

"Good Lord, Annabel," Rick protested. "Most of the staff probably won't even—"

"Yes, they will," she said quickly. "They will come back. Do you need to ask your papa's permission for this?"

"No," Rick said a trifle glumly. "I'll catch hell for it, but too bad. If it's what you want, then it's what *I* want. Father's been after me to marry and settle down, so this is the price he'll have to pay for it. He'll understand that. So do we have a deal?"

Annabel smiled with genuine warmth now. "Yes, we do. And—Rick, I just want you to know—I'll make it *my* business to make you a good wife."

Rick brightened again, in that boyish way in which nothing ever darkened his brow for very long. He reached into his pocket and pulled out a small jewel box. "I hope you like it," he said, as he pushed it across the table. "If you don't, I can always change it."

The ring had a lovely gold setting with a large diamond nestled in it that glowed with subtle superiority. There was nothing showy or ostentatious about this ring. Yet it was a prize.

"It's perfect," she said gratefully.

"Good." Rick slipped it on her finger with the look of a man who'd finally sealed a deal and gotten his hands on a rare work of art that he'd been chasing after for some time.

Annabel tried not to feel like an auctioned-off museum piece already.

"May I kiss you now?" he asked with playful formality.

"Yes," she replied.

He leaned in and kissed her on the lips. He was a pretty good kisser, after all.

From a village off in the distance, they heard a church bell toll. Annabel was startled and thought fleetingly of Jack and the old church high up in the mountains. She told herself that perhaps it was his soul, giving her his blessings, telling her to move on with her life, when, really, there was no other choice.

"To you and me and the Grand Hotel," Rick was saying, as he produced a bottle of champagne and popped it open. "And while we're at it: *vive la France.*"

"Yes. For all of us," Annabel said, accepting the glass he offered her.

EPILOGUE

The Cannes Film Festival
May 2000

A limousine pulled up to the red carpet, and a young publicist from an American movie studio squealed in delighted anticipation.

"That's fine, driver—stop here!" the girl said, and when he did, she hopped out, happy to smile at the bank of photographers who were poised waiting for anyone important to set foot on the path to the main hall. They waited curiously to see who else would emerge.

The French driver got out and opened the door for Annabel, who'd waited patiently for him to help her out of the car. The young publicist turned and remembered her duties.

"Oh, your dress!" she exclaimed. "Let me straighten out the back of it for you. There you go. So pretty!"

Annabel was wearing a vintage Molyneux gown, which had had to be altered a bit because, she discovered, one *did* shrink a bit with age. The woman, not the gown. It was a soft pink silk chiffon affair—and it had not been "vintage" when she'd originally purchased it. She also wore an antique necklace of blue sapphires and pink diamonds, meant to represent the Mediterranean sky. Rick had given it to her, years ago.

"How's it feel to be a success at your age?" someone from the press called out.

Annabel ignored this, momentarily pretending to be hard of hearing as she was ushered inside. But a short while later, when she was seated onstage with a panel of actors and directors at a long table dotted with microphones, there was no avoiding the questions.

The moderator introduced her as one of "the unsung pioneer woman directors of the twentieth century," who was now presenting a new film out of competition at the festival.

"You started your career as a filmmaker relatively late," the young man said, glancing at his note cards, in which Annabel's life had been reduced to a few pithy highlights.

It was true, of course, that she hadn't immediately jumped into making films at the outbreak of the war. The moderator, aware that Annabel had married the heir to a renowned hotel chain, asked questions about her "glamorous life traipsing around the world," which she obligingly answered without divulging the more personal details.

"Your wedding took place in September of 1939," he noted.

It had been a quiet but lovely ceremony in a local chapel. But when the Nazis invaded Paris the next year, Annabel and Rick had already left France, getting Oncle JP and Delphine safely to Switzerland. Oncle JP recovered, and Rick found the clinic for Delphine that specialized in helping polio patients, so after a surgery, the girl learned to walk with the aid of a cane. She still limped a bit, but she went to college in Paris to study medicine, married a fellow French physician, and had an adorable baby girl.

Annabel and Rick stayed with them in Switzerland during the war; and once, on the streets of Zurich, for a fleeting moment Annabel thought she saw Téa slipping through a crowded flower market. But perhaps not. Annabel never saw or heard of her again, so as far as she knew, Téa did not make another film, at least, not one seen by the world beyond Nazi Germany.

When the Second World War had ended, Annabel and her loved ones returned to France—and to the Grand Hotel. The library curtains had been torn and the wine cellar ransacked, first by the Italian army and then by the Germans as they marched through the Côte d'Azur. Rick even discovered an unexploded shell sitting smack in the center of the empty pool.

But with his father's money and Oncle JP's supervision, Rick restored the Grand Hotel to its former glory, and soon, the guests flocked back, like birds returning after a long winter. Winston Churchill stayed for a weekend, then went off to Monte Carlo to pay his 1939 gambling debt to the casino, which never cashed his check but instead framed and displayed it.

And the Cannes Film Festival resumed in 1946, but not without a few technical hiccups—the film reels of Alfred Hitchcock's movie *Notorious* got mixed up and were shown in the wrong order, and *The Three Musketeers* was run upside down. In the end, diplomatically, eleven films were tied for the grand prize.

The Grand Hotel was fully booked that year, but Annabel had no time to ogle celebrities. She was focused on being a good wife to Rick. They stayed married for fifteen years and had two children, a girl first, then a boy. Their son was the spitting image of Rick, with his insouciant blue eyes. And everyone, including Rick, said that the girl looked just like her mother. Yet when Annabel contemplated her daughter's curly hair and intense gaze, sometimes she thought she saw Jack smiling back at her; but she could never be sure.

Rick was proud of the Grand Hotel, and for a while they were happy together, traveling to view all his family's other hotel properties around the world. But eventually the strain of taking over the entire business after his father died created too much stress on the marriage.

Even so, after the divorce, they'd remained friends. He'd kept his word about the ninety-nine-year lease, so Oncle JP lived at the Villa Sanctuaire until he died at the age of seventy-five.

Annabel lived at the Jasmine Cottage whenever she wasn't in Paris. Her children eventually moved to America and wisely stayed out of both show business and the hotel business.

So Annabel's path to filmmaking had not begun until after her divorce from Rick. She'd taken a job as an executive secretary to a film producer in Paris. And there she rediscovered her love of photography and lighting. She'd also met a distinguished professor of classical music who turned out to be her soul mate, and they married. Tonight he was at the Jasmine Cottage, recovering from heart surgery.

"You've made twenty films, mostly shorts and documentaries," the moderator continued. "All critically well received, and the first dramatic film you made was especially memorable. Please tell us what inspired you to make *I'll See You Again*."

That was easy enough to answer. By now she felt comfortable speaking about Jack Cabot. She'd used the footage that she and Jack had shot when they'd gone to Sainte-Agnès all those years ago, to make a mysterious, atmospheric film about a man and woman who'd retreated up there in 1939 at the onset of war and never left it, never looked back. The story was told in a dual time frame, using younger actors to play the grandchildren who grew up in Paris but ventured to Sainte-Agnès in search of their family history.

"But it wasn't until much later that you finally made the film which has brought you here tonight," the moderator said, and the audience murmured. "What inspired this one?"

"I think I was planning it, subconsciously, for decades," Annabel answered.

In the late 1950s when she'd been in New York, she'd gone to see *The Last Time I Saw Paris*, a film loosely based on one of Scott's short stories. Afterward, as Annabel emerged from the theatre and stepped out onto the sidewalk, she'd heard a familiar voice.

"Heavens—it's the girl from the Grand Hotel!" Elsa Lanchester had shouted from down the street, when she spotted Annabel, and she insisted that they dine with Charles Laughton that very night.

It was a festive evening, with Christmas shoppers scurrying about. Annabel and the Laughtons had ducked down a side street and settled cozily into a red leather banquette at a French restaurant. Over champagne and oysters, Annabel told the Laughtons that she thought they'd been especially marvelous in two films they'd recently made together, *The Big Clock*, in which Charles played a murderer and Elsa was a dotty artist; and *Witness for the Prosecution*, in which Charles was an ailing but effective barrister and Elsa was his scolding nurse.

"Elsa is a TV star now," Charles had informed Annabel, telling her about the recent guest spot that Elsa had done for a comedy series called *I Love Lucy*, in a hilarious Florida episode that had just aired.

When they were served their steak with potatoes *dauphinoises* and a fine burgundy, the Laughtons reminisced about their time in France.

This prompted Annabel to ask, "So what happened after you left the Grand Hotel and took the plane to London?" Oncle JP had told her that the Laughtons succeeded in delivering the Enigma replica, but now she wanted to hear the details.

"Oh, the flight in that little aeroplane was ghastly!" Charles moaned. "It's so much better with jet travel now; it's hard to believe what we used to put up with before it."

"And what a fright we had, when we landed in London with your little valise," Elsa said dramatically. "My knees were knocking together like castanets. I was certain that there were German agents lurking around each corner and wanting to stab us with a poison dart."

"And the man from British intelligence who met you when you landed?" Annabel had asked eagerly. "What was he like—did he say the proper coded greeting?"

"He did indeed," Charles replied. "If he hadn't, I should never have given 'the package' to him, for he didn't look at all like a spy. I'd expected a fine false mustache, but he appeared quite nondescript, like an ordinary businessman. You'd never pick him out in a crowd."

"Just between us, now it's all over, what exactly *was* that little package you made us take to London?" Elsa asked raffishly. Annabel hesitated, even then, but decided that she could tell them. She explained it as simply as possible.

"Why, Annabel, we had no *idea!*" Elsa said with mock indignation. "You might have *told* us about that fabulous Enigma! I'd have insisted on having a replica made for myself, just so I could send you dirty limericks in coded messages to confound any spies watching us."

Afterward, when they went outside to hail taxis, it had begun to snow in a magical way, the dancing flakes whirling into the night sky like ballerinas spinning in tulle skirts. Elsa pointed to the window of a posh toy shop displaying multiple plush copies of a popular cat character from a children's TV show.

"Do you know that Sonny's daughter Cissy is the voice of that *Kissy Cat* cartoon?" Elsa told Annabel, pointing at the toy. "She married a cartoon animator, and he found out that she has a marvelous singing voice and could also do funny, squeaky character voices. My dear, she is as rich as Croesus now from those residuals. A good thing she found her 'voice,' too, because her sister, Linda, and brother-in-law, Alan, swindled Cissy out of a good share of her inheritance when their parents died."

They were walking back past the movie theatre from which Annabel had emerged earlier, and Elsa glanced up at the marquee and sighed, "Another film based on Fitzgerald's books. I thought they made quite a hash of it this time, didn't you?" Annabel had to agree.

As his taxi pulled up, Charles commented, "Nice song in that movie, though. They play it on the radio quite often. And having the lovely Elizabeth Taylor starring in it has made the film a success. Too bad that fellow Scott isn't around to collect his share of the profits."

———

Charles's words echoed in Annabel's thoughts when she returned to France. For Scott had died only a year after he'd left the Grand Hotel, at the age of forty-four.

It had caught Annabel by surprise; she and Scott had been writing letters to each other during that first year of the war. He'd told her that *Collier's* and the *Saturday Evening Post* turned down the serial rights for his Hollywood novel after reading his treatment, and his publisher did not give him an advance, either, although his editor made him a personal loan.

So Scott had decided to write *The Love of the Last Tycoon* "for himself," and he'd managed to stay alive by selling his Pat Hobby stories about the hack screenwriter. He kept working on his novel and was optimistic all along, sending Annabel a Christmas card with his usual jubilant flair, just days before he died. In the end, his heart finally gave way, so he did not finish his Hollywood novel.

Annabel was infuriated by the obituaries, which had been shockingly dismissive, as if Scott had been no more important than a fashion trend from the 1920s. She wondered if he had taken his last breath thinking himself a failure. Somehow she couldn't imagine Scott giving up, for despite his unflinching eye on the world, he'd always preserved an unswerving faith that he could make the big leap across the abyss and reach that shining city on a hill just one more time.

At first, it seemed as if he *would* be forgotten. Then, after the Second World War, people started looking at Scott's work again, perhaps because *The Great Gatsby* was a favorite among the books sent to soldiers overseas. Eventually Annabel, still traveling back and forth to the States with Rick at that time, would pick up a magazine and recognize some of the stories she'd typed up for Scott in their summer of '39—now, at long last, making their way into print.

In April of 1949, *Collier's* magazine apparently came to its senses and published a story they'd previously turned down back when Scott had submitted it under his pen name of John Darcy—it was the one that Annabel had typed called "Last Kiss," the sad tale about a director who loves an aspiring actress—and now *Collier's* declared it to be the best story in that issue, even awarding it a $1,000 bonus payment. Which Scott, of course, never got to hear about.

Likewise, the *New Yorker* magazine, which had previously turned down Annabel's favorite of Scott's stories, "Thank You for the Light"—about a tired saleswoman dying for a cigarette who goes into a church to rest—eventually published it to great fanfare and acclaim.

There were also countless biographies, new editions of his work, collected letters, and movie and TV adaptations even of his unfinished novel, *The Love of the Last Tycoon*. And in due course Scott's unpublished stories that Annabel had typed for him would be collected into a book.

Over and over again, Annabel wished with all her heart that such things had happened when Scott was alive. She thought of him so often that it was like a haunting, and she kept recalling Charles Laughton's comment: *Too bad that fellow Scott isn't around to collect his share of the profits.*

Finally, Annabel decided to do something to express her feelings about it, and she made a film based on a simple premise: What if, back in 1939, Scott's magazine and book publishers had actually paid him a true advance on *all* his future royalties, magically calculating what the income would be from these future sales of his work—that is, all the profits his publishers would go on making for so many decades, almost a whole century, after he'd written it?

It was never easy to get financing for an independent film, and it took ten years for this one, but Annabel managed to obtain funds, first from a European film commission, and then when a boutique Hollywood studio kicked in. Tonight was the grand premiere of this movie.

"The press release for your film calls it 'a sprightly and heartfelt homage to Fitzgerald, evoking the joyful fantastic elements of *The Diamond as Big as the Ritz* and "The Curious Case of Benjamin Button."' Did you know the author personally?" the moderator asked her now.

Annabel said, "I was fortunate to work for Scott the year before he died. He was nothing like the clichéd image of a wastrel that is perpetuated about him."

There was a ripple of surprise from the audience, and the interviewer said rather defensively, "Do you deny that Fitzgerald was a drunk? He himself admitted so."

"All I can tell you is that the Scott I knew in 1939 was a sober, devoted professional who never gave up, despite the kind of stress that would have felled any one of us. No, I believe that in the end, it was simply economic deprivation that killed him."

The room had grown quiet. Annabel said gently, "*The Great Gatsby* has been on the bestseller lists for decades now. But in his lifetime it barely earned him pennies. You do the math for what Scott should have been paid for *seventy-five* years' profits on *The Great Gatsby*—and still counting."

A murmur rose from the audience as if they were all calculating that income.

"Well!" the host said brightly. "Let's now watch your film!"

In a lighthearted yet touching way, Annabel's movie envisioned an alternate universe in which Scott, a man of means because of all those "advance royalty payments," lived an incredibly long life, creating more masterpieces as he marveled at all the social and technological changes each decade brought. The audience watched, laughed, cried, then burst into applause at the end.

———

Later that evening, Annabel returned to the Jasmine Cottage. Even though Rick had sold the Grand Hotel to a group of investors just before his death, Annabel's ninety-nine-year lease was still valid. Now and then the new owners contemplated making "improvements" to the hotel and its grounds that thankfully never materialized.

And so, despite the passage of time, the Grand Hotel remained essentially the same, *plus ça change*, an unruffled *grande dame* looking out from her high perch to the sea.

Annabel's husband was waiting up for her, having already heard on television that the screening was a success. "You know, this cottage is a great place to write," he said brightly. "Tonight I finished another chapter on my book about Beethoven. I feel well enough to have a glass of champagne with you."

They sat outside, enjoying the night air and simply glad of each other's company. They could hear music from the terrace of the Grand Hotel wafting toward them on an evening breeze in which the flowers and herbs seemed to be sighing as they released their perfume.

There were film people staying at the Grand Hotel tonight, once again for the Cannes Film Festival. She didn't know most of them.

But there were still some moments, whenever Annabel went for a walk on a moon-filled night, that she would look out across the lawn and see the new guests fluttering down the path like butterflies in their light summer finery; and it seemed to her that, among these bright newcomers, she could still glimpse the ghosts of all those people she'd met in that delirious summer of 1939.

And she thought that, as long as people could still create stories and music and art, there was always solace and hope for the young people who were just discovering how beautiful it was to love one another and to cherish their short stay on this lovely earth.

THE END

ACKNOWLEDGMENTS

A book begins with an author in solitude, but publication is the result of many fine people coming together. And so I give great big thanks to Susan Golomb for her wisdom, friendship, and savvy; and everyone at Writers House, especially Sasha Landauer, and Maja Nikolic and her team. I send heartfelt thanks to Brendan Deneen for his attentive shepherding of this novel at every stage, with unfailing good humor. I also thank the great team at Blackstone, especially Larissa Ezell for her beautiful book cover; Riam Griswold for such intelligent copyediting; my fine publicist, Tatiana Radujkovic; and our terrific marketing and sales team.

I give great thanks to all the lovely booksellers who have supported my novels. And much love to all the book groups I've chatted with, and the many readers who have written to me from far and wide.

I also thank Margaret Atwood for her warmth and encouragement over the years; and Jacques Pépin for his kindness and friendship. To my husband, Ray, I give my thanks and love for all the joy of working, playing, cooking, and living together.